# GALLIANO GOLD

### FRANKI AMATO MYSTERIES BOOK 5

## TRACI ANDRIGHETTI

**Limoncello Press**

GALLIANO GOLD

by

TRACI ANDRIGHETTI

\*\*\*

*This one is for my dogs, Gigi, Vinny, and Ciccio, who help me write by barking, stepping on my keyboard, and continually asking to go outside and come back in. My sweet, fearless Fabi couldn't be there for this one, but I felt her with me nonetheless.*

# THE STEAMBOAT GALLIANO

## THREE DECKS FROM BOTTOM TO TOP

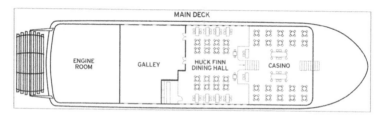

MAIN DECK

ENGINE ROOM — GALLEY — HUCK FINN DINING HALL — CASINO

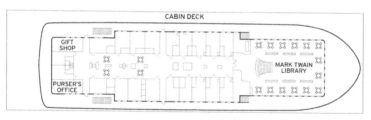

CABIN DECK

GIFT SHOP — PURSER'S OFFICE — MARK TWAIN LIBRARY

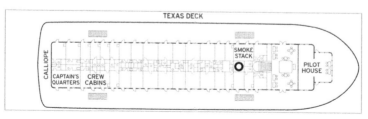

TEXAS DECK

CALLIOPE — CAPTAIN'S QUARTERS — CREW CABINS — SMOKE STACK — PILOT HOUSE

# 1

*Your nonna has hired Private Chicks to investigate why you're a zitella.*

The text message pierced my chest like a bullet that then ricocheted off a rib and tore through my lungs. My elderly Sicilian grandmother had always been a shrewd meddler—but hiring the New Orleans PI firm where I worked to probe my old-maid status? That was Machiavellian.

I sprang from a bench in the plaza of Washington Artillery Park ready for battle. "This time the woman has crossed the line of all lines, and as my name is Franki Amato, I will push her back over it!"

A group of tourists gaped at me as though I'd fired the park's Civil War cannon into the Mississippi River.

I couldn't blame them, really. It was eight thirty in the morning, and I was alone, waving a bag of Café du Monde beignets, and screaming at my cell phone. I figured I should explain myself.

"I'm at war with my nonna, and it's not my fault." I waved my phone as evidence. "She launched the first volley last year when she had some lemons shot at me in church."

The tourists scattered.

"I probably should've left off the lemon part."

A little girl, maybe eight or nine, approached and cocked her head. Except for her posh pink coat and matching patent leather purse and shoes, she could have been a mini-me with her dark eyes and long brown hair. "Why would your nonna have you shot at with lemons?"

I smiled through my anger. After all, the kid was cute. "It has to do with an Italian-American Catholic tradition. On St. Joseph's Day, which is March 19th, we decorate an altar with food to feed the poor. And if an unmarried woman steals a lemon from the altar without anyone seeing her, she'll supposedly get proposed to within a year." I held up my hands. "Not that a woman needs a proposal or anything."

Her brow creased. "But you're not supposed to steal, especially not from poor people in church."

"That's exactly what I said." I knelt, sensing a kindred spirit. "But my nonna thinks it's her God-given duty to get me married. And because I turned thirty last March, she had the lemons shot at me with a T-shirt cannon. I had to take one to make it stop."

"It's February 25th. Have you been proposed to?"

My boyfriend, Bradley Hartmann, hadn't popped the question, and I had mixed feelings about that. Nevertheless, I forced a grin. "Not yet."

She pulled her purse strap higher on her collarbone. "Well, it might be because you're a crazy bag lady."

I catapulted to my five feet, ten inches. Granted, I wasn't in a business suit, but a black turtleneck, blue jeans, and Italian loafers were hardly bag lady attire. On the other hand, I *was* carrying a hobo bag and the bag of beignets. "For your information, young lady, I'm a private investigator."

"Oh. Then I'll bet it's because you're old."

I shoved the last beignet between my teeth and crumpled the bag at her.

She screamed and ran.

A seventyish woman in a puffer coat and knit cap pointed a mittened hand at me. "Shame on you for scaring that sweet girl."

I pulled the beignet from my mouth. "That girl is as sweet as salt. And I hate to be rude, but I've got a big problem I need to deal with."

She harrumphed. "I'll say you do."

I threw up my hands but held tight to the beignet. "Can't a gal be irate in peace?"

"The park is a public space." She parked her mittens on her hips. "And you would do well to change your behavior. As it stands right now, not even a bushel of St. Joseph's Day lemons would land you a man."

I recoiled as though shrapnel had struck me. Apparently, Washington Artillery Park was an active combat zone.

Squeezing my phone, I stormed down the plaza steps and across the railroad tracks to the Moonwalk, a promenade along the Mississippi River. Fortunately, no one was around because I needed some space to collect my thoughts. The text message and unsolicited comments had hit an already wounded nerve.

Bradley and I had been dating for over two years, and even though I was in no rush to get married, I couldn't help but notice that he was in no rush to propose. And his reluctance had triggered old insecurities. *Was he put off by my nonna's meddling? Or was it something I'd done?*

I sighed and gazed at the river. I'd read somewhere that it was a half-mile wide and two hundred feet deep. And because I was in Louisiana, I knew the murky brown depths held a host of sinister creatures. Still, there was something soothing about watching the boats and barges gliding along the water. I closed my eyes and filled my nostrils with the mud-and-tar scented air.

The tension ebbed and flowed from my body.

Tranquility.

A steamboat whistle blasted too close behind me.

My eyes flew open, I started, and my ankle buckled. I lurched toward the river and dropped my phone. My hand slammed onto the rocky embankment, followed by the rest of me. Then I rolled and plunged into the frigid water.

And I sank to the lair of alligators, cottonmouths, and bull sharks.

Fueled by fears of circling predators and a bacterial infection, I rocketed to the surface, gasping and sputtering. I dragged my battered body from the river and stood on shaky feet. My hobo bag was still on my arm, and without thinking I reached inside for a tissue. But it was full of water and...

"A fish!"

"With whiskers!"

The catfish leapt from my bag and into the river, and I stumbled and fell backwards onto jagged rock, which sent a stab of pain through my rear end.

"Fitting," I said through clenched teeth.

I rose and checked for damage. Besides some aches and scrapes, there was a two-inch gash in my jeans and underwear.

With my blood boiling despite my cold, wet clothes, I made my way to the promenade and retrieved my phone. The display had shattered.

I turned and raged at the steamboat. But I did so silently. Thanks to the Mississippi mishap, I'd dramatically upped my bag lady look, and I didn't want to attract attention from the likes of little girls and older women. I did, however, want a word with that whistleblower.

Fists clenched, I hobble-marched to the bow of the white boat. To my surprise, it wasn't the Natchez, New Orleans' only steamboat. "Galliano" was painted in gold on the side, and the giant paddlewheel was the same color. Unlike its competitor, which was popular with tourists, the Galliano looked dark and deserted, like a spooky ghost boat. But someone had blasted that whistle. "Probably a sailor screwing with me for a laugh, the jerk."

I was starting to shiver, so I gave up the manhunt and returned the way I'd come, ignoring the stares as I limped and dribbled river water from my hobo bag. When I reached Jackson Square on Decatur Street, I headed north toward my office— where I should have gone to eat my breakfast beignets—and began weaving through the French Quarter crowds.

My phone rang. *Veronica Maggio* appeared on the cracked display. As my BFF and the owner of Private Chicks, Inc., she shared some of the blame for my predicament.

I pressed *Answer* but said nothing.

Veronica sighed into the receiver. "I take it you still haven't cooled down after my text message?"

Not even a dunk in the river in February had put out my anger embers. "How could you take my nonna's case?"

"We knew she was going to pull some kind of stunt since the lemon deadline is looming, so I thought we should keep an eye on her."

I stepped over a pool of purple, hoping it was a spilled drink. "Watching her doesn't work. She's crafty, and now that you've given her an in, she'll try to shame a proposal from Bradley."

"How was I supposed to refuse her? I've known your family since we were freshmen at The University of Texas."

"We studied Italian together, so you know there are at least two options. An abrupt *no* and an even more abrupt *tch*."

The Italian sound for *no* caught the attention of a drunk who ogled my chest. "Hey, babe. Where's the wet turtleneck contest?"

I swung my hobo bag at him. He ducked, and I kept walking.

"And precisely how do you plan to investigate why I'm not married?"

"I don't. I gave the case to David."

"What? He's a sophomore in college. He's like pasta dough in her hands."

"Not if the only thing he has to do is wait for Bradley to propose."

I went around a slow-moving tour group. "And if he doesn't propose?"

"Franki, Bradley quit a high-paying job to spend more time with you. Does that sound like a man who doesn't have serious intentions?"

It didn't. "But what if he regrets it?"

"I haven't seen any signs of that. Quite the contrary, in fact."

She had a point. Since Bradley had left Pontchartrain Bank, he'd lavished me with daily attention. He'd taken me to dinner and a play the night before, and we had a lunch date in a few hours. "You're probably right, but the lemon tradition is about to sour our relationship."

"My advice—forget the lemons and enjoy your time with him. Sooner or later, he's going to have to go back to work."

Veronica was a wise woman, and I needed to listen to her. "You know what? I will. The next time my nonna calls—"

"Oh, she didn't call. She came to the office."

I stopped dead in front of Molly's pub. "When was this?"

"This morning. Your mother dropped her off."

I gripped the phone so hard that the glass shards crunched. Nonna in NOLA was a no-no, and my mom was well aware of that.

I heard another whistle—but not from a steamboat.

A group of frat boys were checking out my exposed behind.

I grew so hot that I'm pretty sure I let off some river water steam. "There are women flashing their breasts on Bourbon

Street, but you guys are here staring at a few inches of my rear end?" I flicked my bag at them. "Get to class and learn some sense."

They scattered like the tourists had.

"Franki, what's going on?" Veronica sounded concerned.

"Nothing I couldn't handle. Listen, I'm going to come get my car, and then I'll be back after lunch. I need to take care of some personal business." I closed the call and picked up my pace.

There was another tradition behind my nonna's visit, and I had to confront the instigator before she skipped town.

MY 1965 MUSTANG convertible screeched to a stop at the fourplex where I rented a furnished one-bedroom next door to Veronica. My mom's Ford Taurus station wagon wasn't in the driveway, but my sixty-something ex-stripper landlady, Glenda O'Brien, was. It wasn't her pastie-adorned breasts that made me slam on the brakes, it was the giant pastied pair she'd hung from her second-floor apartment railing.

Even though I was anxious to shower and change, I lingered in the front seat. It had already been an epically bad day, and nine thirty was too early for nudity. I glanced in the rearview mirror at Thibodeaux's Tavern, but it was too early for a drink too. Then my gaze drifted to the creepy cemetery next to the tavern. It was definitely too early for that.

I sucked it up and got out of the car.

Glenda held a Mae West–style cigarette holder in one hand and a champagne flute in the other. Unlike me, she had no qualms about imbibing in the morning because day drinking was practically a custom among native New Orleanians. "You look like you crawled from the swamp, Miss Franki."

She was one to talk in her alligator stripper shoes. "Close.

The river." I gestured toward the boob decoration. "I take it those are for Mardi Gras?"

"That was the original plan, sugar, but I might like to keep them up. Carnie made them for me."

The mere mention of her annoying drag queen friend, Carnie Vaul, irritated me. And I silently thanked the gods—or the goddesses, as it were—that the carnival queen was on a world tour with *RuPaul's Drag Race*.

Glenda pulled aside her long, platinum locks and raised her chest. "She modeled them after mine."

I'd thought they were hanging low. I walked to my front door and—case in point—had to duck to avoid hitting my head on one. "Well, before you make any decisions, my nonna's in town for a surprise visit."

Glenda sashay-ran up the stairs, and I smirked as I inserted my key into the lock. She and my nonna were engaged in an ongoing skirmish over clothing. My nonna covered her with bib aprons, and Glenda chafed at the so-called "straitjackets."

I opened the door, and my cairn terrier, Napoleon, trotted out and hiked his leg on my front tire.

"Sometimes I think you're really a rat terrier."

He returned to the entryway and sniffed my leg. His tail lowered, and he bolted beneath the velvet zebra-print chaise lounge.

"Make that a bull terrier because I don't smell that bad."

I shut the door and kicked off my wet loafers and glanced around the apartment, looking for signs of old-world Sicily among the bordello chic décor. But it didn't look like my nonna had been there, which was weird because it wasn't like her to waste time taking over.

I went through the living room to the kitchen and deposited my hobo bag in the sink. Then I headed for the bathroom and called my mom on speaker. I put my cracked phone on the red Louis XVI vanity and stripped off my turtleneck.

The line rang a couple of times, and then I heard the sounds of a car in motion and Bing Crosby's "Deck the Halls."

"Marvelous day, isn't it, dear?" My mother's typically shrill voice was as joyful as the song.

I pulled a Grinch pucker in the oval-shaped mirror for two reasons. First, she was on her way home to Houston without my nonna, i.e., her live-in mother-in-law. And second, she hadn't stopped listening to Christmas music since Nonna, a diehard widow, had invited a man to our holiday dinner. "Mom, could you quit with the carols?"

The fa-la-la-la-laing stopped. "If this is about your nonna, I don't want to hear it."

I wriggled, incensed, from my wet jeans. "Uh, an earful is the least you can expect. You seem to have started a tradition of unloading family members on me, and I want it to stop."

"It was an impromptu trip, Francesca. Luigi Pescatore called last night and asked her to come."

*Nonna's Christmas dinner date?*

"And with any luck," her tone had gone tawdry, "she'll stay with him at the retirement home."

I sank onto the clawfoot tub, and so did my stomach. Nonna and Luigi were both in their eighties, so the thought of them *together* was unsettling. And I wasn't the only one in the family who felt that way. "Dad didn't seem too happy about his elderly mother dating. Does he know you brought her to see him?"

The call ended.

It would be easy to think the line had dropped since my mother was on the road, but I knew her better than that. She'd hung up because I'd caught her keeping my dad in the dark.

I tapped the number again and watched the display until she answered. "Mom—"

"You know that graveyard across the street from your house?" The Christmas joy had left her tone, and it had turned Halloween hell.

"What about it?"

"You screw this up for me, and I'll put you in it, *capisci*?"

I understood. Normally, I would've thought she was kidding. But from the second Luigi entered the scene, a change had come over my mother. She'd gotten an unexpected shot at a mother-in-law-free life, and she was willing to do anything to get it, including sacrificing her daughter.

"That woman has been in my house for twenty-two years, ever since your *nonnu* died. You can't even begin to fathom what that's been like."

Oh, I could—Stephen King-level horror. But my mother's voice was as tight as a violin string, so it was best to agree with her. "No, I can't. But Luigi isn't the only reason she came here, and you know that because you dropped her off at Private Chicks so she could have me investigated—for being an old maid."

"That was for your own good, Francesca. The days are ticking down to your thirty-first birthday, not to mention the end of the lemon tradition. And both are stark reminders that your biological time clock is ticking down too."

I'd heard of mothers who made everything better, but mine had an uncanny ability not only to make things worse, but also to tie all of my problems to my aging reproductive system. "Obviously, I can't expect your help with the zitella case, so at least tell me where nonna is."

"With Luigi." She squealed.

And I half-expected her to break into a chorus of "Joy to the World."

"He was waiting for her at Private Chicks with a beautiful

basket of garlic and chili peppers from his produce company."
She gave a wistful sigh. "So romantic, isn't it?"

It wasn't. In some cultures his gift would be used to ward off
vampires and werewolves. "I'd rather not comment."

"Because you're hard-hearted like your father, which is part
of your problem in relationships."

"That and my old eggs," I muttered.

"You're breaking up, dear. What did you say?"

"Nothing." I moved to the toilet. It seemed more appropriate
somehow.

"Anyway, as I was leaving, I heard Luigi mention something
about a steamboat."

The whistleblower came to mind, as did my need for a
shower. I turned on the water to let it warm up. "He must be
taking her on the Natchez for a jazz cruise."

"No, it was another boat. The Galliano."

For a moment, I wondered whether my nonna had pulled the
whistle that made me fall into the river, but I dismissed the idea.
If she'd done it, she would've been on deck pointing out my
curves to eligible sailors when I'd climbed from the water. "Mom,
I saw the Galliano today, and I don't think it's in operation."

"Well, I'm sure Luigi knows what he's doing. He's extremely
capable for a man his age, and quite the catch."

I wrinkled my lips. Some people would have said the very
same thing about the catfish that had leapt from my purse.

"I just pulled into Steamboat Bill's to get some gumbo for
your father, so I'll let you go. But remember what I said about
that cemetery." Her Halloween tone had returned. "Don't do
anything to interfere with your nonna and Luigi, *or else*."

The line went dead.

I climbed into the tub and closed the shower curtain, slightly
seasick from the conversation. It wasn't my mother's threat or my

nonna's relationship with Luigi that made me queasy—at least, not in that instant. The issue was the recurring steamboat theme, because it seemed like an omen.

And as I rinsed off the dregs of the Mississippi River, I couldn't wash away the feeling that I would have another ill-fated encounter with the Galliano.

The XXXL-sized security guard seated at the door of Mimi's in the Marigny bar flashed a sans-front-teeth smile. "May I tempt you with a piece? It's from Debbie Does Doberge."

I wasn't sure what he was talking about, but it sounded pornographic. I hefted my brow to signal that an explanation was warranted.

He chuckled and shifted his girth, revealing a couple of bakery boxes on a table beside him. "Doberge cake is a N'awlins tradition. If you don't want to try it, I've got some salty balls."

My brows bolted upright. The manager should *not* have let a security guard describe the food. "Thanks, but I'll take my chances with the Doberge. What's the occasion?"

He opened a box that contained a half-eaten chocolate fondant–covered cake with *Willie!* in blue icing. "I was born sixty-three years ago today, so the bar is treating everyone to dessert."

"What a great thing to do. Happy birthday."

"All birthdays are happy, *chère*."

*Not if you had a nonna who counted them and prayed over them like rosary beads.*

He handed me a plate with a huge slice that had six layers of some sort of yellow filling. "Pass a good time."

The French-inspired phrase made me smile. "I will now that I have cake."

I went inside to find my lunch date. If there were such a thing as a cute dive bar, Mimi's in the Marigny was it. The "cute" came from the vintage fireplace, distressed brick walls, and arched windows decorated with Christmas lights, and the "dive" came from the cash-only policy, pool table, and women's restroom with two stall-less toilets. But the décor wasn't what had garnered Bradley's and my affection. It was the gourmet Spanish tapas and artisanal cocktails.

Bradley wasn't at the bar, so I headed to the second-floor dining area. As I climbed each step, it felt like a countdown to something ominous. I blamed the ticking time bomb-themed call with my mom and the plate of cake in my hand, which was yet another reminder that my birthday approached, as did the end of the lemon tradition.

*Did Bradley have anything planned for either event?* I didn't want to ask because that would make me seem desperate for a marriage proposal—and I wasn't. But after the events of the morning, I was pretty darn desperate to stop my nonna's meddling.

I entered the dining room and spotted Bradley holding a newspaper at a two-top next to a window. The sight of his strong profile made my stomach flutter, and his fitted black sweater and tight gray chinos only added to the sexy picture.

Bradley's newspaper was still raised as I slid into my chair. So instead of seeing him, I was greeted with the mug shot of a man with a smile as toothless as Willie's and the headline *Man Stabs Wife at Her Birthday Party.*

Zitella-hood was looking pretty good.

Bradley lowered the paper, and his bright blue eyes widened. "Are you okay, babe? You look pale."

"I'm just cold and annoyed that I had to pay a hundred bucks to replace a cracked phone display."

"Here." He reached behind his chair. "Take my jacket."

"No, no. I'm fine."

He leaned forward and gave me a soft, slow kiss that was definitely inner-glow inducing. Then he pulled back and rubbed my cheek. "I ordered us some starter tapas—the grilled steak, the duck poutine, and the escargot."

I saw an opportunity. "Fancy. Are we celebrating something?"

"Should we be?"

*That attempt fell flat.* "It *is* almost March."

His eyes twinkled. "My favorite day of the year is coming up."

Excitement turned the inner glow from his kiss into a crackling fire. "And what day is that?"

He blinked. "Mardi Gras. What else?"

An icy cold washed over me like I'd fallen back into the river.

His gaze lowered to the menu beside his beer bottle. "Oh yeah, I also ordered the 'Trust Me.'"

He was referring to Mimi's mystery tapas, but the name was ironic since I was no longer sure I could trust him to remember my birthday.

I reached for my fork and cut a huge bite of Willie's cake, thinking that would jog his memory.

"I didn't know you liked Doberge."

"I've never had it, but it's rude not to celebrate someone's birthday." I shot him a pointed stare and shoved the bite into my mouth.

His upper lip curled. "I'm not a fan of the filling. Anything with lemon is a turnoff for me."

The lemon custard curdled on my tongue. *He never told me he didn't like lemon. Was that a veiled message about the lemon tradition?*

He chuckled. "Ruth Walker used to eat a piece of lemon Doberge every Friday. She insisted it was healthy and said it was a type of fruitcake."

Bradley's ex-assistant was a fruitcake herself with an epic ability for denial.

"I wonder if they kept her on at Pontchartrain Bank after I left."

"Let's hope." Ruth had once threatened to make my life hell if I cost her the job at the bank, and since Bradley had resigned because of me, I feared she'd make good on it.

He swallowed a sip of beer. "Speaking of work, any new cases?"

After his lemon comment, I would rather have eaten Willie's salty balls than tell him Nonna was having me investigated for being a zitella. "Not for me." I put down my fork and looked him in the eyes. "But in other news, my nonna's in town."

"What's the occasion?"

That was what I'd asked Willie, who was so beloved that even his manager remembered his birthday. "Meddling, for starters." I looked out the window, irritated. "And according to my mother, she's going for a ride on a steamboat called the Galliano."

"The Galliano's in New Orleans?"

My gaze met his. "You know about it?"

"I helped the captain, Rex Vandergrift, get a loan to buy it right before I resigned from the bank. But the boat was in St. Louis, so I thought the plan was to sail it in Missouri, like Mark Twain."

"What does Mark Twain have to do with this?"

"The captain is a huge fan. He told me all about how Twain was a steamboat pilot in Missouri before hitting it big as a writer." He laughed and spun his beer on its coaster. "Just for kicks, I googled a picture of Twain when he was signing the loan papers, and he even looks like him. Same shock of white hair, crazy eyebrows, and bushy mustache."

"How old is the captain?"

"In his seventies, I'd imagine. Why?"

"Because Luigi Pescatore invited Nonna on the boat, so I was wondering if he knows the guy."

The humor left his eyes. "I'd forgotten about that."

"What?"

"That your nonna's boyfriend is named Pescatore."

I held up my hand. "Slow down on the 'boyfriend' label, Bradley Hartmann. My nonna just reconnected with Luigi."

"Six months ago during Halloween. Then she brought him to Christmas Eve dinner and mass."

*So he remembers Halloween and Christmas, but not my birthday. Interesting.* "Why's his last name relevant?"

He pushed the newspaper toward me. "I haven't read it, but there's an article on page two about a missing man named Nick Pescatore."

My chest tightened. From what my nonna had told me, the name Pescatore wasn't common in Italy, much less in New Orleans. I scanned the article, and my anxiety blasted to steamboat whistle level. "This isn't happening."

"What? Is Nick related to Luigi?"

"No. I mean, I don't know." I drained my sangria and rose from the chair. "I've gotta go."

Bradley grasped my hand. "Franki, what's going on?"

"Nick Pescatore was last seen on the Galliano."

AFTER LOOKING for Nonna and Luigi at the Galliano and my apartment, I pulled into the Private Chicks parking lot and shut off the engine. Then I tapped Bradley's number on my pricey new phone display to find out whether he'd located them.

"Hey, babe," he answered. "Any luck?"

"No, you?"

"I'm at Belleville House, and they're not here."

If they weren't at Luigi's apartment at the retirement home, there was only one place left to check. "I just got to the office, and I'm going to start calling her friends. Do you mind going to the old Mortuary Chapel? Since Nick is missing, Nonna might've taken Luigi there to talk to Father John."

"I'm on my way." He closed the call.

"When will Nonna get a cell phone?" I grumbled as I climbed from the car and slammed the door. I tapped Santina's number and began the three-flight climb to the office. With each step I mentally uttered *please*. Usually, it was a plea for the building's owner, one Veronica Maggio, to have an elevator installed, but in that instance it had a new, dual meaning—please let Nonna be at Santina's, and please don't let Santina's way-too-old-to-live-at-home son, Bruno, pick up.

"Messina residence," a woman answered.

I breathed an already winded sigh of relief. "Hi, this is Franki Amato, Carmela Montalbano's granddaughter—"

"Franki, it's Mary."

Nonna had a lot of nonna friends in New Orleans, so it was hard to keep track of them. "Oh, right. Hello."

"Santina is rolling out pasta dough, so I answered on her behalf. How are you?"

"Honestly, I'm worried because I can't find my nonna."

"Oh? Carmela's in town?"

I gripped the railing. Nonna hadn't informed her friends of her trip, which in the Italian community was a serious slight. "Yyyes, but my mom just dropped her off this morning."

"Hm. One moment."

I listened as she relayed the gist of the call in terse Italian to Santina, who didn't speak English, and with every word the sounds of a rolling pin became more audible.

Mary cleared her throat. "Franki, Santina hasn't heard from her either, and we're surprised to say the least."

"Like I said, she's only been here for a few hours."

"But Carmela doesn't drive, so how would she leave your apartment?"

We both knew that a taxi was out of the question since my nonna thought all strangers were criminals. "Actually, she wasn't at my apartment. She's with Luigi Pescatore."

Silence, the in-church type.

My cheeks burned, as did my thighs from the stairs. Not only did Nonna's friends not know she was in town, they had no idea she'd been seeing a man.

Rapid-fire Italian followed. Then a *Madonna mia!* from Santina and a bang, probably the rolling pin.

Another throat clear. "Is this the first time Luigi and Carmela have been alone together?"

I stumbled on a step. If I lied and they found out, my reputation as a good Catholic girl would be ruined, and I'd be subjected to their suspicious stares for life. "Uh, he might've driven her to midnight mass after Christmas Eve dinner?"

The silence went Vatican level.

Nonna had been in mourning, dress and all, for over two decades. So the news of her and Luigi wasn't merely a shock—it was a calamitous event on par with the Great Flood, which meant that her reputation as a pious Catholic widow was on the verge of becoming extinct.

"One moment."

Sicilian ensued, a sign that the situation was indeed dire.

Unlike Italian, the Sicilian language was virtually indeci-
pherable thanks to its Norman, Greek, and Arabic elements. But
I caught two phrases in English that were fairly alarming
—"catholic.org" and "prayer request."

Mary's throat clear was almost a growl. "Franki, we're going
to make some calls and...take care of an urgent matter. We'll be
in touch."

She hung up before I could reply, which was just as well
because I'd completed my stair climb and was all out of breath.

I entered the lobby, setting off the bell, and let the door slam
behind me.

Our research assistant, Standish "The Vassal" Standifer,
didn't react. He was glued to his computer at the desk in the
corner.

Veronica breezed in from the hallway that led to our offices
wearing an ivory wool pantsuit. "That sounded like one of
David's door slams."

"He's not here?"

"He'll be back from class any minute." She put her hands on
her hips. "You're not going to confront him about taking your
nonna's case, are you?"

"Eventually. But right now I was hoping he'd know where
Nonna is."

"Isn't she with Luigi?"

I tossed my purse on one of the two facing couches in the
middle of the room. "Yes, and they were supposedly going to a
steamboat where a guy went missing."

She put a hand to her mouth. "You mean the Galliano."

"Does everyone except me know about this boat?"

"I read an article about the disappearance this morning and
wondered if the man was related to Luigi. I guess he is?"

"It's looking that way." I jerked off my jacket and hung it on the coat rack. "I just hope Nonna and Luigi aren't missing too. They're not at my place or at Belleville House, and there's no sign of them at the boat."

"Did you call her friends?"

"Yeah, and they were more concerned about her lapsed widowhood. It sounded like they were going to start a national Catholic prayer ring to try to save her."

Veronica swallowed a smile. "Maybe Luigi took her to see Father John."

"Bradley's probably at the old Mortuary Chapel as we speak." I approached The Vassal's desk and saw nudie pics on his computer, which explained why he hadn't pried his lenses from the screen when I came in. "Um, are you looking at porn?"

"Franki." Veronica scrunched her face into a scowl. "He's doing research for Glenda."

The Vassal turned, mouth open, and pushed up his Coke-bottle lensed glasses. Because he was slack-jawed, it was hard to tell whether he was shocked or just breathing. "It's for her book."

I blinked at Veronica. "Are you guys messing with me or what?"

"Since we don't have any big cases at the moment, I told Glenda she could hire him to help with a tell-all she's writing under her stage name. She's in my office now. We're working out how he'll split his hours."

The Vassal's lens-enlarged eyes went wide. "I didn't know about her life as...Lorraine Lamour."

The less he knew the better, although the pictures left little for him to discover. "The tell-all can wait to be told. I need you to look up the Galliano steamboat and Nick Pescatore. Finding my nonna is top priority."

He nodded and turned to the computer.

"Your nonna was at your apartment an hour ago, Miss Franki." Glenda entered the lobby. She'd replaced the pasties with leopard—just the spots—and the Mae West-style cigarette holder with a Sherlock Holmes-style pipe.

I was relieved about my nonna, but Glenda's smoking equipment was troubling. I shot a side-glower at Veronica. "She's not consulting on another investigation, is she?"

"This is my writing pipe, sugar." She took a puff, and the tobacco smelled like strip club. "I don't know if Miss Ronnie told you, but after I saw my breasts on the house this morning, it stirred something in my chest. I felt a deep need to share my story with the public. I just wish I could think of a worthy title."

Debbie Does Doberge came to mind. "We can brainstorm book names later. Did my nonna tell you where she was going?"

"Oh, I kept my distance, Miss Franki." She strutted to the couch and stretched out. "I saw her and Luigi from my living room window. They dropped off a trunk and then left in his Lambo."

"Wait. What?"

"His Lamborghini, sugar. He's got a green one, the color of money."

Stunned, I sank onto the couch beside her. "But he's eighty and sells produce. If anything, he should have a green Ford Fiesta."

Veronica sat on the opposite couch. "He's the owner and CEO of Little Palermo Produce. It's not Dole or Sunkist, but it's close."

My mom must not have known about Luigi's net worth. If she had, she would've ditched my dad and our family deli and married him herself.

"It's hard to believe he started out selling vegetables from a cart like your grandparents."

"And seriously deflating. If he has that much money, why

does he live at Belleville House? I mean, it's in the French Quarter, which is a plus, but it's really rundown."

She shrugged. "My guess is companionship. Or maybe he's frugal when it comes to living expenses."

Glenda puffed her pipe. "Maybe Luigi will get a new place now that he's hooking up with your nonna. He'll need a man den to tame that Sicilian tigress."

*Man den? Sicilian tigress?* Pains punctured my stomach, as though Glenda's ten-inch glitter leopard heels strutted on it.

"Are you all right, Miss Franki? You look as green as Luigi's Lambo."

"Could we not have this conversation?"

"About your nonna's sex life?"

"Yep. That's the one."

Veronica looked at her nails. "Well, I'm happy that Carmela found someone. This morning she mentioned that your nonnu has been gone for twenty-two years. That's a long time to be alone."

Glenda puffed her pipe. "And a damn long time to go without. I hadn't even been alive for twenty-two years the first time I got me some."

I bolted from the couch. "How are you coming over there, Vassal?"

"Very well, thank you."

I rolled my eyes and approached his desk. "No, I mean, what have you found out?"

"The Galliano has a website, and it's due to begin operation as a gambling cruise boat in a few days." He clicked to a Wikipedia page. "This says it was built in Pittsburgh in 1915, which makes it one of the oldest steamboats in the United States. Also, there was a fire onboard in 1922 that killed a crewman and a female passenger. Not only that, in 1934 a sailor fell into the paddlewheel. He was propelled into the stern and pushed underwater. The weird thing is that they never found his body."

"So the Galliano has a dark present *and* past." I pulled up a chair and took a seat beside him. "What about Nick Pescatore?"

He clicked to the *Times-Picayune*. "Besides the fact that he's missing, all I could find was that he's thirty-five and from Slidell."

"Try looking up the captain, Rex Vandergrift."

Glenda slapped her thigh. "Well, I'll be a monkey's sugar mama."

I stared at her over my shoulder. "Let me guess. He was one of your VIP-room regulars at Madame Moiselle's."

"Oh, Rex wasn't local, Miss Franki. The last I knew, he lived about an hour and a half from here in Morgan City. But he used to drive into New Orleans for poker tournaments at Harrah's, and if lady luck smiled on him at the casino, Lorraine Lamour smiled on him at the club."

*On him?* I assumed she was talking about a lap dance. "Do you know how I can get in touch with him?"

"I haven't seen him in ten, maybe fifteen years. He had some bad business back home that cost him his seafood company and his crown."

Veronica tilted her head. "His *crown*?"

"It wasn't official, Miss Ronnie, but everybody thought he had a lock on being King of the Louisiana Shrimp & Petroleum Festival."

The state was famous for unusual festivals, but that one was just wrong. "What kind of bad business?"

"Nothing was ever proven, mind you,"—she pointed her pipe at me—"but old Rex was accused of murder."

A steamboat whistle went off in my head, and I started like I had before I fell into the river. "If Nonna doesn't turn up in the next thirty minutes, I'm going to the police."

"Your nonna has only been missing for a few hours." Veronica leaned against the doorjamb of my office. "It's too soon to call the police."

"The captain murdered someone, Veronica." I sat forward in my desk chair and picked up my cell phone.

"Standish says it was his business partner, not a little old woman like your nonna. And you know as well as I do that the New Orleans PD won't be able to do anything if you call them now."

I scrolled through my phone contacts. "There's a certain Irish detective who would."

"Franki, you can't call Wesley Sullivan."

"Why not?" I attempted an innocent face even though I knew the guilty answer. "He knows Nonna, and he doesn't always play by police rules."

Her chin lowered. "The detective doesn't play by *any* rules. He proved that when he kissed you on Halloween in front of Bradley and then confessed that he was married."

"And how many times have I said that he's descended from one of the snakes Saint Patrick drove out of Ireland?"

"Then why would you call him?"

"Because he's exactly the kind of guy you need to locate a missing person. So I would expect Bradley to put any lingering jealousy aside in the interests of finding Nonna."

She crossed her arms. "For everyone's sake, I hope it doesn't come to that."

"Me too." I wanted to find my nonna, and Veronica was right —any contact with Sullivan would give him an opportunity to slither between Bradley and me and try to swallow our relationship whole.

The phone vibrated in my hand, dissolving a mental image of Sullivan flicking his forked tongue. "It's Bradley. Maybe he's found her." I tapped *answer*. "Hey, any luck at the church?"

"Father John hasn't seen her, so I decided to come to the Galliano and have a look for myself."

I cast Veronica a dark look and shook my head. "I take it she and Luigi aren't there, either."

"No one is. I talked to a guy at the ticket pavilion that handles the boat's bookings, and he said the maiden cruise isn't until this weekend."

"Which company is that? Gray Line?"

"No, Where Dat Tours."

I knew it well because of a murder I'd investigated in October involving one of the company's vampire tours. "Was the guy named Marv, by any chance?"

"I didn't catch his name because he said it through a mouthful of po' boy."

"That's him." I'd never seen Marv not eating something fried and covered in sauce or gravy. "Did you ask him about Nick Pescatore?"

"I didn't think to do that."

I stifled a *How could you not think of such an obvious question?*

"But Marv *did* say that apart from an employee meeting a

few days ago, the only person he's seen at the boat was a drunk bag lady who looked like she'd fallen into the river."

My chin jerked into my neck. *Drunk?*

A beep interrupted the line, and I looked at the display. *Santina Messina.*

"Bradley, I need to take this call. It's one of Nonna's friends."

"Do you want me to ask Marv about Nick Pescatore?"

"No, I'll take it from here. Thank you so much for doing all of this."

"You know I'd do anything for you and your family." His voice was soft, and deep. "I love—"

Another beep busted in, and the lobby bell got in on the mood-killing action.

Veronica went down the hallway.

"I love you too," I said, wondering whether he'd said *you* or something less romantic like *you guys.* Annoyed, I switched to the waiting call. "Hello, Mary?"

"Franki, baby! It's Bruno. I hear you called my house."

I gritted my teeth. It figured that Santina's son had been the one to cut off Bradley. The guy wouldn't get lost, as his mother well knew, because *his* house was actually *hers,* and he'd been living in it for forty-two years. "Uh, yeah. I called about my nonna. She's missing."

"Yeah, that's a bummer," he said, upbeat. "Anyway, are you available for dinner tonight? Mamma's cooking *scacciata.*"

The name of the stuffed Sicilian flat bread meant both *beaten down* and *driven away,* the two things I wanted to see happen to Bruno. "First of all, I'm not going anywhere until I find my nonna. And second, why don't you give it up? I'm staying with Bradley."

"Even if he doesn't propose before St. Joseph's Day?"

The low blow hit my chest like a lemon from a T-shirt cannon. Bruno had been in the church when Nonna had the lemons shot at me, so he understood the gravity of the approaching feast day. "If you weren't such a *mammone*, I'd say you were a bigger snake than Sullivan."

"Who's he?" he asked, ignoring the fact that I'd called him a mamma's boy in Italian. "You seeing guys on the side?"

The hope in his tone prompted me to hang up. Bruno had been pestering me for two years, and one way or another I needed to see to it that he was *scacciata* for good.

Veronica rushed into the room, beaming. "Your nonna is here."

I leapt from my chair, ready to unload my stress on her like I'd learned from my mother.

She blocked my path. "She's with Luigi, so you don't want to embarrass her."

I pulled down my sweater and pulled myself together. "All right. But how do they seem? Did they mention Nick Pescatore?"

"Not a word. I assume they're waiting to talk to you."

I narrowed my eyes. "Is Nonna wearing her black mourning dress?"

She hesitated. "It's gray."

"Dark gray, like at Christmas?"

"More medium?"

I recoiled. "What the hell is going on here? *Fifty Shades of Grey*?"

"Think of it this way—any shade of gray is a neutral color."

"Not for an elderly Sicilian widow." I flailed my arms. "She might as well be wearing scarlet."

She scratched a brow. "Why don't we focus on the Galliano issue since it's the most pressing?"

"Fine. But please tell me Glenda's not still out there in her leopard spots."

Veronica took me by the shoulders and led me to the doorway. "She voluntarily put on my old duster cardigan when your nonna came in."

Bewildered, I headed down the hall. Glenda was dressed respectably, Nonna was dressed scandalously, and I was dressed bag ladily. *What was happening to the world?*

I stopped just before the lobby and motioned for Veronica to stay back so that I could spy on Nonna and Luigi.

They sat stiffly on a couch and stared straight ahead exactly as they'd done on Christmas Eve. The scene was like a TV comedy sketch, and their appearance didn't help. With her short white curls and tight grip on her handbag, Nonna resembled Sophia Petrillo from *The Golden Girls*. And if Luigi had a pair of round glasses and a cigar to go with his suit and bowtie, he could have passed for an Italian George Burns—especially his ears, which were almost as big as hands. But his voice was regular George Burns, raspy from years of cigar smoking.

I marched over to Nonna. "I've been freaking out with worry."

"Why? I can-a take-a care of myself."

"You could've called."

"I had-a some things to do."

"Uh-huh." Sarcasm oozed from my tone like the ricotta from Nonna's cannoli. "And it was important stuff, like hiring David, my own coworker, to investigate me."

"I can-a take-a care of you too." She lifted the handbag from her lap, and I took a step back. It was well known in the family that she had some kind of weight in that thing.

I looked from her to Luigi, who sported a new hearing aid the size of a car motor and dark rings around his eyes the size of tires. "Will one of you please explain what's going on?"

Nonna gave a nod. "Luigi's got a *problema*. It's-a personal."

Glenda rose from The Vassal's desk, pulling Veronica's cardigan around her like a bedsheet. "If it's sexual, honey, you've come to the right place. Psychology was one of my majors at Tulane."

Luigi's hearing aid dropped to the floor.

And my jaw dropped to my chest. "*You* went to *college*?"

"I got a degree in Finance too, Miss Franki. I worked my way through school while I was stripping."

*So that wasn't just a line that strippers used.* "You have *two* degrees? But...why didn't you get a job?"

She blinked. "I went to school to increase my stripping revenue at Madame Moiselle's, sugar. A big part of stripping is counseling your clients. And then you've got to know how to manage the money. I'll talk about all of that in my memoirs."

*How many other surprises would the bare-all book reveal?*

Luigi refitted his hearing aid. Red splotches the size of Glenda's leopard spots covered his face and neck. "My late cousin's kid, Nicky, used to hang out at that club." He pulled a picture from his suit pocket. "You know him?"

Glenda eyed the photo. "I don't remember him. But I'm semi-retired, and I have so many fans it's hard to keep track."

I rolled my eyes.

"Too bad, because he could use a head doctor." He pocketed the picture. "If we find him, I'll hire you to talk to him."

I collapsed onto the couch. It was all really too much.

Veronica cleared her throat. "Luigi, we saw the article about Nick in this morning's paper. Would you like to move to a conference room to talk in private?"

He scrunched his wide, flat nose and waved off the notion. "Nah, Nicky's troubles are common knowledge." He paused, and his small, dark eyes watered. "He lost his mom when he was young and got mixed up with a bunch of hooligans who introduced him to booze and drugs. He's been in and out of jail ever since. Petty crime stuff."

I looked at my lap. Losing a mother was a tough break, and

not one that every kid could process. "When did you last see him?"

"At my cousin's funeral five years ago. But I'm all he's got left, so he calls me from time to time, usually when he needs money. Four days ago, he sent me this text." He pulled a cell phone from his suit pocket and tapped the screen.

I took the phone and looked pointedly at Nonna, silently reprimanding her for not owning one of her own. "Galliano gold." I handed the phone to Veronica and looked at Luigi. "Does that phrase mean anything to you?"

"At first, I thought it was drunken rambling, maybe a drink name. You know, like Galliano with gold tequila or Goldschläger."

It was plausible.

"Then I searched on the Google and found the steamboat."

I shot my nonna another silent reprimand. Luigi also knew how to use the internet, although he wasn't as savvy with the terminology.

Veronica returned the phone to Luigi. "I see you didn't reply to his text. Did you try to call him?"

"I've been trying to reach him since I got it. Yesterday I went to the steamboat, but no one was there, so I showed his picture to a guy at the ticket pavilion." He pressed his fingers to his forehead. "I can't think of his name, but Carmela and I talked to him again today."

I looked at Nonna, who stuck to the statue routine. "Was he eating a po' boy?"

Luigi nodded. "You know him?"

"Yeah, Marv."

He snapped knobby fingers. "That's right. Anyways, he saw Nicky board the Galliano the same day I got the text, but he never saw him get off. That's when I called the police."

Veronica reached for a pad of paper and a pen on the coffee table. "And what have they done to find him?"

"Not a damn thing. They think he's on a bender."

It was a fair conclusion given Nick's background. "Then how did the newspaper learn about his disappearance?"

"I called a reporter to get the word out."

The office door flew open, and David entered. His eyes darted from Nonna to me as his foot hung suspended in mid-air.

I lowered my lids and jerked forward, and he pivoted on the one leg and ran out.

Veronica glowered at me.

But I settled into the cushions, satisfied. David was free to investigate me for Nonna, just as I was free to torment him for it. "Luigi, was Nick a gambler?"

"Yeah, and he had a lot of gambling debts. Why?"

"The current owner and captain of the Galliano is a gambler named Rex Vandergrift. Maybe Nick went to the boat to see him."

He shook his head. "If you ask me, this has something to do with the original captain, Giacomo Galliano."

"Isn't he long dead?"

"Yes, in '25. But legend has it that he stole some of the missing Civil War gold and hid it on the steamboat."

I looked at Veronica. The case had gotten a lot more interesting. "There's missing Civil War gold?"

"Sure. Coins and bullion from the Confederate Treasury. And there were silver coins and jewelry too. It was all loaded onto a train in Richmond in 1865, the day before the Union Army forced General Lee's surrender at Appomattox, and then it disappeared."

The incident reminded me of a case I'd worked that was linked to the Nazi theft of the Amber Room. "How would a steamboat captain get Civil War gold?"

"Galliano fought for the Army of the Two Sicilies against Giuseppe Garibaldi and his thousand men, and he was one of several Sicilian troops who were transported to New Orleans to fight for the Confederacy. Search it on the Google."

My head was spinning from all the G names—and from the image of gold that I visualized myself finding on the steamboat. "I'll take your word for it."

Veronica tapped a pen against her lip. "Besides the Confederate treasure, is there anything else Nick might've meant by the gold reference?"

Luigi held up his palms. "It's got to be that missing gold. A couple of weeks ago I told Nicky that I wasn't going to give him any more money to support his habits. My guess is he got stoned on alcohol or drugs and got the cockamamie idea to go to the Galliano to look for it." His eyes met mine. "I owe it to my cousin to find him, and I need your help."

Veronica turned to me, and Nonna gave me her do-it-or-else-a glare.

"Whaddaya say, Franki?" Luigi pulled out his wallet. "I'll make it worth your while."

It felt awkward taking money from my nonna's sitting-and-staring partner. Then again, he did have a Lambo. "Of course I'll help. Can I have that picture of Nick?"

"It's yours."

I rose to retrieve the photo. "Just to cover all the bases, did Nick have any enemies that you know of?"

Luigi's jaw set. "Maybe the mob."

I stumbled backwards and bounced onto the couch. That not-so-minor detail should have been disclosed *before* I'd accepted the case. "What makes you say that?"

"Those gambling debts I mentioned."

Veronica's eyes had gone wide *and* stayed that way. "Did he gamble at a Mafia-run establishment? Or did he borrow from them to cover debts he'd accrued somewhere else?"

"I couldn't tell ya." Luigi rubbed his chin. "But Marv got uneasy when I told him Nicky was missing. He said it might not be related, but he wanted me to know that the Galliano's chef is a shady character."

Veronica frowned. "I don't understand."

After a run-in with a crazed, knife-wielding chef at Christmas, I did. "He's not French, is he?"

"It's a Sicilian. Alfredo Scalino."

The tense quiet that fell over the room was on par with *omertà*, the Mafia code of silence.

My head spun again with another G name—Gigi "The G-Man" Scalino, brother to Alfredo and one of the most vicious crime bosses ever to darken the streets of New Orleans.

"WELL, if it ain't my second-favorite PI." Marv leaned close to the purchase window of the Where Dat Tours ticket pavilion, his pudgy face and bald scalp reminiscent of Danny DeVito. "No offense or nothin', but Jim Rockford will always be first."

I half-smiled. "I used to watch *The Rockford Files* with my parents, so I'm okay with taking a backseat to James Garner."

"Speakin' o' backseats, you oughta trade your Mustang for a real muscle car like his Pontiac Firebird. You gotta get that gold."

*Get that gold. Is that what Nick had tried to do?*

Marv bit into a fried shrimp po' boy dripping brown gravy and tucked the bite into a cheek. "Hey, you need tickets? You've got time to catch the three o'clock torture tour or the one at the Museum of Death."

My stomach wobbled like I was on the boat. The fried seafood and tar odors didn't mix with the gruesome nature of

New Orleans tours. "I'm on the clock. My client is Luigi Pesca-tore, the elderly man who showed you a picture of his missing relative, Nick."

"Ah, yeah." He dropped his sandwich. "I saw him out here again this morning with some dame."

My head retracted. I told Veronica that Nonna's gray dress was scandalous.

"I wish I coulda helped him more, but I only saw Nick go *on* the boat."

"About what time was that?"

"Six p.m. on the nose. I remember because that's when my po' boy was supposed to be delivered." He gave a sly smile. "Fried catfish."

My eyes narrowed at the smile and catfish reference. *Did he know I was the so-called bag lady at the river this morning?*

"I closed at midnight that night, and I never saw him get off."

I understood why the police hadn't looked for Nick. He could have gotten off the Galliano when Marv wasn't looking or after he'd left. "Luigi said you mentioned an employee meeting that same day?"

"At seven that night."

"Nick could've still been on the boat at that time." I leaned against the counter. "Is there any chance he was an employee?"

"I asked the captain about that, but he said he's never heard of the guy."

I glanced at the Galliano. "Is Captain Vandergrift here now?"

"He's out of town until tomorrow, but you're not going to get any information out of him." He tapped his temple. "That one's a real screwball. Dresses and talks like he's from another time."

I had a bad flashback to Pam, Marv's aging hippie tour guide who'd helped me with the vampire case.

"Your best bet's to go undercover like Rockford. I can get you a job on the boat."

I imagined myself holding a clipboard like Julie, the cruise director from *The Love Boat*. "Thanks, but I don't even know if there's been a crime yet. What I need is to find a way to get onboard so I can look around."

"Why didn't you say so? We're going to offer tours, so I've got a spare key."

Apparently, *The Rockford Files* hadn't taught Marv much about investigations. "Can you let me on now?"

"Sure, but I doubt you'll find that missing guy." He pulled a set of keys from a drawer. "He's probably sleeping with the catfishes."

*Again with the catfish.* "What did you mean by that?"

"It's a mob sayin', but I added a river theme on account o' Gigi Scalino. You heard o' him?"

"Yeah, his clan's into everything from drugs to prostitution."

"Know why they call him the G-Man?"

I shrugged. "Because the G stands for money?"

"No, and it don't stand for government, neither." Marv leaned so close to the ticket slot that his lips almost protruded. "It's for gutter, as in he rips out the guts of his enemies."

My entrails clung to one another.

"Everyone knows that his brother Alfredo, who just happens to be a chef, helps him butcher his victims." He raised a bushy brow. "And guess who the captain hired to work the galley?"

Alfredo was certainly a suspicious hire, but I didn't have any evidence that Nick was dead, much less that the Scalinos had killed him. "If Nick *is* missing, it might not be mob related. My client thinks he was looking for some gold that Giacomo Galliano stole during the Civil War."

He grimaced. "Nothin' but a legend. Talk to the folks at the Confederate Memorial Hall; they'll tell you."

"I will."

Marv exited the pavilion.

I followed him up the sidewalk to the Galliano. "When was the last time you saw anyone on the boat?"

"Apart from the captain yesterday morning, not since the employee meetin'." Marv stepped on the gangplank and bounce-walked across.

I followed behind, grasping the railing and looking at the Mississippi ten feet or so below. *Was Nick Pescatore down in the brown water? Or had he left the Galliano some other way?* "Marv, did you see the captain carry anything off the boat?"

He pointed the keys at me. "Ooh, you mean with a body inside. He had an overnight bag, but that was too small to carry a dead guy. Maybe he chopped it up into pieces and fed it to the catfishes." He laughed and put a hand on his belly. "Like how I did that?"

My eyes narrowed again. Marv was lucky he'd already crossed the gangplank, or I might've pushed him off.

He unlocked the door to the main deck cabin. "Let me know when you're done, and I'll lock up."

"You're not going to show me around?"

"I ain't going in there."

"C'mon, Marv. It's huge."

He headed for the gangplank. "Two hundred and sixty feet long with three decks and forty-four staterooms. And every one of them's haunted."

"Don't tell me you believe your own ghost tours."

"They're a bunch o' hooey." He turned and met my gaze. "But twice when I stayed late for the midnight vampire tour, I heard a guy scream and then a smacking sound, like a body hitting somethin' hard and wet. Same thing both times, and it came from the boat."

I thought of the sailor who'd been thrown into the stern by the paddlewheel, and then I shook him out of my head. "Someone's obviously pranking you."

"Yeah, a ghost. Now I gotta get back to the booth, so be careful. Who knows what's lurking in that thing?" He shot a sideways look at the steamboat and hurried across the gangplank.

On that forbidding note, I stepped inside the Galliano.

"The Love Boat this is not," I muttered as I took in the décor. Instead of a fun cruise-ship interior, the steamboat looked like a combination of a low-rent Titanic and a rundown Vegas casino —complete with the odors of mildew, stale sweat, and broken dreams.

Grimy windows lined wood-paneled walls with tarnished brass fixtures. Above each window was a panel of Tiffany-style glass in brown, green, and peach that matched the worn floral carpeting. In the center of the room, a dusty crystal chandelier hung above a grand staircase. On either side of the staircase were rows of gambling tables—poker, blackjack, craps, and a couple of roulette wheels. In the back of the room was an old wooden bar.

Because of what Marv had told me about Chef Alfredo Scalino's Mafia ties, I decided to search the galley. Assuming it was on the main deck, I made my way to double doors beside the bar. A plaque on the wall read *Huck Finn Dining Hall*, an inauspicious moniker that evoked foods with *corn* in the name, like corned beef, corn pone, and corn dodgers.

The dining room was brighter, but no less sad and spooky. The wood paneling had been painted a dingy yellow, as had the tin ceiling, and the windows were covered in faded floral chintz drapes. Oddly, the tables had full place settings of glassware, silverware, and gold-rimmed china, as though a phantom dinner were taking place.

The wood floor creaked behind me.

I did a 180. "Marv?"

Silence.

"The boat's old, and it's on the water. Of course it creaks."

But my self-reassurance did little to help because I couldn't shake the image of tables full of ghost diners. When it came to spirits, I was a non-believer—until those suckers started acting up.

With my nerves jumping like that catfish I'd caught, I jogged across the dining hall and peered behind a door marked *Staff Only*.

I'd found the galley. It was a gray room with a few portholes, a brown tile floor, and a large chopping block in the center. Stainless steel stoves and ovens were on the left, and shelves for pots and pans were on the right, as was an unmarked door next to a hallway. Along the back wall were three commercial-sized refrigerator-freezers and a first aid kit.

Foreboding spread throughout my body like an oil spill.

I knew what I had to do.

Without giving myself time to change my mind, I walked over to the refrigerators and yanked open the first one.

Then the next.

And the one after.

All empty.

I let out the breath I'd been holding.

My gaze drifted to the unmarked door. I turned toward it, and a rush of air propelled me forward.

I did a full 360, paddlewheel style. "If that's you, Marv, it's not funny."

No one was in the room.

I thought about those ghosts again but came up with a more convincing, not to mention more comforting, explanation. "Old boats are drafty."

The foreboding turned to fear when I gripped the door handle. I turned the knob and kicked open the door.

It was a pantry.

I switched on the light and stiffened. A long white chest freezer was against the back wall.

Transfixed, I went to the freezer and lifted the lid.

Nick Pescatore smiled up at me from a seated position with a queen of spades playing card in his hand. He'd been frozen long enough for a thin layer of frost to form on his face.

# 4

The gangplank buckled with each pounding footstep, but I didn't stop running. I wanted to get off the Galliano and get to a payphone to make an anonymous tip. To find out who killed Nick Pescatore, I was going to have to take Marv up on the job offer and go undercover, so no one on the steamboat could know I'd found the body.

My feet landed on the riverbank, and I veered toward the ticket pavilion, which had a few customers. "Marv!"

He looked up.

"Lock the boat!" I made a neck-slicing motion.

The muscles in his face went slack as though they'd been cut.

And I kept running.

There was no urgency. Nick was subzero. He wasn't going to defrost and come back to life. But the horror of what I'd seen had made my feet flee, and the rest of my body tried to keep up.

I ran through Washington Artillery Park to Jackson Square and downshifted to a jog for the two blocks to Bourbon Street. My feet might've been afraid, but I was no athlete, and the quasi death rattle coming from my chest confirmed my assessment.

Weaving through the minefield of beaded and boa-ed partiers carrying drinks in plastic cups, I made my way to the Tropical Isle bar to use one of the city's few remaining payphones.

I immediately spotted the mascot for the bar's trademarked Hand Grenade, a.k.a. "New Orleans' Most Powerful Drink." He was a huge green hand grenade with big dopey eyes, a goofy smile, camouflage pants, and black clown shoes. And true to his Dancing Hand Grenade name, he was outside the Tropical Isle shimmying to the Bruno Mars song "Grenade" right in front of the payphone.

I approached him, out of steam and out of breath. "I need...to make...a call."

He stood his ground and shimmied forward and backward, trying to entice me to join in.

I added *out of patience* to my list. "If you don't move, I'm going to show you what hand grenades do."

He jolted, held out his arms to steady himself, and looked from side to side. Then he turned it into a dance move.

If I'd had air in my lungs, I would've sighed. The dancing drink was one of many reasons a payphone didn't belong on the famous party street.

Lowering my head like a longhorn, I charged past his Humpty-Dumpty girth. Then I scrounged two quarters from the bottom of my bag and fed them into the phone. I glanced around for the grenade, but he'd disappeared.

I faced the phone and called the police.

"Orleans Parish 911, Operator 27. Where's the emergency?"

"This is an anonymous tip about Nick Pescatore, the guy who went missing on the Galliano steamboat." I looked from side to side before mentioning his murder. "It's a code thirty. His body's in a freezer in the galley pantry." I hung up and turned to leave.

The Dancing Hand Grenade was behind me, air-grinding against my bottom.

My self-preservation instinct kicked in, and I shoved him—hard. I wasn't proud of myself, but in my defense, he *was* really padded.

He went still and assumed the position of a gunslinger at a duel. He yanked the white pin at his temple and went motionless for a few more moments. Then he threw up his arms and flailed them to indicate his explosion.

I rolled my eyes. "You're way too aggressive for a mascot, pal. Why don't you relax and have a drink?"

He put his puffy white-gloved hands on his hips and spun on his clown heels. Then he mosey-waddled to a guy in a cowboy hat and mimed lassoing him.

*That drink doesn't know when to quit.*

"Hey, Franki."

It was a female voice, but I didn't see anyone trying to get my attention.

"I'm on the second floor, so you have to look up to see me."

The instruction seemed like overkill, until I saw Bit-O-Honey waving from the balcony of Madame Moiselle's. She was a chubby, bubbly brunette and not the brightest pastie in the stripper closet. But she'd been a big help to me when I'd worked a homicide case involving one of her former coworkers.

She hung over the iron railing, and so did her pastied breasts. "What are you doing on Bourbon? Investigating something?"

I wasn't, but I was about to because Luigi had said Nick hung out at the strip club. "Yeah, could I talk to you for a second?"

"Wait there, and I'll come out." She threw a strand of Madame Moiselle's signature penis pendant Mardi Gras beads to a bodybuilder in the street. "Business is slow because of the breastfeeding conference in town."

*So much irony in that.*

I crossed the street and went to the club entrance. Then I turned and leaned against the wall. I wanted to make sure the Dancing Hand Grenade couldn't get behind me again.

Bit-O-Honey stepped out in the stripper equivalent of Minnie Mouse shoes. She'd put on a sheer yellow robe that only accentuated her pink-sequined pasties and G-string. "What did you want to talk to me about?"

I showed her the picture Luigi had given me. "I need to know whether you've seen this guy, Nick Pescatore, in the club."

She squinted through two-inch red lashes and held out her hands as though she couldn't see. Then she removed a lash and took another squint. "He comes in every now and then, but he never talks to anyone. The last time I saw him was a couple of weeks ago, and this lady in a gold tinsel wig rushed in and poured a drink on him."

*Gold. Was the color a coincidence?* "What did she look like?"

She shrugged. "Women in clothes all look the same."

That could've explained why I'd never seen Bit-O-Honey in a shirt—she was protecting her individuality.

"Why do you want to know about this Nick guy? Is he a criminal or something?"

I couldn't tell her I'd found him dead in a freezer. "He's missing."

Her eyes narrowed, and she pulled off the other lash. "It might be because of Gigi Scalino. He's a mob boss."

I pulled back, surprised. I hadn't expected her to connect the two men.

"You know I mean the Mafia and not a flash mob, right?"

"I got that. Thanks. But why do you think Gigi Scalino had something to do with Nick's disappearance?"

"Because he was sitting with Gigi when the lady dumped

that drink on him. And that made Gigi real mad because it got all over the tiny white dress shirts he wears on his shoes."

I had to think about that one for a minute, and then I remembered the Edward G. Robinson gangster movies I used to watch with my dad. "Are you talking about spats, the old-fashioned shoe covers men used to wear?"

"I guess so."

"Wow, not even Michael Jackson was able to bring that style back."

She reattached a lash. "Is he a client of Madame Moiselle's too?"

I stared at her for a second, wondering what kind of world she inhabited. "Um, no. Have you ever interacted with Gigi?"

"Sure. I danced for him in the VIP Room, and so have a lot of the other girls. But Mr. Scalino doesn't talk much. Just stares, mostly."

My upper lip crawled to my nostrils. I'd heard plenty of Glenda's stories about what went on in the private stripping rooms, and I never wanted to hear another.

"He's super generous, though. He gives out C-notes as tips. You know I mean a hundred-dollar bill and not like a Post-it Note, right?"

"Right."

"We get another C-note if we give him a little something extra." She winked her lashed eye. "If you know what I'm saying."

I did, and it was disgusting.

She attached her other lash. "You do, right? I mean, get what I'm trying to say?"

"Yeah. He wants more than a striptease."

She nodded. "A shoeshine."

My mouth fell open. "Wait. What?"

"I'll show you." She knelt and pretended to buff my boot,

causing her breasts to buff too. "We only get the tip if we unbutton his spats real slow, like a shoe striptease."

My head recoiled. *What a sicko.*

She rose and adjusted her G-string. "And you know what else we get?"

I was afraid to find out.

"Bit-O-Honey." She squealed and shook her money makers. "My name is his favorite candy. Can you believe that?"

I didn't reply. My attention was focused on the Tropical Isle bar. The Dancing Hand Grenade was in the doorway, pointing me out to a young woman in a bright green wig.

*Was she the same woman who'd poured the drink on Nick?*

We made eye contact, and she shoved a couple of men out of her way and sped down Bourbon on roller skates.

There was no way I could catch her, so I looked back at the bar. The Dancing Hand Grenade had split too. I didn't know what was going on, but I was certain it had to do with Nick Pescatore.

My heart was so heavy it practically weighed me down as I climbed the stairs to Private Chicks. Or maybe it was my thighs, which, other than being large, had been ravaged by all the running. Regardless of the culprit, each weighty, painful step brought me closer to having to call Luigi to inform him that his late cousin's son, Nick, was dead.

*Frozen like a piece of meat.*

Of course, I wasn't going to say it like that. The problem was that I didn't know how to say it.

I passed through the empty lobby bound for my office and the dreaded phone call. And I stopped cold in the doorway.

David's back was to me, and he was rifling through my day planner.

To startle him, I dropped my hobo bag on the floor.

He shot so high that he reminded me of Washington Artillery Park's Civil War cannon. Then he turned, red-faced, and his long, spindly fingers went to his chest. "Dude. You scared me."

"I'm just getting started." I blocked the door and assumed the gunslinger stance à la the Dancing Hand Grenade.

"Help." His cry was feeble, but it elicited Veronica's heels in the hallway.

"Franki." She tapped my shoulder. "Let David out."

"He's investigating me."

"That's what your nonna is paying him to do. If you want him to stop, you'll have to take that up with her."

I would as soon as I'd told Luigi about Nick. I moved to let him pass but imprisoned him with my gaze. As he scurried to the lobby, I saw his LEGO *Star Wars* pen on my desk and shouted, "You can kiss Chewbacca goodbye, buddy."

Veronica gave me the side-eye and took a seat. "You're acting like a child."

"I'm not the one playing with LEGOs."

"Go easy on David. All he wanted to do was find out whether you have a date with Bradley on your birthday. He thought that would placate your nonna for a while."

"Well, my planner is as clueless as I am." I flopped into my desk chair to underscore my frustration. "Apparently, Bradley's mind is on Mardi Gras, his so-called favorite day of the year."

"He always spoils you on your birthday. I'm sure he's got something planned."

It felt wrong to discuss my petty personal problems after the gruesome discovery I'd made on the Galliano. I rubbed my eyes trying to clear the mental visual. "I have some rough news about

Nick Pescatore. I found him dead in a chest freezer on the steamboat."

Veronica looked as frozen as he had, which made the awful memory more vivid. "I went to a payphone and reported it as an anonymous tip."

Her horrified eyes widened. "You left him in the freezer?"

"What was I supposed to do? Contaminate the crime scene by pulling him out?"

"No, it's just that—"

"It seems so cold and callous to leave him there?" I waved my hand in an eraser motion. "Forget I said *cold*." I massaged my temples, which were starting to ache. "Look, Marv said he could get me one of the open jobs on the boat, so I did what I had to do to be able to carry out the investigation undercover."

She reached across the desk and squeezed my hand. "I'm sorry. It's just such a shock."

"Tell me about it." I sat back in my chair, wishing its arms could hug me. "And now I have to call Luigi."

We sat in silence for at least a minute.

The Vassal appeared in the doorway. His mouth was open, so I waited for him to speak. But he began scaling the room with his back pressed to the wall. Veronica and I watched him slide about ten feet in, where he stopped, darted to my desk, snatched Chewbacca, and ran out.

"So, before I make the call," I said leaning forward, "Nick was in a seated position with a queen of spades card in his right hand—smiling."

She went still again. "Do you think he...froze that way?"

"It's possible that he knew he was trapped and waited to die holding the card, but I sincerely hope the killer positioned him like that after he was dead. As for the smile, I don't know how that happened. Maybe a muscle reflex in death?"

Veronica gripped her mouth as though she wanted to

prevent it from moving. "So the card was either a message from Nick or a message from the killer."

"Two things come to mind—Captain Vandergrift's poker playing and the horse-head-in-the-bed scene from *The Godfather*."

"You mean, he's implicating the captain, or it was a Mafia calling card, so to speak, for not paying his gambling debts."

I shrugged. "Or the captain put the card in Nick's hand to expose him as a card cheat. The only other thing I can figure is that the card itself is symbolic. I read once that every card in a playing deck symbolizes something."

"You could ask Chandra Toccato."

I leapt from my seat as though it were one of the flaming toilets that Chandra's husband Lou sold at their plumbing and psychic services company. "Don't even utter her name. You could psychically summon her."

"Well, she *does* do Cartomancy, so she could tell you what the queen of spades means."

"So can the internet, which is faster and doesn't channel psycho spirits who come back to haunt me."

"Valid point." She rose from her seat. "You'd better call Luigi before the police notify him. He left you his contact information." She pulled a business card from her pocket and slid it across my desk. "I'll leave you alone to talk to him."

Veronica left, and I added Luigi to my Contacts list to procrastinate for a few seconds. Then I tapped the number and took a seat as the phone rang.

"Hello? Who is this?"

I half-smiled at his aggressive answer. "Luigi, it's Franki. Listen, I don't know how to tell you this—"

"You don't have to, kid. I knew Nicky was gone."

I fell silent. He'd put up a brave front, but his voice trembled, so the last thing I wanted to do was mention the freezer. "You were right. He was on the steamboat, so you should be hearing from the police soon."

"You okay, kid?"

My stomach churned like the Galliano's paddlewheel. His concern for my well-being only made the situation harder. "I will be, but I'm devastated that this happened."

"Don't take it so hard. Nicky knew the crowd he was running with. I appreciate you sticking your neck out to find him."

I squeezed my eyes shut. "I'm going to find out who did this, I promise."

"I'm counting on that. I'll talk to you soon."

He closed the call, and I put my head on my desk and wrapped my arms around it. I wanted to be in darkness to match my mood. Initially, I'd agreed to look for Nick for my nonna's sake, but after hearing Luigi's reaction, I wanted to find Nick's killer for him.

I heard someone enter my office and take a seat. I knew Veronica had come to comfort me, but I wasn't ready to face anyone.

"I've heard of laying down on the job, but this takes the layer cake."

The dry tone and wry comment were unmistakable.

Alarmed, I raised my head.

Bradley's ex-assistant, Ruth Walker, tightened her graying bun and popped the pull-tab on a can of Pepsi. The laugh lines on her face weren't laughing, and the chains on either side of her black horn-rimmed glasses wagged like fingers repri-manding me. "Speaking of jobs, I lost mine when Bradley resigned from the bank to spend time with you."

I sat up and considered calling for help as David had done. Ruth was obsessed with watching people get justice on court TV shows, so I feared she'd come to seek some of her own—outside the TV courtroom. "I'm sorry. I thought the bank had kept you on. What have you been doing?"

"Buying lottery tickets and rewatching every episode of *The People's Court*." She unzipped a fanny pack and pulled out a small bottle. "But I'm all out of episodes and unemployment benefits, so I'm here for that job."

"We're not hiring."

She unscrewed the cap from the bottle, and I tensed. There could've been poison in that thing. Or acid.

"Fair's fair. You cost me the job, you get me another." She poured the liquid into her Pepsi.

I relaxed, but not too much. "I'm the one who got you the assistant job to begin with, so I shouldn't have to replace it."

Her head swooped into my personal space. "So you're God now, is that it? The Franki giveth, and the Franki taketh away?"

"I would never think of myself as God."

"Darn straight you wouldn't." She slurped from the can. "He's the epitome of charity."

I resented the implication that I wasn't charitable, especially after I'd just reminded her about getting her the job with Bradley.

Veronica entered. "Ruth, we haven't seen you in a while. What have you been up to?"

"Trying to get by after this one"—she jerked a thumb at me —"cost me a job. Now I'm looking for one. You hiring?"

"I already told her we're not."

Veronica smiled and looked at me. "Maybe Marv could get her one of those steamboat positions you mentioned."

Ruth turned with her lips puckered so tightly that her laugh lines threatened to crack her cheeks.

I sank low in my chair. I had to defuse her anger before she tried to sue me on television. "I didn't think you'd be interested.

It's a drinking and gambling boat, and there could be overnight cruises."

"There are casinos and bars on Carnival cruise ships, and I've been on every one that sails from New Orleans." She pulled a plastic card from her fanny pack. "I'm one of their VIFPs."

Veronica eyed the card. "What does that stand for?"

"A Very Important Fun Person."

If Ruth was one of their fun guests, that wasn't good advertising for the company. "Look, I was just hired to investigate a crime on the boat. So why don't I talk to Marv and see if he has something for you at the Where Dat Tours office?"

"And stick me on the admin tasks while you play bingo and eat at the buffet? No sir, I want to cruise."

"Don't insist, Ruth." My tone was testy after that *sir*. "I'm not sure the Galliano's safe."

"You mean Captain Vandergrift's boat? All this time I thought you were talking about the Steamboat Natchez."

I glanced at Veronica. "You know the captain?"

"Not personally. He's a regular at Harrah's."

Glenda had said as much, but I couldn't wait to hear how Ruth would explain her presence at the casino. "How do you know that?"

"I see him there every time I play the penny slots."

Veronica rested her hand on Ruth's chair. "I never realized you were such a gambler."

"Oh, I don't place any bets, so it's not gambling."

*No, just like whatever she'd poured into her Pepsi wasn't drinking.* I knew the answer to the question I was about to ask her, but I wanted Veronica to hear it. "Then what do you call playing the lottery and the slots?"

"Gaming."

Veronica looked away, but I caught the corners of a grin.

Ruth tipped her can in my direction. "Based on what I know

of that crackpot captain, I'm not surprised you're investigating a crime on his steamboat."

"Why do you say that?"

"After a few too many rum and Cokes one night, the captain told half the casino that Civil War gold was hidden onboard." She took a slug of her drink. "I got that straight from Rudy at the craps table."

*Where she wasn't gambling.* "I don't see the crime."

"You will. A couple of weeks ago, I heard the old coot threaten a man if he came looking for the loot."

"Really?" *Is that what Nick had been doing?* "Did you see the man he threatened?"

Ruth glared at me over her horn-rims. "What do you think I am? A nosy parker?"

It was best not to answer.

Veronica bit her lip. "People make a lot of threats. That doesn't mean they follow through with them."

I steepled my fingers. "No, but what did he say exactly?"

Her chains began to rock. "He said, 'You put one boot on my boat, and I'll acquaint you with a new meaning for the cold shivers.'"

Veronica and I exchanged a look. Under normal circumstances, I would've said the captain's threat was tame. But there was nothing normal about the phrase "a new meaning for the cold shivers" when a man had been found dead in a deep freeze.

## 5

"Francesca Lucia Amato." My mother's shrill voice erupted from the phone and ricocheted off the columns of the recessed entrance to the Civil War Museum. "I haven't even been gone for half a day, and you've already traumatized Luigi."

A meat slicer whined in the background, so I knew she was at our family deli, probably imagining slicing me like salami. "Are you seriously blaming me for telling him about his cousin's son? The one he hired me to find?"

"Yes, because you never should have taken that case. It should've been obvious that you weren't to do anything to upset him."

Incredulous, I walked down the steps and away from the building—in case I needed to make a scene. "I thought you'd want me to help Luigi, since you're his biggest fan."

"Do you understand *nothing* about relationships, Francesca?"

"Apparently not the mother-daughter one."

"And now she's back-talking me, Rosalie," my mother lamented to her best friend and long-time customer of the deli. Rosalie was built like a beer keg on two tree stumps, which fit her steam-roller personality, and she always managed to be on standby when there was an issue she could spin into a juicy story. "Where did I go wrong with her?"

"You let her go to public university instead of a Catholic college," Rosalie said, rebuke ready. "They give young women way too much freedom."

"Just like her father."

"What did I do now?" my dad boomed.

"You always let your daughter do whatever she wanted," my mother yelled, "and look at the results."

I thought the results were pretty darn good, especially considering how my brother Anthony turned out. "Hey, Mom, I'm at Confederate Memorial Hall, and they're staying open late for me. So if you're going to talk to everyone in the deli, can I let you go?"

She gasped. "Don't you mouth off to me, young lady."

"Just hang up, Brenda," Rosalie huffed. "That'll show her who's in charge. And look at these invitations. They say, *That's Amore*."

*That's Amore?* The lemon tradition came to mind, and I puckered. *Was she...?* "Mom, are you planning my engagement party?"

"With a cold-footed groom like Bradley?"

Larry from the deli belly-laughed. "I just got an image of him with big blocks of ice on his feet. That's funny."

*Yeah. Hilaaarious.* My feet paced to walk off some steam. "So who are those invitations for?"

"Your nonna."

I slipped off the sidewalk and narrowly missed oncoming traffic. "Are you kidding? We don't even know if they're dating yet."

"Of course they are. And at their age, they don't have much time, so I'm trying to help them speed things along."

We both knew who she was trying to help, and it wasn't

Nonna or Luigi. "You need to put the brakes on this whole fairy tale you've concocted. If you ask me, Luigi has family obligations that—"

"He's married?" Her pitch was somewhere along the spectrum of shriek and scream.

"Who's married?" my father barked in his nervous-indigestion voice.

"Bradley." Rosalie belted out his name so the whole deli would hear. "He remarried that ex-wife of his."

I cringed. That was more than a spin—it was a runaway Tilt-A-Whirl.

"Yo, Joe." Larry's tone had turned Italian-American mafioso. "Maybe we should replace those ice shoes with cement?"

"Sounds justified," an unknown man said.

*Great. They're chatting with customers about killing my boyfriend.* I went and sat on the steps. "So, Mom? Could you help me out here and tell them we're talking about Luigi?"

She covered the receiver. "It's not Bradley, everyone. But that would've been better."

"Mom! What are you saying?"

"I just meant that you've got more time than your nonna does, dear. Although, if you want to have children, not much. Now what are these family obligations Luigi has?"

I had to ungrit my teeth to respond. "All I meant was that an elderly man with a produce company probably wouldn't be in a hurry to remarry. I'm sure he has heirs to think about."

"Well, he couldn't have made much from a grocery store produce job."

I decided to tell her, since she would find out eventually. "He owns Little Palermo Produce, the major corporation?"

"Little...Palermo?" She spoke like her lungs had sprung an air leak. "That's...our...Lu...i...giiii?"

Several loud bonks told me the phone receiver had hit the

floor—and maybe my mother as well. Either way, she wouldn't be returning to the conversation.

*Hm. I should shock her more often.*

I dropped the phone into my bag and climbed the steps to the imposing red-brick building. When I'd googled the address, I read that Confederate Memorial Hall had opened in 1891, which made it the oldest museum in Louisiana. The Romanesque Revival style gave it a fortress feel, which was appropriate given its contents.

I opened the heavy door, and the inside was just as imposing. In the middle of the room was a cannon, and not a replica like the one at Washington Artillery Park. The walls were done in dark wood paneling lined with glass cases containing uniforms, weapons, and various documents. Above them hung paintings of Confederate generals and framed flags. And the peaked roof and rear stage backed by stained-glass windows were reminiscent of a chapel, hence the museum's nickname, The Battle Abbey of the South.

"You must be Franki Amato, the one who called about the missing Civil War gold."

I looked around for the source of the voice.

A forty-something male rose from underneath the cannon with a rag in his hand. He wore a gray button-down shirt and suspenders, and he had a bizarre beard that grew only under his chin and jaw.

"Oh, hair—I mean, hi."

He tucked the rag into his back pocket and extended his hand. "Jefferson Davis, at your service."

We shook, while I tried to figure out whether that was his real name or whether he was in character as the president of the former Confederate States. "Perfect name for the work you do."

"I'm also a Civil War reenactor in the Battle of New Orleans."

That sounded about as fun as reenacting Hurricane Katrina,

but I feigned a look of enthusiasm. "Was that the one where Andrew Jackson enlisted the help of the pirate Jean Lafitte?"

"That was the first Battle of New Orleans during the War of 1812. General Jackson led a ragtag army of militia fighters, frontiersmen, slaves, Indians, and Lafitte's pirates to defeat a vastly superior British Army."

"Oh, I never made the connection that there had been two major war battles here."

"Yes'm." He sucked his tobacco-stained teeth. "And if you're wondering, I'm a progressive."

I hadn't been, but okay. "I haven't met many modern-day Democrats who are so into the Civil War."

"You think I'm a Liberal? Good God, no." His words came out like a rebel yell. "A progressive is what we call a hard-core authentic—someone who's period-appropriate down to their drawers—flannel or osnaburg, which is a coarse, inexpensive linen."

"Ah." I glanced at a sword to discourage an underwear reveal.

His mouth twisted, and he stared into the distance. "The Farbs call us stitch-counters, but what can you expect from guys who show up at a Civil War battlefield wearing polyester and eating po' boys?"

"Right?" I said as though "Farb" was a term I knew and used in everyday conversation.

His face softened. "Hey, next January you should come out to the battle. We could use a nurse or a flag-sewer."

"Didn't women fight in the Civil War? I thought I read somewhere that a few did."

He went as stiff as his beard. "We don't talk about that."

*And he calls himself a progressive.* "So, is this whole missing gold story true?"

"Depends on who you ask. Some of the Confederate assets

were spent paying the soldiers and funding their retreat from the Union forces. But eighty-six thousand dollars in gold coins and bullion was entrusted to Navy Paymaster, Lt. Cdr. James A. Semple to be deposited in a bank in Liverpool to fund the revival of the Confederacy. Historians think the turncoat went and divided it up with two of his friends."

I could see whose side he was on. "Any chance some of it is hidden on the Galliano steamboat?"

"There's a rumor to that effect, but I don't buy it. Old Captain Jack was quite the tall-tale teller."

"You mean, Giacomo Galliano, the original captain of the steamboat?"

Jefferson gave a curt nod. "He went by 'Jack' after he came over from Palermo. Said he was related to Giuseppe Galliano, the hero of the First Italo-Ethiopian War that the liqueur is named after. He also claimed he'd fought with Garibaldi and his thousand men, which was hogwash."

Luigi had said that Galliano's service on Garibaldi's army was how he came to fight in the Civil War. "So, he wasn't one of the Sicilian soldiers sent here to fight for the Confederacy?"

"He fought in the Civil War, all right, but a genealogist proved he was part of an antebellum wave of Sicilian immigration to New Orleans."

"I had no idea Sicilians came here back then."

"They kept coming, too. After the Civil War they replaced freed slaves on the sugar plantations. Eventually, they went from harvesting sugar cane to truck farming and sold their produce at the French Market in the Quarter."

Like my nonna and nonnu, and Luigi.

"In fact, in the early 1900s, the French Quarter was known locally as Little Palermo."

Pride surged in my chest. That must've been where Luigi got his company name.

"The Sicilians were behind the creation of Bourbon Street. They set up illegal gambling operations in the backrooms of bars and clubs, things like pinball and poker machines, all of it controlled by the mob."

Some of my pride surged out.

He pulled a plastic baggie from his front pants pocket. "Care for some hardtack?"

When it came to food, I was definitely a Farb. "I ate some, uh, salt pork before I came."

"That's good eatin'," he said, swallowing my story. He popped a bite of the biscuit into his mouth and tucked it back into his pocket. "Anyhow, Galliano ran with the Bourbon Street mob, and there's some evidence that he bought the steamboat with proceeds from an illegal bookmaking scheme. So if he did hide loot on the boat, I'd say it was gambling money."

The current captain, Rex Vandergrift, apparently believed otherwise.

Jefferson put his hands on his hips. "So, are you part of some sort of festival or theme party?"

"I'm not following you."

"Well, I can count on one hand the number of people who've asked me about Captain Galliano and the gold, and both of you have come in today."

That *was* kind of weird. "Maybe it's because the Galliano steamboat just came to town."

"Or maybe the other lady hit her head one too many times roller-skating."

The woman who'd been talking to the Dancing Hand Grenade skated through my mind. "Why would you say that? About the roller-skating?"

"She came into the museum on a pair of skates. I had to ask her to take the darn things off."

An interest in Captain Galliano's gold could've been a coincidence, but those skates weren't. "I think I know who you're talking about. Was she wearing a wig too?"

He massaged his chin, which didn't disturb his beard underneath. "Yeah, a red one. And a floppy hat pulled down real low."

She hadn't wanted to be recognized. "Did you get her name?"

"Said it was Goldie."

The name hit me like a musket blast, not so much because of the Civil War gold but because of Nick Pescatore's final text, Galliano gold. The fact that she'd come to Confederate Memorial Hall after she ran from me raised two big questions. *Was this Goldie a treasure hunter? And if so, had she killed Nick to stop him from finding it?*

WHEN I TURNED the Mustang around the corner to my house, the sun was setting over the cemetery. I imagined my irate mom emptying the bones from a mausoleum so she could put me in it, and then I rolled my eyes toward the fourplex.

And hit the brakes.

Fiats filled the driveway and spilled into the street, which meant the nonne had converged on my apartment. It also meant that I was in violation of an amendment to Glenda's Visitor Policy that permitted only two nonne at any one time to give Glenda a reasonable chance of avoiding being "tied up" with an apron. The policy was ironic considering that she was standing in the yard with Veronica in an outfit made of whips.

My text tone sounded.

I pulled my phone from my bag. I'd gotten two texts. One was from Bradley, who'd learned of Nick's death on the news and wanted me to call him, and the most recent was from Marv, who'd gotten me a kitchen position on the Galliano starting the next morning. Compared to what awaited me on the lawn and in the house, a haunted and dangerous steamboat sounded nice.

I climbed from the car and walked toward my first hurdle. "Hey, Glenda. I'm sorry about the meeting of the nonne."

She puffed from a spiked cigarette holder. "Miss Ronnie says they're mourning Mr. Luigi's kin, so I'll overlook it. Just like I'll overlook that winged head with three legs covering my Mardi Gras decorations."

My eyes shot to the second-floor balcony. Nonna or one of her friends had covered Glenda's giant breasts with the Sicilian flag. "That's the symbol of Sicily, the *Trinacria*. The head is Medusa, and the legs represent the three points of the island."

"I just thought it was kinky, sugar." She stuck out her tongue and touched the tip to her lip.

Veronica giggled, and the fur muff she held moved.

My eyes widened, and her Pomeranian Hercules's snout emerged from the whitish fur. Somewhere in that dog's DNA was the key to the cure for baldness. "I'd better go in and talk to Luigi."

Veronica put Hercules on the ground. "I've already offered my condolences, but if you want, I can come with you."

"That's all right. If he's up to it, I'm going to ask him some more questions about the case."

Glenda stubbed out her cigarette with a stripper shoe that said *I spank*. "Well, I've got to go change out of my errand outfit and get my writing look on. Maybe that'll help me figure out what to call my memoir."

Veronica smiled. "I suggested *Lorraine Lamour: My Life in the Limelight*."

*The Red Light is more like it*. "That doesn't quite capture her essence."

"Let me know if you have any ideas, Miss Franki. You know me—I'm open."

*A Southern Belle Jezebel* came to mind, but I didn't say it. "I will."

I opened the door to my apartment. The air was somber and filled with the odor of garlic and fried meat, which was awesome because contrary to what I'd told Jefferson Davis, I hadn't eaten salt pork for dinner—or anything since the beignets at breakfast.

Santina, Mary, and ten other nonne were in the living room in full mourning dress. Their eyes were shut tight as they worked the beads of their rosaries. But every now and then, an eye would open and steal a glance at Nonna and Luigi, who sat as stiff as uncooked lasagna noodles at the Baroque dining table in the kitchen. And the prayers would become more fervent.

I crept past them and entered the kitchen, where a nonna cooked at the stove and Napoleon begged at her feet, oblivious to my presence. I approached Luigi. "Can I get you anything?"

"Thanks, kid. But I got a houseful of women trying to feed me. And your nonna has been a real comfort."

I almost fell into my chair. To my memory, no one had ever described Nonna that way.

Luigi's gaze lowered to a plate of antipasti. "I talked to the police a half hour ago. When the medical examiner is done with his investigation, I'm going to follow Nicky's wishes and have him cremated."

Nonna lifted her black lace veil. "But-a first they gotta wait-a for him to defrost-a."

I could see what a comfort she was.

"*Cremato!*" a nonna cried, and the others wailed in unison.

The nonne were lamenting Nick's cremation, and I wasn't surprised. Not only did the Catholic Church frown on keeping loved ones in urns for fear of idolatry, the practice also meant that they couldn't throw themselves on the casket.

I put my hand on Luigi's hunched shoulder. "I'm going

undercover on the Galliano. I report for kitchen duty tomorrow."

"Why don't you leave this to the police, kid? It's too dangerous with Alfredo Scalino onboard."

"After investigating people who live as vampires, I think I can handle him." I immediately regretted saying the *think*, but I did have my doubts. Alfredo Scalino could have been using his chef job as a cover for Mafia activities, just as the TV character Tony Soprano had claimed to be a sanitation worker. Plus, the alleged ghosts on the steamboat had me spooked. In my experience, hauntings were either concocted as a draw for tourists, or they were a shield for something nefarious.

Luigi shot my nonna a lidded look and turned to me. "There's something I need to tell you, Franki, and it's not so good."

I grabbed a salami slice for nervous chewing. "I'm listening."

"There's an old beef between the Pescatores and the Scalinos."

The nonna at the stove heard *beef* and carried a frying pan to the table. She prodded the contents with a wooden spoon. "*Stigghiola.*"

My lips grimaced at the grilled, spiced lamb intestines. I would have rather eaten hardtack with Jefferson at the battle-field. "*No, grazie.*"

"*Mangia!*"

"Uh-uh."

She scowled and returned to the stove.

I grabbed another salami slice. "So, what were you saying about a, um, feud?"

"It has to do with his grandfather's wine press, but I need to backtrack for a minute. You see, our families are from Sambuca di Sicilia, a little town in the Agrigento province of Sicily."

"It's an hour from-a Porto Empedocle." Nonna's tone conveyed her pride in her hometown.

Luigi pushed a wisp of hair over his scalp. "Gigi and I both went to Palermo for work, not together, of course. Like me, he earned money picking fruit and vegetables in the fields and immigrated to New Orleans. I learned how to sell produce, and he learned how to run a Mafia clan."

"I don't get how the two are related to farming."

"If you worked on a farm in Palermo, you ran into the produce Mafia."

"Produce?" I leaned back. "Everyone knows the mob is involved in drugs, gambling, and prostitution. But *lettuce*? That's almost embarrassing."

"They're into everything, kid. If they can make a dishonest buck off it, they've got a black hand in it. And the Mafia started in Palermo because of the British Navy's need for lemons to treat scurvy. It led to a whole citrus Mafia. Search it on the Google, if you don't believe me."

I didn't need online verification. I'd met the New Orleans citrus Mafia—the Sicilian nonne who force their granddaughters to steal lemons from church altars—and my nonna was their capo. "I've always associated Sicily with oranges, and the Amalfi Coast with lemons."

"Palermo has been known for centuries as *Conca d'Oro*, Shell of Gold, because of all the lemon trees in the bay."

*Gold. There it was again. Did it have anything to do with Nick's text?*

"Anyway"—Luigi swallowed a sip of water—"a cousin of mine married Gigi and Alfredo's little sister, Serafina. And when their grandfather died, his father decreed that she would receive the winepress upon his death."

"*Morto*," a nonna shouted, and I jumped in my seat. She had repeated the word *death* in Italian to heighten the tragedy of the moment. For the nonne, life was sorrow, and they never missed an opportunity to call attention to that—or to dish it out to family members like pasta on a plate.

I plucked an olive from the antipasti and popped it into my mouth. "Why did he give the winepress to Serafina and not to Gigi or Alfredo?"

"They were in New Orleans, and I think his father knew they were criminals and didn't want either of them to have it."

Nonna gripped the handles of the handbag in her lap. "That would bring-a shame to his-a father's memory."

"*Vergogna*," a nonna shouted, repeating the word *shame*.

I started and braced myself for the emerging pattern. "Let me guess—Gigi didn't take it well because he was the oldest male and thought the winepress should've gone to him."

"And he was furious that it would be passed down among the Pescatores."

"So what did he do? Threaten your cousin?"

Luigi clenched his jaw, and the skin on his neck tightened. "He had him strangled."

"*Strangolato*," a nonna shouted.

My hand went to my throat. I was prepared for the nonna's cry but not for the shocking revelation.

Luigi loosened his bow tie, as though he too felt suffocated by the murder. "The police said they didn't have any evidence to charge Gigi, much less have him extradited. But everyone knew they were too scared to prosecute him."

"What happened to Serafina?"

"She wasn't home when he was killed. But she died a few months ago, and she didn't have any kids."

"Then what did she do with the winepress?"

He cast a heavy look at my nonna that was underscored by the bags beneath his eyes. "She left it to me, but I never had any kids either."

"Did you leave it to Nicky?"

"Given his lifestyle"—he paused to glance at my nonna—"I didn't think he was the right choice."

I exhaled, frustrated by all the stalling. "So where *is* the winepress?"

Nonna raised her chin. "In a trunk-a in-a your closet."

"Closet!" I shouted it in English because the word didn't exist in Italian. But that didn't make the situation any less dramatic. Because if Gigi Scalino had ordered the strangulation of Luigi's cousin, then I didn't want to imagine what he'd have done to me when he heard that I not only had the winepress but was investigating him for Nick Pescatore's murder.

# 6

I raised my head in the pitch black to roll onto my side, but there wasn't enough room.

*That's weird.*

I reached out on either side of me and touched a cold, hard surface. I definitely wasn't in my bed. *Where was I? Was I inside something?*

The freezer I'd found Nick Pescatore in came to mind, but that wasn't possible because the police had removed it from the Galliano as evidence. And I wasn't even on the steamboat. I was at home.

*Home.* Terror swirled in my chest like a tornado. *I'm in the trunk Luigi and Nonna put in my closet.*

The Scalinos had taken out their winepress and locked me inside. And I didn't need to wonder why they'd done it.

*The trunk is my coffin.*

I heard rustling, like leaves.

*Oh, God. Are they about to bury me in the cemetery across the street? If so, I will haunt Veronica for the rest of her life for tricking me into moving to the fourplex, and I'll haunt her in death too.*

A rushing sound ensued, and freezing water entered the trunk, drenching my feet.

The terror sank to my stomach like an anchor. *The Scalinos threw me into the Mississippi to sleep with the catfishes.*

I thrashed from side to side. I couldn't die yet. I had to turn thirty-one, get married, have babies so that I could find out what life was like without Nonna perched on my back, draped around my neck, and latched like a ball and chain to my ankle.

*Wait a minute...Nonna. I let her have my bed. So I can't be in the trunk, because I'm sleeping in my clawfoot tub.*

I sat up in my sleep shirt. It had all been a bad dream, but the freezing water was real because someone had turned on the bathtub faucet. I turned it off and threw open the shower curtain.

My mother screamed.

I screamed back.

Because she stood stark naked in front of the Louis XVI vanity.

I yanked the shower curtain shut. It was a scene straight out of a French brothel horror film—if that were a genre.

"What are you doing in there, Francesca?" she shouted in the what-have-you-done-*now* tone of my childhood. "You gave me such a fright I almost jumped from my skin."

Her reference to skin brought the brothel scene back, and I rubbed my eyes hard to wipe it out. "The nonne were so loud last night that I had to come in here and turn on the fan to drown out their wailing." *Speaking of drowning...*I looked at my wet legs. "What are you doing in New Orleans?"

"I came to help poor Luigi with Nick's memorial."

*And to help poor Luigi, who wasn't poor at all, propose to Nonna.*

"I got up at three a.m. to drive here—this after staying up until eleven to make your father a lasagna, because God forbid the man who owns a deli would have to eat sandwiches for dinner. Thank goodness Mary's in the kitchen making breakfast, because I'm flat exhausted."

I pulled my knees to my chest and hugged my dripping limbs. Waking up to my mother was a splash of cold water.

"Would you mind coming out of there, Francesca? Everyone's at the funeral home, and I was looking forward to a hot bath and a quick nap before they get back. And shouldn't you be at work? It's almost nine o'clock."

*The employee meeting on the Galliano.* I threw open the shower curtain and closed it again. "Mom, would you please put some clothes on?"

"What for? I just told you that I'm going to take a bath."

With a sigh, I averted my eyes, opened the curtain, and climbed from the tub. I wrapped a towel around my waist and squeezed past her to my bedroom. I opened my closet.

The trunk loomed like the coffin of my nightmare. After I'd recovered from the shock of learning about the winepress, Luigi had said that he wanted me to have it, which was touching. But given its family history, I wanted the winepress back in Italy, or at the bottom of the Mississippi.

"What's that old thing?" My mother stood beside me—still in her brothel birthday suit.

I pointed to the robe hanging from the bathroom door. "Why don't you put that on?"

She strode to the bathroom and slammed the door. "How did I raise such a prude?"

*Uh, you sent me to Catholic School?* was my honest reaction, but I kept my mouth shut so she'd stay in there.

I pulled the hot pink duvet from my bed and tossed it on the trunk, tucking it around the sides. The cover wouldn't fool the Mafia, but it made me feel a little better.

There was a knock on my door, and I closed the closet. "Come in."

Mary entered. She was younger than the other nonne, but no less short, round, and old-fashioned, as evidenced by her mourning dress and coat with the obligatory hat and veil.

"I made some *cartocci*," she said, referring to Sicilian breakfast pastries filled with ricotta cream, "and now I'm headed to the funeral home. But first, I wanted to let you know that Santina and I have a national prayer request underway for your nonna." She touched my forearm to underscore the gravity of the situation. "This has never happened before, so we had to take drastic action."

The "this" she was referring to was the act of an old-school Sicilian widow going rogue from her lifelong mourning duties. "I understand." I used my church voice in accordance with the solemnity of the occasion. "But if I were you, I wouldn't mention this to my mother."

"Why not? I'm sure she'd want to know that we've sought resolution through the church."

My mother would sooner drown Mary and Santina in my bathtub than lose a shot at Luigi's millions. "It's just that it's still such a sensitive matter in the family."

"Ah. Indeed." She turned to leave. "Oh, I almost forgot. The exterminator came."

"I didn't call an exterminator."

She pressed a hand to her cheek. "He said you had. He probably meant your landlady."

Not likely. The one time I'd asked Glenda to exterminate, she said bugs gave the place character. "What did he do?"

"He looked in the cabinets and closets."

The word *closets* hit me like a blast of insecticide. *Had Gigi Scalino sent one of his thugs to find the winepress?* "Did he come in my room?"

"Yes, but don't worry. I wouldn't let him go near the bathroom since you were in there."

Bathrooms drew bugs, and a real exterminator would've known that. "Is he planning to come back to spray in there too?"

"Oh, he didn't spray anywhere. He said you were insect free."

My spider and pill bug roommates begged to differ. The guy was a fraud. "What did this man look like?"

"I was busy cooking, so I didn't get a good look at him. But he was young and seemed shy because his hat was pulled down."

He'd been hiding his face—like that roller-skate girl at the Confederate Hall Museum. *Were they connected somehow?*

Mary looked at her watch. "I need to get to the funeral home. In the meantime, don't worry about your Nonna." She patted my shoulder. "We Catholics have it covered."

"That's so comforting," I murmured as she left the room. But I wasn't comforted in the slightest.

I grabbed a pair of jeans and pulled them on, pondering the exterminator incident. If my suspicions were correct, I needed to get in on a national prayer request.

So that I didn't get murdered, like Nick.

RUTH CLUCKED as I sat at the table in the Galliano's Huck Finn Dining Hall. She pulled up the bill of her orange-and-white sun visor that, combined with her receding chin, made her look like a horn-rimmed-glasses-wearing goose. "I know who's not going to win employee of the month."

I was in no mood to spar after my morning with my mother, but I couldn't resist a comeback. "So what job did Marv get you? Annoying—I mean, assisting—the captain?"

"See this?" She tapped a badge pinned to her khaki vest that said Fun Meter. "Your pointer's going to be set to Min, as in Minimum."

"Uh, it won't because I'm not wearing one of those stupid things."

"You bet your patootie you are, because you're looking at the new cruise director. You spoil my fun, and you'll be talking to Captain Vandergrift."

I wondered whether there was a river equivalent of Davy Jones's Locker, the maritime version of hell, because I had a feeling that was where the Galliano was headed with Ruth at the helm. "Speaking of spoiling, don't blow my cover. While I'm on this steamboat, I'm Franki Rockford."

"Don't you dare compare yourself to Jim. He was the best PI there was."

I didn't think the comparison was that far off. "Jim Rockford is a fictional character, so he can't be the best."

"James Garner *was* Jim Rockford, may he rest in Hollywood heaven. You besmirch his honor again, and I'll revoke your Fun Meter."

Little did she know that my Fun Meter had been revoked the minute she'd gotten a job on the boat.

A thin, sixtyish woman took a seat at our table, and I blinked thinking I was seeing double—and not double my fun. She was practically Ruth's twin with her line frown, too-tight bun, and chained-on black horn-rims. I scanned the room for life jackets. Two Ruths could sink the ship.

Ruth lowered her glasses and gave the woman a skeptical sizing up. "Who're you? The hash slinger?"

Like a mirror reflection, the woman gave her the same going over. "Marian Guidry," she growled. "The gift shop clerk."

Ruth sniffed. "Luckily, I'm not here to tchotchke shop. But since I'm the cruise director, we'll have to talk about stocking troll dolls and rabbit feet for my bingo peeps."

"*I* am a historian. I only stock items that reflect the history of the steamboat, and I definitely don't sell animal parts."

"Well, *I* am the cruise director. And if you talk to me like that again, we'll be selling your parts to my bingo players."

Marian hissed, and Ruth did the same. Then their necks elongated, and their shoulders went back, almost like wings about to flap.

Wanting to avoid a goose attack, I leaned toward Marian. "I'm the new galley employee, Franki Rockford." I pointed to the only other occupied table in the dining hall. "Will any of those people be working with me?"

She cast a disinterested look at the table's occupants. "The baby-faced man in the white sailor suit is Tim Trahan. He used to work on a cruise ship, but now he's the first mate. The chubby one is the bartender, Wendell Baptiste, who plays in a jazz band, and the skinny Katy Perry wannabe is the cocktail waitress, Kate Wilson."

Kate's gaze shifted, as though she'd heard her name. She did a double take when she saw me and jerked her head away.

My hair was in a ponytail, and I wasn't wearing my Sophia Loren-style cat eyeliner, or any makeup for that matter, but I didn't think I looked that bad. I just hoped she hadn't recognized me from somewhere. If she had, my cover and the investigation were blown. "Um, Marian, the guy who got me the job mentioned an employee meeting a few days ago. Are Ruth and I the only ones who missed that?"

"That was just for the captain and the chef. This is the first employee meeting."

If this was the first time the employees had been on the steamboat, that meant Alfredo Scalino and the captain were still my prime suspects. But I had to question the trio at the table on the off chance one of them had known Nick.

Ruth tapped my arm. "Because you were seventeen minutes

late, Roquefort, you did miss Captain Vandergrift's welcome and history of the steamboat."

I glowered at her. "It's Rockford. And it sounds like I didn't miss anything important."

Marian's eyeglass chains came out swinging. "We're helping to carry on a noble tradition." Her tone held a harrumph. "Nicholas Roosevelt, the great-grand-uncle of Teddy, introduced the steamboat to the Mississippi in 1811, when he steered the *New Orleans* into the river from the Ohio."

Ruth nodded, her chains bobbing. "At a speed of ten miles per hour, like we'll be travelling tomorrow for our test cruise."

Marian glanced over her shoulder. "Since the captain was just interrupted by a call from the police, I doubt we'll set sail tomorrow. It's too soon after the discovery of that body."

"Oh, we're setting sail, Negative Nelly. I'm counting on this gig."

Marian hissed, and Ruth elongated her neck.

It was time to debut a line I'd come up with to justify my questioning. "I gotta admit, I'm nervous about working on a steamboat where a dead body was found."

Marian *pshaw*ed. "That was a freak occurrence. The captain thinks he was another rapscallion looking for Galliano's mythical gold."

"Rapscallion?" Ruth perked up. "You into Scrabble?"

"Certainly, but it's the captain's word, not mine. And if you ask me, this Nick Pescatore was stoned on alcohol and fell into that freezer, which is why I never touch the stuff."

Ruth gave the table a tap. "We can agree on that, sister."

I wondered whether Marian was in drink denial like her twin.

"Pardon the flapdoodle, riverboaters." A tall, seventy-some-thing male stood at the microphone on the stage. He cut a striking figure in a white bowtie and suit that matched his unruly hair and mustache. "That saphead detective is getting too high for his nut, interrupting my speech with his blatherskite."

Marv was right. The captain was almost incomprehensible.

"Now, where was I?" He twisted the end of a whisker. "Ah, yes. The mighty Mississippi is a half mile wide and two hundred feet deep, and it's a rogue stream. So your labor on the Galliano promises a grand adventure."

*Yeah,* The Poseidon Adventure, *if the battle of the Ruths was any indication.*

He chuckled and slapped his knee. "Why, just yesterday I saw a bag lady in all her misery take a tumble into the river. She surfaced and tussled with a catfish that was bunking in her purse."

Ruth and Marian honk-laughed, but I crossed my arms. I took offence to the misery reference.

"The brouhaha reminded me of a set-to I once had with a catfish as a whippersnapper deckhand on a steamboat. One summer's day I was lunching on the main deck, enjoying the majesty of this great river, when a ten-foot catfish rose up and snatched a Vienna sausage from betwixt my fingers."

Wendell the bartender's eyes popped and lip dropped, reflecting the general reaction in the room.

The captain's jaw set. "Since I had just begun my repast, I made a lasso and tied the end of the rope around my waist. Then I held up another sausage, and sure as a gun, the slippery sucker returned to thieve the rest of my lunch. I lassoed him with all speed, and he pulled me the two hundred feet to the river bottom."

Ruth and I shared a side-eye. His tale was taller than the ten-foot catfish.

"We scrapped and scuffled," he said, reenacting his side of the battle, "and I was sure the end was nigh from the way he spat and growled. And then the ornery cuss ripped off my britches with his teeth."

The bartender's head snapped back, and I tried to imagine a catfish pucker. And then for some reason, I thought of Jefferson Davis's Civil War drawers.

"By then I was seeing stars from lack of oxygen, so I grabbed his nostril with my left hand and gave him a wallop that knocked him foolish." He gave the air a right hook. "Still bound to the unconscious thief, I kicked and clawed at the water till we rose to the surface. And that catfish became the midday meal he'd tried to rob me of."

Tim the sailor shot up and gave his captain an ovation, while the rest of us managed a few embarrassed claps.

The captain bowed. "Our test cruise has been postponed until the day after tomorrow. In the meantime, riverboaters, you may report to your respective stations."

Marian rose and pursed her lips. "Told you we weren't leaving tomorrow."

Ruth stared after her as she left. "Did you get a load of that old harpy?"

"I did." I stared at Ruth pointedly. "Many times."

"No Fun Meter for her." She stood and shot me a sober look over her horn-rims. "But between you and me, if anyone's too high on his nut, it's that captain."

I agreed even though I still wasn't sure what that meant.

She smacked her lips. "But I do wish I'd seen that catfish take on the bag lady."

That was my cue to report for kitchen duty. I stood and headed for the galley, trying to reconcile the captain's seemingly amiable nature with the murder of his business partner. He was definitely a kook, but he didn't strike me as a killer.

I opened the Staff Only door. No one was in the galley, but dry goods were stacked on the counters and the chopping-block island. I assumed the police had emptied out the pantry while inspecting the crime scene.

The awful image of Nick in the freezer appeared before my eyes. *Was Luigi right? Was it too dangerous to take a possible Mafia case?* Those men weren't amateurs like the other murderers I'd investigated. They were professional assassins who dealt in cruel forms of death.

*Dealt.*

*The playing card.* I had to find someone who could tell me what the queen of spades symbolized. But not Chandra Toccato. No more psychics for me, just a straight up tarot card reader.

I gripped the handle of the pantry door, and after a deep inhale I pulled it open. As I'd suspected, the pantry had been emptied. I spotted a trap door in the wall near where the freezer had been. Cautiously, I lifted the lid to a wide tin tube, probably an old garbage chute. If a weapon had been involved in Nick's death, it could've been the disposal route.

Next, I scanned the shelves and the cracks between the baseboards and the floor. There was nothing to see, not even a scuff mark on the tile.

I exited the pantry and followed the hallway to a small room with a desk and a walk-in refrigerator. Slowly, I opened the door, and a shiver went down my spine. The blast of air from the cooling fan wasn't the culprit, it was the contents.

Lemons.

Crates and crates of lemons.

Given everything I'd been through with the St. Joseph's Day tradition, the sight of hundreds of lemons made me more than skittish. But my anxiety was amplified by Luigi's story about the lemon and the origin of the Mafia. *Was this walk-in full of citrus some kind of bizarre proof that the Scalino clan ruled the boat?*

"Hands in the air!" A throaty female voice cracked at my back.

My feet flew up along with my arms.

"What do we have here? A lemon thief?"

Technically I was one, but I wasn't going to tell that to her. "My name's Franki Rockford, and I was looking for the kitchen manager to report for duty."

"And you thought you'd find me locked in the freezer, did ya?"

She had me there. "Well—"

"Can it. I know you thievin' types. I've been in this business longer than you've been alive. Now put your hands down and let me get a look at ya. I'm Pat Seaman."

I turned to face her, and the name really fit. Apart from her pendulous breasts and five-foot stature, Pat was a cross between a stout sailor and the Sea Hag from *Popeye*. She had a bulbous nose and prominent chin, missing teeth, and a barrel chest that would rival that of Bluto—and my mother's friend Rosalie. And the roots of her bleached boyish hair needed a major touchup.

"We'd best clear out before Chef Scalino comes." She slammed the walk-in door, grabbed my wrist, and dragged me up the hall with a limp-lope that was pure Igor from *Frankenstein*.

Pat released me at the island, and I rubbed my wrist. Meanwhile, she hacked up some phlegm into a handkerchief and stuffed it into her back pocket.

I had to swallow, but all I could think of was that loogie.

"Let's get your training outta the way. You wash dishes and make the shrimp cocktails, and that includes the peeling and de-pooping. Any questions?"

I wanted to ask if she was aware of the term *deveining*, but I had to focus on practical matters. "Yeah, where do I throw away the shrimp peels? In that chute in the pantry?"

One bloodshot brown eye squinted while the brow of the other rose. "I see you had a nice look around."

"I wanted to get familiar with the galley, so I can do a good job."

"As long as that's the reason." She kept the squint eye on me. "That chute in the pantry is called the 'dollar hole' because in the olden days cooks used to throw food waste in it. We don't use it 'cause it goes straight to the river."

So if a weapon had been used to kill Nick, it was gone forever.

"Because I'm the manager, I do the crawdad boils." She paused to let that sink in. "And the chef makes his famous lemon-mint sorbet."

"So that's what the lemons are for?"

"You got some kind o' lemon obsession?"

"What about lemons?" The man's voice shot through the galley—not like a rifle, but more like a BB gun.

Pat sneered. "Our new dishwasher and de-pooper is fixated on 'em, Chef."

I would've suggested "galley hand" as my title, but I was too busy watching Alfredo Scalino pull a knife from a block.

His beady gaze met mine. "Fuggedabout my lemons. They're dead to you, capish?"

I nodded, and he stabbed the knife into the island.

Apparently, he wasn't big on OSHA workplace safety and health standards. And I was certain that he would've had no problem sending an up-and-coming mobster to my apartment to pose as an exterminator. What I didn't know was what he planned to do after he'd learned that the winepress was there.

The chef placed a hand on his forehead, too prominent due to a receding hairline, and looked at Pat. "The captain just told me we're docked tomorrow."

She laid worried red eyes on me. "Come back at 0600 hours the day after tomorrow."

I didn't wait for further instruction. I threw open the galley door and stopped cold.

Kate the cocktail waitress straightened. She touched the sideburn of her cropped dark hair, averted her eyes, and walked away.

She'd been eavesdropping on our conversation. *But why?*

## 7

P*lease tell me Kate doesn't know I'm a PI.* I kept that thought to myself rather than blurting it out bag-lady style as I strode through the empty dining hall. The last thing I wanted to do was disappoint Luigi, but if my cover had been blown, I'd have to remove myself from the case. And no one else at Private Chicks could investigate Nick's death. Veronica wasn't doing much field work anymore, and she wouldn't reassign the case to David. A possible Mafia hit was too dangerous for a college kid, and he was already busy investigating me for my nonna. *The rat.*

I pushed open the door to the gambling area, but Kate wasn't there. I glanced to my left and saw Wendell the bartender crouched behind the bar, stuffing something into a cabinet. "Excuse me."

He started and fell onto his behind. "Lawd a'mighty." He clutched his chubby chest. "I thought Baron Samedi done come to dig my grave."

Any time the voodoo loa of the dead was mentioned, I paid attention. And Wendell was awfully anxious. *Did he have some-*

*thing to hide?* "I just wanted to know if you saw where Kate went. Sorry I scared you."

"It ain't your fault, it's this damn boat. After they found that man in the freezer, I almost didn't take this gig." He pulled himself to his feet. "I sent Kate home just now. Ain't nothing for her to do here today, and the less we're all here the better."

I slid onto a barstool. I wished I could've talked to Kate before she'd left, but I agreed with him about the Galliano. "I'll bet a lot of people backed out of this job. We'll probably have to make do with a skeleton crew for a while."

His brown eyes popped. "Don't never say *skeleton*, now. My people came from Haiti, and we don' throw that word around."

That explained his Baron Samedi reference. I'd been in New Orleans long enough to know that Haitians fled to the city after an eighteenth-century slave revolt, and they brought voodoo with them.

Wendell bent and resumed struggling with the cabinet, and I peered over the bar to see what it was.

A long, hard case. *The perfect size for a rifle or machine gun.*

I sat back and acted casual. "Need any help?"

"Nah, jus' trying to store my bone."

I blinked. "Did you say *bone*?"

He cast a wide-eyed look over his shoulder. "That's one of them words we don' throw around. I meant a *trom*bone." He gave the case a shove and closed the cabinet. "I'm a musician, but I bartend to play the bills between gigs."

"Ah. Where have you worked?"

"All over The Big Easy." He rose and leaned his forearms on the bar. "You name a joint, and I've either played there or served drinks. I even worked on a cruise ship once."

*Like that sailor.* "Did you work with Tim Trahan, by any chance?"

"Sure did. I don' know him well, though. I worked with Kate

too, but I cain't remember where."

I needed to track her down before we set sail on the test cruise, so I concocted a fib. "She looks familiar to me, but I can't figure out where I've seen her."

"Well, if I find out where I know her from, I'll tell you. But right now I need to inventory the liquor, so I can get the hell outta here."

I rose from the barstool but sat down again. "Oh, we've got a lot of lemons in the galley. Did you need some for drink garnish?"

He scribbled something on a clipboard. "All I need is lime, orange, and cherries. We're serving a limited number of pre-mixed drinks to start, mainly bloody Marys, Harvey Wall-bangers, and Hurricane Katrinas."

I wondered whether the Hurricane Katrina used lemon, but I didn't want to mention the fruit again. Word could get back to the Sea Hag and the chef that I really was lemon-obsessed. "Is that like the Hurricane at Pat O'Brien's?"

"It's got the rum and the OJ, but also Banana liqueur and Galliano. We want to make a couple of drinks with Galliano to call out the name of the steamboat."

For me, Galliano called out Nick's final text to Luigi. "Have you ever heard of a drink called the Galliano Gold?"

He stuck out his lower lip. "No, but I oughta make it. Sounds like Galliano and Goldschläger."

*The same thing Luigi had thought. If only that had been the case.*

"Ahoy, mateys!"

Ruth's pirate cry gave Wendell and me both a jolt. He dropped his clipboard, and I spun on my barstool and saw her scurry down the grand staircase. With her pale varicose-veined legs and knobby knees protruding from cargo shorts, long white socks, and spanking new Keds, Ruth looked more like a Girl Scout Troop leader than a pirate or a cruise director.

She approached and gave me the stink eye. "Instead o' parkin' it at that bar, you ought to be touring this fine steamboat."

I limited my reply to a glare.

Wendell shook his head. "I ain't left the main deck."

"Because it's haunted?"

"Say what?" Wendell backed into the bar, and a bottle of Galliano shattered on the floor.

Ruth tsked. "A grown man like you afraid of some bullpucky about ghosts?" She looked down at Wendell as he cleaned up the mess. "The best way to get over that is to take a tour. The second floor's the cabin deck with a library and the purser's office. There's a gift shop too, but you can skip that. It's got a bunch of history books and nautical crap." She hid her mouth behind the back of her hand. "And between you and me, the woman who runs it is a pain in the porthole."

If I'd had a drink, I would've choked on it. Evidently, Ruth had yet to see the similarity between herself and Marian Guidry.

"On the top of the boat, you got the Texas deck with the pilothouse next to the smokestack, the captain's suite, and the crew's quarters. There's even an old steam calliope."

I shuddered. Calliopes reminded me of creepy carnival music, which then reminded me of Glenda's drag queen friend, Carnie Vaul.

Wendell rose with a ragful of glass shards. "Uh-uh. I ain't spendin' the night on no haunted steamboat. They gonna have to drop me at the dock."

"Oh, *pshaw*. It'll be a hoot. Kind of like telling ghost stories around the campfire."

"I never did that," Wendell muttered.

Neither had I, but judging from Ruth's getup, she had.

She leaned on the bar. "Hey, you play in a jazz band, don't you?"

"Yes ma'am. The Treme Tribe."

"Good, because I'm going to need you. I just met with the captain, and we've lost a lot of revenue in ticket sales thanks to the murder. You got a singer?"

"Nah, but I'll ask around."

"You do that." She pointed at him and headed for the grand staircase. "And get someone classy. We want to bring in the high-roller gamblers."

Wendell's brow was on alert as he watched her leave.

I gave him a reassuring smile even though I was thinking about Marv hearing the body of the sailor ghost smacking the paddlewheel. "The haunted stuff is nonsense."

"Spirits exist, trust me on dat." He shook his head. "But I ain't as worried about them as I am the queen of spades card in that dead man's hand."

I was stunned that he knew about the playing card. The police usually kept unusual details under wraps to help catch the killer. "How did you know about that?"

"After our meeting this mornin', I heard the captain tell the gift shop lady that the detective he was complaining about called to ask about that card. He wanted to know if all her playing cards were accounted for."

I was going to have to visit the gift shop myself and find out. "Why would the card bother you?"

"In Haitian Vodou, the houngan and mambo, tha's what they call the priest and priestess, use playing cards instead of tarot."

I hadn't considered a possible voodoo connection to Nick's death, but I should have since we were in New Orleans. "You mean, they use cards to tell your future?"

"No, they don' do that. They use 'em to tell you which of the loa are working in your life."

"So what does the queen of spades mean?"

His head pulled back, and his chest swelled from a fearful

breath. "It means we all in trouble 'cause that man done crossed Erzulie D'en Tort."

I didn't have to ask who Erzulie D'en Tort was. Her name was French for Erzulie of the Wrongs, and she was a vindictive voodoo goddess who'd been invoked in a couple of my cases.

But her aggressive aspect wasn't the problem—or at least not all of it. The issue was that she sought vengeance for wronged women and children, which meant that Nick's murder might not have had to do with gambling or the Mafia, but something that could have been equally dark, like jealousy, betrayal, or abuse.

My legs felt like anchors as I headed for the grand staircase. Erzulie's presence had just darkened the already cloudy waters surrounding Nick Pescatore and the Galliano.

RUTH MUST'VE BEEN HITTING *that bottle in her fanny pack because this steamboat isn't 'fine.'* I surveyed the cabin deck from the top of the grand staircase. *If anything, it's foul.* It wasn't just the shabby décor that elicited my disdain. It was the closed, musty smell that hinted of overflowed toilets.

I looked behind me at the library, which was at the front of the boat. It was an open layout with tall wooden bookshelves, rickety wooden armchairs upholstered in faded fabric, and a huge round photograph of Mark Twain that could have been taken of the captain.

"The lookalikes on this boat are more frightening than the ghosts," I muttered and headed down the wide corridor to the back of the boat.

As I passed the rows of cabins, I was more than creeped out. The entire corridor had been made into a lounge area with old loveseats, a Victorian fainting couch, and the odd backgammon or chess table. The old-timey ambience evoked a long-gone era and long-dead passengers, and the groans from the floor beneath my feet didn't help the creepy atmosphere. I was so tense that I could almost hear the cries of the crewman and the woman who'd been killed in the 1922 fire.

I walked by cabin thirteen and heard a long, slow creak. I spun around.

The door had opened.

"Oh, *hell* no." I broke into a run. If there *were* ghosts on the Galliano, they were haunting that room.

I made it to the back of the boat faster than the steamboat could travel. The Purser's Office and the gift shop were located across from one another. They had glass fronts so I could see inside, and the door to the gift shop was open.

Marian stood beside a register, placing price tags on various items. There was a wall of books behind her, and the other two walls were lined with the nautical items Ruth had complained about—anchors, compasses, ship wheels, and various ropes.

She eyed me from behind the counter as I entered. "If you're here to shop, I've got some cute things to show you."

I glanced at the hideous brass skull with tentacles in her hand. It was either an evil octopus or the mythical kraken monster. "Uh, thanks, but I'm touring the Galliano, on the orders of the cruise director."

She dropped her head and glared over her horn-rims. "Who does that old biddy think she is giving orders on the Galliano?"

Apparently, Marian was as blind as Ruth when it came to their resemblance. "She thought I should know the layout since I'll be working here."

"You work in the galley, so you take your orders from Fredo."

I was startled to learn that Alfredo Scalino, the brother of a mobster, went by the same nickname as the doomed brother in *The Godfather. I mean, why not Al or Fred, or just Chef?* "He's not related to Gigi Scalino, is he?"

"He is. But Fredo's not like his brother." The lines on her face softened. "He's a good, kind man."

The knife he'd stabbed into the chopping block said au contraire. I approached a display case with poker chips, dice, and playing cards. "I didn't realize you'd be selling gambling stuff."

The age lines returned. "That order came from the captain, the old Twainophile."

I stared at her, surprised she'd criticized her captain. But then again, as Ruth's twin she wouldn't have a filter—or even a colander.

"Just look at those cards. His fascination with Mark Twain is bordering on obsessive compulsive."

I picked up a deck. The picture was the same as the one in the library except for the tiny steamboat beneath the author's image, and it was the perfect segue into finding out whether the card in Nick's hand had come from her shop. "Do you happen to have an open deck?"

"What for? Everyone knows what cards look like, and we'd have to write off the cost of the deck as a loss. And I plan on this shop making a considerable profit."

*Not with those krakens, you won't.* I moved to the books on the wall behind her so I could change the course of my questioning. "Do you have any books on the history of the Galliano? I'm interested in the ghosts."

"Goldang it." She threw up her arms, causing her bat wings and turkey neck to wobble. "There are no ghosts on this steamboat, and before you ask about the missing Civil War gold, there's none of that either." She shook her head and her chains. "You're just like that cocktail waitress."

*Kate. What did she know about her?* "How so?"

"This morning she was flirting with the captain like we were at a mixer instead of an employee meeting." She lowered her glasses. "And I heard her ask him about Galliano's gold."

Nick's final text echoed in my head.

Marian harrumphed. "As a historian, I don't stock books that peddle false legends. And I certainly don't encourage treasure hunters"—she paused and shot me a horn-rim look—"or gold diggers."

I resented the implication. If anyone was a gold digger, it was my mother. "Maybe you *should* encourage them to generate business, unless...you think that man who died on the boat was looking for treasure."

Tim Trahan stepped into the shop in a white sailor suit, scowling. "That guy was a homeless drug addict looking for a place to crash."

I struggled to take his sailor-on-the-Cracker-Jack-box face seriously. "What makes you so sure?"

He stormed up to me with a Gestapo gait. "Why aren't you in the galley?"

"The S—" I caught myself before I said Sea Hag. "Pat said I could leave for the day."

"Then follow your orders. That's what we do on this boat." He marched from the gift shop.

Marian stared after him, her eyes wide and narrow like those of a wily octopus. "You don't take orders from him."

"I don't know. He seems really tight with the captain."

"He does, doesn't he?" She rubbed her chin. "Odd since he's new."

"Maybe they know each other from somewhere, like from the cruise ship or their neighborhood or something."

"Not likely." She peeled a price sticker off a sheet. "The captain doesn't sail cruise ships, and he lives in Amelia an hour away."

"I thought he lived onboard."

She fixed the sticker on a severed gator head. "He's moving onto the Galliano in a few days, but if I were him, I'd postpone my move. We don't know whether the Galliano can stay afloat after this murder business."

"Because of the lost revenue?"

"That and the hefty loan the captain took on this boat." Her mouth folded into her face. "And you didn't hear this from me, but that's not all the money he owes."

I moved from the bookshelves to a display of nutria jerky and repressed a gag. "For the boat?"

"Gambling debts. There's a riverboat casino where he lives called the Amelia Belle, and I heard he borrowed to cover some debts he accrued there."

I couldn't imagine who would have told her about the captain's gambling debts—unless he'd borrowed from Gigi Scalino. Marian *was* on a first nickname basis with his brother, Fredo.

She pressed another price sticker onto a dried frog. "I've seen him playing poker, and the man's got a problem."

"You mean, a gambling addiction?"

"That too. But the captain can stay up for days gambling, and he's over seventy."

"Wow. That's impressive."

"Not if you have help from a homeless drug addict."

I turned to face her. "What are you saying?"

She stiffened. "You'd best do as Tim says and scoot." She pointed the dried frog at the door. "Before he comes back to check."

I'd pushed the questioning too far. "Right. Thanks for letting me look around. You've got some, uh, interesting stuff in here."

She nodded, and I exited the gift shop to the corridor, wondering whether Nick Pescatore had come onboard to gamble with the captain—or to deal him drugs.

~

MY PHONE RANG as I crossed the gangplank, and I was so wound up from thoughts of drugs, voodoo, and ghosts that I nearly bounced into the river. I glanced at the display. *Bradley*.

"Hey, babe," I answered.

"Hey, yourself." His tone was playful. "You never called me back last night."

My hand went to my forehead. "I'm sorry. Between the case and the mourning going on at my apartment, I got overwhelmed. And then this morning my mom showed up."

"That was nice of her to come and help."

"Mmm," was all I could muster. I didn't want to tell him the real reason she'd come. Obviously, it was better to let my boyfriend think that I'd come from a non-gold-digger mother.

"Are you at the house right now?"

I resumed my gangplank walk. "Actually, I'm leaving the Galliano."

"What? How'd you get onboard?"

I hesitated because in the past Bradley had gotten upset about me putting myself in dangerous situations. Then I took a deep breath. "As an employee. I'm working undercover in the galley."

He laughed. "Sounds like you're about to embark on a Mississippi riverboat adventure. You'll have to tell me all about it tonight."

I hadn't expected him to be so jovial about the news, but it was a welcome surprise. "Did we have plans this evening?"

"No, but I'd like to stop by and offer my condolences to Luigi and visit with your mom and nonna. I can be your stand-in while you take some time for yourself, maybe a relaxing hot bath."

That sounded heavenly, especially after the cold bath I'd gotten from my mother. "I'll take you up on that offer."

"Then I'll be there at six. What can I bring?"

"Just yourself. The nonne have cooked enough food to feed the Confederate Army."

"That's a random reference."

I smiled. "I'll explain tonight. Love you."

"I love you," he said with passion. "You have no idea how much."

The call ended.

Even though I was back on dry land, I wobbled like I was still on the steamboat. Without warning, tears flowed like the Mississippi. Ever since Bradley had quit his job, he'd put me first, unlike certain members of my family. And it struck me that I finally had the relationship I'd wanted—apart from him forgetting my birthday. But there was still time for him to remember, and after the supportive conversation we'd just had, I was confident he would. So I couldn't allow my birthday doubt—or anything, for that matter—to come between us. Not ever again.

I dropped my phone into my bag and pulled out a tissue. I lifted my head and froze.

The ice blue eyes of the man who stood before me were a colder splash of water than the bath I'd had that morning. In fact, they reminded me of Marian's kraken.

"The minute I heard that the anonymous tip came from a woman who knew police code for Homicide," he said with a snarl, "I begged the commissioner to assign me this case." He leaned low to get in my face. "And I got on my *knees*, Amato."

The steamboat wobble I'd felt turned river-raft lurch. Because the "saphead detective" that the captain had complained about was none other than Wesley Sullivan. And judging from the way he spoke, this time he was out to destroy more than my relationship.

## 8

Once I'd recovered from the shock of seeing the detective, my face grew so hot that my tears dried up. "I'm not surprised you got on your knees, Sullivan. Judging from all the women you've proposed to, you do that pretty often."

His broad chest expanded behind his black suit jacket. "Jealous, Amato? Because I see ol' Bradley still hasn't put a ring on your finger."

The remark hit me like a backhand. He had a knack for IDing my insecurities, but I couldn't let him see that. I started stalking toward the French Quarter where I'd parked since my cherry red Mustang was just as recognizable as Jim Rockford's gold Firebird. But I wasn't going to leave without striking out at him as he'd done to me.

"The next time you get on your knees," I shouted over my shoulder, "make sure it's in a church. That way you can ask forgiveness for all the problems you've caused."

"Problems?" He jogged to my side. "I recommended you for the vampire case, remember?"

"Yeah, and while I was working it, you tried to ruin my relationship."

"Are you talking about that kiss?"

"Quick on your feet *and* on the uptake." I kept my gaze straight ahead. "I'm impressed."

"If I recall, you kissed me back—like a vampire sucking lifeblood."

I stopped, irritated that his analogy matched the nature of the investigation. But then I stormed across the railroad tracks toward Washington Artillery Park. "You took advantage of me when I was vulnerable, and I'm not the only woman you've done that to. What about your wife? Does she know you go around making passes on the job?"

"She's my ex."

"I meant your second wife. Or have you forgotten about her?"

"As of three months ago, she's ex number two."

I stumbled, caught off guard by his admission. He grabbed my arm to steady me, and I yanked free and resumed my marching. "You're nothing but a player. Stay away from me."

"I try, but you keep sticking your nose in my cases."

"If I'm not mistaken," I said as I stomped up the steps to the park plaza with the detective on my heels, "you just said you begged your commissioner to let you stick your nose in *my* case."

"Murder cases are police jurisdiction, Amato."

"Well, if *I* recall, I solved that case. So you should thank me, like the mayor did."

He swore under his breath. "I oughta—"

"What?" I spun to confront him at the Civil War cannon. "Blow my cover?"

"That's right." His hand went to his rock-hard abs, and he

doubled over and laughed so hard I thought he would drop to his knees—again.

"What's so damn funny?"

"You...comparing yourself...to Jim." He struggled to speak through gasps and guffaws. "I'm dying."

I squeezed my handbag and wished the cannon wasn't a replica so I could blast him with it. "I'm serious, Sullivan."

"I know." He straightened and wiped away laugh-tears. "That's what makes it so hysterical."

I sighed. "Okay, you've had a good howl at my expense. Now are you going to out me, or what?"

"I wouldn't dream of it," he said, suddenly serious. "I need you on the case."

My eyes narrowed, and I shifted my weight to one hip. He was too macho to admit he needed my help with an investigation. "Why would you need me? So you can hit on me again?"

The smile slid from his lips, and his eyes went snake-like. "So I can get even."

"I MEAN, seriously, Veronica. Can you believe that guy?" I pressed the phone to my ear and ran across Decatur Street to Jackson Square Park. "Not only did he threaten me, he thinks I'm a joke."

"Do you care what Wesley Sullivan thinks?" Her pitch rose with each word, sounding the relationship alarm.

I gave a frustrated sigh-hiss as I entered the park. "Not in the I-want-him-to-like-me sense, but in the I-demand-he-take-me-seriously sense. I solved that case, and he couldn't. So I deserve some respect."

"You do, but he's a proud Irishman. I doubt he'll ever acknowledge that you bested him."

My feet crunched the gravel pathway, and I imagined myself stepping on Sullivan's ribs. "Well, I'm tired of men not giving women credit for their work, especially arrogant detectives."

"You know I experienced plenty of that as a female attorney, so I share your pain. But if he's acting aggressive toward you, maybe you should step aside from Nick's case. We can hire an outside consultant to take over."

I stopped short at the equestrian statue of Andrew Jackson in the middle of the park. And I thought of Jefferson Davis. "Do you remember the Battle of New Orleans, Veronica?"

"The Civil War battle?"

"No, the first one, when Andrew Jackson led a ragtag army to stop a British invasion."

"What's that got to do with this?"

"That's what I'm going to do."

"Fight the British?"

"No, the Irishman. And I'm going to assemble my own ragtag army to do it."

"*Huh?*"

"Yeah, Ruth Walker. And maybe a trombone player named Wendell."

"Franki, have you been drinking Strega? You know it makes you weird."

"I'm sober, and I need to let you go so I can find a fortune teller." I hung up, fully aware of how insane I sounded.

I exited the park into the small, tourist-packed square in front of Saint Louis Cathedral. I scanned the row of tarot card readers behind their tiny tables. Most of them looked like carnies, hipsters, and retirees, but there was a fiftyish woman with a brown knotted headscarf, shell earrings, and a gold ring in her septum who could've been Creole or Haitian. If she were the latter, she might be able to verify Wendell's vodou interpretation of the queen of spades card.

I sat on the tiny stool at her table and jumped back up.

Instead of cards, she had bones, and I didn't mean *trom*bones. They looked human, like fingers, and they were tied in a bundle with black string.

I pointed but then snatched my finger back. "Where did those come from?"

She waved a hand with inch-long white nails. "Don't worry about where I got 'em." Her voice was low—and local. "Just don't touch."

"I won't." I almost walked, but Sullivan's belly laugh echoed in my head, and my gut burned at the memory. I returned to the stool, determined to solve Nick's murder.

The woman sized me up with big brown eyes that bugged slightly from their sockets. She pursed her chubby lips, making her cheeks even chubbier. "I'm Mama Esther. A throw costs twenty dollars."

I cocked my head. "You mean, a blanket?"

Her cheeks went flat, like her gaze. "I meant a reading."

"Do you do cards?"

She rolled her eyes. "That's so old-fashioned."

"Sorry. I'm not up on the latest fortune-telling techniques."

She *hmphed* and untied the string. "We stopped saying 'fortune-telling' in the eighties. It's divining."

I gave her a hard stare. "Whatever you call it, that's not what I'm here for."

Mama Esther gathered the bones in her left hand and placed a shell on top. She waved her right hand over the items and spoke what sounded like a cross between French and mumbo jumbo. She transferred the bones and shell to the other hand and repeated the gesture. Then she shook them and threw them on the table. She studied them for a moment. "This is not a good throw for you."

My stare got harder. "Awesome, because I just said I wasn't here for that."

"Fine wit' me." She tightened the knot on her headscarf. "You're not ready to hear this, anyway."

I knew she was as fake as the gibberish she spoke, but as with all things mystic, I had a shadow of a doubt.

She reached to scoop up the bones, and I blocked her hand. "Hang on."

"I said, 'don't touch.'"

"Yeah, *those* bones, not *your* bones. Now what do they say?"

"No ma'am. You're confrontational, and this throw is heavy."

"What do you mean?" My hypochondria kicked in. "Is it my health?" I clutched my stomach, which had developed an ache. "Oh, God. Bradley's going to propose, but I'm dying. Or wait. I'm dying, and he's not going to propose."

Mama Esther looked at the next table, where a bearded hipster in a black hat and beige scarf sat with legs crossed sipping a cup of tea and reading a book. "I *told you* I get all the damn crazies."

My lips pursed. I was willing to admit that I'd gotten carried away, but *she* was the one who threw bones for a living. "I'm totally sane, and I didn't come for a *divining*. I have a question about Haitian vodou and playing card readings."

Her head snapped back so hard the knot on her headscarf shook. "Are you racial profiling me?"

Heat crept up my neck. "No, it's just that your headscarf, shells, and bones make you look more like you'd know about voodoo than he does."

The hipster held up a copy of *A Heartbreaking Work of Staggering Genius*. "Hey, I can read and learn, all right? Or do you think I'm dumb because I'm a tarot card reader?"

Honestly, I thought he was a nerd, but under the circumstances

I wasn't going to admit to social profiling. I raised my hands—but folded my fingers. "Look, I didn't mean to offend either of you. I just need to know what the queen of spades means."

Mama Esther's nostrils flared. "It means Erzulie D'en Tort is angry with you, which don't surprise me none."

The hipster leaned in. "It's also a porn term."

For some reason, I thought of Willie's Debbie Does Doberge cake. Then I sat back and stared at them. "Did you see what just happened there?"

Mama Esther crossed her arms against her ample bosom. "Maybe I *do* know about Haitian vodou, but shame on you for assuming. Now what did you do to rile Erzulie—racial profile her?"

"The card has nothing to do with me. A friend of mine got it."

She gave a skeptical *tuh*. "That's what they all say."

The hipster shook his head. "A tired cliché."

I was tired—of the two of them. "I'm telling you the truth, so is there anything else you can tell me?" I glared at the hipster. "And I don't want a description of the porn meaning."

Mama Esther adjusted her headscarf. "Not without knowing the situation. And for that I'd need the person who was dealt the card, so the bones could read their spirit."

"That won't be possible."

The hipster swallowed a sip of tea. "If it helps, in cartomancy spades correspond to tarot's suit of swords, which is the suit of warriors and symbolizes things like courage, aggression, and conflict."

"What about the queen?"

"The queen of spades, the queen of swords, Erzulie—same difference. She's a cold, lonely woman. And hostile. She's out to hurt you, and she'll lie to you just to watch what happens." He tightened his scarf, as though warding off a chill. "She hasn't shown up in one of my readings in a while, but someone asked me about her last night."

My stool wobbled. *The skater?* I needed to know, but I had to formulate my description carefully, so the huckster and the hipster didn't accuse me of some kind of profiling. "Was she a woman in a wig on roller skates?"

His eyes popped. "Wow, are you psychic?"

"If I was, I wouldn't have come here." I shot Mama Esther a look as dry as her bones. Then I rose and threw a twenty on the table.

She frowned at it like she'd done to my bone throw. "After you racial-profiled me, I don't even get a tip?"

Reluctantly, I tossed in a five even though she'd psychologically profiled me—unfavorably. I handed the hipster a ten.

"Oh, thanks." He tipped his hat. "I've got one last tip for your friend—tell him or her that the cards don't lie."

"I'll pass that along." I turned to walk the short distance to Bourbon Street, pondering the hipster-turned-tipster's words.

The only thing the cards said to me was that Nick's death had to do with gambling, and not vodou or porn—although I planned to look that up in private. And if my suspicion was correct, then my bet was on Captain Vandergrift. He seemed decent enough, but as far as I knew, he was the only one on the ship who'd been accused of murder.

I turned onto Bourbon, and the street was unusually packed. It was Mardi Gras season, so I figured the crowd was there to see one of the many marching bands, walking groups, or dance troupes pass through. I weaved my way through the bodies to the Tropical Isle bar, holding my nose from the smell of BO, booze, and vomit.

The Dancing Hand Grenade stood in the doorway, churning his arms at his sides like the dancing gopher in *Caddyshack*. He scanned the crowd, and our eyes met—well, his big fake blue eyes met my brown ones. He stopped churning, raised two puffy white-gloved fingers in a V sign, and did the I've-got-my-eyes-on-you gesture. Then he swiped the V sign across each eye like John Travolta and Uma Thurman's dance from *Pulp Fiction*.

There was nothing that grenade couldn't turn into a dance move.

I marched up to him and scoured his costume for eye holes. I couldn't find them, so I was forced to look him in his fake eyes, which was awkward. And odd. "We need to have a chat about the woman on roller skates you pointed me out to the other day. She's been anticipating my every move, and I want to know why."

He did a lip-locking gesture and topped it off with a tap step and arm flair.

*Naturally*.

"Look, this isn't a dance-off, so why don't you take off your costume so we can discuss this?"

He continued with the lip-locking combo and thrust his hip at me, as though he wanted to knock me flat on the street.

I was already on edge because of Sullivan's threat and the mob of partiers swarming around me. So, I lunged at him—and tried to pull off his head. I wrested and yanked, and he made a grab for my waist. Fortunately, he was too big around to get both hands on me.

"Fight! Fight!" a guy chanted.

"Get her, Grenade!" a woman yelled.

I ignored the incitement. Because I'd come to the conclusion that the Dancing Hand Grenade costume didn't have a head-piece. Which was strange. And unsettling.

A trumpet blasted the opening notes of "When the Saints Go Marching In," and the crowd let out a cheer. I figured a marching band was coming up the street, but I didn't loosen my grip on the grenade.

A car horn honked behind me.

Startled, I let him go and turned around. I was blocking a black-and-gold convertible packed with uniformed New Orleans Saints football players and a dance troupe dressed in team colors. They wore teased black-and-gold wigs, matching minidresses, and shiny gold go-go boots. Two of them carried a sign that read *The Geaux-Geaux Dancers*.

I stepped onto the sidewalk in front of the Tropical Isle entrance.

The Dancing Hand Grenade saw me and lunged for a flier on the door. His fat fingers dislodged it, and he crumpled it between his huge hands.

I tried to snatch it, but he hooked me with one of his clown shoes. I fell flat onto Bourbon—right as the Geaux-Geaux Dancers began to strut to a recording of "Our Lips are Sealed" by the Go-Go's.

The irony of the song choice wasn't lost on me as I curled into a fetal position, not only to avoid getting trampled by the go-go-booted squadron, but also to avoid French Quarter street germs.

A hand grabbed my wrist and pulled me to safety.

One of the football players had come to my rescue.

"You're a saint like your team mascot," I shouted above the music.

He smiled and made his way back to the convertible, and I scanned the crowd for the Dancing Hand Grenade, which was like looking for a big green knitting needle in a haystack. I spotted him waddling down the street and gritted my teeth. *Only in The Big Easy could a Humpty-Dumpty drink mascot evade me.*

"Here you go, champ." A Bacchus in plastic leaves and purple grapes gave me a crumpled sheet of paper. "Your Hand Grenade sparring partner dropped this."

I unfolded the flier. It was an advertisement for the debut of the "Roulergirls" at an upcoming Mardi Gras parade. The name was a play on *rollergirls* that had been inspired by the city's famous phrase *Laissez les bons temps rouler*, Cajun French for *Let the good times roll*. And I understood why the Dancing Hand Grenade hadn't wanted me to see the announcement for the roller-skating troupe.

The wigged woman on skates was front and center on the flier.

A T  S I X  P.M., I pulled onto Maple Street and searched for a parking place amid the FIATs, my Mom's Ford Taurus, Bradley's Mercedes, and Luigi's Lamborghini. To my grim dismay, I had to park in front of the cemetery.

I climbed from the car, exhausted from a lost night of sleep and a wasted day of searching for the Roulergirls. My side hurt from a muscle I'd pulled wrestling with the damn Hand Grenade. So the last thing I wanted to do was endure the exhausting battle that was my family, not to mention the nonne.

To stave off stress, I pulled out my phone and googled "how to find your inner zen" as I walked to my apartment. An article popped up with a list of steps. *Mindfulness, exercise, healthy eating, positive-thinking, and rewarding yourself.*

I did the last one well enough to make up for the other four, but I was pretty sure that didn't count. I settled on a few deep breaths and went inside.

The nonne were decked out in death regalia and rattling away on their rosaries.

I removed my jacket in the entryway, and Bradley exited the kitchen in a black suit appropriate for a funeral or a Milan runway.

His smile was muted to match the occasion. "Hey, babe."

The rosaries stopped rattling.

He gave me the clumsy cheek peck that one would expect from a man being watched by nine no-nonsense nonne.

The rattling resumed.

"How's it going?" I whispered.

The corners of his mouth pulled back. "I got a pretty cold welcome."

"Don't take it personally. It's because they're in mourning."

"I don't think so." He cast a furtive glance at the kitchen table, where my mother sat with Luigi. "Your mom offered Mr. Pescatore wine, but I got lemonade. Unsweetened."

My lips puckered. Bradley was getting the sour treatment, all right.

I looked around for my nonna and saw her in the corner on someone's cell phone. There were only three people she would be talking to, in order of importance—a priest, my dad, and David.

She caught my gaze and pulled the veil over her face.

*David*. I did the Dancing Hand Grenade's eyes-on-you gesture, but without the dance move, and went into the kitchen.

Luigi wasn't looking too smooth. He had on a white short-sleeved shirt and undershirt with belted pants that came to his ribcage, but his old-man style wasn't the issue. His hearing aid was crooked, and his nose was so red that he looked more like an Italian W.C. Fields than a George Burns. In a word, he was schnockered.

He pushed a wayward strand of hair over his scalp. "If I hadn't cut Nicky off, he wouldn't have gone searching for the gold on the steamboat." He leaned forward to put his head in his hands and almost fell over. "And none of this would've happened."

"There, there," my mother said, pushing him upright. "We

do our best with these kids"—she paused and zeroed in on me
—"but it's like they're determined to make mistakes."

Scowling at her wasn't good enough. I pulled down my lower
eyelid, shooting her the evil eye.

She emptied a Marsala bottle into Luigi's glass. "Why don't
you have one of Carmela's meatballs with your wine? When it
comes to cooking, she's...quite a...something."

I narrowed my eyes. My mother was taking a cue from my
nonna's meatballs, which she routinely described as "slick with
grease."

"And have I ever told you what a *(cough)* woman Carmela is?
Yes, she...goes to church, and...keeps a tidy bedroom."

Apparently, my mother had also taken a cue from a used car
salesman, but she wasn't as convincing in the hawking of the
product.

I needed some wine to deal with the spectacle. I opened the
cabinet. *Empty?* I turned to my mother. "You served *my* wine?"

"Well, I didn't have time to go to the store, Francesca." She
furrowed her brow. "Can't you see I'm busy?"

*Yeah, pouring my wine down Luigi's throat.* Annoyed, I
slammed the cabinet shut. "I guess it's a good thing I got that
winepress."

Bradley entered and grimaced like he'd swallowed unsweetened lemonade. "You bought a winepress?"

"It was a gift." I looked at Luigi, who was absorbed in his
thoughts—and his glass. "One I can't accept."

"*Whaaat?*" My mother's head spun toward me.

"It was a nice gesture, but I don't make wine. And for the
sake of the Pescatores and the Scalinos,"—I lingered on the
Mafia clan to drive my point home—"it belongs in Sicily."

She glanced nervously at Luigi. "Well, if he wants you to
*have* it, Francesca..."

Her reaction supported my earlier theory that she'd sacrifice a kid to get rid of her mother-in-law.

"Besides, dear, it's rude to refuse an inheritance. Why, if Luigi were to leave me something," she paused to let that marinate, "I would *treasure* it."

And that one confirmed my theory she was a gold digger.

Bradley leaned into my side. "Can I talk to you in private?"

"Please." I cast a droll look at my mother and led him to my bedroom. As he crossed the threshold, nonne gasped and crossed themselves.

"*Che disgrazia!*"

"*Uno scandalo!*"

Nonna rose with the phone still pressed to her ear and shuffled over to me. "I'm-a not-a gonna ask what you're doing in-a there"—she raised her veil at Bradley—"but it had-a better involve a question."

I closed the door, went to the closet, and dragged the trunk to the doorway.

Bradley smirked. "What's in that old thing, your nonna's dowry?"

Clearly, he hadn't gotten the gist of her question hint. "It's the winepress."

"Ah. That's what I wanted to talk to you about. Are the Scalinos you mentioned related to *Gigi* Scalino, the Mafia *don*?"

I nodded. "The winepress belonged to his father."

Bradley shoved his hands in his pockets as though he were shoving down a comment. "Does Gigi know you have it?"

"I'm not sure." I didn't tell him that I reported to Gigi's brother on the Galliano, or that I suspected the exterminator of being one of his thugs, because he was already worried enough. "But I'm getting rid of it as soon as I can. It's just that right now is a delicate time."

"Yes." He sat on the edge of the bed. "Before you came home, I got a call from Captain Vandergrift."

I was so stunned that I was tempted to join him on the mattress, but I feared the nonne would send in the Swiss Guard. "Why would the captain call *you*?"

"He thought I was still with the bank."

"Did you ask him about Nick's death?"

"Why would I do that?"

I sank onto the trunk. Bradley was turning out to be clueless with questions, which didn't bode well for our future. "Um, because I'm investigating his murder?"

"He was calling to check on his loan. And I didn't have to bring up Nick because he did it for me."

My eyes widened. "How so?"

"He's afraid the investigation might cost him the loan."

"Could it?"

"Not unless he goes to jail and misses a payment." He flashed me a look under his lashes. "Which...he might."

An uneasy sensation settled in my abdomen. "Bradley, what do you know that you're not telling me?"

"I haven't said anything about this to Luigi..."

I stood. "Now I'm worried."

"I am too, Franki." He rose and put his arms around me. "Because you're on the steamboat with that maniac."

"Oh, if you're talking about his murder charge in Morgan City, Glenda told me all about that."

"No." He dropped his arms. "He confessed to throwing Nick from the top deck of the Galliano the night he was killed, so his DNA might be on the body."

My hand went to my chest. If I hadn't known better, I would've sworn that my heart had gone overboard and smacked the paddlewheel.

## 9

Veronica's eyes widened behind the slice of double-stuffed praline and cream cheese king cake I'd brought into the office for breakfast. She sank onto the couch and swallowed her bite whole. "Did the captain say whether Nick survived the fall from the steamboat?"

A huff escaped my lungs. "Bradley didn't ask." From my supine position on the opposite couch, I tore off a hunk of the cake I'd balanced on my chest and sipped from the king cake latte I'd nestled in my armpit. "I'll tell you one thing I've learned in all of this—Bradley could never go on *Jeopardy*. He wouldn't know what questions to ask even with the answers in front of him."

"You should be happy about that, because if he knew what questions to ask, he'd ask you about Detective Sullivan."

*If he knew what questions to ask, he would ask me to marry him.*

The thought took me by surprise. I looked at my king cake, and the purple, yellow, and green sparkles lost some of their luster. Because, evidently, my boyfriend was more concerned with celebrating Mardi Gras than me, my birthday, and our relationship. But I wasn't ready to say that out loud. Instead, I shoved the hunk of cake into my mouth, chewed it, and gulped that thought down.

Veronica cleared her throat. "Was it the cake that shut you up just now, or my question about Sullivan?"

I sighed because I had to come clean. "Bradley doesn't know he's the detective on Nick's case."

"Oh, Franki. You need to tell him today."

"I will, but he's got nothing to worry about." I nestled my head into the couch cushion and stared at the ceiling. "There won't be a repeat of the so-called vampire kiss from six months ago. Apparently, the only advances I have to worry about from Sullivan are battle advances."

"Thus the ragtag army."

My head jerked toward her. "You jest, Veronica, but that guy's gunning for me, and he's got the entire police force behind him. And Sullivan's not the only battle I've got to wage. That cocktail waitress, Kate, could be tracking me too, and don't get me started on the Roulergirl and that damn Dancing Hand Grenade."

She tossed her plate onto the coffee table. "Do you think Kate and the Roulergirl are working together?"

I tore off another cake hunk. "It's too early to tell."

"Well, once you track down the Roulergirl, you've got to find out how she knew about the queen of spades card."

I chewed the hunk while I chewed over the possibilities. "She's been one step ahead of me this entire time, which makes me think she's a PI. And if she is, she could've found Nick's body before I did."

"Or she has a police contact who tipped her off to the card." Veronica kicked off her heels and pulled her feet onto the couch. "I'd love to know who she's working for."

"It's either someone who knew Nick, or someone related to the business partner the captain was accused of killing."

"I don't know. Standish read somewhere that the man didn't have any family."

I sat up and reached for my laptop. "Well, then I'll pick up where I left off yesterday—calling local skating rinks to find out where the Roulergirls practice." I opened the lid, and the screen blipped twice. "My computer's acting weird."

"Oh, I had David install some software updates on it while you were on the steamboat yesterday. If it keeps acting up, let him know."

"I will." I opened the browser and started typing. "And if he keeps acting up with my nonna, I'll let him know about that too."

She snorted and shook her head.

The lobby door opened, and The Vassal entered sporting *Game of Thrones* gear—a T-shirt covered in various types of swords, and a backpack shaped like a shield from one of the houses on the series.

Veronica smiled, no doubt at his geek style. "I wasn't expecting you today, Standish. Are you here to join Franki's ragtag army?"

I cast swords at her with my eyes.

"That sounds like an intriguing enterprise," The Vassal said in diplomatese, "but I'm here to help Miss Glenda with her memoir."

Veronica reached for the king cake box. "Has she thought of a title yet?"

"I believe it's *Stripper Galore: The Glamorous Life and Times of Lorraine Lamour.*"

She cut a cake sliver. "I like the rhyme."

I didn't. The play on Pussy Galore was closer to Tipper Gore, but I kept my mouth crammed with cake because I wanted to stay out of the memoir—in both senses of the phrase. "Hey, Vassal, could you try to find an address for me sometime before you leave? It's for a Kate Wilson, and unfortunately all I can tell you is that she's in her late twenties and looks kind of like Katy Perry."

"I'll see what I can do." He removed his back shield and went to the corner desk to his most prized weapon—the computer.

Veronica rested her head on the back of the couch. "I really should get to work. I need to leave early today."

"How come?"

She wiggled her brow. "Dirk's making me dinner at his place."

Envy wormed into my chest. I took a sad sip of my king cake latte and yearned for king cake ice cream to go with my king cake. "If you don't come home, I've got dibs on your bed. Otherwise, it's back to the tub or Glenda's giant champagne glass."

The lobby door opened, and the devil I'd been speaking of sashayed in like Mae West but dressed like a stripper Marie Antoinette.

I eyed her telltale pouf wig and the *pannier* hoops on her hips and fervently wished she'd opted for more than a pink silk thong and white body makeup to complete the look. Her chest reminded me of the breast mold she had made for the Mardi Gras decorations on our house. "Uh, have you come to warn us that a French Revolution has broken out in the Quarter?"

"*C'est amusant*, Miss Franki. I just came from a pre-parade with the Merry Antoinettes."

"That sounds decadently revelrous," Veronica said. "Who are they?"

"A Mardi Gras krewe of scandalous party queens who celebrate Marie Antoinette's court. They're known for drinking champagne and throwing cake."

Concerned, I glanced at my plate. "I get the champagne part, but what's the deal with the cake?"

"It's their Mardi Gras throw, sugar. They took Marie

Antoinette's line, 'Let them eat cake,' and turned it into 'Let them throw cake.'"

Veronica beamed. "I love that. It's cute *and* clever."

"It's criminal." I picked up my plate. "I don't care if it *is* Mardi Gras. No one should throw cake. Ever."

The Vassal turned in his chair and went as white as Glenda when he saw her body-painted breasts. Ever the diplomat, he removed his glasses. "Throwing cake certainly didn't go well for Agnes Frump."

Glenda jutted out a hoop-adorned hip. "Now who in the world is that?"

I wrinkled my lips. "From the sound of her name, she's not a Merry Antoinette."

Veronica snickered and slapped her knee, and Glenda and I joined in.

The Vassal closed his slack jaw. "She was the female passenger who died in the 1922 fire on the Galliano."

Our merry revelry ceased.

I turned to face him. "Why'd she throw cake?"

"She and a few other guests were invited to Captain Galliano's quarters for after-dinner drinks and dessert. A cook named Rose brought her a piece of cake, but Agnes said it was dry and demanded something else. Rose said that she had personally tasted the cake, and it was moist. Agnes didn't like being contradicted by a cook, so she threw it in Rose's face."

"Lovely table manners," I quipped. "Did the captain stand up for Rose?"

"I don't know. But she brought Agnes another dessert, and as she was leaving, somehow Agnes's dress caught fire. A crewman tried to put it out, and he caught fire too. Both of them burned to death right there in the captain's quarters."

Glenda shook her wig. "And all because of a lousy piece of cake."

I put my plate on the coffee table. The bite I'd taken no longer tasted quite as sweet. "What happened to Rose?"

The Vassal pushed up his glasses. "She was hung in the *Place d'Armes*. That's what Jackson Square was called before it was renamed after the Battle of New Orleans."

The name was French for *Weapons Square*, and it reminded me of my own battles. But they were nothing like those of the countless slaves and criminals who'd been executed there. "I thought they did away with public hangings in the nineteenth century."

"They did, but Rose was lynched. She was from Haiti, so people thought she'd killed Agnes with voodoo."

My mind dealt me the queen of spades card, but it seemed too big a leap to connect Nick's death to that of Agnes. "You mean, because Agnes's dress caught fire?"

"That and because her face didn't burn." The Vassal's naked eyes went Coke-bottle-lens magnified. "One newspaper account said Agnes looked shriveled and wrinkled like an apple-head doll, and the people thought it was Rose's retribution for getting cake thrown in her face."

I touched my cheek. I needed to be better about applying moisturizer.

"Then, shortly after the incident, passengers started reporting the crewman's ghost wandering the Texas deck and a woman's shriveled face surrounded by flames."

Veronica shivered and rubbed her arms. "Franki, didn't you say that Marv at Where Dat Tours told you he'd heard the ghost of the sailor who fell into the paddlewheel?"

I nodded. "Why do you ask?"

"Is it possible that the scream and smacking sound he heard was Nick falling from the boat?"

I slouched into the couch cushions. "No, he would've told me if that had happened the night Nick was killed. Plus, he heard it two different times."

She leaned forward and slipped on her shoes. "Well, I'm sure there's a logical explanation for the sounds."

"Yeah. *Scooby-Doo*."

Her head retracted. "I think you need to lay off the king cake products. The food coloring has affected your brain."

"I'm not kidding, Veronica. In every episode, the villain staged a haunting to cover up some illegal activity."

The Vassal slipped on his glasses. "Like Old Man Simms' pearl-poaching operation."

I unfurled my arm at him à la Vanna White. "See?"

Glenda strutted to the couch and parked her panniers beside Veronica. "You think that's what's happening on the Galliano, sugar?"

"Either that or ghosts are real, which they're not."

"Well, I can't believe old Rex Vandergrift is a murderer, Miss Franki."

"I don't know about that, but he definitely doesn't act like a man who wants to keep away passengers. Yesterday he told Ruth to book entertainment to bring in high-roller gamblers."

Glenda crossed her legs. "Interesting..."

I shot her a look as pointed as her Rococo Baroque stripper shoes. "A jazz singer, not a jaded stripper."

She stiffened and stuck out her Mardi Gras decorations.

Veronica tapped her chin. "I see where you're going with this, Franki. Alfredo Scalino."

"Exactly. He could be running some illegal enterprise for his brother, which means he'd want to keep people off the boat."

"Could be. But if there's no treasure onboard, then why would Nick have texted Luigi the phrase 'Galliano Gold?'"

"Maybe it's code," The Vassal said in keeping with his computer programming background.

Glenda pointed her cigarette holder. "Like black gold from

*The Beverly Hillbillies.* Rex *was* going to be king of the Shrimp and Petroleum Festival."

I kicked up my feet on the coffee table. "I seriously doubt there's oil on the Galliano."

"All right, Miss PI Priss. *You* tell us what it is."

My gaze drifted to the king cake. I stared at the yellow sprinkles, which represented gold, one of the three Mardi Gras colors, and the answer came to me. "The lemon trees in the Bay of Palermo."

Everyone gaped like my face had shriveled and sprouted flames.

"Think about it," I said. "Even though they're yellow, the city was nicknamed the Conca d'Oro, or Shell of Gold."

"Sounds like a luxury gas station," Glenda said, sticking to her oil theory.

Veronica gave an exasperated sigh. "I'm not following any of this."

I was—all the way to the steamboat's walk-in refrigerator. "Galliano gold has something to do with Alfredo's lemons."

Marv exited the Where Dat Tours ticket pavilion with a greasy takeout sack and the key to the Galliano. "It's almost midnight. You sure you want to go on the old girl alone?"

I glanced over my shoulder at the steamboat. In the cloudy, moonless night, it looked especially eerie. "Actually, I'm quite sure I don't. But this could be my last chance to look around before the captain moves onboard. Plus, Detective Sullivan found out I'm on the case, and the cocktail waitress might know I'm a PI. So either one of them could blow my cover, if they haven't already."

"Kate hasn't said nothing. I woulda heard since I hired you."

I took the key from his outstretched hand. "Did you hire her too?"

"Nah, liquor servers have to be certified, so she and Wendell came from the Sazerac Event Staffing agency."

I sighed. A company would never give out Kate's contact information.

He looked at his watch. "Ooh, I gotta run. I'm covering the vampire tour for Pam while she's at a Rainbow Gathering."

"What's that?"

"It's when a bunch of hippies spread peace and love in a forest."

I didn't know how that worked exactly, but it smacked of a bad trip.

Marv's gaze darted to the boat, and he grimaced. "Be careful in there. This is about the time I heard that ghost sailor."

"You didn't hear him on the night Nick was killed, did you?"

"I didn't stay late that night." He saluted me with his sack. "Anyways, I'm off to talk vampires while you hang with the ghosts." He turned and headed for the French Quarter. "Creepy city we live in."

It was, but I didn't appreciate the reminder.

Reluctantly, I faced the Galliano. In the faint glow of a street lamp, the white steamboat loomed before me like a ghost woman with an enormous gold bustle. "The low lighting does nothing for this old girl."

I looked over my shoulder one last time and stepped onto the gangplank. Despite my timid steps, I bounced more than usual. I looked down and discovered the problem—my legs were shaking.

*Not an auspicious beginning.*

I crossed the gangplank and climbed aboard, so wobbly that I would've sworn the steamboat was sailing. I looked from side to side and behind me, and I inserted the key into the lock.

The door creaked open—but I hadn't turned the handle.

*Also not an awesome way to start.*

With my heart and my stomach in my throat, I entered the casino. The musty odor hit me like a phantom fist. I covered my nose and crept past the gambling tables, alert to every creak and groan, and kept my eyes peeled for lurking figures—or floating ones.

Light flashed outside a window overlooking the river.

I approached and peeked out.

The light flashed again over the water. It had come from the rear of the boat on one of the upper decks.

*Was the captain onboard?*

*Or was it the sailor ghost?*

"Not the time to freak yourself out, Franki," I whispered. "Spirits don't exist. But psychopaths do." I paused. "Okay, why'd you have to add that?"

I shook my head to try to pull myself together.

It didn't work.

Stress and fear swirled in my body like a typhoon as I climbed the grand staircase to the passenger deck. Careful to avoid Mark Twain's dead stare, I went up the last set of stairs to the Texas deck.

For the first time ever, I wished I'd followed Ruth's advice. If I'd familiarized myself with the boat like she'd suggested, I'd know where to look for *Scooby-Doo* villains.

*And the killer who deep-froze a man to death.*

I made my way past the pilothouse and crew cabins to the rear of the boat. Off and on, I held my breath to reduce my noise factor—and to avoid the muddy tar smell of the river. Slowly, I peered around the corner. Besides the paddlewheel, the only thing I saw was a calliope.

I exhaled, but I wasn't relieved. I still had to check the other side of the boat, where the light had come from.

As I approached the organ-like instrument, I felt like Don Knotts in *The Ghost and Mr. Chicken* when the organ's blood-spattered keys played their skin-crawling song. Ironically, the only thing more terrifying to me was old-timey circus music that came from a calliope.

I shot the evil instrument a don't-you-dare stare and tiptoed to the corner. I leaned forward and stole a glance.

*No one.*

I tiptoed past a row of windows and came to a door marked Captain's Quarters. I didn't see any lights, so I pressed my ear to the wood.

Silence.

I stepped back and chewed my lower lip. It was possible that the captain was inside trying to sleep. But it was more likely that he was in Amelia, because Marv would've known if he'd been on the boat.

I rested my forehead on the door and gripped the handle.

It turned.

Every cell in my body screamed *Don't go in! This is like one of those horror films where the woman goes back inside the isolated cabin in the woods instead of driving to the police station! And then she falls victim to a crazed hippie killer named Pam!*

The last part would've cracked me up if I hadn't been so scared. Because I had to go in. It could've been my only chance to try to connect the captain to Nick's death. And all I had to do was find a deck of cards with the queen of spades missing.

*Go in. This'll only take a few minutes.*

Obeying my command, I pulled my phone from my back pocket and tapped the flashlight feature. With my cells sizzling, I entered an old-fashioned sitting room that reeked of shoe polish and pipe tobacco. It was sparsely furnished with faded green armchairs, end tables, and a couple of steamboat paintings.

Goosebumps erupted on my skin. I was standing in the room where Agnes Frump and the crewman had burned to death.

And I wanted to get out, quick.

I crossed the room and my lungs ceased to function as I methodically inched my way into the adjoining bedroom.

It was empty.

Apart from a twin bed, there was a writing desk against the far wall, and above it another portrait of Mark Twain. I didn't know whether the captain was a killer, but he was definitely a Twainiac.

I went to the desk to search for the cards. A scroll was held open by two of Marian's horrid krakens. I wrinkled my lips and shone my phone light on the brittle, yellowed paper. It was a map of the ship, and the images of the boat had been hand-drawn in black ink—except for two red X marks on the library and the backstage area in the dining hall.

I ran my finger over the $x$'s. Either the captain believed in the legend of Galliano's gold, or he was looking for something else —perhaps related to the Scalinos.

I raised my phone to snap a picture.

And the calliope started to play.

My body jerked, and I pressed the camera button. The flash went off as the phone fell from my hand, and the white light seared my eyes. Half-blinded, I groped my way to the sitting room while the spooky steam-whistle music continued. I got to the exit and froze.

Fear licked my limbs like a fire that threatened to consume me, and I began backing up.

In the doorway was a shriveled face surrounded by flames.

*The ghost of Agnes Frump.*

## 10

A scream escaped my lips that was loud enough to drown out the calliope. I took another step backward and stumbled into an armchair.

Agnes Frump's flaming ghost head extended a gnarly hand and...

*Switched on the light?*

A lantern lowered.

To reveal Ruth Walker's lined face.

I let out another scream, more bloodcurdling than the first. Because she certainly wasn't wearing her Fun Meter button. The only thing she had on was a super-short T-shirt with the cast of the TV show *Night Court*. Not only that, she wasn't wearing her glasses or her omnipresent bun, which exposed an unsettling resemblance to Kermit the Frog—with Miss Piggy hair.

"Stop your caterwauling, you big sissy," she hissed. "And tell me what in the twain you're doing on the Galliano in the middle of the night."

Something was off about that sentence. "Do you mean *dickens*?"

"We're to replace that term with *twain*, per captain's orders."

I gave an eye roll. The guy had literary issues. "What about *you*? Why are you on the boat—dressed like a TV court tramp?"

Ruth's gaze went half-mast, and she opened her mouth like a frog about to shoot its tongue at an insect.

The calliope reached a crescendo of terrifying tooting.

"Damn freak show music." She threw up her arms. "I can't get a word in edgewise." Her fists clenched, and she stomped into the bedroom.

Confused, I rose and followed her. "What are you doing?"

"Shutting off the power to that blasted calliope." She flipped a breaker near the captain's desk, and circus-free silence filled the room.

"Did you turn it on?"

"Not on purpose. I bumped into the damn thing while I was investigating what I thought was a prowler." She shot me a look worthy of the real ghost of Agnes Frump. "It came on by itself and scared me so bad I broke the safety chain on my glasses."

"How'd you know about the breaker...in the captain's bedroom?"

She raised her Kermit chin. "I don't like what you're insinuating."

"In my defense, you *are* wearing that slinky *Night Court* shirt."

"As the cruise director, I'm in charge of entertainment. So the captain showed me where the switch was."

I smirked. "I'll bet he did."

She sucked in enough air to make her neck balloon like a frog's. "You watch how you talk to your steamboat superior, Missy. Now I'm not done with you, so you park it while I run and get my spare glasses from my cabin."

My aching eyes popped. "You're *living* on the steamboat?"

"Captain Vandergrift let me move onboard early to save on

rent." She twisted a graying brown lock of hair. "The man is a saint."

"Uh, correction—he's a murder suspect with a gambling problem."

"Not everyone's strong enough to be vice-free like me." She picked up the lantern and swung it in my direction. "You plant your rear in that chair until I get back."

I sat at the desk and rubbed my eyes as she left the room. The Agnes Frump scare and the sight of Ruth in the court-themed nightie had given me something akin to sinus pressure.

A couple of minutes passed, so I used the time to rummage through the desk drawers. Pens, tacks, blank envelopes. I opened a bottom drawer, and a slipper-clad foot kicked it shut on my hand.

"Oooowwow!" I howled and leapt up.

Ruth scowled at me from behind red horn-rims with gold chains. "You take Captain Vandergrift off your suspect list." She tightened the belt of the terrycloth robe I was thankful she'd put on. "You've already cost me two jobs, and if you cost me one with free housing, I'll throw you overboard to the gators."

I shook out my hand. "That might be less painful than what you just did. And incidentally, I can't change the fact that the captain might've killed Nick Pescatore."

"You can by focusing on that shady chef." She began winding her hair on top of her head. "You'd be doing society a favor getting a mobster off the streets, so see to it that he's guilty."

"As an avid watcher of court TV, you of all people know that justice doesn't work like that."

"As your cruise director, I know justice on this boat works however I want." She snapped an elastic band over her bun. "So if you don't start investigating that Scalino brother, I'll tell the captain who you are and get *you* fired for a change. That'll be a bigger hoot and toot than the calliope can produce."

I thought about threatening to tell the captain that she had fire onboard his matchstick steamboat, but Ruth was in judge-and-jury mode, so I didn't stand a chance at a fair sentence. "I was planning to investigate Scalino tonight. But I'll need your help because Wesley Sullivan is the detective on the case, and he's out to get even with me for solving a couple of his homicides last year."

Ruth's gaze went from froggish to hawkish. "He's that uppity Irish Romeo that split up you and Bradley and led to me losing my bank job."

I nodded.

"No problemo. I'll bind his hands and feet and make him walk the plank."

Ruth had gotten her boats mixed up. "Um, we have a paddle-wheel, not a plank. And what I meant was, I need your help in the galley to investigate the chef's lemons."

Her mouth puckered like she'd bit into one. "Have you been hitting the casino bar?"

I hadn't, but I would've bet *she* had. "It has to do with the Mafia. They hide things like cash, drugs, and weapons inside everything from gutted fish to coffins."

She pointed to the map. "Is that why you marked that up? To check for hidey-holes?"

"No, it belongs to Captain Vandergrift. I think the red X marks have something to do with Captain Galliano's gold."

Ruth ripped the map from the desk. She lowered her horn-rims, and her chains started vibrating. And the flames I thought I'd seen around her head sprouted from her eyes. She turned and sprinted from the room.

I hurried to the deck and saw her charging full steam toward the pilothouse at the front of the boat. "Hey! What happened to helping me with the investigation?"

"Screw you, woman," she shouted without looking back. "I'm going for the gold, and I sure as hell ain't talkin' about no lemon juice."

I gave a frustrated arm flail. "But there's a murderer on the boat."

"There's also a mobster, but I can't worry about them. That missing Civil War gold is my ticket to cruise-ship retirement in my golden years." She entered the pilothouse and slammed the door.

*So much for recruiting her for my ragtag army.*

I returned to the captain's bedroom and finished my search. His quarters were clean, which wasn't surprising since he hadn't moved in, but I was fairly certain I'd find some dirt in the galley on the chef.

To avoid the calliope, and the risk of it playing spontaneously, I took the mid-ship stairwell to the main deck. I entered the dining hall through a side door and turned on the lights. With Ruth living on the boat, there was no reason to sneak around in the spooky dark.

I pushed open the galley door, flipped the switch, and gave a shiver. And it had as much to do with Pat the Sea Hag's phlegm rag as it did Nick Pescatore's frozen body.

*Nick.*

Whoever had killed him was colder than the deep freeze I'd found him in, and quite possibly the most dangerous killer I'd investigated. As I walked past the pantry and down the narrow hall to the walk-in, I wondered whether I should consider Veronica's offer to hire a PI to take over the case.

But I couldn't let Luigi down, especially not after he'd left me the winepress. And I had a war to win against Sullivan. Because if I didn't beat him once and for all, he'd keep coming at me for more rounds, and my and Bradley's relationship could get taken out in the process.

Resolute, I passed the chef's desk and yanked open the walk-in.

The lemons gleamed in their crates. Like orbs of gold.

I hesitated before going inside. I'd gotten locked in a walk-in at a restaurant over Christmas, and I didn't want to repeat the chilling experience. So I bent over and picked up a couple of lemon crates to prop open the door.

A faint scream came from one of the upper decks.

And a solid splat.

My stomach dropped, and so did the crates.

*Was that the ghost sailor falling into the paddlewheel?*

*Or Ruth?*

MY FEET RAN up the mid-ship stairs, but my stomach had stayed in the galley. And my brain was in overdrive trying to downplay the horror of the scream and splat.

*Ruth is fine. It's that sailor ghost scam.*

*There's no murderer onboard. What you heard was a recording.*

*Like the Pirates of the Caribbean ride at Disneyland.*

*Or the Haunted Mansion?*

"Leave it to my brain to screw me over," I whispered.

I exited the stairwell onto the Texas deck and hooked a right to the rear of the boat—and that creepy calliope. Meanwhile, I tried to control my huffing and puffing. If a killer *was* on the steamboat, I didn't want to out myself, nor did I want to inhale the acrid river smell.

With the stealth of a ninja, I made it to the captain's quarters. I pressed my back against the wall and peered around the corner.

*All clear.*

I crept toward the calliope, willing it not to play.

*Ever.*

I reached the unsettling instrument and shot a nervous glance at the keys.

*Still. Like the night.*

I took another step.

A whoosh of air rushed past my ears, and something struck the middle of my back so hard that I would've sworn it had knocked the lungs from my body. Pain radiated across my shoulders and down my spine in the shape of a red-hot crucifix.

I made like a plank and face-planted on the deck.

And I waited for a fatal blow to the head.

"What're you doing sneaking around like that?" Ruth's outrage cracked above me like a lightning bolt. "Trying to scare me?"

The blow to the head I'd been expecting was metaphorical —the realization that I'd been struck by her and not a killer. I struggled to reply between waves of pain. And rage. "I came...to save you...from a killer."

"*Hmph.*" The paddle of an oar touched down on the deck. "Looks to me like you're laying down on the job again."

I rued the day I'd met Ruth.

She raised the oar. "Let's hop to it, shall we?"

I gritted my teeth and resisted the urge to scream, EASIER SAID THAN DONE YOU OAR-WIELDING LUNATIC. I couldn't risk alerting a possible killer to our presence, or another whack from Ruth.

I pulled myself to my knees and felt my lower back with the hand that still ached from the drawer slam. I wasn't sure, but I thought Ruth had knocked the curve from my spine.

I got to my feet and glared at the oar. "You didn't have a weapon when I came up here before."

"Sure I did. The lantern. I'd planned to toss oil and fire on you."

At least I'd avoided *that*. I rolled my shoulders to make sure my arms still worked. "Did you see anyone or hear anything before the scream?"

"I was in the pilothouse, remember? But I tell you, it's like it came out of nowhere. And I've already circled the deck, and I didn't see anyone."

I scanned the row of crew cabins. Searching them would've been pointless. If someone had been onboard, they could've already left the boat or gone to another deck. "This might sound weird, but is there any chance it could've been a recording?"

"Now that you mention it, yes, it could've been."

I gazed at the gold wheel, and then at the river. The normally brown water was as black as the night. And almost as still. "It's also possible that whoever was on the boat fell into the paddlewheel."

"Suppose we should call the authorities?"

I turned and headed for the mid-ship stairwell. "You live here. That's up to you."

She hurried after me. "Where are you going?"

"Down to the main deck to take a look at those lemons," I said over my shoulder, "then I'm getting off the boat. If you do call the police, I don't want to be here to deal with Sullivan."

"You're just going to leave a defenseless woman onboard with a killer?"

I turned and eyed the oar. "You can come down with me and then wait on land until the cops come."

"What'll I do after they leave?"

I sighed. "You made the decision to move on the Galliano. So, as they say in the industry, batten down the hatches."

Ruth's eyes went Puss in Boots behind her horn-rims.

And Catholic guilt hit me like the oar. I didn't know much

about her, but I'd gathered that she had no money and no family. As much as it pained me—oh so literally—I couldn't leave her alone on the steamboat. My jaw tightened, trying to prevent me from saying the words that I was about to utter. "You can stay with me at Veronica's apartment. But you're sleeping on the couch." I pointed at her legs. "In pajama pants."

"Oh, goodie." She did a jig. "It'll be like a slumber party."

I rolled my eyes and headed down the mid-ship stairs.

"What say we pop by the library and have a look around?"

I grabbed the railing and spun on her. "Do you really think a killer is going to stop and read *Tom Sawyer*?"

She put a hand on her hip. "I meant we should look for the Civil War gold."

My face went flat—like my back. Ruth was a bigger gold digger than my mother. "You live on the Galliano. Do your treasure hunting when we're not potentially onboard with a murderer."

She pulled the sad act again.

"That worked once. It won't work again." I turned and jogged down the stairs. I couldn't let her see that despite my tough act I was kind of a sucker.

We entered the galley, and I led her down the hallway to Alfredo Scalino's lair. I was on high alert for the killer, but I was on higher alert for the oar Ruth wielded behind me.

We made it to the walk-in and took in the scene. One of the crates I'd dropped had split open, and lemons littered the floor. And so did what looked like packages of Pez candy.

In gold.

My back throbbed, so I dipped at the knees to retrieve one of the bags. The candy-sized items said GOLD on one side and 199.9 mg on the other.

I knew what Nick Pescatore's text had been about.

"Are those baby gold bars?" Ruth asked, a note of hope in her tone.

"That's what they're made to look like, but they're some kind of illegal drug." I knelt and examined the crates. They had false bottoms. "And I'll bet every crate in the walk-in is full of them."

We stared at the drugs in silence, and I wondered whether Nick had tried to steal them or even report them to the police. Because something had gotten him silenced—in the freezer.

Footsteps sounded in the galley.

And I imagined them wearing spats.

I got a blast of adrenaline that rocketed me to my feet.

"It's that mobster chef or his brother." Ruth stripped the belt from her robe. "I'll whack him, and then you jump on him and choke him with this."

My look was wry despite our dire circumstances. "I would, but you cracked my spine. Remember?"

The footsteps came closer.

Ruth raised the oar and took a practice swing in my direction.

I ducked just in time.

"Franki? Are you back there?"

I rose, surprised. "Bradley?" I motioned for Ruth to stay back. He didn't know she was on the boat, and this wasn't the time for him to find out. I ran into the galley. "What're you doing here?"

He stood by the island. "I've been trying to call you, but your phone went to voicemail. It finally occurred to me that you might be on the Galliano, and I got worried."

I noticed he'd made no move toward me, and an uneasy feeling settled in my heart. "Has something happened?"

He sniff-laughed. "Yeah. I guess you could say that." He bowed his head for a moment and then met my gaze with laser focus. "I stopped by your apartment to check on Luigi, and he mentioned that Alfredo Scalino runs the kitchen. Why didn't you tell me that when we talked about the winepress this morning?"

"I—"

Ruth entered the galley in a classic case of bad timing.

Bradley's brow bolted at the sight of his ex-assistant. "You're here too?"

"Veronica got me this gig." Ruth gave me the side-eye. "Didn't Franki tell you?"

He stared at me, his face expressionless. "No. She didn't."

She grunted. "She didn't tell me either, even though she knew I needed a job after you quit the bank."

I once again rued the day I met Ruth, and I promised myself that I'd leave her on the steamboat with the ghosts and the killer. "Bradley, so much is going on, that I was too overwhelmed to tell you about it. Look what we just found in the walk-in." I thrust a package of the gold bars into his hand. "They're trafficking drugs on the Galliano. This is what got Nick killed."

He turned the package over. "Everything was so perfect."

My heart fell to the floor and split like that crate. He was talking about our relationship, not Nick or the drugs, and in the past tense.

"Is there anything else you were too overwhelmed to tell me?"

I looked away, and a cold river of fear as powerful as the Mississippi coursed through my veins. And it wasn't because I hadn't told him about Detective Sullivan.

"Bradley, old boy." Sullivan crowed from the galley doorway. "Franki didn't tell me you were still in the picture."

I went limp, but Bradley went as rigid as I had when Ruth had hit me with the oar. He turned to face his nemesis. "She didn't mention you were still around either. But then, she keeps a lot of things to herself."

Everyone stopped and stared at me.

"Bradley—" I stopped short as Sullivan's gaze zeroed in on the drugs I'd put in Bradley's hand.

"Well, well, well." A sour smile settled on the detective's lips. He ambled over to Bradley, never taking his eyes off the bag. "I heard you'd quit your job, but I never thought you'd stoop to this."

"You can't be freakin' serious." Bradley was deathly calm.

But the river in my veins was raging. I knew the detective, and he was capable of anything. "Slow down, Sullivan. You're rushing to judgement, which isn't befitting a police officer."

"Here's a judgement for you," he drawled with delight. "Bradley Hartmann, you're under arrest for drug trafficking."

I was silent, but my head was burning like Agnes Frump's. And inside I was screaming like that sailor when he went overboard.

## 11

"Franki, if you don't stop crying, you'll fill up that glass and drown yourself." Veronica stood in Glenda's all-white living room at the base of the giant champagne flute where I'd taken refuge from the world, and especially from Ruth.

As usual, my best friend was the voice of reason—although anyone hearing her statement out of context wouldn't agree. And at that moment I didn't agree either. I was too drained and depressed to think logically. So I stayed in the glass in a fetal position and continued to sob.

"Do you want to hear what I learned at the police station, or not?"

I did, but I didn't want to look over the glass rim. It wasn't the despair that stopped me as much as the pain in my back from the oar whack—and the floor-to-ceiling stripper action shots of Glenda.

Nevertheless, I pulled myself to a sitting position.

Veronica lowered her chin. "Brace yourself, okay?"

"Oh no." I extended my arms to either side of the glass. "How bad is it?"

"Keep in mind that Bradley hasn't gone before the judge yet, but I know the man who'll preside over his case, and he's really harsh when it comes to drug crimes. Also, he'll take his previous arrest into account when setting bail."

I exhaled at the memory of Bradley being loaded into a squad car outside Madame Moiselle's the year before, after he'd punched Sullivan for tipping me when I'd stripped to try to solve a homicide. "How much do you think it'll be? And don't hold back. God knows Ruth didn't."

She didn't smirk. "It could be as high as a million dollars."

A pain struck my chest like I'd been stabbed by a life-sized cocktail sword. I slid down the side of the glass and hit bottom.

Bradley would never get out of jail.

And he would never forgive me for it.

Veronica paced on the white shag carpet. "I know it sounds bad, but I'm going to do everything I can to get his bail lowered. The judge is a notorious womanizer, so I'll resort to flirting if I have to."

At that amount, it would take a lot more than her famous eyelash batting and hair twirling to get the judge to show any mercy. Tears flowed from my eyes like the Mississippi River. "I want to go to the police station."

"You know you can't do that. Reporters are sniffing around, and they could connect you to the case. Plus, Wesley could always change his mind and arrest you too."

My tears dried up at the mention of the detective, and so did my empathy. "That bastard knew those drugs didn't belong to Bradley. He did this to get even with me, just like he said he was going to do."

"I know." She stopped pacing. "I knew Wesley had a dark side, but this is beyond dark."

I thought of the Civil War cannon and sat up. "And this is beyond war."

"Good." She punched the air. "I'm glad you're getting into combat mode. Now if you're going to wage a 'beyond war,' you need to get out of that glass and eat something. I have breakfast for you in Glenda's kitchen."

"How could I even think of food at a time like this?"

"Because you're a stress eater. I got you king cake French toast with king cake syrup."

My logical thinking returned, and so did my appetite. After all, fighting a dirty detective required sustenance, and king cake products were only available during Mardi Gras.

I wiped my eyes, grabbed my phone, and gingerly climbed from the glass. Pain wracked my back with every movement, and I vowed to wrack Ruth when I got the chance.

As I touched down on the carpet, the phone beeped in my hand. The identity of the texter made my back stiffen. "It's Ruth. She says the Galliano is closed until tomorrow at noon, so I don't have to go to work. I guess the captain must've called her."

"No, when I came back from the police station, she was getting into a cab to go to the boat. That reminds me, why did you sleep here and not at my place with Ruth?"

"Because that nut case, or maybe I should call her a court case, blasts Hulu reruns of Judge Judy to go to sleep. Every time I heard the gavel, I thought about Bradley getting sentenced."

Veronica entered the adjoining kitchen. "She talks in her sleep too. I know because I came home to get my briefcase before I went to the police station."

"What did she say?"

She opened a takeout container. "That you and Bradley got what you deserved for costing her a job."

"That woman put the *ruth* in *ruthless*." I tossed my phone on the table and flopped into a chair. "Bradley's lucky she's not his judge."

My message tone beeped again.

"Oh, so now she wants a place to crash tonight. Hell...to... the...no." I typed the message as I spoke and hit the send arrow.

Veronica shot me a look under her lashes. "Text her back and tell her she can stay at my apartment again."

"Not even if my life depended on it, and that phrase literally applies. Because justice isn't blind, Veronica. She wears a pair of horn-rims and swings an oar instead of a gavel."

Glenda entered the kitchen in a robe so sheer that only the hems were clearly visible—and a few unmentionables. She struck a saucy pose with her cigarette holder. "Can I offer you something to drink, Miss Franki?"

"What have you got?"

"Champagne."

It was tempting, but I needed my wits about me to wage a war. "Just water, thanks."

"Would you like some lemon with that?"

Bitter tears sprang to my eyes, and I cried like I was being juiced.

Glenda put a hand to her all-too-visible bosom. "Oh, I'm sorry, sugar. I should've realized that lemons were a sour subject."

Veronica sat across from me and took my hands. "We're going to fix this, Franki."

I choked back a sob and some snot. "Nonna was right to be worried. Not even the lemon tradition could save me. I'm going to die a *zitella*."

"That tradition is an old wives' tale, and you know it. You also know you're a fighter, so get back into 'beyond war' mode and get your man back."

I wiped my eyes and got a good look at Veronica. She had bags under her eyes, and I felt bad for getting her up in the middle of the night to help Bradley. "I'm sorry for ruining your special evening with Dirk."

"You didn't. We were asleep when you called."

"Then I'm sorry for waking you up."

She reached across the table and squeezed my arm. "You're my best friend. You know I'd do anything to help you."

Tears rolled anew, and so did the snot. "I don't need help, but Bradley sure does."

"And you're just the person to help him." She handed me a napkin, and I wiped my face.

"I'm pretty sure he never wants to see me again."

Glenda delivered the water in a champagne flute, the only glassware she owned. "You show up on release day in a little number I've got in my costume closet, and I guarantee your ex-banker beau will want to see all of you." She gave a too-sheer shimmy. "I call it my get-out-of-jail-see card. I wore it every time I had to get one of my fiancés out of jail."

I should've focused on the last word of that statement, but my mind went back to the plural noun. "You were engaged, and multiple times?"

"Twelve, to be exact, and every one of them went to jail. I'm dedicating an entire chapter to them in my memoir."

"Why didn't you ever marry one of them? Because of the crimes?"

"Oh, I was just in it for the rings, sugar." She squeezed her Mardi Gras decorations and shook her money maker. "I couldn't possibly give all of this to one man. It wouldn't be fair to the others."

Tears teetered on my eyelid rims. I couldn't even get engaged once. But I hadn't tried a criminal—maybe that was the key.

Veronica cleared her throat. "Glenda might be right. For all we know, Bradley blames Sullivan and not you. So, you've got to prove he's innocent, and you can start by finding out how those gold bars got onboard the Galliano. An officer told me that they're a type of Ecstasy from the UK."

I didn't believe that Bradley blamed Sullivan, but it was easier to focus on the case than on my failed relationship and the predicament Bradley was in. "Those drugs belong to the Scalinos, and I'll bet they were planning to use the overnight gambling excursions to distribute them."

Glenda took a seat. "To the gamblers?"

"Or to drug dealers, if we docked somewhere. There are Mississippi river cruises that stop in major cities like Memphis, St. Louis, even Minneapolis, so the captain could be planning to do that too."

Veronica stared at the table. "Do you think Captain Vandergrift was in on the trafficking?"

Glenda lit her cigarette and exhaled a puff of smoke. "I'd be shocked by that, Miss Ronnie. Old Rex is a gambler, not a drug dealer."

"I agree. And I don't think he would do anything to jeopardize his dream of piloting a steamboat like his hero, Mark Twain."

Veronica shook her head. "His fight with Nick suggests otherwise, and so does his 'cold shivers' threat. He could've killed him when he threw him overboard."

"Yes, but if Nick survived the fall then the Scalinos could've put him in the freezer with the playing card to frame the captain and take control of the boat. Don't forget that Marian Guidry, the gift shop clerk, told me Alfredo was onboard that night for the employee meeting."

"Then I just have one question." Veronica crossed her arms. "What prompted Sullivan to go to the steamboat at one a.m. this morning?"

"There's no question there." I cut into my French toast so aggressively that I sliced through the Styrofoam container. "He was staking it out, waiting for the chance to set me up, which is why he begged the captain to give him the case—and why he wanted me to stay on it."

Her blonde brow went dark. "Are you saying he planted those gold bars to get even with you?"

"What I'm saying is that Sullivan knew, just like I did, that Alfredo Scalino wasn't on the Galliano to cook. I mean, his mob boss brother could've set him up in his own fancy restaurant in the city, but instead Alfredo wants to work on a ramshackle steamboat on the Mississippi?" I shook my fork. "No, it was obvious to Sullivan that something was going down on the Galliano—and that it was just a matter of time before I found out what it was. So, he waited like a snake in the river reeds to catch me, and then he doubled his prey by arresting Bradley."

Glenda pulled the lapels of her robe to get air to her chest. "I don't know about you girls, but I'm getting aroused by all this sexy man-talk."

"It isn't sexy. It's just shady."

"That's your opinion, sugar." She blew a smoke heart and stuck out her chest. "I like a down-and-dirty competition between men, particularly when I'm the prize. As the old cliché goes, all's fair in love and war."

I speared a double bite of king cake French toast. "All's fair in war and war too. And if I'm going to die a *zitella* because of Sullivan, then I'll make sure his inevitable third marriage takes place behind bars."

MY HAND INCHED toward my front doorknob but returned to my side. Veronica had informed Luigi of the gold bars and Bradley's arrest, which meant that my mom, nonna, and all the nonne holding vigil for Nick knew too. And in my mourning state, I wasn't ready to go inside and face more mourning, especially when I'd joined Nick as the subject of it.

I turned to the street. Even the atmosphere seemed to know about Bradley. It was almost seven-thirty, and yet the day still struggled to break, as though it couldn't drag itself from bed—or from a giant champagne flute. There was also a chill in the air and scattered rain drops, like a broken-hearted sky was crying.

My eyes shifted left. I'd tried to stop them, keep them directed straight ahead at Thibodeaux's Tavern, but I couldn't. They looked at the creepy cemetery—

—and saw my relationship entombed in a mausoleum.

*What about Bradley's future? Was it dead and buried?*

I shook the horrible thought from my head. No. I wouldn't let that happen. I couldn't control how Bradley felt about me, but I could control the outcome of the investigation. And I wouldn't stop until he was released from jail—and Sullivan was locked up.

Ready to battle the Scalinos, the police, and the nonne, I grasped the door handle and charged into my apartment. The place reeked of *ragù* and regret. Undaunted, I stormed the living room. What I saw whacked the warrior spirit from me like Ruth's oar.

My mom and nonna sat side by side at the kitchen table surrounded by fretting nonne. I wasn't surprised that Nonna had shed the gray shades and gone back to basic black. What took my breath away was my mother's elaborate and antiquated outfit. If Captain Vandergrift had been present, he would have banned me from saying it, but the dress resembled something from a Dickens novel—like a black version of Miss Havisham's wedding gown.

In a stunning role reversal, Luigi poured her a glass of wine and murmured words of reassurance. But my mother stared unseeing through her veil.

She looked like a woman who'd lost a husband.

And she had.

*Mine.*

A nonna with a dowager's hump and a dude's mustache thrust a bundle of fabric into my hands.

I looked down. A black sack dress with ample space for pendulous breasts and a veil so large it could function as a shroud.

*Standard zitella issue.*

My face prickled, probably because it was preparing to sprout little-old-Italian-lady whiskers.

Nonna shuffled from the kitchen. "Franki, it's-a time to get-a dressed."

"I have over a week left on the lemon tradition," I said, shaking the black bundle. "You'd think a bunch of such devout Catholics would have some damn faith."

The nonne stopped fussing over my mom and the ragù and crossed themselves.

"Who's-a talking about-a the *limone*? We have-a to be at-a Nick's memorial at-a nine o'clock."

A nonna wailed an obligatory *Cremato!* And the nonne began working their rosary beads.

I lowered the bundle and my head. The prickling on my face had turned to burning shame. I'd been so focused on the case and my own problems that I hadn't asked the date and time of Nick's service.

"Since-a you brought up-a the tradition, where is-a the lemon?" Nonna waved her arm at my kitchen window, and a nano nonna drew back the drapes in a move reminiscent of a dramatic curtain reveal.

I couldn't fathom what a window had to do with the lemon I'd stolen. "Well, you could hardly expect me to keep a lemon for a whole year. It would rot."

My mother let out a scream more bone-splitting than an oar whacking.

The nonne sputtered and clutched at one other as they struggled to kneel.

"*La Bibbia!*" The nano nonna shuffle-ran for a Bible on the counter and rifled through the pages.

Nonna collapsed into the purple armchair and pressed her palms to her cheeks. "*O mamma mia. Che faccio? CHE FACCIO?*"

"What do you mean, 'What am I going to do'?" I shouted the words half annoyed and half afraid, trying to figure out what kind of non-fresh hell I'd created for myself.

She clasped her hands in prayer. "After you steal-a the lemon, you gotta put it on-a the kitchen windowsill. If-a you don't, it's-a not gonna work."

I sucked in a gasp and pointed at her. "*You* never told me *THAT*."

An awful silence settled over the room as an awful realization settled over me.

I, Francesca Lucia Amato, believed in the lemon tradition.

Despite my common sense and solid education, a lifetime of Nonna's Sicilian home-schooling had implanted crazy superstition seeds in my brain that were sprouting—like my little-old-Italian-lady whiskers.

I looked at the black bundle in my hand. It was fitting that I was going to a memorial, because I had a lot to mourn—the loss of Nick, my beloved Bradley, and all rational thought.

Without a word, I zombie-walked to my bedroom, closed the door, and flopped on my bed. Tears threatened to spill onto my pillow, but I had to pep-talk myself into staying in combat mode. "C'mon, Franki. Hairy chin up. You might talk to yourself like a bag lady, but you could never be a little old Italian lady because" —I wracked my superstition-riddled brain for a reason, and I found one—"you're five-feet-ten!"

I jumped off the bed and stuffed the black bundle into the waste bin in my bathroom. "*Addio*, sack and shroud. It's time to go to your grave in the trash heap at the dump."

Then I looked in the mirror and ran a dry razor over my chin.

Satisfied that all traces of impending *zitellahood* had been eradicated, I marched from the bathroom to find a black dress from the current century—or even the one prior—and opened my closet door.

The winepress lay at my feet.

I seethe-stared at the trunk. It represented all the obstacles in my life, except for the wine part. Old-world superstitions passed down like family heirlooms, criminals like the Scalinos who exploited people for profit, and corrupt cops who couldn't let go of past kisses and case victories.

In a fit of anger, I pulled the trunk from the closet. The hot pink duvet I'd used to cover it got caught under my feet and slid off.

A flash caught my eye.

I couldn't imagine what would have reflected the light so I crouched to have a look. The antique brass hardware was too scuffed and tarnished to be the culprit.

Curious, I flipped the latches and opened the lid. The winepress had been disassembled except for the wooden cage that held the grapes. I rummaged around pieces of wood, bolts, screws and closed the lid.

And I spotted the source of the flash.

A miniature camera was inside the oversized keyhole.

I didn't react. I merely rose and searched for a dress.

But as I sifted through the hangers, my arms trembled. Because the exterminator had indeed been an imposter, and I feared the Scalinos were watching my every move.

LUIGI STOOD outside the main doors to Our Lady of Guadalupe Catholic Chapel in a black suit with a blue carnation on his lapel, greeting friends and colleagues from the grocery business as they arrived for Nick's service.

I stayed inside the entrance, surveying the people coming in. The small Catholic church was packed, but not only for the memorial. Our Lady of Guadalupe served as a type of sanctuary for the homeless who, after a night on New Orleans' streets, slept safely in the pews.

Veronica entered in a chic black-and-white Chanel number that clashed with the modest decor and the nonne's mourning looks. She spotted me and sashayed over. "Hey. Let's go see if we can squeeze in up front next to your mom and nonna."

"No, I'm sticking close to the exit."

She rolled her cornflower blues. "Are you still freaked out that this place used to be a mortuary chapel?"

I scratched my elbow. "That yellow fever epidemic was nothing to joke about, Veronica. But no, I'm not."

"Well," she glanced at my arm, "I see you scratching, so your priest phobia must've kicked in."

I looked around for Father John, the head of the clergy, to make sure he hadn't heard her. "It's not a phobia, okay? Priests *and* nuns make me feel guilty, and when I feel guilty, I itch."

"Uh-huh."

I cocked my head to one side, frustrated. "I'm staying by the door to see if any of the suspects show up for Nick's service. Also, my back is bruised, so I don't want to press it against a hard, wooden pew."

"Whatever you say." She gave a wry smile and headed toward the altar.

I moved to a far corner, next to a statue of Saint Expedite.

For the third time since moving to New Orleans, I studied the image of the unlikely saint—a Roman centurion who held a cross while stepping on a crow. During my first homicide case, Father John told me that locals had appropriated the Catholic saint for voodoo purposes by asking him to "expedite" requests for favors they'd made to Marie Laveau, a legendary voodoo priestess buried outside in the chapel cemetery.

*Was that happening onboard the Galliano? Had a woman Nick wronged appropriated a playing card, the queen of spades, to invoke the wrath of voodoo loa Erzulie D'en Tort?*

In light of the drug discovery, it seemed more likely that Nick had been murdered by the Scalinos than by an angry ex-girl-friend. But I couldn't rule out voodoo. In New Orleans, white and black magic were present in the unlikeliest of places, and Our Lady of Guadalupe Chapel was proof.

Father John exited the sacristy, and the nonne, on cue, began their litany of laments.

I turned my attention to the altar.

The church door closed, and I looked to see who'd entered.

A young woman in sunglasses started at the sight of me, and I stared at her dark lenses.

Until my gaze shifted to her brown wig.

*The Roulergirl, Goldie, sans skates.*

She hit the door with a thwack and ran out.

I took off after her, wishing I hadn't worn four-inch heels to increase the odds against me becoming a little old Italian lady. I skidded on the slick floor and struggled with the door. Then I got to the sidewalk and went as still as the statue of Saint Expedite.

The Roulergirl was gone, but a man with pock-marked skin and a jagged scar under his eye was shoving Luigi into a limousine.

"Get your thieving hands off me, you dirty hooligan!"

Luigi's shout snapped me from my shock, and I lunged for the limo.

The man climbed in after him, and the car door slammed.

As I reached for the handle, the car sped away. And I stood gaping in the middle of Rampart Street.

I didn't get the license plate, but it didn't matter. Before the car door closed, I'd seen something on the floorboard that told me the identity of Luigi's kidnapper.

A pair of men's shoes with white spats.

Gigi "The G-Man" Scalino.

## 12

The 9-1-1 operator hung up, and yet I kept the phone pressed to my ear. In a daze, I glanced around Rampart Street, trying to think of something, anything I could do to help Luigi. I spotted a historical marker for the church that bore the name *The Old Mortuary Chapel*, and my superstitious nature flared.

"Oh, no you don't." I put away my phone and pointed my index and pinky fingers downward in the *scongiuri* gesture Nonna taught me to ward off bad luck. For added insurance I gave the marker a kick. But I should've kicked myself for not telling Luigi to greet his guests inside the church. Instead, I'd left him alone on the sidewalk where he'd been an easy mark for the Mafia. As a result, I stood on that sidewalk in a Mississippi-sized river of regret.

The chapel door opened with a bang, jolting me from my shock. Two men ran out and headed down the street.

*Gigi's thugs?*

They climbed into a black car and placed a flashing blue light on the dash.

I took a breath, relieved. The New Orleans PD had placed undercover officers among the mourners. But like me, they'd been unprepared for Luigi's kidnapping.

I turned and faced the chapel entrance as though confronting the gates of hell. Because an inferno awaited me inside when I informed the guests of the abduction.

The door opened, and my mother appeared in her dark Dickensian wear. Her eyes darted from side to side like they used to do when she suspected my brothers and me of mischief. "What's happening? Where's Luigi?"

She'd already lost my future husband. I didn't know how to tell her she might have lost Nonna's. "Gigi Scalino..."

Her face aged in an instant, like Miss Havisham's—or Agnes Frump's ghost. She spun, threw back her veil, and...

*Howled like a wolf?*

She kicked off a tulle underskirt and sprinted inside the chapel to the middle of the aisle. She faced the image of the Virgin Mary and spread her arms like Jesus on the cross. "Help me, Our Lady of Guadalupe! Luigi's been kidnapped by the mob!"

Shouts and wails erupted, and hymnals went flying. People scrambled from the pews and rushed the exit.

I squeezed past frenzied mourners and homeless men and scanned the church for Nonna and Veronica. I couldn't see them amid the chaos, but I *did* see my mother.

Face-down in the baptismal font.

"Mom!" I rushed over and pulled her from the vessel.

She sputtered holy water, and her knees gave out. "Just leave me here, Francesca. The water's so peaceful."

"If you want peace, try praying like other people." Despite my half-broken back, I half-dragged her toward a pew. We passed a wreath-shaped funerary arrangement, and she ripped out a handful of chrysanthemums and wrested herself from my grip.

"Mom, what are you *doing*?"

As though in a trance, she ran to the statue of Saint Expedite and placed the flowers at his sandaled feet.

I put my hands on my cheeks. My mother had made a voodoo offering to a Roman centurion saint.

"Franki!" Veronica rushed down the side aisle. "Did you see what happened? Was it Gigi?"

I gave a grim nod. "Where's Nonna? Is she all right?"

"She's in the sacristy with the other nonne, seeking counsel from Father John."

If I knew my nonna and her friends, they were using the room as a command post to put out an APB in the Sicilian community and call in reinforcements.

Veronica pulled me to a stained-glass window away from the crowd. "Why would the Scalinos take Luigi?"

"I can't figure it out. I mean, Nick tried to tell Luigi about the drugs with his 'Galliano gold' text, but the secret of the gold bars is out. And even if it wasn't, silencing Luigi wouldn't eliminate his phone records."

She winced at the word "silencing," and I did the same.

Glenda emerged effortlessly from the fray at the door, no doubt due to her decades of strip-club experience and sashayed toward us in an enormous black feather boa and a black mesh dress that let it all hang *way* out. On the plus side, her shoulders were covered in accordance with Catholic tradition, and her pasties and thong said *Censored*.

"This is some kind of send-off, sugar. You Catholics are wild, especially your mother."

I followed her gaze to the altar.

My mother sat spread-eagle on the steps, slugging from a bottle of communion wine.

I'd expected her to maybe sing a funeral dirge in place of a Christmas carol, but not that. Nevertheless, I made no move to stop her from drinking. Booze was a better way to drown her sorrows than holy water.

Veronica leaned in to Glenda. "They're not celebrating Nick's life," she whispered. "Gigi Scalino kidnapped Luigi."

"Well, holy hell." Glenda put her hands on her hips and kicked a leg from a side slit in her dress that went all the way to her waist. "Gigi's got a mansion on St. Charles. Maybe he took Luigi there."

Gigi Scalino was too smart to hide Luigi at his house, but I didn't say that to Glenda. I had a bigger problem to deal with—the nonne were filing from the sacristy like soldiers prepared for battle. Chins raised, chests puffed, they wielded rosaries in one hand and purses in the other. As they marched up the aisle with my nonna in the lead, they reminded me of Mussolini and his Black Shirts, or Black Skirts in their case.

I blocked Nonna's path. "Whatever plan you've concocted isn't going to happen."

Her eyes went ninja. "We're-a going to Gigi's house. And he's-a gonna tell us what he did with-a Luigi, or we're-a gonna work him over, like I'm-a gonna do to you if you don't-a move."

She swung her purse, and I ducked to avoid a probable concussion from whatever was in it.

A siren wailed outside.

"The police are here," I said through clenched teeth. "So you let them handle Gigi."

"If it's-a that-a detective who arrested-a Bradley"—she raised her chin—"we'll-a handle *him*."

The nonne raised their purses and swung them like nunchucks.

Siccing Nonna Mussolina and the Black Skirts on Sullivan wasn't a bad idea. They had over a thousand years of pent-up homemaker rage between them—and purses loaded with heavy Bibles.

The last of the guests made their way from the chapel, and Sullivan blew in like a storm cloud, flanked by two scowling officers. His gaze struck me like a lightning bolt. "What was the tag on the car?"

"I didn't get it, but the car was a black limo."

He pulled a pen and pad from his back pocket. "But you ID'ed Gigi Scalino."

"Not him. His spats."

Sullivan lowered his pen and then his brow. "How in the *hell* am I supposed to get an arrest warrant based on a pair of damn spats?"

The nonne gasped at his language and hoisted their purses, and Nonna stretched out her rosary like a garrote.

I held them back, but only because we were in a church. "No one else in New Orleans wears spats *and* has a motive to kidnap Luigi."

"This isn't a TV show, Franki Rockford. We need actual evidence to incarcerate criminals."

His hypocrisy hit a nerve, and my anger at him erupted. "Like when you falsely arrested Bradley for holding the Scalinos' drugs?"

My words echoed through the chapel, and everyone fell silent.

"Franceshhhca Lucia Amato." My mother tipped her wine bottle at me. "You uszhe your church voishe."

Sullivan's mouth opened at the sight of her but regained its customary sneer. "Your mother's a wise woman, especially since you're shouting slander."

Father John stepped from the sacristy, his features drawn with concern. "Why don't the two of you join me for a moment?"

Sullivan's lips thinned. "This isn't confession, Father. Your services aren't needed."

The nonne charged like horses in Siena's *Palio* race, but Glenda moved in front of them. They dropped their purses and their anger and set about trying to cover her.

Veronica touched my arm. "Why don't I come with you to the sacristy?"

"It's all right." I glowered at Sullivan. "I won't kill him in a house of God." I let the implication lie and stormed up the aisle to the altar, where Father John was trying to rescue the communion wine from my mother. I hooked a right into the sacristy and paced among the vestments, waiting for my showdown with Sullivan.

He entered and slammed the door, indifferent to the holy space. "You trying to land in jail to be close to your boyfriend? Because I'm all too happy to oblige."

*How had a guy who'd made a pass at me a mere six months before come to hate me so badly?* "Admit that you arrested Bradley to get back at me."

"He had drugs in his hand, Amato."

I wanted to scream *Because I put them there*, but the threat of my arrest loomed large in the small room. "You know damn good and well that those drugs belong to Alfredo Scalino—whose brother just kidnapped Luigi."

"The Scalinos had nothing to do with the gold bars."

I lowered my head. "There's no way Bradley was running a drug ring from the Galliano, and you know it. So cut the BS."

"Here's what I know. You introduced Bradley to Luigi, so he started dealing with Nick to finance his life of leisure with you."

It was all I could do not to rip a cross from the wall and hurl it at him. "Drop the charges against Bradley or get ready to lose your badge."

He stepped toward me, and for a split second I was

convinced he would either kiss me or kill me, so I moved back. I wasn't sure, but I thought I saw him flinch.

"Don't threaten me, Amato. You already cost me a promotion. It would be a grave mistake to mess with my career."

"Is that what this is about? Your career?"

"The New Orleans PD is my life, and I'd sooner take down you and your boyfriend before I let you ruin that for me."

Sullivan was out for revenge, but I had to make him see reason. Bradley's life depended on it. "What about the captain? The night Nick died they had a fight, and Nick went overboard. Did you question him about that?"

"No need. As far as I'm concerned, I've got my man."

I stared at his satisfied smirk, fearing that I'd heard him right but hoping I hadn't. "What are you saying?"

His lips spread into a smile that made the Joker's look charming. "As soon as I clear up this Luigi situation, I'm setting my sights back on your boyfriend. I'm not done with him yet."

He left the room, and I sank to the kneeling bench Father John used to pray before mass.

Sullivan was going to charge Bradley with Nick Pescatore's murder.

"WHERE ARE DAVID AND THE VASSAL?" I paced the Private Chicks conference room like a drill sergeant in my olive-green sweater, even though my back still ached from that oar wallop. "It's almost noon."

Veronica's eyes were guarded as she observed me from the head of the rectangular table. "I called them at ten thirty, before we left the chapel, but they were still asleep."

"Do people still do that? Sleep, I mean?"

She fidgeted with the bow at the neck of her white blouse. "I know it isn't the time to say this, but you have to get some rest. If you don't, you won't be able to help Luigi or Bradley."

An ironic laugh leapt from my lips. "Even if I could sleep, my mom and Nonna wouldn't let me. When I dropped them off, my mom passed out in my bed, and Nonna and the nonne went to work setting up a *Find Luigi* command center—and you won't believe where."

"Your bedroom?"

"Nope. My place is the mess hall." I began circling the room. "They marched upstairs and seized control of Glenda's spare apartment—after tying her up with some aprons."

Veronica's hand moved to her mouth. "They didn't really tie her up, did they?"

"No, of course not. They just put the aprons on her as usual. But you know Glenda—she's a stripper superhero, and clothes are her kryptonite."

"What about her costumes and props? That apartment was full of them."

"The nonne were moving those into her living room when I left."

She inhaled and shook her head. "You'll have to sleep at my place, I guess."

I sank into a chair. "How can I do that with Luigi missing and Bradley in jail?" A funeral veil of tears covered my eyes. "Has he even gone before a judge?"

"That can take up to 72 hours."

"Three days? In a New Orleans jail?" My pitch climbed toward hysteria. "He'll never recover, and I know from experience. I still have PTSD from the skin slougher who used me as a pillow in jail last year."

Veronica stood. "Why don't I give you a massage?"

"Just don't touch my mid back. I haven't looked at it yet, but

I'm sure it's as black as my mood." I laid my forehead on the table and remained tense as she worked my muscles.

"You're going to make yourself sick if you don't calm down."

"Calm isn't going to happen until Luigi and Bradley are home and Sullivan is strung up like that poor cook, Rose, after she set Agnes Frump and the crewman on fire."

"That's pretty extreme, don't you think?"

"That's the point." I lifted my head and shrugged off her hands. "And it's the least violent thing I'd do to the guy. It took everything I had not to crucify him in the sacristy."

She sighed and sat down. "It *is* hard to believe that Wesley would take things this far."

"I know. For a man who's so tied to his career, it doesn't make sense that he'd risk it over an old case."

"Oh, I think it's jealousy." She leaned back in her chair. "I saw how he felt about you when you two collaborated on the vampire case."

I flashed back to our kiss on the balcony of the Bourbon Orleans Hotel. For a moment, I'd felt a flicker of something too. But fortunately, I'd glimpsed his dark side before he'd sucked the blood from me.

The door flew open, and David entered followed by The Vassal.

"Yo." David slipped off his *Ghostbusters* proton pack backpack. "Sorry we're late."

I eyed the takeout bags in their hands, annoyed that they'd stopped for breakfast. "What took you so long?"

"Parade traffic in the Quarter. The Krewe of Cork is doing their street stroll in giant champagne bottle costumes and wine barrels."

My mother should've been a member. "Well, take a seat. Veronica and I have assignments for you."

They sat next to each other at the conference table. David

pulled three jelly doughnuts from his takeout bag and lined them up on napkins.

The Vassal opened his *Game of Thrones* shield backpack and pulled out a plastic knife, a spoon, and a calculator. He reached into his takeout bag and removed a Haydel's hand pie. He carefully unsealed the package rather than tear it open. Then he cut the pie in half and used the spoon to scoop out the filling—one bite at a time.

I caught a whiff of lemon, my nasal equivalent of a red cape to a bull. I tossed the pie in the trash. "Son," I said, going all Texan on him, "do you want to die?"

His slack jaw slackened, and his eyes darted to the jelly doughnut in David's hand.

"It's filled with Nutella," David shouted. "I swear."

I eyed the other two on the table in front of him. "Are they all Nutella?"

"Yes."

I snatched them up. "Good, because they're mine now."

David's jaw hung lower than The Vassal's.

I bit into the doughnut to rub it in. "You guys should've eaten before you came. This is work, and your focus is on finding Luigi and linking those gold bars to the Scalinos, so we can free Bradley. Now get ready to take notes."

They pulled tablet computers from their backpacks.

As soldiers went, they were as ragtag as it got. And their drawers were definitely cotton, not Civil War-era flannel or osnaburg.

David tapped the touch screen, and The Vassal fiddled with the blinking red light on a stylus he'd tricked out to resemble R2-D2.

The tapping and blinking frayed my last nerve.

"That's enough!" I confiscated their devices.

The Vassal started so hard his glasses went crooked. "But

how will we take notes?"

I put my hands on the table and leaned in close. "You'll use pen and paper and like it."

Their heads snapped back. My voice had dropped to Darth Vader level.

"We're at war with Detective Sullivan and the Scalino clan, so we've got to strategize." I returned to my seat. "This is Operation All Hands on Deck."

Veronica passed out paper and pens to the boys. "I'll be working on getting Bradley released, so that leaves the two of you to...carry out Franki's orders."

I flipped open my laptop and consulted the screen. "Vassal, you're going to help Veronica by researching gold bars in the U.K. I want to know where they're made and anything you can find about drug smuggling from England."

He picked up his pencil—first like a chopstick, then an eyedropper. After a few unsuccessful attempts, he jotted a note.

I shook my head. Ruth put the *r* in ragtag, and Wendell the bartender was a coward, but compared to David and The Vassal, they were the Army Delta Force.

David raised his hand. "What's my, uh, mission?"

"Focus on the Scalino clan and their bases of operation. I want to know their headquarters and every warehouse and storefront they've been associated with in the press in case they're holding Luigi somewhere."

"Sir, yes sir."

I half-raised from my seat.

He lowered in his. "Ma'am, yes ma'am?"

That wasn't much better, but I let it slide. "I'll be at work on the Galliano, so make sure you email me anything you find out —no texts or calls. I can't risk Alfredo Scalino seeing or over-hearing our conversation. I know he and his brother are watching me because they planted a camera in a trunk in my closet."

David's eyes went wide, and The Vassal's slack jaw was already so low that he had no choice but to snap it shut.

Veronica opened her laptop. "That reminds me. Did you cover the camera?"

"No, I looked right at the thing, so covering it would've tipped them off that I'd spotted it. The weird thing is, Alfredo didn't act like he knew me when I met him, and yet he and his brother are spying on me in my bedroom, the pervs."

David and The Vassal exchanged a look, and The Vassal raised his stylus. "What about the skater girl, Goldie? Do you need us to keep checking the skating rinks?"

David gave him an elbow, and The Vassal turned as red as R2-D2's blinking light.

I didn't know what the elbowing was about, but I wrote it off as something geeky between them. "Goldie is most likely a PI, so she's the least of our concerns right now. With any luck, she'll find something that helps Luigi and Bradley."

My text tone sounded, and I pulled my phone from my purse on the table. "It's Ruth. Galliano staff have been cleared to report to work in the morning."

The screen on my laptop began to flash.

"Dang it. My computer's acting up again." I shoved my phone into my bag, and my purple Ruger slid out. "David, what did you install on this thing?"

The Vassal shot to his feet, as rigid as his R2-D2 stylus. "Please don't kill us. We knew about Goldie and the skating rinks because we hacked your computer to spy for your no—"

David clamped a hand over The Vassal's mouth, but the dirty secret was out. They took cover behind The Vassal's shield backpack as though that would stop my bullets.

I swooped over them like one of the *Game of Thrones* dragons. "My Nonna's investigation is over"—I fire-breathed my words—"like my relationship with Bradley."

"That's cool," David said.

The Vassal straightened his glasses. "Absolutely so."

"Good because anyone who investigates me again gets this." I grabbed the Haydel's pie from the trashcan and squeezed it until yellow goo ran between my fingers.

"Seriously, Franki?" Veronica grabbed some tissues and took the crust from my hand.

She looked at the boys, who remained hunkered behind the shield. "You two get to work on your assignments. I need to speak with Franki alone."

They rose and glanced at the devices I'd confiscated.

I mock-lunged for my gun.

The Vassal flung the shield into the air and ran into the door. David pushed him aside, yanked open the handle, and they both tried to exit. After a couple of joint thrusts, they made it through to the hallway at the same time.

Veronica closed the door. "I've tried talking to you as a friend, but apparently I have to talk like your employer. I don't want you carrying a gun in your current frame of mind. You could be a liability to the company."

My chin retracted, but my mouth went on the offensive. "That's not fair. My life could be on the line. And friend or boss, you know I have a right to protect myself."

She tipped her head and held up a hand. "Carrying a gun for protection is understandable, but from things you've been saying, this sounds like revenge—against a police detective, no less."

"I'm days away from setting sail with a homicidal steamboat captain and a member of a Mafia clan." I threw up my arms for emphasis. "I think that falls under the freakin' protection category."

Her eyes bore into mine. "As long as the captain and Alfredo are the reason for the gun, then fine."

"They are. Trust me."

She nodded in agreement.

But she shouldn't have. Because if anyone, I was gunning for Wesley Sullivan.

## 13

Captain Vandergrift looked like the ghost of Mark Twain beneath the harsh lighting of the Huck Finn Dining Hall stage. His white suit and bowtie only accentuated his ethereal glow as he stood at the microphone studying a sheet of paper that presumably held his morning speech.

A coquettish laugh rang out, and my gaze lowered to the table in front of the stage.

*Kate.*

Moments before, she'd entered the dining hall, passed the center table I shared with Wendell and Ruth, and parked herself next to Tim. She fiddled with her short, dark hair and touched the sleeve of his sailor suit, flirting with him as she had the captain.

Ruth bit into a beignet and swung what remained of the pastry in the direction of their table. "Would you look at that hussy cocktail waitress?" She chewed as though the powdered sugar topping were salt. "It's disgraceful the way she's carrying on, and in front of the captain."

Wendell leaned forward and rubbed his knees. "Young love. What're ya gonna do?"

Ruth's head jerked toward him with such force that her Fun Meter pointer moved from Max to Med. "It's lust, not love. And I'd best not catch them in a stateroom or a crew cabin together. As the cruise director, I'd boot them off the boat."

If the Galliano had a plank, I was sure Ruth would make them walk it on their way out. What I wasn't sure about was how she'd attained Very Important Fun Person status on the Carnival cruise line.

I scanned the room. Not surprisingly, Alfredo Scalino was absent, as was Pat. He was probably keeping a low profile, and she was just a galley dweller—the kitchen equivalent of the Hunchback of Notre Dame in the bell tower. What did surprise me was Marian's absence. She was a stickler for the rules, like Ruth.

Another throaty laugh echoed through the hall.

I turned my attention back to Kate, trying to figure out her angle. Unless she'd fixated on Cracker Jack the sailor as a kid, her end goal wasn't a date with Tim Trahan. Was she looking for the missing Civil War gold? Or was she after something else?

Captain Vandergrift tapped the microphone. "Good day, riverboaters. As you know, the Galliano has been the victim of hooliganism—multiple villainies involving murder and drugs." His bushy white brow creased. "It was a sore blight to learn that the culprit was none other than the banker who loaned me the money to buy this fine steamboat."

I seethed in my chair. Apparently, the captain had bought Sullivan's story that Bradley was a drug dealer who'd murdered Nick to silence him.

"But now," he bellowed, "that scoundrel banker is behind bars thanks to the persistence of a local detective."

Tim and Kate stood for an ovation, but I stayed seated and wrenched the edge of the white tablecloth.

"Don't worry," Ruth growled in my ear, "I'll set the captain straight on Bradley." She gave my thigh a pat. "The only crime that poor man ever committed was hooking up with you."

I shot her a shut-it stare, and not just because she risked blowing my cover to Wendell.

"Much obliged." The captain nodded at Kate and Tim as they took their seats. "As my name is Rex Vandergrift, we shall have no more delays. This Sunday, we'll embark on our maiden voyage for the Galliano gambling tournament. Just like Twain, we'll sail up the mighty Mississippi on a floating palace."

"Palace?" Wendell gave a low laugh. "Dat's a good one."

I had to agree.

The captain raised his arm. "We'll pass Civil War battle-grounds, plantation homes, and sugar cane fields."

"And chemical plants and oil docks," Wendell muttered.

"You'll see wildlife as you've never known it," the captain said. "Beavers, alligators, and catfish, fat from the spoils of this great river. And the waterfowl get so thick you can see them on the radar like oil spills on the water."

Wendell and I exchanged a look. We both sensed that a whopper was coming.

"By the by, they're ornery cusses, especially the geese. I once rumbled with three ganders, must've weighed 150 pounds between them. They swooped on deck and came at me like a pack of gangsters, walking in time and clicking their beaks."

My mouth twisted. The tall tale sounded like the finger-snapping fight scene in *West Side Story*.

"One of the rascals even—"

"Excuse me, Captain." Marian stepped onto the stage to the relief of everyone present. She whispered something, and he turned to the microphone. "Take a five-minute break, river-boaters. I shall return."

Marian followed him from the stage, glaring at Tim and Kate as she descended the steps.

Wendell turned to his chicory coffee. "Old Cap'n Rex lives in a world of fiction."

Ruth eyed him through her horn-rims. "Because he reads Mark Twain?"

I reached for my beignet. "He's talking about the captain's stories, not to mention his take on the crimes. I mean, how could he suspect a banker of murder and drug dealing when a mobster's brother runs the galley?"

Wendell's eyes popped. "Say what?"

I took a bite of the pastry and scanned the room for Alfredo. "The chef is related to Gigi Scalino."

"The Italian dude who wears the sweet spats?"

I nodded, but not about the *sweet* part. "Yesterday he kidnapped a relative of Nick Pescatore, the guy who was found dead on the boat."

Wendell fell against the chair back like he'd taken a bullet to the chest. "I got to get me another damn job."

"Until you do, we've got to band together, keep an eye on things." I looked from him to Ruth. "Whatever happened on this boat isn't over as long as Alfredo Scalino is the chef."

"Don't forget the ghosts," Wendell said.

"I won't." I stared at Ruth.

She wrinkled her mouth, and her Agnes Frump lines deepened. "By the way, I asked the captain about those screams we heard."

Wendell's bottom lip dropped. "Those say what?"

"The sailor ghost. Franki and I heard him on the Texas deck."

Wendell's face blanched like he'd just heard the screams himself.

I swallowed a beignet bite. "What did he say?"

"That Marv at Where Dat Tours had mentioned the screams, but he thought it was the tomfoolery of some scalawags."

"It's got to be the tomfoolery of some Scalinos." I glanced at the table by the stage. Kate was still there, but Tim was about to pass us en route to the casino.

"Hey, brah." Wendell stood and shared a soul shake with Tim. "How's ya mom'n'em?"

The local greeting reminded me that they'd worked together on a cruise ship.

"Good, man." Tim tugged at the waistband of his white sailor pants. "You ready to set sail?"

"I'm a landlubber, remember?"

Tim's mouth smiled, but the rest of his face didn't. Without a word, he strode to the exit.

I stared after him. "That guy's weird. He didn't even say goodbye."

"Aw, he's jus' stressed out." Wendell dropped into his seat. "I think he's trying to get back into the cruise industry, and I wouldn't blame him after this experience."

Ruth lowered her horn-rims. "Why do you think that?"

"I saw him down the dock at the Southampton Spitfire a week or so ago. He met up with another sailor and went onboard." He tapped the table. "That reminds me, I remembered how I know Kate. My band played a couple of gigs at a joint she worked at, the Gold Mine Saloon."

The word *gold* kept coming up. "Did you mention that to her?"

"I did. But she said she never worked there."

Ruth's turkey neck tightened. "A woman would remember

where she worked." She cast me a side-eye. "And where she lost her jobs."

I reached over and set her Fun Meter to Min.

Wendell shrugged and swallowed the last of his coffee. "Kate's hair is different, so I might o' confused her with someone else. But I was sure it was her on account o' her T-shirt."

I sat forward. "What shirt?"

"From the Gold Mine Saloon. That's how I remembered. She brought an overnight bag onto the boat this mornin', and it fell out.

Something didn't sound right. If Kate had a shirt from the saloon, then she could have worked there. But why lie about it, especially to a man who'd seen her on the job?

The captain took the stage. "Pardon the interruption, riverboaters. I have one more announcement before releasing you to your stations. Detective Wesley Sullivan has graciously volunteered his days off to work security during the gambling tournament."

I looked at the tablecloth and saw red instead of white. When I raised my eyes, I saw black—Sullivan's suit as he stepped onto the stage and had the audacity to take a bow.

Everyone clapped. But my hand moved to the hobo bag hanging on my chair—where I'd put my gun.

Ruth leaned in. "Why in the devil would the detective want to work free security?"

Sullivan's gaze targeted mine and told me the answer to her question. He hadn't made the offer out of the kindness of his heart. He was coming for me, and I had to be ready.

～

"Now that the galley's all put back together and clean," Pat the Sea Hag limp-loped around the island in a pair of pink Capris, "you can start the shrimp."

I'd spent the past seven hours restocking the pantry and sterilizing the kitchen, and I was ready for the torment to end. Rivers of sweat flowed from my hairnet to my kitchen clogs, and thanks to the rubber bib apron I was required to wear, I finally understood why Glenda felt so restricted in the things. "We don't set sail for two days. Wouldn't we want to peel the shrimp fresh?"

She squinted a bloodshot eye. "What do you think this is, Long John Silver's? We don't have the luxury of a big, fancy crew, so we've got to work ahead."

*Fancy* was more than a stretch, but she was entitled to her opinion.

"While you were dilly-dallying with the dishes, I had to get your workstation ready." She gestured to a couple of white plastic buckets she'd placed beside the island.

I could see why she was so put out. Arranging two whole buckets must've taken some effort. "Can I have a chair?"

"That's it right there." She kicked one of the buckets with the toe of a dirty green clog.

I took a seat on the hard, bumpy lid and stripped off a latex glove.

"Just what do you think you're doin'?"

I followed her glare to my glove. "You can't expect me to peel shrimp in these."

"I don't, but Detective Sullivan does."

My heart hardened like the lid I was sitting on. "Why is that, exactly?"

"So you don't contaminate any evidence."

Evidence my aching rear. The crime scene had been processed. Sullivan had issued that order with the sole intent of making my life miserable—more so than it already was. I yanked on the glove and ripped off the bucket lid imagining that it was his huge Irish head.

*Crawfish.*

Pat Popeyed the semi-frozen shellfish. "Those are for my crawdad boil. The cops must've moved the buckets when they were looking for them gold bars. You keep your butt parked while I look for the shrimp."

I nodded. I was being micromanaged, probably at the insistence of Chef Alfredo. The Scalinos were surveilling me at my house, so they were definitely watching me on the Galliano. But why? The drugs were gone, so what were they afraid I would find?

She disappeared down the hallway, and I stared at the crawdads. I hadn't eaten them since my first date with Bradley because they'd caused my lips to swell to the size of boxing gloves. I smiled at the memory of him rushing me to the emergency room, and tears clouded my eyes. I'd had the relationship I'd always wanted, and I'd lost it. And not because I'd gotten him arrested for drug dealing, but because I hadn't trusted him enough to tell him the truth about the winepress and Sullivan.

*When would I learn?*

"What're you blubberin' about?" Pat dropped a bucket in front of me. "Is galley work too tough for you?"

"No, I got attacked by a crazy woman, so my back hurts."

Evidently, getting attacked by crazy women was par for Pat's course because she didn't bat a squint eye at my explanation.

She sucked the gap in her teeth. "You don't know pain till you sit on one of them buckets after you've had your uterus yanked. Let me tell you, it goes from your dollar hole straight to your molars."

The last thing I wanted was to discuss female anatomy with

Pat, and particularly in steamboat garbage chute terms, but I had to play along. "Uh, sorry you had to go through that."

She recoiled, and her eye quasi relaxed. "Yeah." She hacked up some phlegm and spit it into her rag. "Hang on. I've got something that'll make de-pooping the shrimp easier. It's called a shrimp de-pooper."

I stared at her for a moment and not because of her unexpected kindness. How was it possible that she'd never heard the word *deveiner* working in the New Orleans culinary industry?

She handed me the slim metal tool, and the eye squint turned slant. "That was a gift. Don't try to steal it."

I gritted my teeth. "I won't. I have one at home."

"Whoa. Big shot." She lifted a box marked *Swampfire Seafood Boil* from the supply rack and carried it to the opposite side of the island so that she could keep a squint-eye on me and her precious de-pooper.

It was the opportunity I'd been waiting for to try to figure out whether she was involved in Nick's murder and the drugs. I picked up a shrimp. "So, is the chef still going to make his lemon-mint sorbet?"

"Why wouldn't he?"

"I thought he'd have to throw out the lemons after that guy stashed drugs in them."

"Nah." She picked up a knife and cut open the box. "The cops took all the crates that had the gold bars. There were only six, so that left plenty for the sorbet."

I squeezed the shrimp to peel it, and it shot up from my gloved fingers and down to the bucket. I reached for another. "I still can't believe that banker picked the Galliano to deal his drugs."

"He done it on purpose to discredit Captain Vandergrift. Killed that guy Nick they found in the freezer too."

"Why would he do all of that?"

"Must've had something against the captain."

I gripped the shrimp, and it flew into the air and plummeted to the floor. *Slippery suckers.* "Maybe, but Nick had a playing card in his hand, so his death could've had something to do with gambling."

Her squint-eye squinted, and she pointed the knife at me. "You best not be implying that the captain killed the guy."

"Oh, I'm not."

"Good. Because he's the one who gave me that shrimp de-pooper."

It didn't take much to buy Pat's loyalty. "And that queen of spades card could've been a voodoo offering."

She dropped the knife. "You been living in New Orleans too long."

I couldn't argue with that while I was peeling shrimp in latex gloves on a crime-ridden steamboat.

"With any luck," she pulled spice bags from the box, "that banker guy'll get life, and we can all get on with our work."

Angry at her "life" comment, I pinned a shrimp to my thigh and tried to rub off the shell. Pieces of shrimp squished out, but the shell stayed intact. "If the banker's guilty, then why did the chef's brother kidnap one of Nick's relatives?"

She stiffened. "Whoever that witness was made a mistake."

"Why do you say that?"

"Gigi Scalino ain't no kidnapper. He's a gentleman. He paid for my hysterectomy bills and testosterone supplements."

So many questions came to mind—about Pat's reasoning skills, the men who gave her presents, the doctor who thought she needed testosterone. And, since I was making a list, why hadn't she done anything about that phlegm issue?

But the questions died on my lips.

Alfredo's beady eyes studied me from the doorway. Then he went to the island and picked up Pat's knife.

My abs tensed, fearing a stabbing, and I tightened my grip on the deveiner. *Did he hear what I said about Gigi? Or had he found out that I was the one who called the cops on him?*

Tim pushed open the door. "Captain wants to see you both."

Alfredo swore and shoved the knife into a block.

My abs released, as did my breath.

Pat removed her hairnet and apron, her Sea Hag face as pink as her Capris. She didn't act like someone who had crimes to hide, but rather a woman who had the hots for the captain.

Alfredo bit the skin around his thumb and stole a glimpse of Tim. Then he ran a hand through his greasy hair and exited followed by Pat, whose limp-lope had turned limp-gallop.

Tim glanced around the galley and shot me his usual scowl before letting the door swing closed behind him.

I stood frozen, torn between finishing my Franki Rockford shift and running for my Franki Amato life.

"Hey there, sailor."

*Kate's voice.* I tiptoed to the door.

"What're you doing on our day off tomorrow?" Her tone was flirty but forced.

"I've got a buddy coming in from England. Why?"

For a guy who was getting propositioned, Tim sounded oddly defensive.

"Well, I was hoping we could have lunch."

"Yeah," he hedged. "I don't know."

"At my place?"

"He docks at six," he gushed. "I can be there by noon."

I bet he could.

"On second thought," Kate purred, "why wait until tomorrow when we could start tonight?"

My text tone blared from behind my bib apron. In a panic, I sprinted down the hallway. I removed a glove and fished my phone from my T-shirt pocket, and my heart flip-flopped at the message from Veronica.

*Bradley has a bail reduction hearing tomorrow afternoon. He could be out tomorrow night or early Sunday. Fingers crossed!*

My knees buckled, and I sank into a chair. If he made bail, then what? Should I call him? And if I did, what could I possibly say to make up for ruining his life?

I put my head down—and realized where I was sitting. My phone fell from my hand and clattered beneath the desk.

*Mannaggia me*, I said, cursing myself. If Alfredo found me snooping in his office, he'd finish me off with that knife.

I dropped to my knees and felt underneath the low desk. My fingers touched something furry, and I jerked my hand back, suppressing a scream that would have rocked the steamboat. I glanced behind me to check for Alfredo and put my glove back on. Then I held my breath as I pressed my cheek to the dirty floor, hoping I didn't come eye to eye with a rat or get infected with E. coli.

Fortunately, the furry creature was a moldy carrot top. I scanned the filthy tile for my phone. I spotted it near a far corner, and there was something above it—taped to the bottom of the desk.

I squinted like Pat.

*A picture of Mark Twain?*

I reached for the photo. As soon as my gloved fingers wrapped around it, I had a feeling that I knew what it was. I pried it from the wood, and the tiny steamboat beneath Twain's image confirmed my suspicion.

It was a deck of playing cards from Marian's gift shop.

I didn't have to open the box to know that the queen of spades was missing.

## 14

E very brain cell I had screamed *Get the hell out of Alfredo's office.*

Holding the pack of cards by the tips of my latex glove, I ran up the hallway. Alfredo and Pat hadn't returned from their meeting with the captain, so I darted to the supply rack, dropped the deck into a plastic baggie, and threw it into my hobo bag. Then I gave my gloves a good washing in the sink and hurried back to my bucket.

The obvious course of action was to give the cards to the police so that they could dust them for the killer's fingerprints, but that wasn't an option. Sullivan was dead set on framing Bradley, so I feared that he might make the cards disappear from the evidence room.

Which raised an important question. Assuming Alfredo was Nick's killer, why hadn't he thrown the cards into the Mississippi? While he was stuffing Nick's body into the pantry freezer, he could've tossed them down the dollar hole.

A shudder racked my spine, not because of the memory of Nick in the deep freeze but because Pat's anatomy came to mind

—and it wasn't pretty. "From now on, I'm calling the dollar hole the 'garbage chute.'"

I started at the sound of my voice. I had to stop talking to myself, especially on the Galliano. And I had to get back to work.

I grabbed a shrimp, and it catapulted from my fingers straight to my lips. I sputtered and wiped my mouth with a stinky shellfishy glove. "Oh, God. I could've just gotten a sea tapeworm."

Stripping off the gloves, I rushed to the sink and blasted my lips with the spray nozzle. After a solid twenty seconds of spraying, water dripped from my hairnetted hair, and my face burned —from hot water and hot rage. And I made a promise to myself. When Sullivan was behind bars where he belonged, I would take any money I earned from Nick's case and bribe a prison official to put him on permanent kitchen duty.

I glanced at the clock. Fifteen minutes remained of my shift, but in my current state—and with the evidence in my purse—I felt like a boiled shrimp waiting to be peeled by a crazy bag lady in latex gloves. It was time to abandon ship so I could talk to Veronica about what to do with the cards and find out whether David had any updates on the Scalinos' bases of operation. Every minute that passed lessened the likelihood that we would find Luigi alive, and I couldn't let that happen.

I removed my wet hairnet and apron, grabbed my bag from the supply rack, and entered the dining hall. As I approached the door to the casino, I heard a man's voice and paused to listen.

"Ain't no ghosts 'round here. No sir."

*Wendell.*

"It might look like that bar rag moved by itself, but it's jus' your imagination, Wendell."

*Talking to himself.* It was so unfair that there wasn't a masculine equivalent for *crazy bag lady*.

I pushed open the door and approached the bar. "Hey, Wendell."

He jumped like I was Agnes Frump's flaming head—after she'd been doused with water to put the fire out. "Girl, you can't be comin' up on me like dat. Not on no haunted boat."

"Sorry about that." I eyed the gris-gris bag he wore around his neck to ward off the ghosts that weren't on the Galliano. "Is Kate around?"

"I sent her to make groceries. We're short on bar snacks."

I slid onto a bar stool. "Could you do me a favor?"

"Long as it don't involve me pokin' around dis old boat."

Wendell was going to have a rough time on the Galliano's overnight gambling trips. "I just need you to keep an eye on Kate. She's up to something."

He leaned onto the bar. "What kind o' somethin'?"

"That's the thing. I don't know. But she's acting suspicious. First, she flirted with the captain, who's way too old for her, and now she's switched to Tim, who is way too surly for any woman."

He cleared his throat and began wiping the spotless counter.

I knew what that meant. Slowly, I spun on my stool.

Tim stood at the foot of the grand staircase looking like Cracker Jack about to get in a shore-leave fight. He surged toward me, as did the smell of the Old Spice he must've poured on for Kate's benefit. "You done with your shift, or are you slacking off?"

"I'm off work."

"Then you're off the ship."

"Who are you, the cruise director?" I meant to say *captain*, but Tim was about as fun to work with as Ruth—oar wallop included.

"I'm the first mate to the captain, who doesn't approve of staff hanging out at the bar after hours."

I wanted to ask whether the captain approved of a staff member carrying on with the cocktail waitress, but I knew when to cut and run. "If it's the captain's rule, then fine."

Wendell tossed the rag over his shoulder. "She wasn't drinkin'."

"See to it that she never does." Tim turned to me. "I'd better not find you on this ship until the day we set sail. Is that clear?"

*Was Tim trying to tell me that he knew I'd been on board the night the gold bars were found?* There was no way to know, and with a gun and the cards in my bag I had to avoid a possible escalation. So I rose and headed for the exit. Outside, I stomped to the gangplank and, against my better judgement, looked back.

Tim watched from a casino window.

I glared, and he turned away.

As I bounced across the gangplank, I thought about how despicable he was. There was no way Kate was interested in him. And I couldn't fathom how he had any friends, especially ones who would travel from as far away as England to see him.

I stepped onto land and spotted Marv walking toward the Where Dat Tours ticket booth with a Central Grocery takeout bag. It had to be a muffuletta sandwich.

He raised the bag in a greeting. "I was just thinking about you. Last night I watched *The Rockford Files*. Did you ever see the episode called 'There's One in Every Port?'"

"Like I said, I just caught the occasional rerun when my parents watched it. I don't remember much about the show."

"Well, you should watch this one. It's about a ship called the Golden Star."

The word *gold* was coming up too often. My newly embraced superstitious self thought it might be a sign, especially since the reference involved a ship. "What was the episode about?"

"It wasn't your typical bad guy investigation. Jim gets conned by his ex-con friends who want to buy the ship, and he runs a con of his own to get even."

"But he's a PI."

"Sure." Marv ran a hand through his thinning black hair. "Before that, though, he went to the slammer."

I couldn't judge Jim Rockford. I'd gone to the slammer too.

He smacked his lips. "That's the thing about ol' Jim. You expect him to be the good guy, and he is, just not in the way you'd think." His eyes took on a wistful look. "They don't make shows like that no more."

"Right?" I said, distracted. My mind was still on Tim, who wasn't a good guy, and his British buddy. He'd said the guy *docked*, which meant he was arriving by boat, and I wanted to know which one. "While we're on the subject of ships, does New Orleans get a lot of cruise business from England?"

"Not much, no. Norwegian has a Copenhagen–New Orleans cruise that stops in England, I think. The only other one is the Southampton Spitfire."

*The cruise ship that Wendell saw Tim boarding with a sailor a week or so before.* "Know if it comes to town tomorrow?"

"Sure does, Franki Rockford." He chuckled and rested a hand on his belly. "Why? You going on a cruise? Or are you thinking of setting up a con like ol' Jim?"

"No, nothing like that." More like a stakeout. I needed to find out whether Tim's British buddy was coming for a visit—or delivering a new shipment of gold bars from the U.K.

"It's Happy Hour," a young brunette shouted as I walked through the French Quarter. She wore only two items of clothing, a pair of shorts and tennis shoes, but her topless state wasn't what caught my attention. It was her green plastic Hand Grenade cup.

"I'm not done with that damn Dancing Hand Grenade," I muttered as I headed up St. Peter.

But I couldn't fool with the huge green Humpty Dumpty at the moment. It was too late to catch Veronica at the office, but it was the perfect time to stop by the Gold Mine Saloon, where Wendell had worked with Kate. My conversation with Marv about Jim Rockford's character and the Golden Star ship had convinced me that I needed to figure out what kind of game she was playing on the Galliano. And after the day I'd had in the galley and the evening at home that lay ahead, a drink was definitely on my agenda.

I rounded the corner onto Dauphine Street and stepped inside the dark saloon. The scent of dive bar hit me, as did the sight of a creepy clown trashcan that made me think of the calliope, neither of which made for a good time.

The saloon appeared empty, so I scanned the room while I waited for an employee. There was an old wooden bar that had seen its share of hard times. Arcade games lined the exposed brick walls, and a disco ball hung from the ceiling.

The door to the ladies room opened, and a short, sixty-something woman with a rat's nest of dyed black hair, badly applied blue eyeshadow, and red lipstick emerged. She stepped behind the bar and began filling a plastic cup with cherries from a garnish tray.

I walked over, but she didn't look up. "Hi, I—"

"You here for a flaming Dr. Pepper shot? The Gold Mine invented 'em."

"No, I—"

"What's your name?"

"Franki. I'm looking for a woman—"

"You a lesbian?"

I recoiled at her directness. "I just need some information—"

"Does this look like a library to you?"

I grimaced and took a deep breath. "Obviously not. I think she used to work—"

"Who is it?"

"Kate Wilson." I spit out the name before she could interrupt me again.

She moved from the cherries to the orange slices. "What is this, some kind of setup?"

I was starting to wonder whether this woman spoke only in questions. "No, I just need to ask you a few questions about her."

"You a cop?"

It was looking like I was right about the questions. I reached into my wallet and pulled out a business card. "I'm a PI."

Her eyes moved from the card, to my eyes, to my wallet, where they stayed.

I sighed and pulled out a twenty.

She snatched the bill from my fingers and stuffed it into her bra. Then she stepped from behind the bar and headed for the door.

"Hey, where are you going?"

She continued walking without even bothering to pick up her pace.

"Listen, lady," I shouted, "I answered all of your questions. You need to answer mine. Where are you going with my money?"

She spat on the concrete floor, and I leapt backwards to avoid splatter.

"What's all the yelling about?" a male voice boomed.

I turned to a manager type, around forty, in a Gold Mine Saloon shirt and jeans. "Your employee just took off with my money."

"What employee?"

I looked back at the door, but the woman was gone. "The one with all the blue eyeshadow and red lipstick."

"Oh, you mean Marlene." He grinned. "She's a crazy bag lady who comes in and eats our garnish."

I stared at him, stunned. I'd been conned by one of my own kind, like Jim Rockford.

"Did you need a drink?"

Did I ever. But after getting conned out of my twenty dollars, I couldn't afford one. "Actually," I flashed my business card, "I'm a PI, and I'm here about Kate Wilson."

His brown eyes crinkled. "She's not missing, is she?"

That wasn't the reaction I'd expected. "Why would you ask?"

"I told her she'd either end up dead or in jail thanks to her loser boyfriend. She hooked up with him and got herself fired for drug possession and possible dealing."

*Drugs?* "And this is Kate? Kate Wilson?"

"We called her Goldie."

*Goldie.* My head began to spin like the disco ball. That was the name the woman on roller skates had given to Jefferson Davis at the Civil War Museum. But she and Kate couldn't be the same person, could they? "Just so I know we're talking about the same woman, can you describe her?"

"I can do better than that. We've got a picture of her over there." He led me to a wall covered with pictures and pointed to one close to the floor. "That's her."

I crouched and stared at a picture of Kate balancing a tray of drinks—in a yellow wig and roller skates.

Kate, a.k.a. Goldie, was the Roulergirl, the woman in sunglasses who'd been anticipating my every move like a PI and running from me with the help of the Dancing Hand Grenade.

The manager shoved his hands into his pockets. "She skates in the roller derby and with a group during Mardi Gras. She came up with the name Goldie Brawn, like Goldie Hawn, while she was working here at the Gold Mine. She was always real clever like that."

So clever that I hadn't even recognized her. I rose slowly, because my head was in a disco-ball spin.

"You never said why you were looking for her. Is she in trouble?"

"It's about a case I'm working. So no, she's not in trouble." But I wasn't so sure about that.

Because if Kate had a history of dealing drugs, then it was possible that she had something to do with the gold bars.

GLENDA FLAGGED me down from her second-floor balcony—literally. She waved her cigarette holder while draped in a Sicilian flag, just like the Mardi Gras decorations.

I leaned back in the front seat of my Mustang and regretted not springing for that drink at the saloon—if not the flaming Dr. Pepper shot, then at least a Goldmine Lager beer. I sighed and opened my car door.

"I need you to come up, Miss Franki," she whisper-shouted. "We've got two big situations."

*Yeah. Each of those giant boobs hanging from the house.* I slammed the car door, climbed the stairs, and followed Glenda into her living room, where I promptly stopped and shifted my weight onto one hip.

My mother was sprawled in the giant champagne glass, humming a honky-tonk tune in between swigs from a Chianti bottle. And the worst part was that she was still wearing her black Miss Havisham dress.

I knew I should have done something, but with Bradley in jail and Luigi missing, it didn't seem like a big deal that my mom was in a glass bottom. "What's she humming?"

"An old country song by Bobby Bare." Glenda's eyes narrowed behind a cloud of smoke. "It's called 'Marie Laveau.'"

My head snapped back. My mother was taking the voodoo thing seriously. I couldn't believe it, but I kind of missed the Christmas carols.

"I don't mind her using the glass, sugar, but red wine doesn't belong in a champagne flute."

My teeth tightened, and I longed for a swig of my mom's Chianti. "Maybe you could look the other way under the circumstances?"

She widened her eyes and flung one end of the flag over her shoulder. "I've already been looking the other way on The Visitor Policy, what with all these Lilliputians running around. And that's the other big situation, Miss Franki. I don't mind them using my spare apartment for an emergency, but I draw the line at my acsexsories."

"Say what?" I not only copied Wendell's line but also his lip drop.

"Go see for yourself. I'm not going into that den of non-heathens."

I would have rather spent the night alone on the Galliano with the ghosts and the drug-dealing killer, but I didn't have a choice in the matter. Besides, the scene in Glenda's costume apartment couldn't have been any worse than the one in her living room.

Without so much as a glance at my mom, I went outside to the balcony and pressed my ear to the door.

It was quiet, which was odd given that there were at least ten busy-body Sicilian nonne in the place.

I turned the handle and peered inside.

The costume racks had been pushed to the sides of the room, and Nonna stood at the far wall studying a map of New Orleans on the wall. The other nonne sat with their backs to me, observing Nonna from a table they'd made with a surfboard that said *Stripping Safari* and a huge hoop skirt that Glenda had once loaned me for a plantation investigation.

I couldn't understand what Glenda had been so upset about until I realized that the nonne had stuck her pasties on various points on the map and that Nonna was using her whip as a pointer.

Except for the stripper acsexsories, the scene was eerily reminiscent of the wax museum in Rome's infamous recreation of a meeting of Mussolini's cabinet.

Nonna turned and smacked the tip of the whip against her hand. "Franki. Where you been-a?"

I took a step back. The woman shared a lot of Il Duce's qualities. "On the Galliano. Those places you've got pastied on that map aren't Scalino properties, are they? Because I've got David looking into that,"—I paused and narrowed my eyes as a warning—"and he doesn't need any help."

She opened her arms wide. "Relax-a. They are the chapel and Gigi's-a mansion. We're re-enacting Luigi's abduction."

"Have you come up with anything?"

"The man you saw in-a the limo was-a not-a Gigi Scalino."

I was skeptical. "And the map told you that?"

"No. His-a maid. We went-a to his-a mansion."

I imagined the Black Skirts marching on his home like the Black Shirts had marched on Rome in 1922, when they'd helped Mussolini rise to power. "You shouldn't have done that, Nonna. Gigi Scalino is dangerous, and don't forget that we have his father's winepress."

She paced, tapping her whip. "He's-a not-a going to touch-a the nonne."

Mary leaned forward. "It goes against the code."

They had a point. No self-respecting Mafia don would dare go after a bunch of grandmas. That would be bad publicity, and they liked to appear to be good, generous men in their communities—John Gotti being a prime example. "So what did the maid tell you, exactly?"

Mary clutched her cross necklace. "She said Gigi was having an emergency appendectomy yesterday morning when Nick's memorial was supposed to start."

I took a seat at the surfboard. "And you believed her?"

Nonna nodded. "We went-a to the hospital. It's-a true."

Then Gigi couldn't have kidnapped Luigi. "I guess we need to get the names of everyone who rented limos on Sunday."

"Gigi has his own-a limo. It was in-a the garage."

I flashed back to the shoes and spats I'd seen on the floor of the backseat. "That means Alfredo was probably the guy I saw. He's the only person who could've gotten Gigi's men to help him abduct Luigi."

Santina Messina curled her mustached lip. "*C'è un'altra possibilità.*"

I couldn't wait to hear who this other "*possibilità*" was.

Nonna's eyelids lowered to you're-not-a-going-to-believe-a-this mode. "His *consigliera*."

The term referred to a mob boss advisor, like Robert Duval's character in *The Godfather*, but I'd never heard it with the feminine *a* ending. "You mean, *consigliere*?"

She raised the whip and waved it left to right. *Tch.*

The sound was a hard *no* in Italian, which meant that whatever she was about to tell me was serious.

"Word on-a the street is-a," she bowed her head and then raised her chin, "Gigi take-a the advice of a woman."

A tall nonna spat on the wood floor.

Far too much spit had been raining down around me, but I didn't say anything. In the old Sicilian culture, the notion of a man, and especially a Mafia boss, taking the advice of a woman was equivalent to blasphemy—unless she was his mother. "Who is she?"

"We don't have-a no idea."

Realistically, the consigliera could have been anyone. But I had a definite idea of the woman I wanted to investigate first.

## 15

W aves lapped against the dock at the Julia Street Cruise Terminal. I couldn't see them from inside the empty shipping container, but I could hear them. And the sounds of frogs. Or birds. No, it was dark out. Crickets? Actually, just whatever insects and animals lived on the river and made noise before dawn.

Unlike the water and those damn river creatures, time stood still—and silent. I'd turned off my phone when I'd arrived at five a.m. to avoid the display signaling my location like a beacon. And even though the container was at least nine feet high and eight feet wide, I had to sit quietly in the stuffy space, slightly nauseated from the stink of tar and fish, listening and waiting for the Southampton Spitfire.

And Tim.

*What was his role in the Galliano crimes?* He was such a stickler for steamboat rules that I wouldn't have been surprised if he were simply an overzealous sailor. But given the British origin of the gold bars, his meeting with the buddy on the Spitfire was a red flag, as was Kate's interest in him.

Kate was even more of an enigma. I didn't know whether she

was a gold digger after Captain Vandergrift's money, a treasure hunter after Captain Galliano's Civil War gold, a PI after justice, or a civilian after drug money. *But could she be a consigliera for the Scalino clan?* Somehow I had a hard time envisioning the likes of Gigi and Alfredo taking advice from a twenty-something woman, even if she *was* tough enough to be in the roller derby.

Alfredo was another question mark. He was definitely behind the gold bars. *But had he killed Nick and kidnapped Luigi?* The cards taped beneath his desk weren't necessarily proof that he was the killer. Someone could have put them there to frame him.

Like the captain. Because of the queen of spades card in Nick's hand, he was the most obvious suspect. But I didn't believe he would risk his dream of sailing the Mississippi like Mark Twain—at least not intentionally. And there was always the possibility that the card was related to voodoo.

That left Pat, Marian, or Wendell. But I had no reason to suspect them of Nick's murder. They weren't onboard for the managers' meeting the night he was killed, and there wasn't any evidence to incriminate them. Plus, Wendell didn't have the stuff of a killer. He would've been too afraid that his victim's ghost would come back to haunt him.

In terms of the evidence, Nick had either been killed by the captain, Alfredo, or a mystery woman who'd invoked voodoo loa Erzulie D'en Tort for revenge.

*But why kidnap Luigi? And where was he?*

I rubbed my face. It was all so frustrating.

And exhausting.

I yawned and leaned the back of my head against the container wall. It figured that the one night I could've gotten some sleep, thanks to my mom spending the night in Glenda's glass, I had to do a stakeout. And I needed sleep to be able to piece together the details of the case.

My thoughts drifted to Bradley.

*Was he sleeping?*

*Would he make bail today?*

*And would he ever speak to me again?*

I certainly planned to talk to him, to explain. *But if he didn't want to listen, what then? Were we really through?*

A tear rolled down my cheek.

I didn't want to imagine a future without Bradley. Or a future with my nonna post-failed lemon tradition. The former foretold a cold, harsh winter, but the latter foretold fire and the apocalypse.

Light entered the end of the shipping container, snapping me out of my-life-is-over mode. I crawled to the opening and peeked at the river. A cruise ship lit up the sky.

The Southampton Spitfire.

The sound of an engine sent me ducking inside the container. A car had pulled onto the dock.

*Tim?*

My breathing increased, which was unfortunate given that fish smell.

Minutes passed, five, maybe ten.

The engine cut off, and a car door slammed.

Slowly, I peered out again.

The Spitfire had pulled lengthwise along the dock, and Tim strode toward the middle of the ship, looking over his shoulder every so often.

I needed a better vantage point.

Empty shipping containers lined the dock, so I waited until his head was turned and crept to the next container. And then another.

Two loud clicks caught my attention.

I flattened against the container and peered around the corner.

A sailor had opened a mid-ship door for boarding passengers. He looked from side to side and disappeared inside. Seconds later he emerged with two dark suitcases and handed them to Tim. He took one last look around and closed the ship door.

No words were exchanged, which told me what I'd come to find out.

The Southampton Spitfire was the source of the gold bars, and I'd just witnessed another delivery.

Meanwhile, Tim headed to the car.

I went back the way I'd come, creeping behind the shipping containers. My foot hit something fleshy, like a human arm or hand, and a squeak escaped my lips.

I looked down.

A dead catfish, about the size of the one that had jumped from my purse after I fell into the river.

*What was it doing back here?*

*More importantly, was it a sign of my fate?*

Panicked, I made like a leach against the side of the container and held my breath. But I couldn't hear Tim—or even the river creatures.

Only waves lapping against the dock.

Fear ran along my body in streams. *Had Tim heard me? Was he coming this way?*

I had to move.

Fast.

On tiptoes, I slipped inside a half-open door of a shipping container and peered through the crack.

And I let out my breath.

Tim was at the car. He unzipped one of the suitcases.

The passenger window lowered, and my head recoiled.

*Kate.*

Tim smirked and held up a bag of gold bars.

THE PRIVATE CHICKS door closed behind me, and I didn't bother to lock it. It was seven a.m., which meant the French Quarter would be deserted until nine—the socially accepted hour to start drinking.

I tossed my bag onto the couch and went to my office. With the stakeout of the cruise ship out of the way, I had one day to look for Luigi before reporting to the Galliano for the overnight gambling cruise. I was hoping David had updated Nick's case file with a list of the Scalinos' properties. If he hadn't, I would have to consult the pasties on the nonne's command center map, which, truth be told, might've been more accurate. Anyone with a nonna knew they operated in vast and powerful networks that rivaled the police, the Mafia, even the Catholic Church.

While I waited for my laptop to fire up, I sat at my desk and texted Veronica about the drug delivery and Kate's identity. What I didn't know was whether Tim and Kate had dropped the suitcases off at the Galliano. By the time I'd walked downriver to the steamboat, there was no sign of them at the dock.

Nor was there any sign of the police, and I knew the reason. Wesley Sullivan had already decided who was behind the crimes on the Galliano, and he was making sure that no one found evidence to prove otherwise—like the deck of cards sans queen of spades in my purse. That deck was my sole weapon in the war. I just hoped it was enough.

Footsteps pounded the stairs, shaking me from my thoughts. They sounded like more than one person, which brought me to my feet. *Veronica said Bradley would make bail today. Had she brought him here for some reason?*

Anxiety squeezed my stomach. Veronica wouldn't know I was in the office because I'd parked on a side street, and there was a strong possibility that Bradley wouldn't want to see me. Nevertheless, I practically ran to the lobby.

Shadows were visible through the frosted glass of the door. I decided to call out to alert them to my presence. "Veronica?"

"Shhh."

It was a woman, and not my BFF and boss. *But who else would be outside the door? And why would they shush someone?*

An answer hit me like Ruth's oar.

*Kate.*

*With Tim.*

My anxiety turned to panic. If they'd heard me semi-scream on the dock, they could've driven off, parked out of sight, and followed me to the Galliano and then the office, which meant my cover was blown.

And the Scalinos would've ordered my hit.

The squeeze on my stomach turned vice grip, and my head spun. I held out my arms to steady myself, tiptoed to my purse, and drew my gun. Then I darted to the wall beside the door and pressed my back to it. My heart pounded so hard I was sure they could hear it.

*Was this what had happened to Nick? He'd figured out the source of the drugs and gotten killed for it?*

I couldn't think about him now. I had to save myself.

Mentally, I counted to three. Then I threw open the door with one hand while aiming my gun with the other. "Freeze, or I'll shoot."

The stairwell was empty.

Footsteps came from the conference room on the opposite side of the stairs, followed by a knock—*from inside the door?*

A male cleared his throat. "Uh, it's David. You know, I work here? So please don't shoot."

I lowered the gun and opened the door.

And I rolled my eyes.

Behind David sat the usual suspects—Nonna, who wore her traditional mourning dress with her usual black handbag, and my mother, who'd ditched the dark Miss Havisham look in favor of a mom-jeans ensemble and an icepack that she wore on her head like a hat.

"What's going on in here?" I tried to read their faces, but none of them would look at me—not even David. I gasped. "You're not still investigating my zitellahood, are you?"

My mom moved the icepack to her forehead. "Put that gun away, Francesca. And stop shouting."

I'd spoken in my usual pitch, but it had been amplified by the aftereffects of her two-day drunk. "Don't worry about my gun, Mom." I shoved it into the waistband of my pants. "If I shoot anyone, it'll be myself."

Nonna waved off my suicide threat. "Calm-a down, Franki."

"I can't calm-a down. A man is missing. And not just any man—a dear friend and"—I glanced at my nonna, who refused to meet my gaze—"whatever else he is. And instead of looking for him, you guys are looking for my husband. Does that not strike you as seriously misguided?"

My mother sniffed. "That's not all we're doing."

"So you admit it."

"Of course." She threw up her hand and winced at the sudden movement. "We're trying to solve two crises at one time. What's wrong with that?"

I looked at David, who was hunkered by the door. "Can we have a minute?"

"Totally." He fled from the room and down the stairs.

Apparently, he wasn't coming back.

I sat at the table and laid a hard stare on my mother. "What's wrong is that my relationship status is not a crisis."

She lowered the icepack—then her eyelids. "You got your

best chance at getting married sent to jail and probably prison. If that's not a crisis, what is?"

"I'll-a tell you, Brenda," Nonna said in a mock-tragic tone. "In seventeen-a days your daughter will-a be the first Italian-American in-a New Orleans history not to get a proposal from-a the lemon tradition. For-a years, maybe centuries, she'll-a serve as a warning to young-a Catholic women everywhere."

I grabbed the icepack and put it on my head. It was a crisis.

My mother raised her chin in a stiff-upper-lip move. "Veronica left for Bradley's bail hearing right before we came to meet David. All we can do now is pray for a miracle."

Nonna crossed herself and kissed her fingers.

I wasn't ready to believe that Bradley's fate was out of my hands. Sullivan had set him up, and I would be the one to prove it. I looked at my mom. "What was the other reason you came to see David?"

"Well, you told the nonne that he was looking for properties where the Scalinos might be hiding Luigi, and we wanted to know if he'd located any."

I had the same question. "Did he?"

She shook her head. Then her hand went to her forehead, and she grabbed the icepack.

Nonna leaned over her handbag. "Santina heard that-a Gigi sold all of-a their properties, and-a soon even his-a house."

"Why? Are he and Alfredo planning to leave New Orleans?"

"We don't-a know."

"Well, I hope not. If they're leaving, they could—" I cut myself off. I couldn't bear to finish the thought.

Nonna put her hand on my arm. "Fredo's not-a going to kill-a Luigi, and neither is-a Gigi."

"Why? Because Luigi's so respected in the community?"

"No, because Gigi want-a the winepress."

I blinked and looked at my mom. "That can't be right. The kidnapping has to do with Nick's murder, not the winepress."

"It's true, Francesca. Father John went to see Gigi at the hospital this morning, and Gigi told him that he knows who kidnapped Luigi. He'll see to it that he's released unharmed in exchange for the winepress."

"He knows who did it, because it was his brother. So what are we supposed to do, take the winepress to his mansion?"

Her face hardened. "We're not going to give it to him, Francesca. Luigi gave that winepress to you."

My mouth dropped open. I knew my mother could be greedy, but that comment made Scrooge look generous. "You can't be serious."

Nonna raised a knobby finger. "This is a feud, Franki. Luigi would-a rather die than-a see you give-a Gigi that-a winepress. It's a matter of honor, something young-a people today"—she paused and shot me a look—"and-a not so young-a, don't-a know nothing about."

I let the age jibe go because I was still trying to comprehend the Luigi situation. "Is how Gigi receives the winepress also a matter of honor? Because he sent a fake exterminator to my apartment who could've just stolen the damn thing instead of installing a video camera in it."

"There's a video camera in the winepress?" My mother shrieked—then she cringed.

"Yeah. In the keyhole of the trunk."

Nonna's brow formed a hard line. "That-a wasn't the Scalinos. Gigi told-a Father John that they thought-a Luigi had-a the winepress in-a storage somewhere."

"I walked around naked in front of that thing," my mom whispered. "Now some pervert will probably put a video of me on a porn site, and filthy men will do nasty things while they watch it."

My mind reeled, and not solely because of the awful images my mother had just put in my head. If the video camera didn't belong to the Scalinos, then I had no idea who was watching my family and me.

"WHOEVER YOU ARE, YOU CREEPY PERVERT"—I paused and glared into the trunk keyhole—"you're going to rue the day you installed this video camera in my bedroom—if you don't already after that nudie shot of my mother."

I inserted a screwdriver into the opening and twisted it until I heard the camera crunch. Then I rose and walked to my nightstand to check my phone.

The display glowered at me, accusing me of ruining Bradley's life and being fool enough to think he'd call after making bail.

With the phone in hand, I faceplanted on the bed. I was upset about Bradley, but even more upset that I had no clue where to look for Luigi. I tried to take comfort in Nonna's conviction that the Scalino clan wouldn't kill him, but I felt like I'd failed him, just as I had Bradley.

My ringtone went off, and I jumped. A number I didn't recognize. *Bradley from jail?* I tapped *Answer* with my heart in my throat. "Hello?"

"This is Standish."

My heart dove to the pit of my stomach.

He cleared his throat. "You know me as The Vassal?"

'I know who you are. There aren't a lot of Standishes running around." *Thank God.*

"Am I interrupting your nap?"

I rolled onto my back and massaged my forehead. "What

makes you think I'm taking a nap at eight in the morning on a Saturday?"

"Oh, well, you sound tired."

"I always sound tired, because I always *am* tired." I wondered whether his concern for my sleep status had anything to do with the crush I suspected he had on me. "So, what's up?"

"You wanted to know where the gold bars are manufactured, but I don't have a precise answer for you. Apparently, they're as easy to produce as crystal methamphetamines, so they're being made in homes all over England."

There was a knock at my door.

I ignored it, thinking it was my mom or Nonna. They weren't welcome after that scene at the office hours before. "That's all right. I already know the drugs came from Southampton. The sailor picked up a shipment from a cruise ship this morning with the cocktail waitress, who, incidentally, is also the Roulergirl. What we need to figure out is how they're planning to distribute them."

"Franki?" Veronica called. "Can I come in?"

"Sorry, Vassal. I've got to go." I closed the call and sat up as my heart leapt from my stomach back into my chest. "Door's unlocked."

Veronica entered in a navy skirt suit, and one look at her face laid me out. "He doesn't want to see me. I knew it."

"That's not it."

The edge in her tone brought me to my feet. "What happened?"

She sank onto the side of the bed. "The bail hearing was postponed after new evidence came to light."

"How can there be new evi..." There was no need to finish the question because the answer was horribly obvious. I'd been outmaneuvered by Wesley Sullivan.

"Detective Sullivan got a search warrant for Bradley's apartment." She paused, and her brow creased as though she still hadn't processed what he'd found.

My heart was on the precipice again. "And what did he supposedly find?"

"A deck of Mark Twain playing cards with the queen of spades missing."

I grabbed my purse and rummaged inside, and my heart not only took that dive, it threatened to stop.

The deck of cards that I'd found taped to Alfredo's desk was gone.

## 16

Veronica pushed a Bloody Mary in front of me and slid to our booth at Thibodeaux's Tavern. "Now that we have some much-needed refreshments, we've got to figure out how Wesley Sullivan got access to your purse."

"It's my fault." I looked out the window at our fourplex across the street, feeling like one of the giant boobs hanging from the balcony. "I put it under my front seat when I went to wait for the Southampton Spitfire, so he obviously tailed me, broke into my car, and took the cards. He's probably the one who put the camera in the winepress trunk too."

"The detective would certainly know how to do those things," she said wryly. "Do you think he went to the dock?"

I shrugged. "If he knew that's where I was headed, yes. He could've hidden in one of the shipping containers like I did."

"If he had, then surely he would've arrested Tim and Kate when he saw the drug deal go down."

I turned my head to meet her gaze. "Unless..."

She covered her mouth to keep from spitting a sip of mimosa and then choked it down. "You think he's involved with the gold bars?"

"Why not? Maybe he's framing Bradley for two reasons—to stick it to me and to cover his drug crime."

"It's possible. But where do Nick's murder and Luigi's abduction fall in all of this?"

My answer was one that even I had a hard time believing. "If Sullivan is involved with the drugs, then we can't rule out his involvement in everything else."

She took a deep breath. "This is scary, Franki."

"Tell me about it. Sullivan volunteered to work security on the gambling cruise, and if he's not going to investigate the homicide and kidnapping, then either he's planning to do something drug related, or he's planning to do something to me." I took the straw from my Bloody Mary and stabbed the lime.

"That's it." She pulled her phone from her Chanel bag and started typing a text.

"What are you doing?"

"Canceling plans with Dirk and his parents. I'm coming on that cruise."

My head hit the back of the booth. I'd been so busy with the case that I'd somehow missed that she was meeting her boyfriend's parents. "But you haven't met them before."

"I can do it another time."

Guilt and a tinge of envy double-teamed my gut. I'd never met Bradley's parents, and it looked like I never would. The last thing I wanted was for my best friend to miss such a huge relationship milestone and on my account. And I also wanted her to be available to help Bradley, if she could. "Don't cancel, Veronica. I can navigate the Sullivan situation."

"No, I don't want you alone on that steamboat."

"I won't be alone. There'll be other passengers, and I've got my ragtag army, remember?"

She tossed her phone on the table. "I don't know. The name of that army is hardly comforting. What if I send David?"

"No, I don't want him on a steamboat with a killer. Besides, a ramshackle group of people can beat formidable foes, just ask Jefferson Davis at the Civil War Museum."

Glenda sashayed to the booth in a crop top—cropped above the breasts—and a pair of stripper shorts that she wore in defiance of the cool March temperatures. Thankfully, she clutched a notebook and her writer pipe to her chest. "I didn't know you girls were here. I've been in a back booth doing some morning writing."

Veronica eyed the notebook. "How are your memoirs coming?"

"Fine, but right now I'm working on the answers to the interview questions Ruth Walker sent me for the gambling cruise."

I resisted the urge to beat my head against the padded seat. "Ruth hired *you* for the entertainment?"

"Don't sound so surprised, Miss Franki. Captain Vandergrift wants something classy, like those interview tours that Sophia Loren did, and who better than *moi*?"

*Sophia Loren, for one.*

She pointed the pipe at me. "And don't you begrudge me a steamboat trip. Lord knows I need to de-stress, and a handsome gambler or two will do the trick."

"The nonne will be out of your costume apartment as soon as we find Luigi."

"It's not them, sugar. It's Father John. There's no phone in that apartment, so he calls my place and sends me into the Lilliputian den to fetch your nonna."

Veronica smirked. "That puts you in a compromising position."

"Truly, Miss Ronnie. If word gets out that a priest is calling my house, my reputation in New Orleans is ruined."

The corners of Veronica's mouth curled.

But I couldn't even begin to smile. I wanted to know why

Father John was still calling Nonna. "What does he want? Does he have more information about Luigi's kidnapping?"

"No, he's trying to help the Lilliputians figure out the Scalinos' favorite hangouts. I think Alfredo's hiding Luigi right under their noses, like that time the sultan kidnapped me and held me captive in my own boudoir."

Veronica gasped. "You were kidnapped by a sultan?"

"He wanted me in his harem, naturally." She flipped her platinum hair. "I talk about it in the 'Seduction Abductions' chapter."

Despite all that was logical, I wanted to read her memoirs. There was some sizzling stuff in there. "So, how'd you get away?"

"He released me after my clients at Madame Moiselle's appealed for my safe return on the news. They said it wasn't right to hide me away when I did so much good for the world." She jutted out her crop top. "This body has healing powers."

That psychology degree she'd gotten had affected her head. Still, I wondered whether she was right about Luigi being held nearby. *If so, where?*

"Now, if you girls will excuse me, I need to go plan my parade costume. The Krewe of Muses roll tonight, and I need some inspiration to help me finish these interview questions."

I remembered the flier the Dancing Hand Grenade had tried to hide from me. "Do you happen to know if the Roulergirls skate with the Muses?"

"They sure do. My girls, the Organ Grinders, march with them too."

I flashed back to an art auction featuring a painting of Glenda as a stripper organ grinder—complete with monkey—and slugged from my Bloody Mary.

Following my lead, Veronica reached for her mimosa. "I wonder if the Roulergirls have a throw."

"They don't, Miss Ronnie. They skate for tips, like the flambeaux, so they each carry a skate full of envelopes that they pass out."

I wrinkled my lips. "First, who are the flambeaux?"

Glenda bit her lower lip and shook her Mardi-Gras makers. "The hot, sweaty men who carry flaming torches to guide the parades."

I shielded my eyes. "Uh, getting back to the envelopes. What's in them?"

"Who knows, sugar. Probably candy or free passes to the skating rink or something."

I had an idea about what could be inside Kate's envelopes, and it wasn't candy or free skate passes.

As I DROVE my Mustang along the parade route looking for a parking spot, Glenda sat behind me in the backseat, holding my huge tawny-colored bouffant wig in place. "Could you let up on the vice grip?"

Veronica eyed the wig through her purple Venetian mask. "She can't, Franki. The wind is catching the board, and you don't want it to blow away."

"That's exactly what I want." I glared in the rearview mirror at the eight-inch board covered in newspaper that was nestled on top of the crawfish-boil-themed wig. Paper towels jutted out like handkerchiefs from either side of the board, and on it were three lacquered crawdads, a red plastic cup, and a lemon—as if to announce to the whole city that I'd failed at the lemon tradition. And to add insult to my bad hair day, the bouffant was so high that there was room above the board for a red bandana bow. "If you'd given me a normal-sized wig, Glenda, I could've kept the convertible top up."

"And if the Lilliputians hadn't taken over my costume apartment, I could've come up with something else."

In a way, I was relieved that hadn't happened. As costumes went, this wasn't the worst she'd loaned me, even though it did remind me of Pat the Sea Hag's crawdad boils and my shrimp de-pooping job. "Let's just hope these crawfish don't give me an allergic reaction."

Veronica rolled her eyes behind her mask.

Irritated, I gripped the steering wheel. "Where did you get this monstrosity, anyway?"

"It's one of Carnie's drag wigs, sugar."

I should've known. Even though Carnie was on tour with RuPaul, she still haunted me like the ghosts on the Galliano. "Well, keep your eyes peeled for Detective Sullivan. I'm sure he's following us, but when I look in the rearview mirror, all I see is this big ugly wig."

"Stop your bellyaching, Miss Franki. You don't want Kate to recognize you, otherwise she won't give you an envelope."

I hooked a right onto Napoleon Street and then glanced over my shoulder at Glenda. "If anything, I'm headaching, not belly-aching, because this wig weighs a ton."

Veronica lowered her mask and gave me the onceover. "Well, it looks adorable with that bib apron."

The apron was one of many that the nonne had tied around Glenda, and there was nothing adorable about it. It had a crawdad on the front and the vaguely pornographic saying, *Suck da head, squeeze da tip, now you eatin' crawfish.*

"There's a spot, sugar."

I parallel-parked and shut off the engine.

Glenda climbed from the car in a gold headband, a barely-there toga, and strappy Roman stripper sandals. Instead of her writer pipe, she clutched a cigarette holder, a stylus, and a notebook. She looked like the famous Pompeian fresco of Sappho—only a smoking stripper version.

Veronica slammed the car door and adjusted her green tutu. "What time is it?"

I looked at my phone. "Six twenty-seven."

"We'd better get to Magazine Street. Glenda and I are hoping to catch one of the Muses' bedazzled shoes."

We set off, and I tried to keep a lookout for Sullivan. But the wig was so heavy that I had to turn my entire body to see behind me. It was a situation that I was sure Jim Rockford had never found himself in.

"Uh-oh." Veronica wiped her arm. "I just got hit by a couple of raindrops."

Glenda pressed her stylus to her lip in a studied move. "There is a storm in the forecast, Miss Ronnie. The parade might get rained out."

I shot her a look. "With any luck these crawdads will swim away and take this hideous wig with them."

Veronica rolled her eyes behind her mask again.

"I can see what you're doing, Veronica."

She smirked and kept walking.

We reached the parade starting point, and the crowd was four people deep on either side of the street. We selected a spot in front of a gated Catholic church that had porta-potties for paradegoers in the yard, as well as a statue of Mary with a light directed on her. The effect was intended to make the shadow cast by her extended arms look as though she was reaching for her flock. But given the parade environment, Mary looked like she was reaching for one of the hurricanes being sold at the drink stand across the street.

Glenda pulled a wad of bills from the bosom of her teeny toga. "Dollars out, ladies. Here come the flambeaux."

As the torch holders approached, she strutted amongst them

and deposited the money in their waistbands rather than their hands, as was the custom.

Someone needed to tell her that we weren't at a strip club, but I wasn't that person. Instead, I scanned the crowd for Sullivan. Most of the attendees weren't in costume, which made us stick out even more. In fact, the closest things to costumes were T-shirts that said *Just krewe it* and the Sir Mix-a-Lot inspired *I like big beads and I cannot lie.*

"Franki!" Veronica tapped my arm. "It's the Bayou Cuisine float."

I spun and stared in horror at the giant gumbo pot making its way up the street. As I'd feared, local plumber Lou Toccato beamed in the okra costume he'd embellished with flames, just like the toilets he sold.

"Look at that, sugar. Your crawdad boil costume fits right in with that gumbo pot. You should jump in."

I gave her the side-eye. I had no plans to call any more attention to myself in case Lou's psycho psychic wife, Chandra, was in the area. She'd wreaked considerable havoc on my life, so running into her was more terrifying than any encounter with the ghost of Agnes Frump, or even a killer. I scoured the parade-goers again, for Chandra as well as Sullivan.

There was no sign of them, but I couldn't rest easy. I was being watched. I could feel it.

I turned and saw Glenda spinning in a motorized La-Z-Boy chair on wheels driven by a Laissez Boy, another name inspired by the city's famous phrase *Laissez les bons temps rouler*, like that of the Roulergirls. I scanned the parade for Kate and the other rollergirls, but all I saw was more Glenda bait interspersed between Krewe of Muses floats—the caped and jumpsuited Elvi, the plural of Elvis, on motorcycles and the Dead Rockstars marching as Prince from the *Purple Rain* period.

No sooner had I thought of the famous album than drops

fell from the sky. I looked up. It was about to pour. I scanned the parade line again. Still no Roulergirls.

Glenda sashayed toward a giant pink high heel float. "Throw me something, sister!"

A masked silver-haired woman on the krewe dangled a New Orleans Saints-themed boot, and a crowd of women gathered to catch it. Glenda towered above them in her six-inch stripper heels, and she snatched the sparkly shoe from the woman's hands.

She walked back to Veronica and me, scowling at the bedazzled throw. "The heel on this thing is only two damn inches. Now why in the hell would I want that?"

I opted to leave the shoe drama to Veronica and looked behind me. And my stomach felt as though it had been kicked by the Muses boot.

The Dancing Hand Grenade was in the churchyard peering around the side of a porta-potty. His dopey, dead blue eyes were fixed on me, and he had a cell-phone pressed to his earless green head.

I knew that grenade could talk, and he was probably calling Kate and warning her not to skate with the drugs.

I whirled around. "Veronica, the Dancing Ha—"

Someone clubbed the back of my head.

The last thing I saw was a thundercloud, and then everything went black.

THE WINDSHIELD WIPERS of my Mustang whipped back and forth, upping the throb in my head. I tried to turn in the passenger seat to glower at Glenda in the backseat, but my neck only made it to Veronica, who was hunched over the steering wheel trying to see the road through heavy rain. Then I remembered that I could use the rearview mirror since the wet wig was at my feet.

I grabbed the mirror and frowned into it. "I still can't believe you launched that boot at my head."

"Like I said, I wasn't aiming for you, sugar, I was trying to hit the woman who had the gall to use that godawful Naturalizer as a Krewe of Muses throw."

Under normal circumstances I would've agreed with her, but because of the knot on my skull I couldn't let on to as much. "Given what happened, I think you should cancel your appearance on the Galliano."

Glenda pressed her hand to her chest like I'd stabbed her in the heart with her Sappho stylus.

Veronica glanced at me for a split second. "Franki, that's pretty harsh."

"Is it? Stripper Sappho here cost me a chance to find out whether Kate was dealing the gold bars at the parade."

"No, she didn't. I told you that when the Bearded Oysters came out, the parade was called off due to this storm. The Roulergirls never even got to skate."

"Well, I can't risk another mistake. Nick's dead, but Luigi's life is still on the line."

Glenda stuck her head into the front seat. "I'm a professional, Miss Franki. In all my years, I've never canceled a performance, and I don't plan to now. Besides, the Evening with Lorraine Lamour is an opportunity to practice for my book tour."

The wheels in my probably concussed brain began to spin. A book tour would mean Glenda would be on the road for weeks, even months, and that was my opportunity to practice for a more normal life. "Fine, but you'd better steer clear of me on the steamboat."

"Don't worry, child." She raised her cigarette holder to her lips. "The talent doesn't mix with the galley hands."

"This mudbug nest says otherwise." I reached for the wig to toss it into the backseat, and the Mustang made a hard U-turn, slamming my head into the window. "Hello! I've got a head injury here."

Veronica shot me a grim look. "I'm sorry, but the streets are starting to flood. We're going to the office to wait out the storm."

"Is that a good idea, Miss Ronnie? You know how often the French Quarter floods, and I read the other day that only two of the thirty pumps in the quarter are working."

I rubbed the new knot forming near my temple. "She's right. I've seen the quarter get a foot of water in minutes."

"So have I, but I don't think we can make it home." She turned onto Bourbon Street, which was eerily empty. The Weed World van wasn't even seeing any action, which was telling considering that they sold marijuana lollipops for five bucks.

"The water is rising, Miss Ronnie."

Veronica slowed the Mustang to a crawl.

I leaned my head against the seat rest, and under the awning of the Tropical Isle bar I saw a giant green blob and gold sparkles. I bolted upright and looked again.

The Dancing Hand Grenade was with Kate. She wore a gold tinsel wig and a purple mask to go with her Mardi Gras-colored roller derby costume. And in her hand was a roller skate full of envelopes.

I threw open the door and stepped into musty-smelling water up to my shins.

"Franki," Veronica shouted eyeing the unlikely duo. "This isn't the time."

"This is exactly the time. Go on to the office." I grabbed the wig from the floorboard and slammed the door.

Glenda rolled down the window. "If you don't make it to Private Chicks, sugar, I'll see you on the steamboat."

Veronica drove off before I could react, and Kate glided away like a swan, apparently still wearing her roller skates. But the Dancing Hand Grenade danced his ground, doing The Super-bowl Shuffle to the beat of "Stayin' Alive."

Adrenaline shot through my limbs like rocket fuel. I'd had enough of the grenade and his goofy dance moves—and with people interfering in my investigation. I pulled the wig on, gripped either side of the board, and charged. My head made contact with his mid-section, and he tipped over like the Little Teapot—and floated on his back down Bourbon Street.

I gaped at him in shock. I hadn't expected the wig to do the trick, but it had, and the extra bouffant had padded my head.

"Hey!" He raised a puffy, gloved hand. "Help a guy out."

My shock gave way to guilt. The guy could drown in that costume. I lifted my foot to run, but the water had risen to my knees, and there was an undertow. I tossed the wig at him. "Grab onto that board."

"I can't," he shouted. "It's too far away."

"Put those puffy hands to use and paddle over to it, or to a streetlamp. You can hang on until I can make it to you."

"They're like big cotton balls. They're soaked."

I plodded through the water, looking for anything I could use to rescue him. But the only things around were floating booze bottles and the odd flip flop.

Kate emerged like a superhero skater from a side street one block up. "Don't freak, Danny! I'm coming for you!"

*Danny the Dancing Hand Grenade?*

She tossed the roller skate and pumped her arms to travel through the water faster, and the white envelopes spread across the water.

There was no way I could reach Kate and the grenade, so I

jog-splashed toward the closest envelope, still wearing the wig. My head throbbed, my thighs burned, and the spot where Ruth had whacked me ached. But after a few minutes, my fingers curled around an envelope. It was fat, and full of drug promise.

I tore the wet paper.

A keychain with a roller skate that said, *NOLA Roulergirls.*

"No, it's a foil," I said in crazy bag lady mode. I tossed it into the water and spent twenty minutes collecting envelopes, tearing them open, and finding the same prize. I was in such a frenzy to find gold bars that I didn't hear the motor until it was right in front of me.

I looked up and saw a flat boat with a red crawfish emblem and the words *Cajun Navy, Louisiana Strong.*

A man in a camouflage jacket and matching pith helmet extended his hand. "Nice bib apron, *chère*. Climb aboard."

I saw a flash of gold as a wave hit my face. I spat at least ten times in case I'd gotten staphylococcus or the flesh-eating bacteria in my mouth, and then I opened my eyes.

Kate stood before me in the water without her mask.

I looked from her to the man in the boat. Another man in fishing waders who was clearly the camouflaged man's identical twin was in the back—and so was the Dancing Hand Grenade, looking green around the gills.

"Franki Amato," Kate's tone dripped contempt, "we haven't officially met."

I didn't flinch at my last name. "I know who you are. Kate Wilson, a.k.a. Goldie Brawn."

She grabbed my hand, collapsing my bones as she shook it. "A.k.a. Nicky Pescatore's ex-fiancée."

## 17

"This is your stop, *chères*." The camouflaged Cajun Navy man pulled the flat boat in front of Veronica's building on Decatur Street. We'd already been to the Tropical Isle bar to drop off Danny the Dancing Hand Grenade, who'd turned out to be a short, pudgy guy shaped like his costume.

The boat rocked ominously as I rose to my feet. With the help of his twin in the fishing waders, I jumped into the knee-deep water. Then I turned and laid a don't-try-anything look on Kate.

She glared and stood in her roller skates, and then she climbed from the boat as gracefully as a ballerina in *Swan Lake*.

The camouflaged man handed us both a business card. "You need any help, you give us a shout."

The names on the card were a mouthful. Jean-Thibault and Jean-Toussaint Froiquingont. "Merci beaucoup for the rescue, uh," I glanced at the card, "Jeans."

They tipped their pith hats and motored away.

I tucked the business card into my semi-dry shirt pocket and gestured to the open door of the stairwell. "You first, Goldie. A.k.a. Kate."

Her perky mouth curled. "It's not like I'm going to run."

"You mean, skate? By the way, I suggest you take those things off because Private Chicks is on the third floor."

"And risk a cut on my foot in this raw sewage?"

Bile rose in my throat like the floodwater in the French Quarter. I hadn't known about the sewage, but now that I did my gut seized up, hopefully not from giardia or hepatitis.

Kate clomped up the steps on her toe stops, and I followed gripping both handrails to block an escape attempt—and to steady my stomach. Both of us reeked of eau de Vieux Carré sewer.

Glenda stared at us from the top of the stairs. "From the ruckus you two are making, I thought the cavalry was coming."

"Nah, just the roller derby queen here." I stepped onto the landing. "Although, we were rescued by the Cajun Navy."

Her eyes popped like the green of her olive branch pasties, and she rushed down the stairwell.

"They're gone, Glenda."

"Well, *merde*, sugar." She climbed the stairs. "I should've jumped into the water with you."

I imagined her on flooded Bourbon Street, her feet so high in the strappy Roman stripper heels that she seemed to walk on the water.

Veronica appeared in the doorway with towels. "You must be Kate."

I lowered my lids. "A.k.a. Nick Pescatore's ex-fiancée, a.k.a. quite possibly the scorned woman who killed him and left the queen of spades as a voodoo calling card."

Kate spun on me in her skates. "For your information, until yesterday I thought the scorned woman was you."

"Me? I never even met Nick."

Veronica shoved a towel into my hands. "Let's take this inside, Franki. There's a pot of chamomile tea on the coffee table."

We entered, and Kate sat on a couch next to Glenda. I walked over to her, dripping water and spitting mad. "How did you come to the horribly mistaken conclusion that I killed Nick?"

Kate reached for a teacup.

"Uh uh." I wagged my finger. "No tea till you talk."

Her eyes sparkled like her tinsel wig, and it wasn't from Mardi Gras spirit. "Danny heard you report Nick's murder on the pay phone at the Tropical Isle bar, which made you my number one suspect. Then you started stalking me, and you even got a job on the Galliano. I figured you were some giant tramp—"

"Giant?" I loomed over her and realized I'd objected to the wrong word.

Veronica pushed me onto the opposite couch, smoothed her tutu, and took a seat beside me. "So, Kate, you assumed that Franki killed Nick because he'd jilted her for you."

"Exactly. And I thought she was coming for me next. I mean, she did chase me out of Nicky's memorial."

"I chased you because you ran."

"And I ran because I thought you were going to kill me."

Glenda pressed her stylus to her lip. "That does sound plausible, Miss Franki. A Bond Girl pulled a gun on one of my fiancés when he started dating me. I'm writing about her in my memoirs."

My interest in Glenda's memoirs was waning, and so was my patience with her. I turned to Kate. "You said you thought I killed Nick until yesterday. What changed your mind?"

"I couldn't find anything on a Franki *Rockford*,"—she paused to smirk at my name choice—"so I followed you here from the Galliano."

Irritation pricked my chest. That must have been when I'd gone looking for her after the drug drop-off at the dock.

"Then I googled this place and found an article with your picture about a vampire murder you solved."

Veronica tipped her head. "For an amateur sleuth, you're pretty good. If you ever need a job, let me know."

I jolted like I was back in the French Quarter undertow. "Uh, slow down there, partner, because Kate got the story mostly wrong. She also got fired from the Gold Mine Saloon for drug possession."

Kate shot Glenda the side-eye. "See what I mean about the stalking?"

Glenda nodded. "It does look that way, sugar."

"I'm a PI." My tone was dry, unlike the rest of me. "It's my job to follow people, remember?"

Kate crossed her leg, resting a skate on her knee. "In all fairness, Franki, you got my story mostly wrong too. The drugs that got me fired were opioids that Nicky was dealing. He stashed them in a bag in my closet that he didn't think I was using anymore."

I crossed my arms. "All right. But if you're so innocent, why would you date a drug dealer?"

"I didn't know. He told me he worked at his uncle's produce company. But believe me, I broke off the engagement as soon as I got fired. And who didn't have a lousy boyfriend in their twenties?"

Glenda nodded. "Ain't that the truth, child?"

It *was* true, and my lousy ex-boyfriends Todd and Vince were proof. I sank into the couch cushions and scrutinized Kate. As skeptical as I was about her story, she reminded me of Marv's comment about Jim Rockford—she was good, just not in the way one would think. "Let's talk about Nick. Why was he on the Galliano the night he got killed?"

Kate rubbed her forehead as though trying to erase a bad memory. "To get money Captain Vandergrift owed him from a card game. Nicky owed me back rent, and I was about to get evicted from my apartment. So I went with him to the Galliano, and I waited outside. The whole night."

I leaned forward and glanced at Veronica, who bit her lower lip. "Did you hear him—"

"Scream?" Kate's eyes teared up, and she looked at her shorts.

I hesitated to tell her what the captain had confessed to Bradley, but she needed to know. "Captain Vandergrift threw him overboard."

Her head shot up. "I thought it was Alfredo Scalino."

"Why? Did you see him there?"

"Yeah. After Nicky screamed the captain went down to the river, and Alfredo was with him." She raised her hands before I could protest. "I don't know him personally, but I've seen him and Gigi in the Quarter. Anyway, the captain got into a car and drove away, but Alfredo went back on the boat. I would've called the cops if I'd had my cell phone, but it was turned off because I hadn't paid the bill. And I was too afraid to go find a phone in case Nicky was alive and needed my help."

"Is your phone on now?"

She nodded, and Veronica handed her a tissue.

"I guess Nick didn't text you that night?"

"No, he knew my phone wasn't working. Why?"

"He texted his uncle, my client, the words 'Galliano gold.'"

Kate dabbed her eyes. "I guess we know now that he was referring to the gold bars. But when I heard him scream, I thought maybe he'd started looking for the Civil War gold and gotten caught or something. He mentioned the gold to me before he went on the boat. But then when I saw Alfredo, I wondered if it had something to do with the opioids. Alfredo is the one who sold them to him."

Veronica cradled a teacup. "Sounds like Alfredo has always been involved in Gigi's drug business."

Kate shook her head and blew her nose. "Nicky said Gigi didn't know about Alfredo's dealing—at least, he didn't until the gold bars turned up on the Galliano. Apparently, Alfredo has always resented Gigi being the head of the family. But Gigi is retiring and moving to Italy, so Alfredo wants to take his place as the *capo di tutti capi*."

*The boss of all bosses.* Alfredo was double-crossing Gigi while he was hospitalized with appendicitis. Not a smart move when your brother was a mobster. "What did you do after Alfredo left the Galliano?"

She tugged at her skate laces. "I went on the boat. And I found Nicky." She clenched her jaw. "I figured he might be in the galley because Alfredo was wearing a bib apron like yours."

Glenda slapped her thigh. "Is that what those things are called?"

"Yes," I said. "They're used for an activity known as cooking." I turned back to Kate. "Look, I can see that you're genuinely distraught about what happened to Nick, but I have to question why you were at the Julia Street Cruise Terminal yesterday morning with Tim."

"You followed me there too?"

"Sugar, honestly," Glenda chided. "Miss Kate could get a restraining order against you."

I shot styluses at her with my eyes. "And you're surprised that I don't want you on the steamboat?"

She crossed her arms and legs and bounced a stripper-sandaled foot.

Kate cleared her throat. "I know the Tim thing looks bad, but after I found Nicky, I vowed to him and to myself that I'd get even with Alfredo and the captain for what they did to him. And Tim is making it pretty easy for me because he can't stop bragging about his involvement in the drug ring."

"You think the three of them are in this together?"

"I don't know about the captain, but Alfredo and Tim for sure. And not just them. I saw a woman come down the gangplank after the captain left the boat that night."

I collapsed into the couch, stunned. Someone else had been onboard during the managers meeting.

Veronica leaned forward. "Did you see what she looked like?"

"No, she was wearing a long wool coat with the hood up, but she was average height, thin. And the crazy thing is, she got into a limo, and then Alfredo came out and got in with her."

Glenda chewed her stylus. "Who do you think she is, sugar? The scorned voodoo woman?"

I poured chamomile tea for Kate and me because both of us were going to need something soothing after I answered Glenda's question. "The more likely scenario is that Alfredo has teamed up with Gigi's consigliera. And now that Gigi knows about the gold bars, members of the Scalino clan will probably be on the Galliano for the overnight gambling cruise."

My hand trembled as I raised the teacup to my lips. I took a sip and swallowed, hard. "And if that happens, at least one person is going to get whacked."

VERONICA STOOD at the bottom of the stairwell surveying the flood situation on Decatur, and Glenda, Kate, and I were single file behind her. She pulled my car keys from her purse. "The water has gone down enough that we should be fine to make it home."

I yawned as we descended the stairs into the street. It was two a.m., and I was anxious to get a few hours of sleep before I had to be on the Galliano for the gambling cruise.

Kate did a skater spin on the wet sidewalk. "I'm staying with friends over on Dauphine, so I'm going to head out." She gave me a salute as she skated backwards. "See you on the steamboat, Rockford."

I eyed her as she rolled away. I didn't think she was a murderer, but she was killing me with that sarcasm.

"I'll drive, Franki." Veronica opened the Mustang door, and she and Glenda climbed inside.

I walked toward the car and stopped short.

Two eyes—no, six—watched me from the floodwater in the street.

The exhaustion must've been making me hallucinate. I rubbed my brow and looked again.

The eyes were still there and with a huge head of fur, or...*hair?*

I squinted, and my hands flew to my mouth.

The ball of hair had a red bandana bow.

"Look out, sugar! It's Miss Carnie's wig."

Something in the floodwater—maybe chemicals from the sewer—had caused the wig to grow into a giant mudbug monster. And it was after me, probably because I'd thrown it to the Dancing Hand Grenade on Bourbon Street and hadn't tried to retrieve it.

The eyes began to rise. The cup surfaced, then the lemon and the board. Next came antennae and an open chasm with gnashing claw-like teeth.

I had to get to my car, but my feet were stuck to the sidewalk.

Two enormous crawdad arms emerged from the water and

waved giant pinchers in the air. One pincher ripped the plastic cup from the board and scooped up some of the filthy water.

I screamed, and the wig monster poured the water into my mouth. I gagged and clutched my neck as the other pincher picked up the lemon and shoved it deep into my throat.

As I gasped for breath that wouldn't come, I thought about how ironic it was that with so many dangers around me—the Scalinos, Captain Vandergrift, Detective Sullivan—the thing that was going to kill me was a lemon.

The wig monster grabbed me with its giant claws and shook me hard. "Franki!"

*Wait. How does it know my name?*

My eyes flickered open. I was in the backseat of my Mustang, and Veronica was shaking me awake.

"You fell asleep on the way home." She turned in the driver seat and pulled the keys from the ignition. "And you were having some kind of nightmare."

Glenda stuck her gold head-banded head in the backseat. "We've got an emergency, Miss Franki. My breasts are gone."

I looked at Veronica. "This is still part of the nightmare, right?"

"No, her Mardi Gras decorations have been stolen right off the front of the house. Can you believe it?"

I really couldn't. Surely I was still asleep.

"Get out of that car, sugar. I'm in dire need of your investigating help."

I climbed from the backseat into our driveway. Sure enough, the balcony railing was bare.

Glenda lit a cigarette in her holder and blew out the smoke in a huff. "I'm telling you, it was Carmela and those other Lilliputians. For reasons that are beyond me, they never liked my decorations."

I straightened my shirt. "There's no way they could've taken them. Those breasts were huge."

"I've got the good Lord to thank for that, child."

Veronica scanned the yard. "She might be right, Franki. The Sicilian flag is gone too, and I doubt a thief would have taken that."

"If he was Sicilian he would've, and there are plenty of Sicilians in NOLA. Just look at all the nonne."

My apartment door opened, and the capo di tutte nonne came outside in a granny gown that would've done Sophia from *The Golden Girls* proud. "What is all-a the shouting about-a?"

Glenda pointed her cigarette holder at the balcony. "Someone took my breasts. Was it you?"

"Why the hell-a would I want-a yours? I don't even want-a the two I got."

I pinched my arm. Nope. I was painfully awake.

"Well, someone stole them." Glenda strut-paced in the driveway. "Maybe it was the Scalinos."

I snorted. "Not unless there were drugs in those breasts."

She stopped and struck a pose. "This entire body is a drug, Miss Franki."

Nonna smacked her hands together in a praying motion and shook them up and down. It was the Italian gesture for *What in God's name is this one talking about?* "Luigi's-a missing, and you are-a looking for your boobies?"

Glenda crossed her arms over her olive branch pasties. "You make me sound selfish."

"You think-a?"

She took a deep drag from her cigarette. "If those mobsters took my breasts from the house, how do I know they're not going to take me next?"

Nonna pressed a hand to her stomach and chuckled, and

Glenda gave her a glare that made it clear she wouldn't be extending the olive branches any time soon.

Veronica held up her hands. "Now Glenda's got a point. It never occurred to any of us that Alfredo would've kidnapped Luigi, so it's possible that Glenda, or any of us, really, could be next."

I shook my head. "If either of the Scalinos had come here to steal something, it would've been the winepress, not Glenda's boobs. But they don't know where it is, remember? That's why Gigi's holding Luigi."

Veronica chewed her thumbnail. "Do you suppose Luigi told him it was in your closet under duress?"

Her question shook all of us awake. Because if Luigi had told Gigi where the winepress was, then he should've been released —unless Gigi had reneged on the deal.

"I'll go check my closet." I turned and entered my apartment with three pairs of eyes watching me like the wig monster. I went to my room and found my mother asleep on her back, her head thrashing from side to side, and the bedding in knots. She was having a nightmare of her own, and I considered turning on the light to wake her up.

She jolted and kicked the covers. "Save me, Jesus. You don't know what those women are like to live with. Bring the men back."

On second thought, I decided to leave her in the nightmare. The woman couldn't even give it a rest when she was asleep, so there was no way I was going to wake her up.

I switched on my phone light and opened the closet.

The trunk was still on the floor.

"So far so good," I whispered as I crouched and lifted the lid. The wine press was inside, which meant that someone else had stolen Glenda's breasts. The weirdo.

I closed the lid and froze. The brass lock was bent. I shone the light on the keyhole and fell back onto my haunches.

The Mardi Gras boobs weren't the only thing that was stolen. The video camera was gone too.

I felt cold and dirty, like I'd been dunked in floodwater. Someone had come into my home while my mom and nonna were sleeping, and I didn't know who or why.

But one thing was certain. Whatever was going on was about to come to a wig monster-sized head on the Galliano.

## 18

My stomach rose and fell like the steamboat as I pulled my overnight suitcase across the gangplank. Most likely it was a combination of the tarry river smell and apprehension about the gambling cruise, but I couldn't rule out a floodwater-induced salmonella infection or the sight of Ruth Walker in her Fun Meter.

"Well, well, well." Ruth scowled at me from behind a card table labeled Welcome Station with her arms crossed against her safari vest, tapping the toe of her Keds. "Look who's late to work."

I looked at my phone. "It's one-minute past eight."

"Employees were to board by eight a.m. sharp before the guests start boarding."

I seriously didn't know how she justified setting her Fun Meter to Max.

She shove-handed me a key from the table. "This is to your crew cabin on the Texas deck."

"Where's my Fun Meter?"

"I'm a little short, so they're reserved for the guests."

My mental Fun Meter moved from Min to Med. "What are

these?" I reached for some brochures next to a stack of bingo cards.

She gave my hand a slap. "They're the guests' schedules. We have a safety drill before we set sail, and I have an activity planned for every hour." She frowned beneath her sun visor. "It's going to be a blast."

"Yeah. Sticking to a strict schedule on vacation is tons of fun."

"I didn't earn Very Important Fun Person status on Carnival for nothing, party pooper."

"You're right. You paid for it in the price of your ticket."

She cocked her jaw open, and then she pulled a sheet of paper from a clipboard with a snap. "You're to report to the galley at nine. This has your cabin number and instructions for how staff are to behave onboard. You'll note that it says no fraternizing with the guests."

"You know I'm not here to fraternize, Ruth."

"In theory, but a lot of wealthy men are coming on the cruise. And after Bradley's drug bust, you're single."

I tightened my grip on my suitcase handle. "You really like to kick a girl when she's down, don't you? Or should I say, *whack*?"

She leaned over the Welcome Station, and the chains of her horn-rims swung. "I thought you were an intruder. But if that oar knocked some sense into you, so be it. Maybe now you'll try a little harder to hang on to your next boyfriend."

I opened my mouth to reply, but nothing came out. Because the name Ruth was in the word truth, and she spoke it, albeit a lot more directly than I would have liked. But I hadn't been truthful with Bradley, and when I'd opted not to tell him about the Scalinos and Sullivan, I'd essentially let him go. So there was nothing left to do but move on and allow him to do the same when he made bail.

With my heart queasy like my belly, I decided to take a few minutes in my cabin to lie down.

"Ahoy, missies." Glenda waved from the gangplank in black cat-eye sunglasses and a miniscule ivory halter dress and matching stripper slingbacks.

I sighed. So much for lying down.

Glenda sashayed across the deck like she was walking the red carpet.

Ruth lowered her horn-rims. "Miss O'Brien—correction, Miss Lamour, I'm thrilled to have you on the Galliano. And I do like those sunglasses."

*She would.*

"Thank you, Miss Ruth. They're part of my Hollywood look. Recognize this dress?"

"The pleats give it away. It's a version of the one Marilyn Monroe wore in *The Seven Year Itch*."

In Glenda's case, it was more like *The Sixty-Seven Year Itch*. And the dress was so short that she didn't need the wind from the subway grating to expose her underwear.

Ruth reached for a key. "Where's your luggage?"

Glenda gestured toward land. "I'm having it brought up now."

"Then I'll go get someone to escort you to your stateroom. Be back in a jiffy." Ruth hurried inside the casino.

With Ruth gone, I decided to give Glenda my own set of instructions for how staff were to behave onboard. "When you're not onstage, you need to stay out of trouble."

She struck a pose with her cigarette holder. "Now why on earth would I do that, sugar?"

"Because if you don't, you could jeopardize the investigation and maybe even get hurt—or worse."

"Relax, Miss Franki. I'm going to spend the morning getting situated in my stateroom, and after that I'm going to flirt with the crewmen before the gamblers board. Then I'm going to flirt with them."

Relief washed over me like the French Quarter flood. So many men would be on the ship that she'd probably be tied up for the entire cruise—possibly literally, if I knew Glenda.

But my relief was short-lived.

There were two passengers crossing the gangplank who made the rise and fall of my stomach turn to heave. My Nonna in her mourning dress and a wide-brimmed sun hat, and my mother in a green Hawaiian muumuu and a flower hair wreath.

I spun on Glenda like the Tasmanian Devil in a game of *Twister*. "They'd better be here to carry your bags."

"We've got Bruno for that, sugar."

An oil tanker couldn't have given me a bigger jolt. My gaze darted back to the gangplank. Bruno Messina, my nonna's long-time backup for Bradley, trudged across loaded with baggage. He wore the Italian-American version of seersucker—his white and black *Saturday Night Fever* suit complete with the gold horn necklace and a gold cross for extra emphasis.

I speed-walked to my mom and Nonna. "Really? You're still matchmaking even with Luigi missing?"

Nonna stared straight ahead as she walked to the Welcome Station. "Like-a Brenda said, we can-a work on-a two crises at-a once."

My mother nodded her flowers. "And according to David's investigation into your zitellahood, one of the biggest mistakes you made was turning down the dates your nonna arranged when you moved to New Orleans."

And to think I'd kept that rat off the ship to protect him from getting murdered. "Who's taking care of Napoleon?"

My mother parked a hand on her hip. "Veronica. And if you worried about your relationships as much as you worry about that dog, we wouldn't be in this mess."

"'We' wouldn't be in this mess if you two would butt out of my private life."

Nonna put a hand on her hip. "We will-a, as-a soon as-a Bruno resolve-a the crisis."

"Franki, baby."

A chill went down my spine at the sound of his voice.

Bruno dumped the bags on the deck with a thud and opened his arms wide. A bead of sweat dribbled from his Neanderthal brow to his nose hair and dropped into the fur on his chest.

I took a step back.

Undaunted, he flashed a smile and pulled a couple of Butterfingers from a suitcase. "A little gift from my concession stand."

My mother winked. "He really knows how to butter a girl up, doesn't he, Francesca?"

Under duress—and the weight of that bad pun—I snatched the Butterfingers and stuck them in my pocket. Not that I was a materialistic person, but candy bars didn't have the same sparkle as the ruby necklace Bradley had given me. "Uh, I need to report for duty soon. Bruno, why don't you carry the bags to the cabin deck on the second floor?"

"My pleasure." He gave a smile that resembled a leer. "Let me know when you have a break later. I'll buy you a drink and a shrimp cocktail."

"We'll see." Of course I wanted to avoid him, but I also wanted to avoid the shrimp. Given my track record, the odds of me deveining those suckers was slim.

Bruno collected the baggage and entered the casino, and I turned on my mom and Nonna. "You cannot be here while I'm investigating a homicide. It's too dangerous, and too much is at stake. So gather up Bruno and your bags and go home. While you're there, focus on the real crises, which, incidentally, are finding Luigi and getting Bradley out of jail."

Glenda cackled. "I can't wait till you hear this, Miss Franki. You're going to have to eat your words about not wanting me on the boat, because it turns out that my writing skills haven't dulled my sleuthing skills in the slightest."

"What're you talking about?"

"That thing I said about Luigi being right under their noses."

I looked at Nonna.

She glanced from side to side and lowered the brim of her sun hat. "We got a tip-a from-a Vito Tomasino at-a the gift-a shop across-a the street. The morning of-a Nicky's memorial, he saw the Scalinos' limo here at-a the Galliano."

"So? Maybe Alfredo was here before the memorial."

"No, dear." My mother removed her wreath. "It was after."

"How do you know?"

"Because-a Vito saw two men-a taking a man in a trench-a coat and a hat on-a the steam-a-boat. He didn't think-a nothing at-a the time, but when he heard that-a Luigi had-a been kidnapped, he came-a to have a look-a. And-a he found a blue carnation on-a the ground."

*The one Luigi wore to Nick's memorial?*

If so, Luigi hadn't been right under the nonne's noses. He'd been under mine the whole time.

MY CREW CABIN was next to the mid-ship stairwell, which was ideal. Because if that creepy calliope started playing in the middle of the night, I wanted to be near an exit.

I slipped my key into the lock and glanced at my phone. I'd missed a call from Veronica, but she'd have to wait. It was eight-twenty, so I only had forty minutes to look for Luigi before I had to deal with Alfredo, Pat, and those shrimp.

I shouldered open the door and pulled my suitcase inside.

"What took you so long?" a familiar voice drawled.

My phone hit the floor.

Sullivan lay on the bottom bunk in nothing but a pair of briefs. He held out a yellow rose. "For you."

My hands stayed at my sides, but I felt as though the rose's thorns had pricked me. That was the flower Bradley always gave me, and Sullivan had ruined it. And frankly, I would've rather eaten Bruno's Butterfingers than accept anything from the detective. "Get out of my cabin."

"This is my cabin, Rockford—I mean, Amato." He put his arms behind his head to show off his pecs. "But you're welcome to shack up with me."

"Rot in hell." I bent to retrieve my phone, and he latched onto me like an octopus—or a kraken. I struggled. "Let go of me, you pig."

"You know you want this, Amato." He pulled me to the bottom bunk and held me on top of him. "You've wanted it since you stripped for me at Madame Moiselle's."

"For you? Your ego's bigger than the Galliano. You know I stripped to solve a—"

His mouth smothered my protest. The last time he kissed me, I'd felt desire tinged with danger, but now it was revulsion mixed with rage. I put my hands on his chest and shoved, but his arms stuck to me like tentacles.

"Detective?" Ruth entered the open door. "There's been a—" She looked at me and her jaw went slack, then it drew up and clamped. "—mistake."

Sullivan shoved me to the floor and reached for a blanket.

I grabbed my phone and sprung to my feet. "I'll say there's been a mistake—letting a corrupt cop work security."

Sullivan tensed as though he were about to lunge, but Ruth stepped between us.

"You shush, missy." She snapped her fingers at me. "I'm sorry for the confusion, Detective. I'll show her to the correct cabin."

"That's fine, Miss Walker. You couldn't have known that she'd try to take advantage of me during my nap."

"If I ever do find you sleeping, be afraid." I grabbed my suitcase and stormed to the deck. I didn't know where I was going. I just wanted to be far from that man.

Ruth chased me down. "Not twenty minutes after I tell you not to fraternize with the guests, I find you swapping spit with the detective."

I spun around. "You're off base here, okay? He pounced on me when I went into what I thought was my cabin."

"Well." She tugged at her safari vest. "I ought to have him thrown off this steamboat."

"Don't. He's an enemy I need to keep close—just not in my cabin close. But how could you make a mistake like that?"

"I didn't. This morning the captain changed the cabin assignments because he wanted the detective near the pilot-house instead of downstairs. But it's not a big deal because you and I are practically best friends."

I ignored the best friends comment because there was something more alarming in her statement. "What do you have to do with this equation?"

"With Sullivan on the Texas deck, we're short a crew cabin. So the captain suggested you bunk with me."

A night of court TV and Ruth shouting verdicts in her sleep was enough to make me leap overboard. "I assume you've heard the expression 'never the twain shall meet?'"

"Of course. It means things are too different to coexist."

"And lady, that's you and me."

"Nonsense. It'll be a ball." She tapped her Fun Meter as evidence and pulled my suitcase to the cabin next to the captain's quarters, right by the damn calliope.

Reluctantly, I went inside. Sure enough Ruth had a TV with a DVD player—and a poster of the late Judge Joseph Wapner. If I didn't need to keep my cover on the boat, I would've actually preferred to bunk with my mom and nonna.

"Knock, knock." Kate entered with Wendell in tow. They were in uniform, crisp white shirts and black slacks. "You two look cozy."

I sank onto the bottom bunk. "You mean, queasy."

"Hypochondriac much?"

Yeah, but I didn't see what business that was of hers.

Ruth snickered. "She probably thinks she caught dysentery from that floodwater."

I stared at Kate. "How does she know about that?"

"I filled her and Wendell in on the events of last night."

Ruth shot me an accusatory look. "And I told them about Bradley."

"That's why we're here,"—Kate sat cross-legged on the floor—"to formulate a plan of attack."

I gave them a stare worthy of a drill sergeant. "All right. But now that you're all in the know, remember that loose lips sink ships—and steamboats. Understood?"

They nodded.

"Good, because there's been a major development in the case. In all probability, Luigi Pescatore is being held captive somewhere onboard."

Ruth and Kate shared a look of shock, and Wendell's eyes popped like he'd seen a ghost.

"So now we each have two objectives. The first is to keep an eye on our assigned people. Since I'm in the galley, I'll take Alfredo. Kate, you watch Sullivan because he'll be hanging around the casino and the dining hall. And Ruth, you work with the captain, so you've got him."

She flushed and lowered her visor.

Kate frowned. "That leaves Wendell covering Tim. How's he going to do that if he's stuck at the bar?"

"He's not. We're all going to have to keep an eye on the shifty sailor. Wendell, I need you to watch the gamblers and find out which men interact with Alfredo, because they're probably members of the Scalino Mafia clan."

"As long as they ain't ghosts, I'm cool. But what about Marian? Shouldn't we bring her in on this?"

Kate leaned back on her hands. "I vote no. She can't surveil anyone from the gift shop."

"Not only that," Ruth barked, "I find her rather off-putting."

I put the tip of my tongue between my teeth and bit it. "Okay then, let's enter our numbers into each other's phones." I handed my cell to Wendell. "We'll communicate via group text, and be sure to delete the message after you've read it in case it ends up in the wrong hands."

Kate handed me her phone, and I typed in my number. "The second objective is to look for Luigi whenever possible. But be careful because mobsters will be watching, and they're all killers."

Wendell pulled a handkerchief from his shirt pocket and wiped his brow.

Ruth eyed us over her horn-rims. "If you get caught looking for Luigi, say you're hunting for Captain Galliano's Civil War gold."

I leapt from the bunk. "That's it—the map we saw on the desk in the captain's bedroom."

Ruth put her hands on her hips. "What about it?"

"It had red Xes on the library and the stage."

"Yeah, $x$ marks the spot where the treasure might be hidden." She snorted. "You're a PI, and you don't know that?"

I sighed. This ragtag army thing might not work out. "What I mean is, those Xes could also mark potential hiding places for Luigi."

"Oh, foo." Ruth waved off the notion. "He hadn't even been kidnapped when we found that map. And I told you, the captain isn't a killer."

"Maybe not. But I'd be willing to bet one of those missing gold bars that you and I weren't the only ones who saw that map. And whoever else happened upon it could've gotten the idea to hide a kidnapped man in one of those spots."

Wendell looked at Ruth. "They'd be good hidey holes since hardly no one knows about 'em."

Kate's gaze bore into mine. "It had to be that scumbag Alfredo."

"Possibly. It depends on how long the captain left the map on his desk."

Ruth crossed her arms, and her chains started swinging. "But the only person you and I saw on the boat that night was Detective Sullivan."

"Precisely. And right after that, he volunteered to work security for the gambling cruise."

MY FEET FLEW DOWN the mid-ship stairs. The impromptu strategy meeting had eaten twenty minutes, so I didn't have long to look for Luigi before I had to be in the galley.

I opened the door to the cabin deck and scanned the hallway. No one was around, so I ran to my main objective—the old Mark Twain photo in the library.

I stepped onto the chair beneath the photo, balanced my foot on one of the arms, and felt above the round frame.

"What are you doing, Francesca?"

I started, and the chair cracked. My mother's jarring voice

was enough to break me and wood too. "What do you think I'm doing?" I hopped to the ground and eyed her bathing suit, tote bag, and flip-flops. "And never mind me, what are *you* doing?"

"I'm going to get some sun."

"Mom, this is *not* a vacation."

"Well I *know* thaaat. But nothing's going to happen until the other passengers arrive, and if you want me to be of any help, then I need to take care of myself. I raised you three kids, so believe me, I know how to handle three crises at once."

I did a mental eye roll. Then I reviewed the crises I knew of —Luigi's abduction and my zitellahood. "What's the third crisis?"

"My stress level, that's what."

*The woman had no idea.*

She slipped on a pair of Jackie O sunglasses. "I'll be on starboard deck, if you need me."

I wouldn't. I climbed back onto the chair and examined the wood paneling beneath the photo. No latch. I scanned the shelves. There was row after row of books by Twain, collections of his work, essays on his writing, biographies. One by one I pulled them down to see if a bookcase would swing open.

"Franki, baby!"

I jumped, and the chair arm separated from the frame. I fell, and a leg jammed into the exact spot on my back where Ruth had whacked me with the oar.

Bruno knelt so close that his nose hair tufts almost brushed my cheek. "Speak to me, doll."

I couldn't. The wind had been knocked from me in a gust.

A light went on in his dark brown eyes when he realized I couldn't talk. "Let's just have a feel to see if anything's broken."

I bent his fingers backwards.

"Ow, ow, ow, ow, ow."

When he'd backed off, I sat up.

And I saw the man with the facial scar who'd pushed Luigi into the limo. He'd exited a stateroom and was heading toward us.

I sucked in a panicked breath. He would recognize me since I'd run to the limo door. I jumped up and did the only thing I could to hide my face. I wrapped my arms around Bruno and locked lips—mine, as I pressed them to his.

He broke out in an instant sweat. "I haven't been able to get you outta my head since you stripped to solve that case."

*Would no one let me forget that?* I peered through my lashes and saw the man going down the grand staircase.

I pushed Bruno away. "I feel better now, thanks."

He came back at me, all arms and hands. "I'll make you feel even better."

The guy was as bad as Sullivan.

Nonna exited her stateroom, and I saw my opportunity. "Oh, God. My nonna's coming."

Bruno did what every nonna-fearing Sicilian male would do in that situation. He ran like a baby, probably to call his mamma.

Nonna pursed her lips as he sprinted down the grand staircase. "I see you already scared-a him away too."

*Little did she know.* "I just saw the man who pushed Luigi into the limo."

"What-a? Where-a?"

"He came out of the stateroom across from yours." I took off down the hall and led her to the room. "Cover me."

She nodded.

The door was locked, but the knob was old and cheaply made. I inserted my cabin key, and after some jiggling, the door opened.

Nonna and I exchanged a look, and I slipped inside.

The room was terrifying. A floral bedspread in pinks and blues that matched the wallpaper, old-fashioned wall sconces, and a white-and-gold armoire. I went into the bathroom, which looked and smelled like something out of a state mental hospital —a sterile white sink, toilet, and tub with no shower curtain.

My hands shook as I opened the medicine cabinet.

Nothing.

I went back into the room. I didn't see any luggage, so I checked under the bed and the pillows. I stuck my hand under the mattress and touched something small and plastic. I pulled out the item and stopped breathing.

A hearing aid the size of a quarter.

I'd only seen one that big—on Luigi Pescatore.

"*Buongiorno.* It's-a nice-a day for a cruise, no?"

I stiffened. Nonna wasn't nice to strangers, or anyone, for that matter.

"Yeh, real nice," an irritated male replied. "Now if you'll, uh, move, I need to get in my cabin."

*The thug.*

I shot to my feet. If he found me in his room, he would kill me and Nonna.

"Give-a me a minute. I don't-a move-a so fast no more."

I scoured the room, but there was no way out. The windows didn't open, and there was no closet to hide in. Frantic, I looked at the door and broke into a Bruno-style sweat.

The handle was turning.

The thug was coming in.

## 19

The door opened, and the thug spotted me near the bed. But his black eyes didn't widen. They fixed on me with a dead stare.

He closed the door and leaned against it.

My pulse kicked up a notch.

"I'd love to hear why you're in my cabin." His voice was soft but lethal, like toxic gas seeping into the room. "And it had better be good."

"Galliano crew, sir." I pointed to the bedding that I'd pulled back and to Bruno's Butterfinger on his pillow, hoping he didn't notice my arm trembling. "I'm here for turn-down service."

His eyes narrowed to slot-machine-sized slits. "It's not even nine a.m."

"Y-yessir, we're short staffed, so we have to get the rooms done before we start dining service. Now if you'll excuse me, I have to report to Chef Scalino."

At the mention of Alfredo, his hard squint eased up. He rubbed his jaw and licked the corner of his mouth. Then he moved aside and gestured for me to go.

My arm hair stood on alert as I walked to the door.

"Hold on a second."

The hair on the nape of my neck joined my alarmed arm hair.

"Take this." He grabbed the Butterfinger from the bed and slapped it into my hand. "I'm a diabetic."

"I'll note that in your guest file." I opened the door and lunged into the hallway, where I inhaled a deep breath of freedom—that was promptly knocked from my lungs.

By Nonna's handbag.

"Owwmmm." I semi-swallowed my cry after my shoulder took a hit from the weight of whatever was inside her purse. Fortunately, the thug had closed the door behind me, so I didn't think he'd heard.

With my one good arm, I pulled her to the Victorian fainting couch by the backgammon table. "What did you do that for?" I whisper-hissed. "You saw me coming out."

She slipped her purse onto her forearm. "I had-a to swing-a early in case you were the thug-a. But since it happened, that's-a for getting Bradley arrested."

The pain from my broken heart and oar-whacked back were enough, I didn't need a shoulder injury to add to it. I rotated my arm socket and then leaned in to tell her what I'd discovered— but not too close because the woman was a wild card. "I found Luigi's hearing aid."

"*Brutto criminale!*" She raised her handbag and rushed the "ugly criminal's" door.

I covered her mouth and pulled her back to the couch.

And she bit me.

I ground my teeth and kicked myself for the tactical error. I'd tussled with Nonna long enough to know that when it came to getting her way, she was lowdown and bitey.

Marian came out of the gift shop at the stern of the boat. Her brow arched and then downturned, and she returned inside.

I took that as my cue to go to work. "Nonna, I've got to report to the galley. Please do something safe and normal while I'm gone, like keeping an eye on things in the casino."

"I'm-a here to find-a Luigi, not-a to gamble."

I didn't want her poking around where the wrong people could see her. "Fine, then search the backstage area. The captain has a map of the ship that makes me think there's either a secret room or a compartment under the floor."

She rose from the couch, but I blocked her.

"One more thing. Do your searching when Glenda's backstage before her performance. And help her get ready so no one suspects what you're up to."

"What's-a there for me to do? She's-a not gonna wear any clothes-a."

*True.* "So brush her hair, or something."

"Bah!" She shuffled to the grand staircase.

And I sprinted to the mid-ship stairs. On my way down, I sent a text to the group warning them about the thug and returned Veronica's call. The line dropped after one ring. I wasn't sure what was going on with the phone service, but it didn't portend smooth sailing for a cruise emergency.

I exited the stairwell into the empty dining hall, and the galley door opened. I took cover in a dark corner by the stage.

Tim emerged with a plate of croissants and went to the stairs. I wondered whether the food was for Luigi, but more than likely it was for the captain in the pilothouse.

I rushed into the galley expecting an earful from Pat. She wasn't around, so I slipped on my bib apron and went to my "workstation."

My phone vibrated. It was a text from Wendell that a man with a scar under his eye had just entered the dining hall.

*Was the thug coming to tell Alfredo that I'd been in his stateroom?*

"What're you doing on your damn phone?"

I jumped at Pat's voice and shoved my phone into my back pocket.

She was in full Sea Hag mode in a black ensemble with a matching scarf on her head. "You've got shrimp to peel and depoop."

For once, I didn't take issue with the icky term. I sat on the bucket with my back strategically turned to the door and put on my hairnet. But I ignored the latex gloves. If Sullivan wanted me to wear them, he'd have to shove them on me himself.

Pat halved red potatoes for the crawdad boil with a rhythmic knife whack.

"Is the chef in?" The thug's silky serial-killer voice was unmistakable—and unnerving.

She didn't miss a whack. "In his office."

I reached for a shrimp and lowered my head as he walked past, but I felt his dead eyes drill into my back.

After a moment, the two men began talking. Their voices were low, which was telling, even though I couldn't make out a word they said.

Minutes elapsed, and the tension in the galley mounted. Pat glanced at the hallway as though waiting for something bad to happen, which heightened my fear that the delinquent duo had discovered who I was.

"Pat!"

We both jumped at Alfredo's bark.

She spat into her phlegm rag and limp-loped to the hallway, and I strained my ears to listen.

"You called, Chef?"

"Obviously," he snapped. "Change of plans. We're serving Bananas Foster for dessert, so we'll dock in White Castle to pick up some Galliano."

"What about the lemons for your sorbet?"

"Go to the pantry." His speech had slowed, and his tone had

lowered an octave. "Tell me how many boxes of bananas we've got."

"Right away, Chef."

I pulled out my phone and texted the group about the unplanned booze stop. Wendell replied immediately, and I wasn't surprised by his answer. No one had asked him about his Galliano stores, and given the name of the steamboat, he'd stocked enough for two gambling cruises.

The text reminded me of Nick's—Galliano gold. The chef's unplanned stop was a ruse to deliver the suitcase of gold bars that Tim had collected from the Southampton Spitfire.

"Attention, guests and staff." Ruth's voice blasted throughout the galley on loudspeaker. "It's your Cruise Director, Cruisin' Ruth."

That nickname made her sound like she was looking for a sex partner—or a bruising, which I would've happily supplied. I put away my phone and grabbed a shrimp while I waited for her announcement.

"We've got so much fun planned for our inaugural voyage that you'll wish you could stay on the Galliano forever."

"There is *no* amount of fun that would keep me on this ghost trap," I said as I ripped off the shrimp's tail.

"In fifteen minutes, we'll kick things off on the main deck with a mandatory safety drill. After that, the staff will head back to work—I'm talking to you, Franki."

I paused the peeling to shoot the finger at the ceiling speaker.

"Then I'll lead the guests to the dining hall where we'll square dance to Mississippi-River-themed karaoke. When our toesies are too tired to do-si-do, we'll recharge with some fruit punch and blackout bingo."

With fun like that, my toesies would do-si-do back to the galley to work. But the safety drill was the opportunity I needed to make myself scarce before the thug emerged from Alfredo's office. I tossed the shrimp into the bucket, pulled off my hairnet and bib apron, and hot-footed it from the galley.

My shoes screeched to a stop as soon as I stepped into the dining hall.

On the floor outside the door was a candy wrapper—not from a Butterfinger but a Bit-O-Honey.

Gigi "The G-Man" Scalino's favorite candy, and it didn't come from the diabetic thug.

"Line up for a fun safety drill, people." Ruth smiled and directed an elderly couple farther down the main deck. "I need you silent and single file with exactly one foot between you, no more no less."

Her smile went south when she spotted me leaning on the boat railing. She marched over and raised a bullhorn to her lips. "What is it about the word *safety* that you don't understand?"

I moved to the center of the deck, but what I wanted to move was her Fun Meter—to Min.

She lowered the bullhorn, checked to make sure no one was listening, and turned her horn-rims on me. "Like I said on the loudspeaker, this drill is mandatory. And who are the two no-shows? Why, your family. Go figure."

Nonna was probably searching the backstage area, even though I'd asked her to wait. And if I knew my mother, she was investigating whether the Galliano had spa services. Nevertheless, I made a show of scanning the guests, who were mostly retirees. And judging from their canes and walkers, they didn't look like they'd be do-si-doing to karaoke. "You're right. I don't see them, but I'm sure they're on their way. There's no way they'd miss all of this fun order and discipline."

The chains on her glasses shook. "I run a tight steamship, missy. If they're not on deck in five minutes, they're off the boat."

"Really?" For the first time since Nick's murder, I broke into a smile. "Awesome."

Ruth raised the bullhorn. "Move those tootsies, *now*."

Against their will, my tootsies entered the casino. As I passed the gaming tables, I wondered whether Cruisin' Ruth had scheduled time among all her fun to let the guests actually use them.

The dining hall door swung open, and Marian emerged, clipping a nametag to her pale green cardigan. "Shouldn't you be going the other way?"

"Oh, uh. Right." I couldn't tell her about my family, so I happily abandoned the search. It was no skin off my aching back if Ruth shipped them back to shore. In fact, it would probably save my skin *and* aching back if they went home.

I followed Marian to the main deck and lined up beside her.

Sullivan stood by the gangplank in dark sunglasses, a black windbreaker, and matching slacks. He looked the part of a security guard impassively observing the scene. But I knew he was on the Galliano for another reason.

To get me, somehow.

What I didn't know was whether Gigi Scalino was on the steamboat too. The Bit-O-Honey wrapper could've been dropped by a guest. But if not, I feared the worst. If The G-Man had come onboard so soon after having his appendix removed, it was to take someone out, and possibly Luigi.

A frigid gust of wind blew across the deck, and I crossed my arms for warmth—and self-comfort.

Marian buttoned her cardigan. "A cold front's coming in." She pressed her lips as tight as her bun. "I hope that maniac cruise director doesn't keep us out here too long. Otherwise, we'll all be covered in frost like Nick."

I shivered, more from analogy than the chill.

"Franki, baby!"

I cringed as Bruno sidled up beside me and pressed his hip against mine.

"You look cold, doll." He tilted his head toward my ear. "When you're off duty, I can keep you warm."

As could a shot of whiskey, which I was in desperate need of.

"Between you and me," he whispered, "I got some beer from my concession stand in my cabin."

I would almost rather drink French Quarter floodwater, but his concession stand gave me an idea. "Did you happen to bring any Bit-O-Honey on the boat?"

"No, but I brought plenty o' peanuts." He reached into his pocket. "And I found this Butterfinger outside my stateroom."

It must've been the one I dropped when my Nonna purse-whacked me.

He widened his eyes and his nostrils. "I can't believe whoever dropped it didn't pick it up. You should see the candy prices in that gift shop upstairs. And I say that as a concession-stand man."

*The gift shop.* If Marian sold Bit-O-Honey, then whoever dropped that wrapper could have bought it onboard. I turned to ask her, but she was gone, probably driven away by Bruno's charm, and in her place stood Ruth, tapping the toe of her Keds.

"I ask you to do one thing, and instead I find you makin' a play for a new man."

Bruno beamed, and I glowered. I worked hard to constantly remind him that he wasn't Bradley's replacement, so I didn't need Cruisin' Ruth to put the promise of sex into his head.

She jerked the bill of her sun visor. "If you don't find our missing guests ASAP, I'll inform the captain that you volunteered to run a five a.m. Zumba class tomorrow."

I was caught between the devil and the deep blue sea—or

rather, the deep brown river. But if I had to choose between being on the boat with my family and early morning exercise, I'd opt for the former because I could avoid them.

"Be back in ten." I dashed through the casino and up the grand staircase. But before I looked for my mom and nonna, I planned to make a pitstop at the gift shop.

The door was closed but unlocked. The creepy krakens seemed to watch me from a shelf above the wall of books as I checked the candy selection at the counter.

No Bit-O-Honey.

I turned to see if I'd overlooked any other candy displays, and I toppled a stack of Steamboat Galliano hat pins in packages by the cash register. I picked them up and looked behind the counter to see if I'd missed one. Sure enough, I had. I reached for the package.

But I retracted my hand.

On the floor next to a shelf labeled "New Orleans History: Mafia" lay a Bit-O-Honey wrapper.

No doubt about it. Gigi Scalino, notorious mob boss and sicko who was into shoe stripteases from strippers, was on the Galliano.

~

"MAKE LIKE A SHRIMP COCKTAIL AND CHILL," I said to my reflection in the cabin bathroom mirror. "You've investigated plenty of dangerous homicides, so you've got this. Besides, there's safety in numbers, and especially after Cruisin' Ruth's fun safety drill."

But my advice had no effect. As I pulled my blow-dried hair into a ponytail, my fingers looked like the shrimp I'd peeled and shook like the crawdads Pat had boiled. Dinner had been served and dessert had been delayed, which meant the drug deal was about to go down. And with Gigi Scalino onboard, more crime would follow.

As in cold-blooded murder.

I swallowed and adjusted my black turtleneck. It was seven p.m., so I had an hour and a half to look for a secret room behind the library before returning to the galley to serve the Bananas Foster. I also needed to be on the main deck when the steamboat stopped to pick up the Galliano, i.e., deliver the gold bars.

I grabbed my key and phone and exited the cabin. Darkness had descended, as had the cold front. And the night air reeked of the same swamp smell that I'd just showered off after my shift and smoke from the smokestack. As I walked the length of the Texas deck, I checked for the usual suspects, Sullivan, the thug, Gigi Scalino—and Bruno, who was a born-and-bred lurker.

The pilothouse glowed like a beacon at the bow of the boat. Tim was at the helm in place of the captain, who'd gone to dine and mingle with the guests until dessert and Glenda's performance at nine o'clock.

I took a stairwell to the cabin deck. A man was reading in the library, so I couldn't search for Luigi. I made a detour down the grand staircase, keeping an eye out for Cruisin' Ruth. She'd give me another oar whacking if she caught me on the fancy steps.

Kate was alone at the bar adding ice to a row of Harvey Wallbangers, so I went to check in. "Hey." I climbed onto a barstool. "Where's Wendell?"

She angled her eyelids. "Doing a dress rehearsal with Ms. Lamour in her stateroom."

"Yikes." I felt kind of bad for the guy. It took courage for a man to be alone with Glenda, and he didn't have much of that. "What's his role in the show? The interviewer?"

"They're doing an adaptation of the Sophia Loren thing.

Instead of answering audience questions, Wendell's going to play his trombone while Glenda recites lines from her memoir."

"Sounds like a bad beatnik trip."

"Yeah. Not sorry I have to stay at the bar." She stabbed a cherry with a drink sword. "What's our chef up to?"

I shrugged. "He sat in his office the entire day while Pat and I did all the work. I literally never saw him."

"Gigi hasn't shown his face, either. But his thug, Scarface, went into the dining hall forty-five minutes ago."

Around the time I went to shower. "I'm sure he went to meet with Alfredo about the drug deal. What about Sullivan?"

"He slipped out at least an hour ago, but I haven't been able to leave the casino to look for him. These gamblers are really guzzling the booze."

"I'm on it." I slid off the barstool.

"Stop right there, missy." Ruth rushed me in a dress that looked like Judge Judy's court robe—black with a white lace collar—and a pair of heels so modest that a nun wouldn't have worn them. "Kate, pour me a shot of Galliano. I need a good herbal tonic to calm my nerves."

My chin dipped. "Herbal tonic?"

"Sure. It's all saffron and anise and stuff." She swigged from the glass. "I tell you, between that godawful gift shop harpy and your mom and nonna, I'm tempted to drop anchor and call it a cruise."

"What are you talking about?"

Kate gave me a wry look. "She's just worked up because Marian do-si-doed with Captain Vandergrift in a red square-dancing dress with pettipants."

I was shocked. I didn't know Marian had a flashy side—or that pettipants were a thing.

"It was shameful," Ruth hissed. "And apparently, you came by your man-eating ways honestly. Just look at your women."

My gaze followed her finger to a roulette wheel by the casino entrance.

And I grabbed a Harvey Wallbanger and tossed it back.

My women, as Ruth called them, were flirting with the captain in what had to be accessories from Glenda's costume closet—a black feather headpiece on my nonna, and on my mom, a money boa.

I didn't dare approach them while they were with the captain because I had to remain undercover—and because I didn't want to be seen with them in those outfits. "Ruth, I need you to hang in there a little longer while I look for Sullivan. Keep an eye on them, all right?"

"I've been hanging in there so long that I haven't had time to look for the damn gold." She hiccupped. "I mean, Luigi."

That was the herbs talking, and they didn't lie.

I entered the empty dining hall, thankful the square dancing was over, and ditto for the karaoke. The list of people who'd sung about the Mississippi had turned out to be as long as the river and just as twisted—from Conway Twitty to Kid Rock.

Glenda poked her head through the stage curtains. "There you are, Miss Franki. I was looking for you earlier to help me get into my dress."

"Oh." I really wanted to avoid the next question, but I was trapped. "Do you still need help?"

"Hit it, Mr. Wendell."

The curtains opened.

And I choked on some spit.

Wendell, who looked a bit peaked, averted his eyes to his trombone.

"Well?" Glenda prompted. "How do I look?"

Her dress, if one could call it that, consisted of a clear crystal mermaid skirt, a see-through plastic bowl that encapsulated the torso, and pasties shaped like bubbles. Instead of the diplomatic approach, I opted for a descriptive tack. "Like a champagne glass with half a woman inside."

She beamed, positively effervescent. "Marvelous, sugar. Now, I've been practicing my grand entrance, but for some reason, I can't seem to get my sea legs."

I blamed the six-inch stripper heels under her skirt/stem. "In that glass, no one will notice," I said. "But did you happen to see Sullivan pass through?"

"No, but your mom and nonna were backstage a little while ago. They couldn't find any sign of Luigi."

"I'm not surprised."

"If I were you, I'd try the galley, though. I heard noises in there when I was looking for you. I opened the door, but the lights were off. I got so spooked, I about jumped out of my clothes."

I didn't comment. It was too easy.

Wendell rubbed his head and looked at me. "You think it was dat detective? Or Mr. Pescatore?"

It didn't seem likely that Alfredo would hide Luigi in such a high-traffic area. "It was probably Sullivan, but I could use some backup while I check it out."

He exhaled a long stream of air, as though blowing his trombone, and came down the stage steps like he was going to meet Baron Samedi.

Given his reluctance, I led the way into the galley, switched on the light, and scanned the room. It was exactly as Pat and I had left it an hour before, pristine and reeking of ammonia. I looked over my shoulder at Wendell, who held his trombone like a bat. "Let's try the back."

He wiped sweat from his forehead. "I'll go first."

I was touched that he would offer to protect me. "Thanks, but"—I patted my hip—"I've got a gun."

"Then by all means,"—he gestured to the hall—"ladies first."

I nodded, and we crept down the narrow hallway to the pantry. I reached for the door handle.

His eyes popped. "Do we have to?"

I nodded and put my finger to my lips. Then I moved one hand to my gun and pulled the door open with the other.

A faint light came through the porthole.

The pantry was empty.

Wendell blew out another breath, and I continued to the walk-in. I stopped breathing as I peered around the corner to Alfredo's office.

It was empty too.

I exhaled like Wendell. "It's clear."

His eyes upturned, and he passed his hand over his face, pulling down his lips. "Miss Glenda musta been hearin' thangs."

"Yeah, this boat's old and creaky." I took a look at Alfredo's desk, and on my way out, I yanked open the walk-in.

Wendell's trombone hit the tile and rolled.

And so did Wendell.

I knelt and patted his cheek while I looked up at Alfredo and struggled not to pass out myself.

In a scene straight from the movie *Goodfellas*, he hung by the back of his shirt from a meat hook. Like Nick Pescatore, he had frost on his face, but he wasn't holding a playing card. Still, the symbolism was clear—a mob hit.

I glanced around the walk-in, woozy with shock. I had to keep my wits about me to look for evidence that would point to his killer. But all I could see were the lemons.

And the thug, who hung from a hook behind the chef.

## 20

A s I gaped at the bodies of Alfredo and the thug in the walk-in, I felt cold and lightheaded as though I were suspended from a meat hook alongside them. Their murders had effectively killed everything I thought I knew about Nick Pescatore's case, and all I had left were questions that left me in a chilling state of limbo.

*Had Gigi Scalino come on the Galliano to whack his own brother?* Not even Michael Corleone had shown that much cruelty in *The Godfather*. He had his men kill his brother Fredo, which could have been what the thug had come onboard to do. But if so, who'd whacked the thug? And did this mean Alfredo hadn't killed Nick?

Clenching and unclenching my fists to keep from keeling over like Wendell, I entered the walk-in. There were no signs of trauma on the front of the men's bodies, but when I examined them from behind the cause of death was clear—their skulls had been crushed. The thug didn't have frost on his face like Alfredo, but that was because he'd been alive within the past hour. Alfredo had been killed much earlier, which explained why I hadn't seen him all day.

I had to feel for the thug's pulse, but I sure didn't want to. My hand inched toward his wrist, and bile churned in my gut like the river below the Galliano. I was as grossed out as if I were about to touch Pat's phlegm rag. It took a few seconds, but my fingers finally landed.

His wrist was warm.

And it moved.

I let out a scream that could be heard downriver, even though I knew I'd caused the movement, and fell into a crate of lemons. Juice oozed through the seat of my jeans, a bitter reminder that no matter how bad things were, there could always be a lemon lurking that would make things worse.

I heard a groan and a thud in the office, and my body went from cold to deep freeze.

*Had Wendell been whacked too?*

I pushed myself from the crate and peered with my gun aimed outside the walk-in door.

And I relaxed.

Wendell had moved, which meant he'd come to and fainted again.

I went back inside the walk-in and checked for the thug's pulse. He hadn't survived the skull fracture.

With a shudder, I slid my gun into my waistband and sent a text alerting Ruth and Kate to the murders. Then I left the walk-in and tried again to revive Wendell, but he was out cold— almost to the extent of Alfredo and the thug. I rose to check the galley first aid kit for smelling salts.

And I saw Pat.

She blocked the hallway, her eye twitch going ten miles an hour, like the steamboat.

*Had I been wrong about her innocence?*

"You're the murderer."

*Evidently not.* "No, Pat, I found them dead a few minutes ago."

"You're a big 'un. You killed 'em and hung 'em up like sides o' beef." She turned and limp-loped up the hall.

"I'm not big, I'm tall," I protested, following after her, "and my size doesn't make me a murderer. I'm a PI, and I was hired to investigate Nick's death. Wait till Wendell wakes up. He'll tell—"

My mouth clamped shut when I entered the galley.

Pat was behind the island, wielding a chef's knife. "I could tell there was somethin' shifty about you the day you started this gig."

This from a woman who looked like the Sea Hag and walked like Igor from *Frankenstein*. "That's probably because I was undercover."

"Yeah. An undercover assassin."

I raised my hands and approached the island. "Pat—"

She raised the knife. "One more step, and I'll carve out your heart and liver and make boudin outta ya."

*That was unnecessarily graphic.* "Try it. I'm packing a Ruger."

"So you *are* a killer."

"I carry a weapon to protect myself." I heard a noise behind me and glanced over my shoulder, hoping Wendell had regained consciousness.

"*Pour le Roi et pour la France!*"

I turned as Pat charged with her raised knife. I ran to the opposite side of the island, wondering why she'd shouted about the King and France. "What are you yelling?"

"My ancestors were Bourbon monarchists who helped defeat Napoleon. That was their battle cry."

"Yeah, well, the king is dead, and that French won't work on an Italian-American."

She growled a *hmphf* worthy of the Sea Hag herself. "Because you're a dirty mobster."

"Don't confuse me with Alfredo and Gigi."

Her eye twitched. "There you go trashin' the Scalinos again." She rotated the knife. "Keep it up, and I'll cut out your spine for a nice backbone stew."

Pat might not have killed anyone on the Galliano, but I was starting to think she was a female Hannibal Lecter in her free time.

We sized each other up across the island.

She hunkered into a linebacker position and growled.

When she'd lost her uterus, her testicles must've dropped. It would be a tough fight, but if I could get my arms around her barrel chest, I was sure I could subdue her without firing a shot. But all bets were off if I ran into that phlegm rag.

Her eyebrow cocked as though she'd heard my thoughts, and she darted along the side of the island.

The galley door opened, and before Pat could turn the corner, Kate rushed in and delivered a hip check that knocked her into the supply rack and sent the chef's knife skidding.

Kate stooped to retrieve the weapon. "As we say in roller derby, 'Win some, bruise some.'"

I stepped from behind the island. "Nice hip work."

"Thanks. When I was training to make my team, I practiced on Danny in his Dancing Hand Grenade costume."

I wished I'd been there to see the green drink go down.

Pat pulled herself from the supply rack and touched her teeth to see if she'd lost another. "What're you gonna do to me?"

Kate shrugged. "Franki?"

I eyed the Sea Hag. "First you're going to answer some questions. And remember, Kate's got your knife, and I've got a gun, so don't try to BS us."

"What do you want to know?"

"Whether you've been withholding information about any of the murders or the drugs."

Her eyes met mine, and they didn't twitch. "Chef Scalino never said nothin' to me that wasn't an order."

*Another reason to adore him.* "What about Nick's uncle, Luigi Pescatore? Alfredo was holding him hostage onboard. Do you know where?"

She rubbed her thighs. "The chef had me make meals for someone, but I don't know if it was him."

Kate shook the knife. "Who delivered the meals?"

"Gerald."

*Was she talking about a passenger?* "Who's Gerald?"

"The dead guy hanging behind the chef in the walk-in."

He had to be Irish. No Italian mobster would give his son a name like that. "What about Detective Sullivan? Have you seen him with Alfredo or Gerald?"

She shook her head. "I ain't seen them together, no."

Kate ran a hand through her short hair. "This is going nowhere. What should we do with her?"

I narrowed my eyes at Pat. "We'll lock her in the pantry for the night. We can't trust her given her blind loyalty to the Scalinos." And my army wasn't so ragtag that we'd take a woman with a rag soaked in phlegm. "I'll take care of her if you help Wendell. He fainted by the walk-in when he saw the bodies. But first, put away that knife, or he's likely to go down again."

Kate returned the knife to the block, and she strode into the hallway.

I drew my gun and ushered Pat to the pantry, keeping at least a foot between me and the rag. She entered without a struggle, and I locked the door and returned to the galley to keep watch for the killer until Kate and Wendell were ready to leave. While I waited, I pulled out my phone to search for a number for the coast guard.

*Veronica Maggio* appeared on the display. "Finally." I tapped

Answer before it even rang. "Veronica, you're not going to believe—"

"Franki, can you hear me?"

"Yes, can you hear *me*?"

"Barely. I've been calling to tell you—"

The line went dead.

"Seriously?" I tapped her number, but it didn't ring. I sent a text and got a *Not Delivered* message.

Kate led a grimacing Wendell and his trombone into the galley.

I couldn't tell if he was in pain or embarrassed. "Why don't you go to your cabin and lie down?"

His eyes threatened to blast from their orbits. "By myself? Uh-uh. Not on this boat I won't."

Kate looked at me. "Do you think we should tell the passengers to go to their rooms?"

"We'd have to tell them about the murders, and pandemonium could break out."

"An' dis is Loosiana." Wendell raised his trombone. "People got guns."

Kate chewed her lip. "But if we don't warn them, innocent people could get killed."

I leaned against the island. "This is a Mafia thing. They typically only kill each other."

"Are you sure about that? The detective could have done this."

I gazed at the floor. Sullivan was a snake, but I didn't think he was a killer—at least, not yet. "All I know is there's safety in numbers. So why don't you guys go back to the casino and try to keep the passengers there? Offer door prizes every half hour or something like that."

Wendell scratched his brow. "What about Miss Glenda's performance?"

"I'll tell her it's canceled."

His cheeks ballooned as he blew out a breath and wiped his forehead.

I shared his relief. We both knew that Glenda's stories were best left in her memoir. "I'm going to the pilothouse to tell Tim the jig is up, so he's got to stop the boat. And at some point, I've got to look for Luigi. Time's running out to find him. That reminds me, do either of you have cell service?"

They reached into their pants pockets.

"Dang, brah." Wendell held up a shattered screen. "I done smashed my phone when I fell."

"And I have zero signal bars," Kate said. "They've been coming and going."

"Same here." I glanced at my phone. "When your service comes back, call the Coast Guard and let them know we need help."

"Got it."

We headed to the door.

And it flew open.

Ruth emerged, swaying like the chains on her glasses—proof that Galliano wasn't herbal tonic but just plain tonic, like the kind Granny distilled in *The Beverly Hillbillies*.

She lowered her chin, and her eyes lasered in on Wendell and Kate. "I shoulda known thiss one's sslacker ways"—she jerked a thumb at me but hiccupped and knocked it off course—"would rub off on you two." She grabbed the door jamb to steady herself. "But with all these murders, iss not the time to ssway around."

"It sure isn't." My tone was as dry as her last shot glass. "Where's the captain?"

"Thass what I came to tell you." She let go of the doorjamb to gesture but latched onto it again. "I tol' him about the murders, and he locked himself in the pilothouse."

Kate took a step forward. "What? Where's Tim?"

"He's sstill in there. The captain tied him up. Ssaid this gamblin' cruise'll go on come hell or high liquor."

Of course she meant *water*, but I couldn't waste time correcting her. "I'm on my way to the pilothouse. Kate, Wendell, you guys get to the casino. And brace yourselves. Even though we're only going ten miles an hour, it's going to be a wild ride."

~

"But, Miss Franki. We can't cancel my debut speaking engagement. The guests came on the Galliano to hear my story."

They came onboard to gamble, but there was no reason to point that out. "I hate to burst your, uh,"—I cast a glance at her pasties—"bubbles, but something I'd rather keep quiet has happened, and we need everyone together in one place. So please go find my mom and Nonna in the casino and stay with them."

She gave her platinum Cher hair a flip. "I'm sorry, sugar, but this glass act will go on."

With Luigi's life on the line, I didn't have time to argue or deal with any puns. "There have been two more murders onboard." I pointed to the door. "So get your glass to the casino *now*."

At the mention of murder, Glenda got her sea legs and split.

I ran up the mid-ship stairs, my mind firing questions like bullets from my Ruger.

*Who was behind the murders?*

*Gigi Scalino? The captain? Tim?*

*And what was Sullivan's role in all of this?*

*What about Luigi? Was he still alive?*

*If so, could I crack the case before his and other lives were lost?*

At the top of the stairwell, I pulled my Ruger from my waistband and threw open the door to the Texas deck. Franki Rockford was gone, and Franki Amato was onboard. The killer had to reckon with me.

A ragtag army of one.

The smell of rain was in the air, and clouds had obscured the stars. But the light from the pilothouse illuminated my path.

I crept along the deck on high alert. Gigi or Sullivan could have been lying in wait to exact their revenge—Gigi for the winepress Luigi had given me, and Sullivan for the humiliation he'd suffered when I'd solved his case. And there was always the possibility that Boozin' Ruth was on the prowl with that oar.

I reached the pilothouse and crouched beneath a window in the door. Little flecks of ash rained from the smokestack, and the occasional spark. The Galliano was all kinds of dangerous.

Slowly, I rose and looked through the window. Captain Vandergrift stood at the old wooden ship wheel, a ghostly vision in white, gazing with admiration at his beloved Mississippi River, and seemingly indifferent to the gore below deck. Tim was on the floor beside him, bound and gagged. His brow formed a scowl as he worked the rope around his wrists. He was probably calculating all the money he'd lose on the drug deal if the captain didn't stop the boat.

Tim lowered his head, revealing a trickle of blood. He'd been struck with some sort of object like Alfredo and Gerald the thug. It was time to stop the madness and the steamboat. I rose and pounded on the door. "Captain, you need to dock in the next town."

He turned and waved me away. "Get back to the galley, girl, you have dessert to serve."

"First of all, don't call me *girl*. I'm almost thirty-o—" No matter how dire the situation, there was no need to get ahead of the birthdays. I was thirty for eight more days. "And second, with the chef and another man dead, the Bananas Foster isn't going to happen."

"There's nary a thing we can do for those louts now. They'll keep in the walk-in till we dock in the morn. So I trust you and Pat will see to our guests." He returned to the wheel, and a trance-like look came over his eyes as he stared at the Mississippi.

Captain Vandergrift had never been cleared of the murder of his business partner, and he'd confessed to Bradley that he'd pushed Nick off the deck, not to mention threatening to give him "the cold shivers." I had to know whether he'd committed the other murders. "Did you hit Alfredo and Gerald over the back of the head like you did Tim?"

Tim's head jerked toward the captain. He was afraid, which told me he had no idea who'd killed the men.

The captain approached the window. "What the dickens are you prattling on about? I'm not some rogue miscreant who bought this steamer to commit malfeasance. The Galliano has a storied history, and she belongs on the river, as do I. I bought her to sail, and sail her I shall."

I believed him. If he'd killed Alfredo and Gerald, then he would've killed Tim as well. Also, he'd broken his own order by betraying Twain with that Dickens-inspired expression, so he must've been genuinely shocked and appalled by my question.

The only thing to do was find Ruth and have her ask him to stop the steamboat. She seemed to have influence over him—or hold sway, as it were—for some unfathomable reason. And because of Tim's involvement in the drugs, he was best left tied up with the captain until the ship docked and the authorities came onboard.

I figured Ruth was probably at the bar or a bingo table, but I ran to our crew cabin just in case. I opened the door to the sound of court TV.

*Was she asleep?*

I switched off the DVR player by the bunks and froze.

A yellow rose lay on my pillow.

*Was Sullivan in our cabin?*

I raised my gun and kicked open the door to the bathroom.

Luckily for him, he wasn't inside.

I shoved my gun into my waistband and glared at the top bunk. Ruth was up there, but she was out and still wearing her horn-rims and her Judge Judy dress.

"Ruth." I gave her a shake.

She rolled to face the wall. "I need ssome shut-eye."

"This is no time for shut-eye, Popeye." I shook her harder. "You're the cruise director, and passenger lives are at stake."

"What doess he ssee in that harpy?"

I knew who she was talking about, but I wanted to engage her in conversation to wake her up. "Who? The captain?"

"He ssays Marian has perssonality. Know what I ssay to that?"

"No, what?"

"Whatever floatss your ssteamboat." She raised her arm and made a pulling motion. "*Toot toot.*"

I widened my eyes. Cruisin' Ruth was really crocked. I had to say something that would snap her sober. "I'm not sure how this has escaped your horn-rims, but you and Marian Guidry look and act so similar that you must be twins separated at birth."

She rose up like a zombie from a grave. "I'm gonna tell Bradley to ssue you on *Couples Court* sso I can tape that episode."

I recoiled, and she flopped onto her back and snored.

Someone knocked on our cabin door.

I pulled my gun. "Who is it?"

"Bruno. Your knight in shining armor."

*More like a nuisance in shining gold chains.* I opened the door, but he missed my glare.

His roving eyes went from my breasts to my Ruger—and lit up like the pilot house. "I came to take you for that drink and shrimp cocktail, but I'm down for staying in and playing bad cop."

"Of course you're down—*low down*." I closed the door, but he got a leg in first. Nevertheless, I pushed.

"Hold on, baby." His voice was strained as he worked his arm into the opening. "What about our date?"

"There won't be a date. Two men have been killed in the galley, so I need you to—"

His arm and leg slipped from the cabin, and his feet pounded the deck.

*And I was just about to ask the coward to watch over my mom, Nonna, and Glenda.*

I closed and locked the door and pulled out my phone. Still no signal. With any luck, Kate had gotten her cell service back and called for help. Otherwise, we'd be on this boat for another twelve hours, and I didn't want to think of how many others could die in that time.

I sat on my bunk and put my face in my hands. *What if I couldn't solve the case?* The Mafia and a corrupt cop were involved, so I was in trouble as deep as the Mississippi River. Plus, I didn't always have the best track record when it came to figuring things out. Bradley was a perfect example. I couldn't save our relationship even with an army of God-fearing nonne and the lemon tradition on my side.

Ruth turned over, shaking the bunk. "It'ss time for your ssentence, Marian."

The justice-dispensing portion of the evening was my cue to get a grip and look for Luigi. If I could find him, he could probably tell me who killed his nephew. And then maybe he could talk some sense into the captain.

I went to the door and reached for the knob.

"To the hoossegow for you, harpy, till hell freezess over."

My arm dropped to my side.

*Freezes.*

*What was it Marian had said during the safety drill?*

A horrific scream interrupted my thoughts.

Then a splat.

It was a man, and obviously not the sailor ghost.

But it wasn't a recording, either.

Someone had fallen into the paddlewheel.

Or they'd been pushed.

I opened the cabin door and aimed my gun. The deck was clear, so I tiptoed toward the bow, wishing the light from the pilot house extended the length of the boat.

The temperature had dropped, and my breath came out in frozen bursts that I feared would out me to the killer. As I passed the captain's quarters, the wood beneath my foot gave a loud creak.

I stopped and listened for movement.

All I could hear was the splashing of the paddlewheel.

I resumed my approach and made it to the end of the captain's quarters. I took a breath and extended my shooting arm and eye around the corner.

A figure in a dark, hooded jacket stood in front of the calliope, peering over the rail at the paddlewheel.

"Hands in the air, or I'll shoot."

The figure turned, removed the hood, and flashed a reptile smile.

Sullivan.

## 21

"Man overboard!" I kept my gun aimed at Sullivan's chest while I waited for Captain Vandergrift to stop the Galliano.

But the hell-bound voyage continued.

Either the captain had ignored me, or we were on a runaway steamboat. I took a step toward Sullivan. "Did you push the captain overboard? Or was it Tim?"

"You don't actually believe I did that." He lowered his hands.

I pulled the trigger, and a bullet blew past his head.

His hands shot up, and he went as white as one of the Galliano's ghosts.

It was the first time I'd seen him scared, and if I'd been sure the boat had a captain, I might have shot at him again for fun. "Answer me, Sullivan. We have a steamboat full of passengers, including my family and friends."

"The captain's in the pilothouse. I saw him when I came up the stairwell."

"So it was Tim."

"I don't know who the hell it was." His shock had turned to anger. "I came to find out, like you."

I knew better than to listen to his forked tongue. I motioned with the gun. "Back up."

"Oh, for Chri—"

"Back. Up. Or this time I shoot a leg."

He swore under his breath and moved backwards.

I waited until he was past the calliope and looked over the back of the boat. The paddlewheel turned, and I didn't see anyone around it. I remembered the blood on Tim's head and shuddered. "Tim's probably gator food by now. That was the plan, wasn't it?"

His nostrils flared. "I've been locked in an unmarked room backstage for the past two hours. I assumed you knew."

"Why would I know that?"

"Because your nonna clocked me with her handbag, and your mother tied me up with a money boa."

"You expect me to believe—" I stopped before I embarrassed myself. Anyone who'd met my mom and nonna knew they were more than capable of taking out the detective, and probably the entire police force.

"I can tell by the look on your face that you believe me, Amato, so why don't you put the gun down and help me investigate what happened? For old time's sake."

I stayed silent and kept the gun trained on his chest. He was playing the nostalgia card, but I wasn't fool enough to fall for his bluff. And the money boa was a convincing detail, but he could've seen my mother wearing it in the casino and fabricated the locked-in-a-room story.

A corner of his mouth rose. "You come from strong women. If things had been different, you and I could've done great things together."

This time I replied—by refocusing my aim on his head. "Were you in the walk-in when Alfredo and his thug were murdered?"

His chin jutted forward. "Have the ghosts on this boat gotten you spooked, or something? Because the Franki I know would never suspect me of killing anyone."

"You don't know me at all. And clearly, I don't know you either. But from what I've figured out, you're involved with the gold bars somehow. Is that why you pushed Tim into the river? So he could never testify against you?"

He stared into my eyes and pulled a wounded look. "I know I've given you reason to suspect the worst of me, especially after the way I behaved about that case last October, but I didn't push anyone off this boat."

I gave a bitter laugh. "Setting up Bradley on a bogus drug trafficking charge doesn't warrant a mention?"

"It's your boyfriend who doesn't warrant the mention. Face it, Amato. He's a lemon."

His choice of fruit stung like citric acid on a wound, and I was certain that had been his intention. "He's the finest man I've ever met, which is why you arrested him. You couldn't have me as your booty call, and it galled you to see me with a real man since you could never be one yourself."

He laughed and lowered his head. "I see how it is. A man who quits his job to spend time with a woman is a *real man*." He snorted. "I'll bet that real man didn't even remember that you've got a birthday coming up."

The citric-acid sting turned burn.

"It's March twelfth," a voice replied.

One I thought I'd never hear again. I turned.

"Franki, look out!" Bradley darted from around the corner, as Sullivan kicked the gun from my hand.

The Ruger slid toward the calliope.

I lunged and crashed on the deck at the same time as Sullivan and Bradley. Through a tangle of arms and legs, I spotted the gun a few feet ahead. Each of us slapped and shoved and elbowed as we tried to gain ground. Bradley was the closest to the weapon, so I latched onto Sullivan's leg to hold him back and pulled a Nonna—I bit him.

He writhed like the snake he was and jammed the butt of his hand into my nose.

A crack echoed in my ears. I cried out as pain pierced my brain.

Bradley turned to check on me.

And Sullivan grabbed the gun.

He scrambled to his feet and aimed at us. "Get up, and back against the calliope."

I wiped my throbbing nose, and blood wet my fingers. With Bradley's help, I got to my feet and leaned against the instrument, pressing the backs of my thighs into the keyboard for support.

"You hit her on purpose, you bastard." Bradley's voice was as taut as his fists. "She needs a doctor, something to stop the bleeding."

"Ever the gentleman, eh, Bradley? By the way, those yellow roses were a sweet touch. Too bad Franki thought they were from me."

The butt of his hand might as well have jammed into my stomach, and I was certain Bradley had felt the same gut punch.

Sullivan moved the gun to Bradley. "Now to what do we owe the pleasure?"

I wanted to know myself. Veronica must've been calling to tell me he'd made bail, but I couldn't understand why he'd stayed hidden.

"I came to make sure you didn't lay a hand on Franki."

Sullivan chuckled. "Judging from the size of her nose, I'd say it's too late for that."

Numbness had spread to my brain, but what my head

couldn't feel was more than made up for by my heart, which pounded like a war drum.

"You're reprehensible." His gaze moved from Sullivan to me. "I also came to prove he's skimming drugs from evidence. The night I was arrested, I heard him downplay the amount the police confiscated from the walk-in when he was talking to his superior. He said they'd only found six bags, but when he was interrogating me, he told me that there were seven."

Sullivan's face was as hard as the metal of his gun.

I wiped my nose. Pat had told me there were six bags of drugs, so Sullivan must've slipped up when he was talking to Bradley.

Bradley's gaze returned to Sullivan. "And now he's on the boat pretending to be a security guard so he can steal a cut of the next deal too."

So I hadn't been his sole target. He was also after the gold bars.

"Look at you being an amateur sleuth," Sullivan drawled. "Too bad Franki's the last one who'll ever hear your theory."

My nose might've been swollen, but I could still smell trouble. "What are you talking about?"

"Well, I can't have your boyfriend telling the Mafia I stole their drugs, now can I, Amato? And since he just snitched to you, it's time for him to go to sleep with the fishes."

I swayed, both from pain and shock.

Bradley's eyes met mine, full of sadness and an apology.

One I couldn't accept because he'd done nothing wrong by confiding in me. "Don't add to your crimes, Sullivan. Stop while you're ahead, and turn yourself in."

His hand went to his abs, and he laughed. "No can do, Amato. You know my story. I've got two ex-wives to feed, and the money I'll make off the gold bars will get me early retirement and a fishing boat I've had my eye on."

I swayed backwards and braced myself on the calliope keys.

And a thought occurred to me.

"Now Bradley, old boy," Sullivan gestured to the railing, "normally I would say ladies first, but I'd like a little time alone with your woman after you're gone."

Bradley growled and lurched forward.

And I grabbed the back of his jacket. "Don't fall into his trap. He wants to goad you into hitting him so he can plead self-defense."

Bradley slumped, and I moved my hands behind me and pressed the calliope keys. "How are you going to explain his death to your colleagues?"

"Being the decent guy he is, he jumped overboard to try to valiantly save our dear Tim."

My stomach heaved, but I continued to press the keys.

"Let's go, Bradley. Otherwise, I'll have to shoot Franki while you watch."

Bradley moved to the rail. He turned, and his eyes sought mine. They glowed in the pitch black—with love.

My tears could have flooded the river. "I love you."

"I love you too." He put one leg over the rail.

I sobbed and pressed the keys, frantic.

Bradley sat on the rail and pulled his other leg over.

I ran my fingers over the keys like Jerry Lee Lewis.

Then I heard a scream.

And a splat.

Sullivan's mouth opened in shock, and I rushed him like a longhorn at a roundup.

He and my Ruger went over the rail.

I waited until I heard him splash.

Horror rose up in my throat like ash from the smokestack.

But I didn't yell *man overboard*.

"How did you make that scream and wet splat sound happen?"

I raised my head from Bradley's chest and looked at the calliope. "It's supposed to be a recording of the ghost of a sailor who fell to his death on the paddlewheel. The switch was one of the keys."

"Quick thinking, as always." He gazed into my eyes with the same love I'd seen before he climbed onto the rail. "You literally saved our lives."

I returned my head to his chest but turned to face the river, half-expecting Sullivan to rise up like a kraken and take us in his tentacles down to the murky bottom. And even though I knew that was impossible, I felt no relief. Sullivan had met his end at my hand, and that would stay with me for a long time.

Bradley kissed my hair. "Veronica said you thought I blamed you for my arrest. But I didn't. I just wanted you to confide in me."

Tears clouded my vision. "I will from now on. I promise."

He squeezed me and rubbed my back. "I knew Sullivan was bad news the first time I met him, but I never would have thought he was a killer."

"He was about to kill us, but he wasn't responsible for the murders on the Galliano. That was Marian Guidry."

He pulled away. "The gift shop lady who looks like Ruth?"

"The one and, I hope, only. Marian is Gigi Scalino's consigliera."

"And she whacked his brother?"

I nodded and pulled out my phone. Finally, I had a faint signal. "Gigi is about to retire in Sicily, and we all know what happens when Mafia bosses retire."

"A power struggle for control of the family."

"Precisely." I typed a group text.

"What are you doing?"

"Alerting staff to what just happened with Sullivan." I tapped the send arrow and pocketed my phone. "Alfredo made a fatal mistake when he started dealing drugs behind Gigi's back."

"So Gigi looked the other way when Marian killed him?"

"Yeah, only she had his thug do the actual killing, and then she whacked the thug. Now she's made her bones, to put it in mobster terms, which clears the way for her to become New Orleans' first female mob boss."

He grimaced. "Well, if she's anything like Ruth when she was my secretary, she could run this town."

Based on Ruth's cruise director stint, I had my doubts about that.

Bradley stared at the river. "What about Nick? Why'd Marian kill him?"

"Alfredo did that." I followed his gaze, wondering whether he was looking for Sullivan, like me. "Nick came to the Galliano to get some money the captain owed him, not realizing that Alfredo was on the boat in the guise of a chef. My guess is that before he and the captain had the fight that ended with him being thrown overboard, he tried to warn him about Alfredo by telling him that he used to deal drugs for him. So Alfredo fished him out of the river and finished him off in the freezer."

"Like he was a giant catfish."

I withheld comment. After my experience on Nick's case, my fried catfish days were over. "The only thing I haven't figured out is why Alfredo put a queen of spades card in Nick's hand." I shivered from the cold and ran my hands over my arms. "Anyway, we'd better go look for Luigi. Marian and Gigi are still onboard, so he's not out of danger."

Bradley reached for my hand, but I went to the railing and took one last look at the paddlewheel. I had a foreboding feeling, like Sullivan was clinging to the back of the boat, waiting to climb onboard and get his revenge.

A dull thwack sent tremors up my spine, like tiny kraken tentacles tickling my skin.

I knew Sullivan would come back.

I spun.

But it wasn't him.

It was Marian in a red square-dancing dress with pettipants, wielding the pistol she'd used to club Bradley.

MY GAZE DROPPED to Bradley's crumpled body as my heart dropped to the Texas deck.

*Had Marian crushed his skull like Alfredo's and the thug's?*

"Hand over your cell phone."

I reached into my back pocket and complied.

She tossed it over the railing, ending my group texts, and with them, probably my life.

"Well, Miss Franki Rockford—"

"Amato," I corrected.

She sniffed. "You're a better PI than our not-so-trusty cruise director led me to believe. Incidentally, that playing card was my idea. I told Fredo it would implicate the captain, but I like to think of the queen of spades as me."

I gave her square-dancing dress the onceover. "An evil, petti-panted ruler who digs people's graves?"

Her eyes narrowed behind her red horn-rims. "In Cartomancy, she represents intelligence and practical judgement, something you and your boyfriend don't have."

"Leave Bradley out of this."

"I can't. You just involved him when you told him my plans to take over the Scalino family."

I knew what I'd promised Bradley, but if he and I survived the night, we *had* to stop confiding in one another.

"Too bad he came on the Galliano after he made bail. A man with sound judgement would have gone straight to his attorney to see about suing you on *Couples Court*."

If Marian wasn't Ruth's long-lost twin, she was at least her cousin. "So what's your practical plan for me?"

"You're walking the plank."

And I thought Ruth had used a metaphor when she'd threatened to make Sullivan walk the plank. "There's actually a plank? On a steamboat?"

She flipped a switch on the calliope, and a board emerged below the railing. "I had it installed at the same time as the sailor ghost recording. It's another deterrent for curious onlookers...and PIs."

Disappointment mixed with dread. The sailor ghost trick wouldn't work on Marian like it had Sullivan, and I didn't have anything else in my trick bag—except to hope that Bradley had survived the pistol whipping and woke up.

I gazed at him, lying on the deck. He didn't look like he was going to open his beautiful blue eyes again. But if he did, I'd be gone. The thought of losing him so soon after we'd been reunited was too much to bear. I threw back my head and screamed bloody murder for both of our lives.

Marian slapped me hard, hitting my nose.

I gasped and fell to my knees.

"You pull that again and I'll blow a hole through your throat. The captain's not going to stop the steamboat, and Cruisin' Ruth's not coming to your rescue. I saw to that when I slipped an Ambien into her Galliano."

*That's why Ruth was so out of it—a sleeping pill. Well, that and the booze.*

Marian smoothed her poofy skirt. "I did us both a favor by

taking care of that insufferable woman."

Given my track record with Ruth, she was probably right.

"All aboard." She waved the gun toward the plank.

I glared at her as I pulled myself to my feet and climbed onto the narrow board, thankful the Galliano traveled so slowly that I had a chance at maintaining my balance. "How are you going to explain all of these deaths?"

"I think they're fairly self-explanatory, don't you?"

I didn't have to ask what she meant. She could tell the police that Sullivan killed Tim to silence him, Gigi whacked Alfredo and the thug for betraying him, and I murdered Sullivan for framing and killing Bradley. Then, distraught over losing the love of my life, I jumped to my death.

"Start moving those tootsies."

I smirked at the Ruthism. Using my arms like a tight-rope walker, I took a couple of small steps, trying not to look at the river below.

"Keep going."

I swallowed and slid my feet along the plank. The only thing I could do to save myself was jump. People dived off nine-story cliffs all the time, so I ought to be able to handle a three-story steamboat, but I wasn't as confident about handling the alligators and water moccasins.

"That's not fast enough."

A bullet whizzed past my head.

My arms flailed.

And I fell.

I grasped at the air, hoping to catch hold of the plank. I landed belly-first onto the board and wrapped my arms around it—and heard a crack.

"I ssentenced you to prison." Ruth's voice rang out like a shot, or a judge in court.

Slowly, I raised my head and strained to look over my shoulder at the bow of the boat. And I couldn't believe my eyes.

Ruth held her lantern-weapon in one hand and gripped Marian's bun with the other. Marian still held her gun—and Ruth's bun. And the two women were twisting and turning in a square-dance move.

"Please don't break." Carefully, I turned around on the plank and slid toward the railing, keeping my head low to avoid any bullets.

Ruth and Marian were still locked in their square-dance battle, moving toward a corner of the boat.

Music blasted from the calliope.

I jerked, and the plank cracked again. But after everything I'd been through, I was damned if a possessed carnival instrument would steam-toot me to my death.

Using my feet, I catapulted myself forward. My hands clamped onto the rail like vice grips.

And the plank gave way.

I heard a crash as the board hit the paddlewheel and was plowed underwater.

Like that sailor long ago.

And Tim.

And Sullivan.

But not me.

With a strength I didn't know I had, I pulled myself on deck. Then I crouched and approached the square-dancing duo.

Their heads were pointed down, as they twisted one another's hair. But Marian spotted me and aimed her gun at the easiest target—Bradley, who lay not two feet from her.

"Okay. I give." I backed up and raised my hands.

"I sure as hell don't." Ruth gave Marian's bun a yank, pulling her aim off target.

I lunged and grabbed the gun, twisting Marian's hand like Ruth did her bun. "Ruth, back off. I've got this."

She showed no sign of hearing me over the creepy carnival music even though I was beside her. She raised her lantern like a weapon and struck Marian in the back of the head, exactly where Marian had hit Alfredo, the thug, and Bradley.

Glass shattered, spilling kerosene.

A flame emerged from Marian's bun, and her eyes went as wide as the ship's wheel as she suffered the fate of Agnes Frump.

The scream that came from her mouth was like none I'd ever heard—except for maybe my mother's when she'd learned her one shot at marrying off my nonna had been kidnapped.

I couldn't stand by and watch a human being burned to death, regardless of what that person had done. I pulled my turtleneck over my head and ran to Marian.

She ran to the railing—and hurled herself overboard.

She didn't make a sound on the way down.

Just a splash.

I rushed to the railing and scanned the black water.

But the Mississippi had swallowed her, as it had Tim and Sullivan. And almost Bradley and me.

I knelt beside Bradley but stared up at Ruth. "Why would you do that? I had it under control."

"I'm late for court, and I've got ssentences to hand down. The ssafety of this ssteamboat depends on me." She raised her broken lantern and walked away with a mechanical gait.

And I realized she'd been sleep-walking on Ambien the entire time.

## 22

"**O**pen your eyes, Bradley." I patted his hand instead of his cheek to avoid moving his injured head. "Please."

The moon had emerged from the clouds, and in the blue-white light he looked pale, ghostly.

And it was terrifying.

I looked behind me at the calliope, which had shut off as freakily as it had come on, and willed it to blast a spooky steam-whistle song to frighten him awake. I turned to caress his handsome face, and my tears dripped onto his cheeks. "You've got to wake up. You've just got to. I don't know what I'd do without you."

His eyelids spasmed.

And with them, my heart.

Slowly, they opened.

A tsunami of emotion swept over me.

He gazed at me with eyes the color of moonlight. "I don't remember agreeing to going camping."

*Okay, so he had a concussion.* "We're on the Galliano, remember?"

"The liqueur?"

*Maybe partial amnesia.* "It's a steamboat, and you hit your head."

"Did you hit your nose?"

The moment definitely wasn't playing out like I wanted. "Let's get you downstairs to bed."

He raised his torso, and I helped him to a standing position and wrapped my arm around his waist. I had to get him to a safe place so that I could look for Luigi. Because Gigi Scalino was still onboard, and so was Ruth—doling out "ssentences" on her Ambien.

We hobbled along the deck, and my anxiety grew with each step. I kept an eye on the railing and turned every few seconds to look behind us. I felt like that catfish I'd caught in my purse when I fell into the river—trapped in a small space waiting to be shot like a fish in a barrel.

Bradley grimaced and touched his head. "Where are we going?"

"My mom and Nonna are staying in a stateroom on the deck below. They'll take care of you."

His eyes enlarged.

I wasn't surprised that he'd remember to be afraid of them. "I meant that they'll take care of you in a good way."

"Are you sure? I haven't always been their favorite."

I started to tell him not to worry because Glenda was with them, but that would've scared him further, and he hadn't even heard her memoir stories. "Don't worry. They won't try anything since you're already hurt."

"All right. I guess?"

I knew it was hardly a comforting answer, but if he was looking for comfort, he'd picked the wrong family.

We reached the mid-ship stairwell, and I shouldered open

the door. When I was sure the coast was clear of Gigi and Ruth, I cast a glance at the pilothouse.

Captain Vandergrift stood at the helm, lost in whatever Mark Twain novel he was living.

We descended the stairs and walked to my family's stateroom. I tapped on the door. "It's me," I whispered. "Open up."

"Francesca?" My mother called as shrill as a steamboat whistle.

"Yes, Mom," I hissed. "Who else?"

"Well everyone can say 'me,' dear. And you don't sound like you."

Probably because of my swollen nose. "Would you just open up?"

The door opened an inch, and my mother peered out. Horror flickered over her face as though the hit from Sullivan's palm had transformed me into Gigi Scalino. Then she saw Bradley and smoothed her hair. "Why, Bradley. I had no idea you were on the boat."

Nonna shuffled toward the door. "Let's-a hope he's-a here to propose."

I blew an exasperated exhale from my nostrils and instantly regretted it. "He's got a concussion, Nonna."

"It's-a good-a thing-a. Maybe he won't-a notice the size of your schnoz-a."

*And she* actually believed *she could help me land a husband.* "Could you just take care of him while I look for Luigi?"

"Of course, dear." My mom stepped aside.

"Lock the door." I helped Bradley to the closest bed. "Where's Glenda?"

"We couldn't get her out of that champagne glass, so she went to Bruno's room to see if he could help."

I was positive that wasn't all she'd gone there for.

My mom and nonna gathered around Bradley and examined his wound.

"I'm going to the library." I volleyed a warning look at both of them. "Don't try to manipulate him while he's got a head injury."

"Honestly, Francesca. What makes you think we would do such a thing?"

"Uhhhh, all the times you've done such things?"

She averted her eyes and entered the bathroom.

Nonna grabbed her handbag from the nightstand.

"By the way, did you hit Sullivan with your purse and tie him up?"

"*Sì*. What's-a the problem?"

My mom exited the bathroom with a wet washcloth. "After what he did to Bradley, dear, he deserved that. It's clear he's up to no good."

Not anymore, but I wasn't ready to tell them that. I turned the lock. "Don't open this door unless it's me, understood?"

"You mean 'me' as in 'Francesca'?"

I grabbed the door handle and squeezed.

"Franki, wait." Bradley rose on woozy legs. "I'll come with you."

"No, you need to rest."

"I'll-a go," Nonna said. "I found-a the lever for the secret-a room back-a-stage. I'll-a find one in-a the library too."

My mother pressed the cloth to Bradley's head. "It's probably an old book you pull down, like in the movies."

Bradley's face tightened in concentration. "Look for *Life on the Mississippi*. When I helped the captain get the steamboat loan, he said it was the Twain novel that inspired him to buy the Galliano."

I smiled, relieved. He, and his memory, were going to be fine.

As long as we survived the steamboat.

Nonna speed-shuffled to the library, and I was happy to follow. My nose injury was messing with my head, so the only means of defense we had between us was her handbag —and her.

I surveyed the shelves. Nonna was too short to read the titles on the upper rows. "You keep watch while I look for the book."

She gripped her handbag and nodded.

On tiptoes, I scanned the top shelves. Even though Nonna was standing guard, I stopped every so often to look over my shoulder. I hadn't forgotten that Gigi Scalino had ordered Luigi's cousin in Sicily to be strangled for accepting the winepress— and that he'd had his house burned down too.

I finished the upper shelves and moved to the middle. The book had to be on the shelf somewhere. But there were so many.

I dropped to my knees and checked the bottom shelf.

*Life on the Mississippi* was the last book.

I pulled it down.

Nothing happened.

I removed the book from the shelf and discovered a light switch on the wall behind it. I flipped it.

A shelf began to open.

Luigi sat bound and gagged in the dark suit he'd worn to Nick's funeral five days before. His eyes were closed, and his head drooped low onto his chest.

"*Oddio*," Nonna whispered. "Luigi!"

He didn't budge.

*Were we too late?*

~

THE BOOKSHELF OPENED ENOUGH for me to slip inside the secret room.

"Luigi. It's me, as in Francesca." I blamed my mother for that odd clarification. I tugged at the knot on the handkerchief gagging his mouth.

His eyes opened, and he raised his head.

Nonna crossed herself. "*Grazie a Dio.*"

I untied the knot, and the gag dropped into Luigi's lap.

"My glasses." His voice was hoarse. "In my shirt pocket."

I pulled them out and slipped them onto his face.

His pupils constricted behind the lenses. "I knew you gals would find me."

"I'm sorry it took us so long."

"Eh?"

*His hearing aid.* I pulled it from my pocket and clipped it onto his ear.

"Thanks, kid. The hoodlum who kidnapped me from the church took my hearing aid so I wouldn't be able to hear anyone in the library and make noise with my chair."

"His name is Gerald." I moved behind him to untie the rope around his wrists. "And he won't bother you anymore. Neither will Alfredo."

"Got themselves whacked, did they?"

I freed his arms. "Yes, in the walk-in."

"I'll bet it was Gigi Scalino's doing. He's on the boat, you know."

Nonna entered. "That's-a why we're trying to get-a you outta here."

I knelt and worked the knotted rope around his ankles. "Nonna, would you please keep watch for Gigi?"

She waved her hand and faced the hallway.

Luigi rubbed his wrist. "Gigi was going to hold me on this rat trap until I told him where the winepress was. He said if I didn't, I'd have to walk a plank before we got back to New Orleans. Did you know this steamboat has a plank?"

"I'm familiar with it, yes." I untied one foot and started on the other. "Did you ever find out why he's so obsessed with the winepress?"

"He's retiring to Sicily and wants to take it with him. It reminds him of his mother."

Nonna looked inside. "Was his-a *mamma* shaped like a wine-a barrel?"

I got a vision of Pat with black hair and a mustache.

"Nah." Luigi swept a stray gray tuft over his scalp. "She made her own wine with it."

If Gigi and Alfredo had been my sons, I would've made my own wine too. "The only thing I don't understand is how a man who has eyes and ears all over town wouldn't know that his brother was dealing drugs behind his back."

"Alfredo told him he was on the steamboat to find Captain Galliano's gold, and Gigi bought it hook, line, and sinker. I think that's why he's retiring." He tapped his temple. "He's slipping."

I freed his other foot.

"You're my saving angel." He tried to stand and fell onto the chair seat.

Nonna shuffle-rushed to his side. "What's-a the matter?"

"I can't feel my feet."

I dropped to my knees and removed Luigi's shoes. "Nonna, how are you going to watch for Gigi with your back to the hallway?"

"There's-a no one out-a there. I just-a looked-a."

"Let's hope it stays that way." I rubbed Luigi's ankles to get the circulation moving.

"That feels better, kid. I think I can make it now."

I looked to my left to grab his shoes.

And I jerked like the steamboat had hit a pothole.

Because unless Luigi's shoes had put on the "tiny white dress shirts," to quote Bit-O-Honey, then I was looking at Gigi Scalino's spats.

MY EYES WORKED their way from the spats to the black pin stripe suit, lingered on the machine gun, and stopped at the wide, puffy mug beneath the cream fedora. Gigi "The G-Man" Scalino was a reincarnation of Al Capone if he'd made it to old age.

"Look at you, Luigi, surrounded by the ladies."

He even sounded like a 1920s gangster.

Nonna and Luigi were as stiff as the collar of Gigi's shirt.

And it was so quiet in the secret room that we could have heard a pin stripe drop.

Gigi propped the machine gun under his arm and peeled a wrapper from a Bit-O-Honey. He popped the candy into his mouth and leaned his head outside the opening to cast his black eyes on the Mark Twain books. "I don't know how anyone could read this garbage. Most of these books ain't even got pictures. But if you like readin', they got a picture book about me down the hall in the gift shop."

The spider veins on Luigi's nose turned purple. "Does it list all the crimes you committed?"

"Don't be fooled by the non-fiction label. All them stories they tell about me being a heartless hitman ain't true. I'm a businessman." His fleshy mouth stretched into a still-lippy smile. "And I'm very generous, as long as you don't double-cross me."

*Double-cross?* The guy wasn't a fiction character, he was a cartoon.

"*Hmph-a.*" Nonna crossed her arms. "Now that's-a fiction."

I shot her a zip-it look. Her handbag was deadly, but it was no match for Gigi Scalino's machine gun.

"Speakin' of fiction, Luigi here tells me my father's winepress is somewhere I'll never find it."

Luigi rose on unsteady legs. "I'm an old man, Gigi. I've lived a good life. I'd rather go to my grave early than see you with that winepress."

"Being the stand-up guy that I am, I can accommodate that." He raised his gun, but his face contorted, and he clutched his abdomen.

The incision from his appendicitis surgery. "You might've popped your stiches. You should see a doctor."

"Ah, the PI."

I blinked, wondering what else Gigi knew about me.

"That's some good sleuthin' to know about my operation. Maybe you could use that honker of yours to sniff out where my winepress is."

He was one to talk. And I wasn't stupid enough to give away my only bargaining chip. "I can take you to it if you let Luigi and my nonna go."

"Don't-a do it, Franki." Nonna pointed a knobby finger at Gigi. "This-a scum-a-bag don't deserve-a the fruits of his-a padre's hard-a work." She stepped forward.

And she spat on his spats.

Gigi bowed his head.

My stomach sank as though it had been torpedoed. *Would he mow her down with his machine gun?*

After a moment, he raised his head. But instead of a face contorted with rage, it was streaked with tears. "You're right, and so was my father. I don't deserve the winepress."

The G-Man wasn't just slipping—he'd gone soft.

He wiped his eyes. Then he stiffened and aimed the gun at her. "But that won't stop me from takin' it back to Sicily."

Luigi raised a shaky finger. "If you hurt either these women, you won't make it back to Sicily."

"That's-a right." Nonna pointed at me. "My *nipote*, Franki, she won't-a let-a you get away with-a this."

Gigi smacked his Bit-O-Honey and shifted his aim to my forehead.

Honestly, the woman really needed to rethink her sales pitches where I was concerned.

Luigi stuck out his bony chest. "Shoot me, Gigi. I'm the one you've got a beef with."

He shifted his aim to Luigi. "I'm gonna countdown from three."

Luigi closed his eyes and swayed.

"*Three.*"

Nonna shook her fist. "You're a *ruffiano*, Gigi."

I had to get Nonna away from him before she either smacked him or spat again, and I had to stop him from slaughtering Luigi. I scanned the room, looking for something, anything I could use as a weapon.

*But what?*

"*Two.*"

*Luigi's shoes?* If I threw them at Gigi, he'd riddle me with with enough holes to turn me into a human spaghetti attachment for a pasta maker. But it was my only option, so I stretched my arm and grabbed a shoe.

"Miss Franki!"

*Glenda?*

Gigi dipped inside the room and lowered the machine gun.

"Your mother said I'd find you here." Glenda squeezed inside in nothing but Bruno's white Saturday Night Fever jacket and a thong. She saw the gun and raised her arms, and her Mardi Gras decorations popped out.

Gigi's eyes followed suit.

I grabbed the gun and jammed it into his incision.

He doubled over and collapsed onto the floor.

I aimed the gun at him while Nonna and Glenda helped

Luigi out. Then I backed out myself. "Glenda, flip the switch and get Luigi to your room."

The bookshelf slowly began to move.

I aimed at the opening until it snapped shut.

For the first time in a minute, I breathed.

I lowered the gun—but kept my eyes raised—as I turned to look at Glenda. "Thank God you came when you did. Gigi was about to kill us all. Now let's get to the pilothouse and pull your Saturday Night Fever move on the captain."

"No need, sugar. That's what I came to tell you."

"Why not? We need him to stop the boat."

"It's already in the works. Come on. I'll show you."

I glanced at the bookshelf. Gigi wasn't going anywhere, and I still had the gun, so I followed her outside to the deck.

And I uttered silent thanks to Kate.

At least twenty crawdad-emblazoned Cajun Navy vessels surged toward the Galliano. Leading the fleet was the flat boat of my French Quarter flood rescuers, Jean-Thibault and Jean-Toussaint Froiquingont.

Glenda whipped off Bruno's jacket and waved it like a surrender flag. "Hooyah, *chers!*"

## 23

"Where have you been?" Veronica gave me the evil-employer eye from her fuchsia office chair. "I asked you to be here at ten a.m. sharp, and it's almost eleven."

"Sorry." I eyed her gold party dress and wished she'd chosen another color. "I had to run an errand."

"On Mardi Gras day?"

"A few places are open." I threw my bag on the armchair in front of her desk to pre-punctuate my next point. "Like Private Chicks?"

"I told you, this staff meeting is important. Now what was this errand?" Her powdered brows narrowed. "You have that look about you."

"You mean, the look of a person with a cracked nose and bruised back?"

"You're stalling. Out with it."

I raised my swollen nose in an attempt to look dignified and smoothed my purple skirt before I took a seat. "If you must know, I took the winepress to the Galliano."

"You didn't," she breathed.

"I did. Gigi Scalino's in jail now, but he'll get out. Mafia bosses usually find a way to evade hard time. And when he comes looking for the winepress, I'll figure out something. But in the meantime, I don't want the whack-worthy thing in my house."

She pressed her hand to her forehead. "Luigi was held captive for five days because he wanted you to have that winepress. What are you going to tell him?"

"Nothing. The only ones who know are you and Marv from Where Dat Tours. He helped me carry it to the secret room backstage while the captain was at the police station."

"Oh, Franki. This is bad."

"Why? Luigi will never know, and if anyone on the Galliano ever finds it, they'll just think it's an old prop." I crossed my legs and leaned back—gingerly. "And Marv isn't going to tell anyone because the threat of Gigi returning with a machine gun would jeopardize the Galliano's ticket sales. He said they're selling like gangbusters since the news broke last night."

"I'll bet." Veronica picked up a pen and twirled it between her fingers. "A throw-back captain, mob murders, and a Cajun Navy rescue are big attractions."

"Marv said the biggest draws are the plank, which they're repairing, and the calliope."

She wrinkled her lips. "Why the calliope?"

"Because some reporter dug up the story about the ghost of that cook, Rose, being lynched after Agnes Frump and the crewman burned. And he ended his news report by theorizing that Rose had turned on the calliope to save me from an unjust death like the one she suffered."

Veronica stole a glance at me from the corner of her eye. "It *is* weird that the calliope came on when it did."

I shrugged. "Snoozin' Ruth could have turned it on and off from the switch in the captain's bedroom. If not, then it was a mechanical problem." At least, those were the explanations I was going with. "Regardless of how it happened, Marian would be furious at all of the so-called 'curious onlookers' the story is attracting."

"I still can't fathom how she made it out of that river alive, especially with third-degree burns on her scalp."

I looked at her under my lashes. "What about Tim? He broke his arm on that paddlewheel and swam to shore."

"That's different. He's a young man." She fell silent and stared at the pen.

And I knew why. I didn't know what to say about Sullivan either. "Got any plans with Dirk tonight?"

"Actually, yes. We're planning our engagement party."

"What? Oh my gosh. Congratulations." I got up and threw my arms around her. And we hugged for what seemed like a minute. "When did this happen?"

"The night of that special dinner." She pulled back and took a ring box from her desk drawer. "I didn't want to tell you since Bradley was in jail."

I felt awful that our drama had spoiled her excitement. "I wish you hadn't done that. You know I would've been happy for you."

"I do know that. But that night Bradley got arrested, and then I found you crying in Glenda's champagne glass because you thought it was over between you two. And to top it all off, there was your nonna's investigation into your zitellahood and the whole lemon tradition."

"Just a normal day in my life."

She smirked and opened the box to reveal a huge marquise diamond.

"It's stunning."

She sparkled like the ring. "Isn't it?"

"When's the wedding?"

"We don't have a date, but it's in Venice. Will you be my maid of honor?"

"Do you even have to ask?" I hugged her again and shed a few tears. Then I raised my arms and shook my hips. "We're going to Italy."

"And we're going early to have some girl time."

The lobby bell sounded, and the door slammed in classic David style.

We shared a smile. Our moment had ended, but we'd be best friends forever.

Veronica picked up a file from her desk. "Let's get this meeting started so we're not late for Bradley's lunch."

I came crashing down from the wedding-in-Venice high. "I told him that he shouldn't be hosting this thing with a concussion."

She looked at me from the doorway. "The doctor said it was mild, and it's the perfect day to celebrate having the charges against him dropped."

"It's also the perfect day to celebrate my mom and nonna going home to Houston, but now they're staying because of his Mardi Gras fixation."

"I would say 'it's just one more day,' but with your mom and nonna..." She left the implication hanging and left the office.

I entered the hallway, pondering the potential fallout. There were two weeks left in the lemon tradition, so Nonna was more desperate than ever. A scenario struck me that was so terrible I had to lean against the wall.

*What if she slipped me an Ambien so I'd sleep-walk to the altar and marry Bruno?*

"Franki," Veronica called, "we're waiting."

I entered the lobby, and David and The Vassal rose from one of the couches and saluted. I sat across from them next to Veronica. "At ease, men."

David flipped his bangs and flopped into his seat. "Tell us what happened when the Cajun Navy cruised up."

I grinned at the memory. "The captain thought they were pirates, so he was delighted to surrender. He grabbed a white jacket Glenda had and jumped up and down like a kid while he waved it."

The Vassal pushed up his glasses. "I'm not surprised. It's well documented that Mark Twain fantasized about being a pirate."

David bounced his leg. "What about the passengers? What were they doing while everything was going down?"

"Kate and Wendell kept them in the casino by giving away free drinks *and* free future cruises on the Galliano. The captain wasn't happy when he found out about all the money he'd lost."

"That is a bummer." David shrugged. "But it's awesome that you guys kept everyone safe."

"Yeah." I nestled into the couch cushions. "It's funny, isn't it? A ragtag group of Louisianans beat the Mafia just like the ragtag army in the Battle of New Orleans that beat the British."

Veronica opened the file and pulled out some envelopes. "And thanks to you and your army, Luigi Pescatore gave you a generous bonus. Not only that, he's decided to invest in Private Chicks."

I took the envelope, more excited about the investment money than the bonus. "That's terrific. What are you going to do with the money?"

"Purchase some new technology, for starters."

David looked at The Vassal, and their faces lit up like computer screens. "Yo, we can help with that."

"I'm counting on it." Veronica looked at me. "I'm also going to bring on a new PI."

I wondered whether she was considering Kate, but instead of asking, I shot death rays at David. "Well I hope it's not someone who'll investigate their coworker. I still can't believe you hacked my computer." I turned to The Vassal since I was sure he'd helped, and the last question I had about the case turned into an exclamation mark. "You! It was you."

He cowered, and I got up to tower over him.

"Franki," Veronica's tone was tense, "what are you doing?"

I spun to face her. "When I first met The Vassal, he told me he wanted to major in Radio, Television, and Film, but his parents wouldn't let him, so he majored in Computer Science."

"So?"

"Isn't it obvious? He put the video camera in the winepress— in my bedroom."

Veronica looked from him to David. "Someone had better start explaining."

The Vassal's slack-jawed stare was unchanging, but his glasses lenses started to fog.

David held up his hands. "Okay, so, I wanted to put a camera in her apartment, but it was The Vassal's idea to put it in the winepress."

The Vassal's lenses were completely opaque. "Because I didn't want her to suspect us if she found it."

Given his probable crush on me, I had my doubts about that explanation. "So which one of you came to my apartment, pretending to be an exterminator?"

David pointed to his head. "I borrowed the outfit from a man who worked at our old dorm. Then when your mom and nonna came for the investigation update, I heard your mom yelling about being videotaped, uh, naked and told The Vassal."

I scowled at The Vassal, even though he couldn't see me. "And you orchestrated the reconnaissance mission."

He nodded.

"But why take Glenda's Mardi Gras decorations?" Veronica asked.

I shot her a smirk. "Remember the strip club case when The

Vassal wanted to cash out his college fund to pay for that sugar baby's boob job?"

Veronica's jaw mimicked The Vassal's. "Standish, is this true?"

"I confess, and I apologize." He removed his glasses and wiped the lenses on his shirt. "Miss O'Brien's decorations are hanging at the Gamma Epsilon Epsilon Kappa fraternity house."

Veronica pressed her lips together to look stern, but I could tell she was stifling a laugh at the thought of Glenda's boobs hanging at the boys' Comp Sci frat. "Well, spying on Franki in her bedroom and stealing from Glenda warrant disciplinary action."

David's mouth opened, and The Vassal's closed.

"But I've never established a company policy for that sort of thing, so I'll overlook it this time. In the future, however, you two will discuss any and all investigatory methods with me in advance of implementation, understood?"

Their heads bounced like David's leg.

She licked her lips. "Good. As for Glenda's Mardi Gras decorations, you need to return them immediately."

Their faces drooped, a lot like the decorations.

And so did mine. "Can't we just leave the boobs at the GEEK frat house? I mean, do you really want them back on *our* house?"

Veronica looked from the boys to me. "You're right. Better to leave them where they are. But if any of you ever tell Glenda, you're fired."

David, The Vassal, and I exchanged high-fives.

Veronica looked at her watch. "We'd better get going, Franki."

The four of us rose, and a copy of the *Times Picayune* fell from The Vassal's backpack.

I stooped to pick it up and saw the front page.

And my stomach bounced as though I were white-water rafting.

I handed the paper to The Vassal and left the office.

But as I descended the stairs, I could still see the picture of police divers at the river and the headline.

*Body of Local Detective Still Missing.*

VERONICA SIPPED from her rosé glass and ran her hand over a brick archway in the wine cellar at Brennan's restaurant. "I read that this was a stable in 1795. It's fabulous, isn't it?"

It was, but I couldn't take my eyes off the fabulous check from Luigi that lay on the cypress-wood table. "Thirty. Thousand. Dollars."

"One thousand for every year you've been alive...for another week, anyway."

I was so enamored of the check that I didn't mind the birthday reference or the fact that I was turning thirty-one.

The wooden stairs creaked.

I looked up and saw my mom and Nonna coming down the stairs. My mother wore Mardi Gras colors, but Nonna was back in black, presumably mourning my single status.

My mother pressed a hand to her cheek. "This wine cellar is gorgeous. It looks like something you'd see in Italy, doesn't it, Carmela?"

Nonna surveyed the room with a face as dark as her dress. "Let's-a hope they have-a pasta to go with it."

I rose from the table, reluctantly. "Is Luigi coming? I want to thank him for this amazing gift."

"He's on-a bed-a rest."

"Doctor's orders," my mother chimed. "I think she should stay in New Orleans for a couple of weeks to look after him."

*Of course you do.*

"I don't-a have-a time. The lemon tradition is about-a to end."

I visualized myself asleep at the altar with Bruno, holding a bouquet of Butterfingers. "It's Mardi Gras, Nonna. A day to let your cares slip away."

"*Hmphf-a.* That-a day will come-a when I die. Until-a then, I've got to find-a you a husband and-a mourn your nonnu."

My mother's hand hit the table like Judge Judy's gavel. "But... what about Luigi?"

"What about him?" Nonna turned up her palms. "We're-a friends."

My mom looked like Bradley had after Marian pistol-whipped him. Because that engagement party she and her friend Rosalie had been planning was never going to happen.

"Nonna, did your friends guilt you into this with their national prayer request? Or Father John?"

She raised her chin. "I do what I want-a."

That she did.

Nonna gave a small smile. "There's just-a one man-a for me. Your *nonnu.*"

I teared up. "There's just one man for me too." I paused and then figured I'd better clarify. "Bradley, not Bruno."

"Oof-a. I don't-a blame you. Bruno is-a so annoying with that-a concession stand-a candy."

I squeezed her hand, and she winked. We'd finally come to an understanding.

Bradley descended the steps in a blue suit with a dozen yellow roses. I flashed back to Sullivan in my cabin with the yellow rose Bradley had left me, and I shook my head. I didn't have to worry about him anymore. He was gone.

*Or was he?*

Bradley gave me a peck. "You look worried, babe. Is every-thing okay?"

I had to come up with an explanation unrelated to Sullivan. "The flowers are beautiful, but I was thinking...about how much you're spending."

"Don't. This is a holiday, and it's worth every penny."

A pang of guilt, or maybe hunger, gnawed at my stomach. I shouldn't have told him the fib so soon after I'd promised to confide in him. On the other hand, sharing every detail hadn't worked out too well for us on the Galliano.

A waiter emerged from the adjoining cellar. "I've informed the chef that you're ready to begin, Mr. Hartmann. Would you like me to put the flowers in a vase?"

"That would be great, thanks." Bradley handed him the roses.

"Before you go,"—I put my hand on the waiter's arm and pointed to my mother—"that woman over there has just gotten some bad news, so could you please bring her something strong, like a Sazerac?"

"I'll bring it right out." He exited through an archway to the bar.

Glenda made her grand entrance. Since it was Mardi Gras, she wore less than usual. Her entire outfit consisted of a cigarette holder and a few strands of beads.

My mom and nonna were so absorbed in their problems that they didn't even notice her nudity.

Glenda sidled up to Bradley. "Thanks for the invite, handsome."

"My pleasure."

She licked her lips. "I have no doubt."

He grinned and put his arm around her, careful to avoid her Mardi Gras decorations. "I hear you're working on your memoirs."

"I am, indeed. And some of my wildest escapades happened on this holiday."

My hand shot up. "No spoilers, please."

Veronica came over. "Have you decided on a title, Glenda?"

"I thought about *Rise and Grind* or *Stripped Bare*, but they're too cliché. So I settled on *Like a Polecat at a Garden Party*. Get it? Stripper pole and cat?"

I did. "It's the essence of you."

Veronica took Glenda by the arm. "It's purrfect, and speaking of your essence, let's get you some champagne."

They headed for the bar as Ruth bounded down the steps in her cruise director suit.

I blinked and looked at Bradley. "What's *she* doing here?"

"I invited her for you."

"Uh...why?"

Ruth leaned in to my ear. "It's all right. He knows we're best friends, but I told him to keep it on the down-low since Veronica's here."

I had to set her straight once and for all—not for Veronica's sake, but for mine. Because the woman was dangerous. "Ruth, Veronica is my best friend. You and I are...members of the same army troop."

"I understand." She turned her Fun Meter to Min. "You don't want to hurt her feelings."

Bradley cleared his throat. "So what's next for you, Ruth?"

Pink tinged her cheeks. "Rex asked me to stay on...as the Galliano's cruise director, of course."

Bradley and I shared a look. Apparently, the almost king of the Shrimp and Petroleum Festival had found his almost queen.

I took a sip of Chianti. "Well, the steamboat *is* your home."

"*Pfff!* I'm staying for the gold. Captain Galliano's treasure is on that steamboat, and I'm going to find it."

"But we found both of the hidden rooms on the map, and it wasn't in them."

"Rex said those red Xes marked the two secret rooms he'd found. He claims there are more. If not, I'll move to plan B."

"What's that? Win the steamboat in a poker game?"

"I don't gamble, remember?"

The waiter passed by with the vase, and Ruth flagged him down. "I'll take a cider."

*And she didn't drink, either.* "What? No Galliano?"

"Listen here, prissy missy, I was sleep-walking the other night, not drunk."

"Uh-huh."

Bradley swallowed a grin. "We're having Bananas Foster for dessert. I thought it was fitting since they light the Galliano on fire."

I appreciated the symbolism.

Ruth smacked her lips. "Bananas Foster reminds me of poor Pat. She's taking over the chef position as soon as she recovers from her dollar-hole accident."

"Her what?" Bradley asked.

I sighed because Pat's anatomy came to mind again. "After I locked her in the galley, she tried to escape through the garbage chute. She got stuck and cracked a couple of ribs."

Bradley winced.

Several waiters delivered soup to the table.

"That's the first course." Bradley took my hand. "I'm sitting at the head, and you're to my right. Everyone is having crawfish bisque, but since you're allergic you're having lobster bisque."

I gave him a long kiss.

My mother passed by. "It's so thoughtful of you to remember her allergy, Bradley."

Nonna shuffled to the table. "How could he forget-a after their first-a date? *Che disastro.*"

The *disaster* was the direction the conversation had taken.

"Why? What happened?" Ruth asked—from the seat next to mine.

Veronica and I shared a look, but I didn't tell Ruth to move. It was best to have Veronica at the end of the table with Glenda, so she could stave off any Mardi Gras memoir stories.

Nonna took the chair across from Ruth. "Franki's lips swelled up-a like-a Genoa salami after she sucked the head of a mud-a-bug."

I took my seat, regretting the conversation *and* the guest list.

My mom sat beside Bradley. "Before we knew what had caused the swelling, some of our deli customers said she probably had hand, foot, and mouth disease or a bad case of herpes."

"Mom,"—I raised my spoon—"we're about to eat?"

Ruth poked her head around. "Why didn't you tell me that? We *are* best friends."

Veronica took a sip of rosé and looked away, and I shoved a spoonful of bisque in my mouth.

Bradley's eyes twinkled. "We've had some adventures, haven't we, babe?"

"We certainly have. The only thing that could've made this last one better would have been finding Captain Galliano's gold. When I was little, I always wanted to find a treasure chest full of coins and jewels."

"I think I can help you there." Bradley reached into his suit pocket and pulled out a Tiffany's Blue Box.

The size of a ring.

My stomach jumped up and hugged my heart.

And my lips started to tingle, which was odd.

From the corner of my eye, I glanced at my soup.

And spotted a crawfish tail.

Ruth leaned forward. "Consider it payback, for sneaking that mobster's winepress onto the Galliano."

My hand went to my mouth. My lips were starting to swell—to match my nose.

Bradley dropped to one knee.

A flush joined the tingling.

He looked up at me, his blue eyes bright. "This is why I told you that Mardi Gras is my favorite day. Because I knew I was going to ask you this question." He opened the ring box, and it held a gold band with a ruby and diamonds. "Francesca Lucia Amato, will you marry me?"

With my hand still hiding my lips, I tried to say yes.

But my tongue had swollen.

I felt like I was sinking to the murky depths of the Mississippi River. *Bradley had finally popped the question, the obvious question, and I couldn't answer him.*

Panicked, I turned to my mother and moved my hand.

"Oh, no." She leapt from the table. "No, no, no, no. You answer that question this minute, young lady."

Bradley rushed to my side. "What is it?"

Ruth lowered her horn-rims to feign a look of surprise. "She took a bite of my crawfish bisque by mistake."

I couldn't speak, so I growled. And bared my teeth.

She pushed up her glasses. "We'd better call an ambulance. The allergy has gone to her brain."

Bradley put his arm around my waist, guiding me from the chair. "I'm taking you to the hospital."

"Carmela!" my mother shrieked. "Do something!"

My nonna pulled a lemon wedge from her water glass and shoved it between my lips. "That should cut-a the allergy."

If I could have spoken, I would have reminded her that a lemon had just landed me a proposal, which was already more than we could've expected from a mere citrus fruit.

"Bradley's-a waiting, Franki. *Rispondi.*"

I wanted to *rispondi* so badly I could taste it—that and the lemon.

"Come on, Franki." Veronica punched the air. "Spit it out so we can plan our weddings together."

Glenda fingered her Mardi Gras beads. "I'd be happy to answer for her."

"Time to go." Bradley scooped me into his arms like a groom about to carry his wife over the threshold and strode to the stairs.

I knew I had to do something to ensure that he *did* carry me over a threshold one day. So I latched on to the railing like I had when I'd saved myself from the broken plank and spat out the lemon.

"Uhhhh. Uhhhh." I kicked my feet.

Bradley looked into my eyes. "What is it?"

I motioned to Ruth.

She angled a glance at Veronica. "I think she wants *me* to come to the hospital."

"Mm-mm. Mm-mm." I thrashed my head and pointed to Ruth.

Bradley carried me to her.

I grabbed ahold of her safari vest and pointed to her Fun Meter. When I was sure he was watching, I pushed it to Max.

He gave me a tender look and kissed my salami-sized lips. "I'll take that as a *yes*."

I sighed and laid my head on his shoulder, happily engaged.

As he carried me up the stairs, Nonna dropped to her knees in prayer. And my mother threw back her head and serenaded us with an operatic rendition of "Hark! The Herald Angels Sing."

# FREE MINI MYSTERIES OFFER

Want to know what happens to Franki after *Galliano Gold*? Sign up for my newsletter to receive a free copy of the *Franki Amato Mini Mysteries*, a hilarious collection that contains "Cremoncello Cream" (Franki #5.5) and five other fun short mysteries. You'll also be the first to know about my new releases, deals, and giveaways.

Here's the blurb for "Cremoncello Cream:"

Franki Amato's BFF and boss, Veronica Maggio, takes her to sunny Sicily for a PI conference but neglects to tell her about their teambuilder, a trek up Mount Etna. And the volcano isn't the only earth-shattering surprise in store for Franki. Next her engagement ring is stolen, and then she learns her life is in danger. She has to find out who took the ring, and why people on the island seem to know her. If she doesn't, she could end up in hot lava—literally.

And don't forget to follow me!

BookBub
https://www.bookbub.com/authors/traci-andrighetti

Goodreads
https://www.goodreads.com/author/show/
7383577.Traci_Andrighetti

Facebook
https://www.facebook.com/traciandrighettiauthor

# BOOK BACKSTORY

*Galliano Gold* is in the books, and I'm ecstatic. My life took so many twists and turns during the writing of this book that I felt like Franki Amato. I adopted a puppy, a family member had major surgery, and I was recruited out of nowhere for a job—fighting actual crime. That's right, I'm no longer just a crime writer, I'm also a crime fighter (who likes to rhyme). Funny how life works, isn't it?

But back to *Galliano Gold*. The title is important to me because Galliano L'Autentico Liqueur, known simply as Galliano, reminds me of my childhood. And no, I wasn't drinking back then! My parents had at least one party in the 1970s where they served *the* drink of the decade, the Harvey Wallbanger. Ironically, neither my mom nor my dad is a drinker, so the tall, tapered bottle with the bright yellow liquid hung around our house for decades—it even moved with us from West Texas to Houston. And I'm glad it did because now my mom uses it to make Bananas Foster, which is one of the best desserts ever invented.

The strange thing about Galliano is that Americans often use it as a banana liqueur, but Italians claim it's vanilla. Both flavors seem like a stretch considering that vanilla is only one of the thirty herbs, spices, and plant extracts used to make the liqueur. The other known ingredients (the recipe has been a closely guarded secret since 1896!) are anise, juniper, musk yarrow, lavender, cinnamon, and peppermint. If you ask me, that definitely doesn't sound like banana *or* vanilla. But again, I digress.

I'm also excited that *Galliano Gold* is done because the book has been in my head for *years*. Back in 2014 when my husband, son, and I took Italian friends to New Orleans, I realized that if I wanted to do The Big Easy justice, I needed to write a mystery on a plantation and another on a Mississippi River steamboat. I wrote *Prosecco Pink*, which is based on Oak Alley Plantation, that same year. But the steamboat mystery, inspired by our cruise on the Steamboat Natchez, has been waiting to come to life ever since. And it was worth the wait, because it takes Franki Amato on a heck of a ride and sets up an ending that is not to be missed.

While I'm on the subject of New Orleans sites, they're not all that make the city so memorable and mysterious. The people are the best part, and I celebrate them with every book I write. For *Galliano Gold*, I would especially like to call out the Dancing Hand Grenade mascot at the Tropical Isle bar on Bourbon Street, the Mardi Gras dance troops and krewes, and the Cajun Navy for keeping New Orleans so weird, wild, and wonderful.

I would also like to thank a few people for their help with this book, starting with my mom for reading every chapter and making comments that sometimes inspire plot twists, and my long-time editor, Sally J. Smith, for getting my sense of humor and letting me leave it in the books! I'm also grateful to Barbara Hackel, one of my favorite readers, for suggesting that I incorporate elements of a NOLA trip gone horribly, awfully wrong, and to Madeline Mrozek, my multi-talented (and multi-voiced) audiobook narrator, for suggesting that I have Franki investigate in an outrageous wig I posted on Facebook and for asking me to bring the character of Ruth Walker back. Their suggestions were so good that I found myself laughing as I wrote *Galliano Gold*. Here's hoping you enjoy the book as much as I did.

*Cin cin* (Cheers)!
    Traci

# A COCKTAIL AND DESSERT

## HARVEY WALLBANGER

The name of this drink is so weird that it practically asked to be in a Franki Amato mystery, which is why Glenda offers to buy one for Franki the first time they meet in *Limoncello Yellow*. The story goes that the Harvey Wallbanger was created in 1952 at Duke's Backwatch Bar on the Sunset Strip in West Hollywood. Owner Donato "Duke" Antone allegedly named it after a local surfer named Tom Harvey, who got so drunk he ran into walls. Sounds like someone should have cut old Tom off!

*Ingredients*
> 1 ½ ounces vodka
> 4 ounces orange juice
> ½ ounce Galliano
> 1 orange slice and 1 maraschino cherry

Add the vodka and orange juice over ice in a tall glass. Float the Galliano on top. Garnish with a skewered orange slice and maraschino cherry.

## BANANAS FOSTER

Like the Harvey Wallbanger, Bananas Foster is a product of the 1950s and is perfect for a Franki Amato mystery—because it has a crime connection. New Orleans was a major port of entry for bananas, so Owen Brennan, the founder of Brennan's restaurant, asked Chef Paul Blangé to create a dessert with the fruit. Brennan named the dessert after his good friend Richard Foster who served with him on the New Orleans Crime Commission, a civic group created to clean up the French Quarter. Franki thinks they need to come back and finish the job, so she doesn't have to.

*Ingredients*
   ¼ cup butter
   1 cup brown sugar
   ½ teaspoon cinnamon
   ¼ cup banana liqueur (Galliano)
   4 bananas cut in half lengthwise then halved
   ¼ cup dark rum
   4 scoops vanilla ice cream

Combine the butter, sugar, and cinnamon in a flambé pan or skillet. Place the pan over low heat and stir until the sugar dissolves. Stir in the Galliano, then place the bananas in the pan. When the bananas soften and begin to brown, carefully add the rum. Cook the sauce until the rum is hot, then tip the pan slightly to ignite the rum. When the flames subside, remove the bananas from the pan and place four pieces over each scoop of ice cream. Generously spoon warm sauce over the ice cream and serve.

# ABOUT THE AUTHOR

Traci Andrighetti is the *USA TODAY* bestselling author of the Franki Amato Mysteries and the Danger Cove Hair Salon Mysteries. In her previous life, she was an award-winning literary translator and a Lecturer of Italian at the University of Texas at Austin, where she earned a PhD in Applied Linguistics. But then she got wise and ditched that academic stuff for a life of crime—writing, that is. Her latest capers are teaching mystery for Savvy Authors and taking authors on writing retreats to Italy with LemonLit.

To learn more about Traci, check out her websites: www. traciandrighetti.com
www.lemonlit.com

# SNEAK PEEK

If you liked this Franki Amato mystery, read the first chapter of:

## MARSALA MAROON
Franki Amato Mysteries Book 6

by
Traci Andrighetti

### CHAPTER 1

"Is it me, or is the lemon tradition haunting us?"

My fiancé's question came through my cell phone like a splash of cold water, and I gripped the granite rim of the Jackson Square fountain where I was sitting. The St. Joseph's Day lemon tradition had played a key role in our engagement. *Was he souring on the decision to ask me to marry him?*

I rose and paced the French Quarter park's gravel walkway. "'Haunting' is an interesting choice of words, Bradley. Mind expanding on that?"

"I said it was haunting *us*, Franki, not *me*. And you have to admit that after the pressure to get engaged within the tradition's one-year time limit, things haven't calmed down. Your mom and nonna are pushing us to fast-track the wedding, and weird things have been happening, like my new car breaking down the last three times we've had plans. It's like it's, well, a lemon."

I understood the pressure part, but the car thing was ludicrous. Then again, so was the Sicilian-American custom of stealing a lemon from a church altar for the poor to land oneself a husband. "Surely you don't believe that my taking a piece of citrus fruit is the cause of your car problems?"

"Of course not." He sighed. "I'm sorry. I just want us to be able to enjoy our engagement, which is why I proposed on Mardi Gras. But that party ended as abruptly as the parades."

I sunk back onto the fountain. Bradley was frustrated, and I could relate. My mom and nonna had been laying on the wedding pressure as thick as ricotta cheese. I had to do something to bolster his spirits. I glanced behind me at the equestrian statue of General Andrew Jackson in the Battle of New Orleans to summon my combat instincts. "Mom and Nonna are excited, that's all. Give them another couple of weeks, they'll settle down."

"Will they?"

The honest answer was *Not a chance in Dante's inferno.* Those women would squeeze us like a garlic press until we produced a bambino, but I couldn't say that to Bradley. He might've gotten cold feet for real and hotfooted it from my life.

I stared at the St. Louis Cathedral overlooking the park and got a divine inspiration. "We have to have faith, that's all."

"I'll try-y."

His two-syllable "try" wasn't convincing, and I couldn't blame him for being skeptical. Because I knew that it would take more than God and a general-turned-president to slow my mom and nonna's march to our wedding altar. "Why don't you go deal with your car, and I'll meet them for lunch? It'll give me a chance to tell them to back off."

"All right, but we've got another problem coming—on Thursday, to be exact—because my mother and grandmother are flying in to talk to me about the wedding."

That statement was foreboding. After two years of dating, I still hadn't met the Hartmann family, so I would have expected him to say that they were arriving from Boston to meet me, their future daughter-in-law. "Is this about the rehearsal dinner?"

"The entire wedding, I'm afraid."

The St. Louis Cathedral bell tolled, and I didn't appreciate its timing. The bell announced the Sunday noon mass, but it could have been a sign that his family was against our marriage.

I licked my lips. "I hope you told them that my parents are super traditional and insist on paying."

"I did, but my mother and grandmother are...particular."

"You mean, about the wedding theme?"

"Among other things."

*Did those 'other things' extend to his choice of bride?* I gripped the phone a tad tighter. "Well, if they'd like a say in the decorations, I'd be happy to oblige."

"You'd do that?"

The relief in his tone brought a smile to my face because it indicated that the so-called problem coming on Thursday had been solved. "I'd do anything for you and your family. After all, I'm going to be a Hartmann soon."

"I'm so lucky that you agreed to marry me."

The cold-water splash of before turned cozy-warm snuggle. "True. And after I tell my mom and nonna to stand down, I'll send them home to Houston so I can show you just how lucky you are."

"I'd like that." His tone had gone sexy. "Very much."

The creak of the park's iron gate broke the seductive spell. A male in dark jeans, a gray hoodie, and sunglasses entered and headed straight for me. Despite the unusual attire, I recognized the long, lanky figure of my college-student coworker from Private Chicks, Inc.

"Bradley, I've got to run. David Savoie's here to talk to me about a case."

"That's fine." The sexy had turned serious. "Good luck with your mom and nonna."

I stopped myself from saying that I'd need something a lot stronger than luck, like voodoo, and limited my reply to "Love you."

As I closed the call, a flash from the fountain's concrete basin caught my eye. Sunlight had reflected off one of the pennies scattered along the bottom.

*Why not? I could use the insurance.*

I stood, fished a penny from my hobo bag, and made a wish —more of a plea, really—that my family would give Bradley and me some space during our engagement. I tossed the coin into the fountain and watched it drift down...

*And slip through a hole in the drain grate!*

I blinked, incredulous.

Then the water stopped flowing.

A tidal wave of shock rolled over me as I realized what had happened.

My penny had clogged the Jackson Square fountain.

*What did that mean for my wish? And out of all the pennies in the basin, why had mine gotten sucked up?*

Anger swelled in me like the pent-up water in the fountain pump. I tied my long brown hair into a knot, knelt on the rim, and plunged both hands into the water.

"Yo, uh, what's goin' on?"

I recognized David's college-speak but didn't look behind

me. I was too busy running my hand over the grate, feeling for a knob. "I'll tell you what's going on—this freaking fountain is trying to ruin my wedding."

Silence.

Balancing on both hands, I glanced over my shoulder to ask for his help, but he was opening and closing his mouth like a fish out of water. "What is it, David? Spit it out." I glowered at the fountain. "That goes for you too."

"Um, yeah. So...I don't think you're supposed to take money from a fountain."

I worked my finger into the grate hole and pulled. "After taking a lemon from the poor in a church, this doesn't seem so bad, especially since it was my money to begin with."

"Riiight. Although, I think it's illegal?"

I turned my head and gave him a hard stare. "I'm a private investigator, David, and before that I was a rookie cop, so I'm well aware of the law. But after everything Bradley and I have been through, I'm not going to let a fickle fountain cheat us." I returned my attention to the grate and yanked. "It's going to give me my damn penny *and* my wish for a peaceful engagement."

"Gotcha. But, could you maybe wait and get arrested after our meeting?"

His request hit me with the same cold-water splash as Bradley's lemon tradition question. I'd been arrested once before—on my thirtieth birthday, no less—thanks to a run-in with a woman who'd claimed to be a three-hundred-year-old witch, and I had no desire to return to a Big Easy jail.

I cast a side-eye at the fountain, and then I stood and wiped my hands on my jeans. "While we're on the subject of criminals, why are you dressed like a gangbanger?"

"I didn't want anyone from the office to see me. I've been thinking about your case offer, but, like, I don't feel right about taking it."

I put my hands on my hips to keep from shaking a finger at him—or shaking him. "You owe me after you investigated why I was still a *zitella* for my nonna. Do you know how humiliating it was to have you running around town looking into why I was an old maid?"

He lowered his head, and the hood obscured his sunglasses.

"Besides, you're a professional PI, so your feelings are irrelevant." I pulled a check from my purse and stuck it under his nose. "But this should make you feel better."

His head popped up, and so did his eyebrows. "This is, like, a month's salary."

"For a job that'll take half that at most."

"I don't get it. Veronica's an awesome boss and your best friend. Why would you want me to investigate who she's interviewing for the PI position?"

"David, you sweet innocent boy." I rested a hand on his shoulder. "Have you forgotten the consultants she hired to help me with my homicide cases? An ex-stripper, a drag queen, and my eighty-year-old grandmother?"

He took the check and crammed it into his pants pocket.

I gave his cheek a pat. "I'm glad you're seeing things my way, despite those black shades."

My phone rang. *Amato's Deli* appeared on the display. "It's my father. Not a word about your new case to Veronica, you hear?"

"Chill, okay? I don't want to get fired." David tugged his hood low and slunk away.

I tapped Answer. "Hey, Dad. What's up?"

"Your mother isn't answering her cell phone," he boomed in his gruff, I-need-an-antacid voice. "I don't know why she has the blasted thing if she's not going to turn it on. Is she with you?"

It was one of the few times I'd been able to shake her since my engagement two months earlier. "Actually, she and Nonna are at Our Lady of Guadalupe Church for mass, but I'm meeting them at Central Grocery for lunch in an hour."

"I'd imagine they're closed."

"On a Sunday afternoon? That's prime muffuletta-sandwich-selling time."

"There's been a tragedy in the New Orleans grocer community. That's why I'm calling."

I frowned and pressed the phone closer to my ear.

"A customer just came in and told me that our biggest competitor, back when I was still at Central Grocery, has been killed. His funeral is today, and there's no way I can make it from Houston in time, so I'd like for your mother and nonna to pay my respects."

My Sicilian grandma attended funerals like an it-girl attended parties, so that wouldn't have been a problem. Plus, she'd been wearing a mourning dress since my *nonnu* had died twenty-two years before, which meant that she was already dressed for the occasion. "I'll let them know. Did I ever meet this man?"

"No, his name was Angelo LaRocca, of LaRocca's Market on North Rampart Street. He inherited the business from his father back in '85 when he was in his mid-twenties, and like Central Grocery, it's one of the last Italian grocery stores from the old days."

"What did he die of?"

"He was murdered, and I was hoping you could look into it for me."

The St. Louis Cathedral bell tolled, giving me a jolt. I didn't remember it ringing on the quarter hour.

"I'm not asking you to do any investigating, just keep your ears open. The police aren't releasing any details, but there's a rumor going around that the crime scene was bad—gruesome, in fact."

The bell tolled again, and I glared at the cathedral. I didn't know what was going on, but if the bell pulled that stunt again, I would personally climb the central tower and clock the thing.

"What do you say, Franki? Can you do it?"

"Sure, Dad. I'll get right on it."

"Thanks, honey. I'll let you go. I've got customers at the counter.

He hung up, and I checked the time. My mom and nonna wouldn't get out of church for forty-five minutes, so I had time to kill.

*Kill.*

I felt sad for Angelo LaRocca and for the community, but also concerned. Because my gut told me that I'd need to do more for my dad and the late grocer than keep my ears open.

A peal of laughter shook me from my worry. I glanced across the park at a group of women enjoying the spring day while window-shopping at one of the two block-long Pontalba Buildings that formed either side of Jackson Square.

And I saw my mom and nonna enter the Creole Delicacies Gourmet Shop.

An alarm bell tolled, and it wasn't the one at the top of the St. Louis Cathedral. The odds of my nonna swapping prayer for pralines were about the same as those of the Catholic Church replacing communion wafers with cookies. If she was missing mass, then something big was going down—like meddling.

I rose to go investigate, and I paused to scowl at the fiendish fountain. Between my mom and nonna's antics and my dad's somber request, it was obvious that I needed a break in the luck department. Without it, my hopes of a stress-free engagement were in danger of going down the drain like my penny.

～

The vanilla-and-toasted-pecan odor inside the Creole Delicacies Gourmet Shop filled my nostrils and seduced my sweet tooth. I put my mom-and-nonna investigation on hold and helped myself to some praline samples. A sugar high could only help when confronting Machiavellian meddlers.

As I munched, I spotted my nonna talking to a saleswoman at the rear of the shop, and my mother was at a sale table in the center. Her back was to me, but it wasn't hard to recognize her. Even though she lived in Houston, her dyed-brown salon do had grown to Dallas proportions.

I snuck up behind her. "Uh, Mom?"

She started and went as stiff as her lacquered hair. Then she turned and lowered her readers. "What are you doing here, Francesca?" she asked in her shrill voice. "Aren't you supposed to be at a work meeting?"

Deflection was one of her standard tactics. "It ended early. Why aren't you and Nonna in church?"

"We felt terrible about missing mass, dear, but we had an urgent errand to run."

My brow rose, along with my suspicions. "In a candy and kitchen shop?"

"Well, yes." Her eyes widened to justification-of-a-lie size. "Your nonna and I have some cooking to do for a church function, and you desperately need a new..." She grabbed a gadget from the table. "...garlic press."

I recoiled. I knew she couldn't really squeeze Bradley and me with the thing, but her timing was disturbing nonetheless.

She reached for another item. "While we're here, dear, what do you think of this spaghetti fork?"

I wrested the pronged utensil from her hand and returned it to the shelf. It was well known within the family that my nonna thought spaghetti forks were instruments of the devil. "If Nonna sees you with that," I whisper-hissed, "she'll have Father John call in an exorcist."

"This isn't about Carmela, dear, it's about you and what you like."

My eyelids lowered. There was only one reason I'd need new kitchen accessories. "Are you two picking items for my wedding registry?"

"Now Francesca, you know we'd never pick your kitchen-ware. That's a personal decision."

Not only would they *pick* my kitchenware, they'd organize it in my drawers and cabinets and use it to serve Bradley and me a "suitable meal."

"Oh." My mother pressed her hands to her cheeks. "Look how adorable this is." She raised a plump lavender sachet topped with the head of a veiled bride.

"It looks like a severed head on a silk cushion."

"Well *I* think they'd make darling *bomboniere*."

The Italian term for *wedding favors* exploded in my head like the word's first four letters, and I began to sweat like a pressed garlic clove. As Italian-American traditions went, the bomboniere made the St. Joseph's Day lemons look like harmless citrus fruit. The bride had to choose the bomboniere, and all aspects of the newlyweds' life hinged on that choice—their health, wealth, happiness, fertility, and longevity. That was an awful lot to put on a gal, not to mention on a tchotchke with some Jordan almonds.

"Mom, I know you and nonna are excited about the wedding, but it's way too early to talk bomboniere—or wedding. I told you that Bradley and I are waiting to set a date until we know when Veronica and Dirk are getting married."

She bit the earpiece of her readers—and bared her teeth. "I don't see why you have to wait just because she got engaged first."

My mother *did* see—but she chose not to. "I want both of our weddings to be special, so I won't even consider getting married for at least six months after she does."

"Then you might want to go with *this* for your bomboniere." She picked up an hourglass kitchen timer and flipped it over. "It's for two minutes, which is about all your biological time-clock has left."

I bared *my* teeth—and growled. "I'm thirty-one, not forty-one, so stick a spaghetti fork in it."

She sniffed and resumed browsing. "That's a bad analogy for someone who's reproductive days are almost done."

I squeezed my fists and took a breath. The woman was lucky that I'd put the fork back on the shelf.

She gasped and held up a yellow tulle bag. "Little lemon-shaped soaps. They're perfect for your theme."

Yes, the theme of a woman whose relatives kept shoving lemons at her, making her more and more bitter. "Mom, drop the merchandise *and* the meddling. Bradley and I are going to enjoy our engagement for the time being. In the meantime, Dad called and he needs us to go to a funeral this afternoon for a grocer named Angelo LaRocca."

She waved me off with the lemon. "That can wait, Francesca."

"Uh, how do you figure?"

"Because this is about the rest of your life, and that man's already dead."

With logic like that, the only thing to do was go outside. "I'll wait for you and Nonna out front. You don't need me to plan my wedding, anyway."

She huffed like I was the one behaving badly.

I stormed from the store—after grabbing a couple more praline samples—and ran smack into a chubby man wearing a strap-on snare drum.

He leapt backward. "Careful, baby. This instrument is my livelihood."

"I'm sorry." I read the band name written on the drum, *The Tremé Tribe*. "Hey, is Wendell Baptiste still playing with you?"

He ran a hand over his clean-shaven head. "Dat's what me and the rest o' the band wanna know. You seen him today?"

"Oh, we don't hang out. We worked on a steamboat together a couple of months ago." I neglected to add that Wendell had helped me with a homicide case.

"Well, if you do see him, tell him to give his bandmates a shout. We got a gig playing a jazz funeral, and we cain't find him nowhere."

That didn't sound like Wendell. "Is it like him to miss a gig?"

"No ma'am, especially not one dis high profile. It's for a guy who was murdered, so the whole town'll be watching."

I had a feeling I knew who he was talking about. "You mean, Angelo LaRocca?"

"Dat's him. We linin' up now." He pointed a drumstick toward Decatur Street where a hundred or so people had formed a line behind a horse hitched to a glass carriage, and he shook his head. "It's closed casket 'cause dey said his skull was all jacked up."

I grimaced at the mental image. "'Jacked up' how?"

"Someone attacked him with somethin' while he was sleeping. Probably an ex-wife or girlfriend." He sucked his teeth. "Anyways, I gotta git. You have a blessed day." He set off toward the procession, pounding his drum.

On that note, I turned to go get my mom and nonna and noticed an old woman in a frumpy dress and apron watching me from the doorway of the New Orleans Cajun Store.

She opened her mouth, revealing missing teeth. "A *cauchemar*."

I thought she'd coughed up some phlegm, but based on the

way her black eyes drilled into mine, she expected a response. "I'm sorry. Were you talking to me?"

"A cauchemar killed dat man."

It wasn't phlegm she'd coughed up, but rather a French word. "What's that?"

"A nightmare witch, who attack people in deir beds at night." Her eyes went horror-story. "She saddle dem up and ride 'em like a horse. And if they don' wake up, dey die."

That sounded like a local folk legend. "I don't believe in that sort of thing."

Her eye twitched, and she rubbed a wart on her chin. "You sleep tight now."

I stared, dumbfounded, as she returned inside the store, because her tone had held a threat.

A trumpet sounded. The jazz funeral was underway on Decatur Street. The horse, owing to the weight of the carriage and casket, took halting steps before settling into a reluctant trot.

The image reinforced exactly how I felt—like I too had been hitched to dead weight that I wasn't prepared to carry.

78261086R00184